Haldar
uncondi
out her
black ha

'Liste
the Underground. It is true I put a thought in your mind,
Haldar – but you were not betrayed. I caused you to swear
by the Key, because I *have* the Key, the Key itself of the
Marmian Wizard's Manse. It is this one. Now I come to
you to offer what you seek. I'll give you your life's transcendent feat – your greatest exploit – and I will not ask your
life in fee, though you have sworn it. Instead I shall fee
you – I'll give you the Wizard's Key. For this, you must
bring down to me one living man, one man still living
down to me in the Winds of Warr, down where I dwell in
the Place of the Raging Dead.'

She pointed again and again to the ground . . .

By the same author

MICHAEL SHEA

Nifft the Lean

PANTHER
Granada Publishing

Panther Books
Granada Publishing Ltd
8 Grafton Street, London W1X 3LA

Published by Panther Books 1985

Copyright © Michael Shea 1982

ISBN 0-586-06499-0

Printed and bound in Great Britain by
Anchor Brendon Ltd, Tiptree, Essex

Set in Baskerville

All rights reserved. No part of this publication may
be reproduced, stored in a retrieval system, or
transmitted, in any form, or by any means, electronic,
mechanical, photocopying, recording or otherwise,
without the prior permission of the publishers.

This book is sold subject to the conditions that it
shall not, by way of trade or otherwise, be lent,
re-sold, hired out or otherwise circulated
without the publisher's prior consent in any
form of binding or cover other than that in
which it is published and without a similar
condition including this condition being imposed
on the subsequent purchaser.

Shag Margold's *Eulogy of Nifft the Lean, His Dear Friend*

Nifft the Lean is no longer among us, and I have at last confessed to myself that, hereafter, he never will be. Consequently, I have tried to do for him all that remains in my power to do, little though that is. The man is gone, but here, at least, is some record of what he saw and did in the world. It is a bitter thing that each of us must finally be blown out like a candle, and have the unique ardor of his individual flame choked off, and sucked utterly away like smoke in the dark. Do we ever accept this in our hearts, any of us? The waste of knowledge! It never ceases to be ... infuriating. In Nifft's case I find it galls me cruelly, and the documents I now present to my country-men – records which Nifft, or Barnar the Chilite, or others of our mutual acquaintance have put in my keeping over the years – have given me great consolation for the loss of him.

In strict truth, I do not say that Nifft is dead. This cannot be known. But for all that he was dear to me, when I consider the Thing which took him from us I *wish* him dead. Escape he cannot. He was a man who made some deep ventures and yet always found his way back to the sunlight, but this time I do not look for my waybrother's coming home.

Nifft was an affectionate man, watchful for his friend's advantage, and hence my present possession of his records. Nifft relished making record of his exploits (simply vanity his sole motive, he insisted), and so did his friends, and from our first acquaintance he contrived to make me the guardian of all such manuscripts, alleging his unsettled life

5

barred his keeping them. This was tactful altruism. He had other friends to leave his papers with, but to me, an historian and cartographer, they could be of unique benefit. Indeed, my latest effort, the *Second Revised Global Map*, owes the kind praise it has reaped mainly to the wealth of new and detailed information which Nifft's papers put at my disposal during its drafting. From time to time I remonstrated with him, offered payment for his material, until one day he put his hand on my shoulder. (He had huge hands – they were the reason for his preeminence with all forms of dart, javelin, lance or spear.) Solemnly he said to me:

'Enough of this please, Shag. I can't take money from a man I admire as much as you. You're the most widely traveled *honest* man I know.'

If Nifft was not entirely honest, he was entirely honorable, and it is futile to push moral assessment further than this in the case of a thief. That Nifft was one of the master thieves of his generation stands beyond dispute. The reader must note that I write in Karkmahn-Ra, jewel of the Ephesion Chain and much frequented by Nifft's guildfellows. To know his professional standing I need not travel far, and can have it from the lips of such legendary talents as Taramat Light-Touch, Nab the Trickster, and Ellen Errin the Kadrashite. These, and their peers, judge unanimously that Nifft stood in the very vanguard of his guild's greatest luminaries.

He was a limber, gaunt man, a full span taller than the average. Though he was spare, he was densely wrought – rope-veined, gnarl-muscled, and unusually strong. His face was long and droll, the big nose battered, the wide mouth wry. This face was a marvelously expressive instrument whenever Nifft chose, as he occasionally did, to entertain us with some piece of comic pantomime. He was highly accomplished in this art. At the age of thirteen he had finagled an apprenticeship in it with a traveling acrobatic

6

troupe then visiting the town of his birth, therewith commencing the peripatetic career he was to pursue so illustriously and which, though it took him far across the face of the earth, never brought him back to his native city. By his twentieth year he was a thorough adept in all of what we may term the 'carnival arts,' and already a widely traveled young man. From mastery of the mountebank's larcenous skills to the study of outright felonious appropriation, and all its subsidiary sciences, proved but a short step for Nifft, who always credited his early 'dramatic training' with his success as a thief, vowing it had given him a rare grasp of his trade's fundamentals: lying, imposture and nimble movement. For the latter, Nifft had a particular capacity, and was known for a certain inimitable, restive carriage of body. His way of moving – taut, flickering, balanced – made his friends liken him to a lizard – a similitude he professed to deplore, but which I believe he secretly relished.

It is hard indeed to think him gone! He was one of those men whose death one hears of frequently and always, as it proves, falsely – the kind of man who always pops up into view like a cork upon the after-turbulence of storms and shipwrecks, bobbing unharmed out of the general ruin. There was a period of about five years when I and all who knew him believed him dead. During this time I attended a number of anniversary revelries held by his guildfellows in observance of his memory – bibulous festivities which they decreed without allowing themselves to be limited by the strictly calendrical notion of an 'anniversary,' and of which I had attended no less than eleven when, a lustrum after his 'passing,' I set out on my first extended cruise of exploration in the southern oceans. I was one of a coalition of Ephesionite scholars. The vessel we had chartered for our year of reconnaissance was rigged with elaborate signal beacons on a scaffold in the foredeck, for we sought parley with every vessel we sighted at sea, and inquired into their crews' affairs – their travels, homes, and modes of life – as studiously as we logged coasts, climes, and oceanic phenomena. In our second month out, as we skirted the Glacial Maelstroms, we spied a brig of exotic design. We hailed her and, shortly, hove alongside her for our habitual trade of amenities and news.

The brig's masters were two wealthy carpet merchants from Fregor Ingens, and there was a third man with them who was in the manner of a junior partner and clerk. This man poured out the drinks for our convivial little assembly. I looked at the broad, rawboned hand that tipped the beaker to my cup, looked up along the stark length of arm, and into Nifft's black, spark-centered eyes. He had grown his hair long and wore it pulled back into a braided club on his neck, in the style of the Jarkeladd nomads, and this revealed that he now lacked his left ear, but Nifft it surely was. Our conversation on this occasion was one of covert looks only, for I quickly perceived his association with the merchants he so deferentially attended was of a type which sudden disclosure of his identity could jeopardize. I did not compromise him, though I smiled to myself to think of all I would hear from my friend the next time we sat at liquor together.

And I would not have compromised him now, as these volumes must do were Nifft ever to reenter the world of men. I would have delayed this work interminably out of reluctance to acknowledge his loss by completing this verbal monument to his life and deeds. But I am old, and my health is more than a little imperfect. No one knows his term, and I have been compelled to accomplish this labor while labor lay still within my power. From this, the great importance I attach to this work should be obvious. At the same time I must confess that during the months I have devoted to these documents, I have been no stranger to the despairing cynicism with which all men must grapple in the winter of their lives. Mockingly I have asked myself my labor's aim. Is it to set my friend's excellence before the eyes of Posterity? But 'Posterity' – what a hair-raising gulf of time is masked by that word! An illimitable boneyard of Histories lies already behind us. Worlds on worlds of men have flowered, died and drifted on their time-islands into the desolation of eternity, and worlds more lie ahead of us – that, or the end of all. I have seen archaic maps which showed me the faces of earths utterly different from this, minutely rendered geographies which no man will find today in any of the five seas. Whither, on what unguessable currents, do I launch this man's fame, and what eddy will it end in, an impenetrable fragment in a tongue unknown to the wisest scholars, if it is preserved at all?

But I have set aside this cynical lassitude as a wasteful and childish mistake. Though a light burn comparatively small in the darkness, its first and consuming necessity is to broadcast all the illumination in its power. While it is foolish to deny the dark around us, it is futile to exaggerate it. And I make bold to say that I am not the only one of my countrymen who could profit from taking this admonition to heart.

I have in mind the notion that is so fashionable nowadays, namely that we live in a Dark Age where puny Science quails before many a dim Unknown on every hand. Surely this sort of facile pessimism dampens the energy of inquiry even as it leads to obscurantism – toward a despair of certainty which encourages us to embrace truths, half-truths, and the most extravagant falsehoods with a promiscuous lack of descrimination.

What responsible person denies – to speak only of the cartographic science – that vast tracts of land and sea remain mysterious to the wisest? The great Kolodrian mountain systems are an instance. The Thaumeton Island Group, the hinterlands of the Jarkeladd tundras, are further examples. But mark in this how clearly we can define our ignorance. The fact is, our world's main outlines – coasts and climes, seas and currents – are known. It is the same in other disciplines. We have sufficient fragments of sufficient histories to know that man has been both far more powerful and far more abject than he is today. If our tools and techniques are crude compared to the fabulous resources of ages past, they are also marvels of efficacy to what our race has muddled through within yet other periods.

Granting that our knowledge be limited, what can it profit us to traffic in lurid fantasies and errant imaginings? When – certainty failing us – we *must* speculate, let us recognize the difference between careful enumeration of reasonable hypotheses, and the reckless multiplication of bizarre conceptions. To illustrate with a classic instance, we cannot say what demons are. If the knowledge ever existed, it is lost to us now. Consequently, we must acknowledge several theories which continue to dominate the discussions of serious students of the question. Demons, few of whom lack some human component, may have been the parent stock of Man. Or they may have been spawned by man, his degenerate progeny. Possibly, they are his invention run wild, artifacts of a potent but diseased sorcery he once possessed. And, conceivably, the sub-worlds were populated according to Undle Ninefingers' suggestion, which holds that the demons arose as a 'spiritual distillate' of human evil, a 'coagulation' of psychic energies into the material entities we know today. The judicious man, though he have his private leaning, must grant all of these some claim to credence. But must he entertain the idea that demons come from seeds which are rained upon the earth at each full moon? Or that each demon is the 'vital shadow' of a living man, engendered below in the instant of that man's conception, and extinguished in the moment of his death?

The spirit in which I offer my prefatory notes to each of the following narratives should now be clear. I shall present as certain only those data corroborated by exhaustive research, or by my own personal investigations, as I am not untraveled for a bookish man. Wherever doubt exists, I shall unambiguously state its degree and nature, along with whatever grounds I may have for preferring one hypothesis over another. If, despite all I have said, the reader disdains such honest ambiguity, and stubbornly prefers the unequivocal assertiveness to be found in factitious travelogues penned by raffish 'explorers' or in the specious 'natural histories' compiled by crapulous and unprincipled hacks who have never left their squalid lofts in Scrivener's Row, then there is nothing further I can do, and I leave him, with apologies, to his deception.

Herewith, then, I dedicate these volumes to the memory of Nifft the Lean. Had there been a funerary stone marking his remains, I would have had it inscribed in accordance with the only preference he was ever heard to voice on the subject – namely, with those verses he loved above all others, written by the immortal Parple, the bard's 'Salutation to the World.' So let them be written here, since the stone is lacking.

Salutation To The World As Beheld At Dawn From Atop Mount Eburon

Long have your continents drifted and merged,
Jostled like whales on the seas,
Then cloven, and sundered, and slowly diverged,
While your mountains arose and sank to their knees.

Long and long were your eons of ice,
Long were your ages of fire.
Long has there been
The bleeding of men
And the darkness that cancels desire.

What hosts of hosts – born, grown, and gone –
Have swarmed your million Babylons?

How many pits has Mankind dug?
How many peaks has he stood upon?

Many and long were your empires of blood,
Fewer your empires of light.
Now their wisdoms and wars
Lie remote as the stars,
Stone-cold in the blanketing night.

Now even your wisest could never restore
One tithe of the truths Man's lost,
Nor even one book of the radiant lore
That so many treasured so long, at such cost.

For it's many the pages the wind has torn
And their hoarded secrets blown –
Tumbled and chased
Through the eyeless wastes
Where the wreckage of history's thrown.

Part 1

Shag Margold's *Preface to Come Then, Mortal – We Will Seek Her Soul*

The manuscript of this account is in a professional scribe's hand, but it is unmistakably of Nifft's own composition. This is not automatically the case, even though a given history be recounted as if in Nifft's voice, for two of his dearest friends, in repeating tales he told them but did not himself record, enjoyed adopting his persona and reproducing – or so they conceived – his narrative manner. (See, for example, the chapter concerning his encounter with the vampire Queen Vulvula.) In the present instance, however, I am convinced we have our information direct from the master-thief himself.

The Great Cleft Lake lies in Lúlumë, near the center of that continent's northern limb, and Lurkna Downs is the only really large city on its extensive perimeter, occupying The Jut, a sharp salience of the southern shoreline which extends to within half a mile of the northern shore, almost bisecting the vast body of water. Numerous small fishing hamlets rim the lake, for its waters teem with many delectable or otherwise valuable species, the most notable being speckled ramhead, skad, grapple, deepwater lumulus and pygmy hullbreaker. But as the great size of most of these creatures might suggest, fishing those waters on a commercial scale requires large vessels and elaborate equipment, and northern Lúlumë as a whole is too poor and thinly populated to mount such enterprise. Lurkna Downs owes its beginning to the wealth of Kolodria, whence entrepreneurs from the Great Shallows came some two centuries ago and endowed the then-minor settlement with its first large fishing fleet. And, having seeded the

15

Great Cleft Lake with ships, it is Kolodrian merchants who today bear its finny harvest back across the Sea of Agon in their argosies, and market it throughout the Shallows.

These economic matters are not entirely remote from the love of Dalissem for Defalk, and its dreadful issue. Everything Nifft tells us of that volcano-hearted temple child marks her as a classic specimen of northern Lúlumë's self-styled First Folk, a people who, though not truly aboriginal, migrated from the Jarkeladd tundras in the north of the Kolodrian continent more than a millennium ago. They came across the Icebridge Island Chain, and brought into Lúlumë a nomad stoicism and uncouth but potent sorcery with which, where it survives today, the fiercest Jarkeladd shaman would still feel an instantaneous kinship and empathy.

But indeed, this tundra-born culture is now half-eclipsed in the Cleft Lake region. The habit of wealth and property which the Kolodrian merchants brought to Lurkna Downs, the urbanity and cosmopolitan conceits which two centuries of trade with Kolodria have since fostered there, have deprived the First Folk values – their ferocious passions and proud austerities – of the general reverence they once enjoyed. And Defalk belonged to this latter-day Lurkna Downs just as surely as Dalissem did to the First Folk. That she was a temple child in itself argues this. This cult – to which Dalissem would have been born, and not admitted through any voluntary candidacy – is one of the few still-vigorous First Folk institutions that is allowed a conspicuous existence in Lurkna Downs. The cult's name is never uttered by its initiates in the hearing of the uninitiated, and its tenets remain obscure. But the learned Quall of Hursh-Himïn is probably correct in saying that it centers on a rigorous votive asceticism – virginity paramount among the self-abnegations required – and that its annual mysteries involve further physical rigors. These trance-inducing group ordeals' aim is a visionary ecstasy (one sees again the tundra influence) wherein is revealed – to herself and her sisters at once – the identity of the worshipper to be honored as that year's sacramental suicide. Dalissem's actions – though rebelliously secular in their frame of expression – undeniably tend to corroborate this report.

Though this is the extent of our reliable information about the cult, I feel I must go out of my way to point out that we have no reason to credit the usually trustworthy Arsgrave's preposterous assertion that the cultists' alleged virginity masks the most unvirginal practice – the cult's 'chief end' he calls it! – of mass orgiastic copulation with water demons in the lake's deeps. No serious student of the *Aquademoniad* can be unaware that fresh-water demons have been extinct for at least three millennia. My own opinion is that Arsgrave's sexual pride – which he seems incapable of suppressing, even in contexts utterly remote from that issue – renders him powerless to believe that the pleasures of 'normal' copulation can be forgone by any but those devoted to wholly grotesque passions.

Finally, as to the world of the dead, I will neither misrepresent my faith – which is absolute – in Nifft's veracity by expressing doubt of its existence, nor compromise my editorial impartiality by expressing conviction thereof. It is, however, perhaps relevant to note that both Undle Ninefingers and the great Pandector – drawing on wholly independent sources and writing without knowledge of one another – affirm its existence; and that Pandector's account in particular describes a mode whereby the living may enter that realm which in every essential feature agrees with Nifft's description.

Shag Margold

Come Then, Mortal.
We Will Seek Her Soul

I

Nifft the Lean and Barnar the Chilite had agreed not to sleep that night. Darkness had overtaken them in the swamp. They might rest their bodies, but not their vigilance – not here.

They climbed up in the groin of one of the massive, wide-spreading swamp trees. Here there was room to recline, and to build a small fire which seemed scarcely to affect the tough, reptilian bark of the giant supporting them. They did not risk a fire big enough to warm them against the numbing, clammy air. At the spare little flame they dried their boots and kept the blood in their hands and feet, but came no closer than this to comfort.

The two friends talked quietly, pausing often to read – brows intent – the wide, wet noise of the swamp, and to listen for the silken progress of a treelurk down one of the branches they sat on. Both were men inured to hard and various terrain, and in the manner of such men they seemed able to achieve a subtle bodily harmony with whatever surroundings they had to endure. Nifft sat with his arms folded across his knees. His gauntness, his loose, jut-limbed repose, called to mind the big carrion-eating birds they had seen so many of during their day's march across the fens. Barnar was more suggestive of the water-bulls of the region. He sat four-square, thick and still as a boulder, yet following everything with flick of eye and nostril.

There came a long pause in their talk. Barnar squinted at the wet darkness around them for a long time, and shrugged, as if to throw off ugly thoughts. 'Study it how you will, it's a foul piece of the world and not meant for men, not sane ones.'

Nifft waved his hand vaguely and didn't answer, gazing at the swamp with more complacency than his friend. Barnar poked the fire discontentedly. Talk was what he needed; he was in too glum a mood for silent musing. He cast about for a subject. He found one which he would have shunned as indiscreet in a less gloomy mood – for one did not ask even one's esteemed partner about his past; among thieves such information must be volunteered.

'You used to know a man from these regions, didn't you? A guidefellow who'd won a high name – Haldar it was, wasn't it?'

'Haldar Dirkniss.' Nifft answered him with a look of benign humor. This prodding was sufficiently unlike Barnar's style to make Nifft aware of its cause, and after a moment he sat up a little straighter and spoke more expansively. 'He was my partner for six years, Barnar. You would have loved him. He had a marvelous imagination, and withal he was so solemn. You should have seen him at work laying the groundwork for some exploit – grave, intense . . . he was so *studious*! And he loved the form as much as the dross, loved an inspired trick as much as the gold it won. We would have made the Black Crack's own trio!'

'Where is he now?'

'In the land of the dead.' Nifft said this with an odd intensity, looking at Barnar with a watchfulness the Chilite didn't understand. Nifft's metaphorical turn of speech also seemed out of place.

'My regrets,' Barnar said uncertainly. 'It's where we'll all go sure enough and all too soon.'

'But never in the same way, Barnar – never as Haldar – and I – went there. We went down alive!'

If Nifft had said this gravely Barnar would have known

19

he jested. But he said it with the evil smile he reserved for true and terrible matters, a taunting smile that dared his hearer's disbelief. Barnar knew his friend's humor: a scoffing reply now, and Nifft would laugh, as if in acknowledgment of fraud and say no further word. Barnar had seen him do as much amid colleagues at more than one tavern where the men of the guild drank and gossiped. He'd seen skeptical laughter lose men the hearing of several adventures which perhaps he would have mocked himself, had he not experienced them at Nifft's side.

Still Nifft grinned at him, his last words hanging like a challenge that must be taken up if he was to proceed. So at last the Chilite rumbled grudgingly:

'Well, if such a thing can be done, you're as likely a man for the job as any I know, though in truth it's a hard matter to swallow. Does the Guide of Ghosts pass traffic thru his gates, then?'

This was enough – Nifft sat up, warming to speech. 'Now that it's said, I find it easy to tell. All the time I've known you I've hesitated to try. I was afraid you'd mock the notion and anger me and bad blood would be made between us. I've been remembering that exploit ever since we entered the swamps.

'You see, Barnar, there is no *gate* to that place. You enter it through an instant of time. You must stand near someone when his death comes, and in the instant before he goes there is a spell you must speak which lets you into the dying man's moment. And then, you see, you are present when the Guide of Ghosts, and the Soul-taker, come for him.

'And though there may be other living men around the deathbed, they will be to you as statues. For them, the man's passing is a single blink of time. You who have entered his moment through the spell move within the Time beneath time – the Time where the dead endure.'

Barnar opened his mouth to ask a question, but closed it

20

again on seeing his friend's self-absorbed stare. Nifft would give the whole tale now, and would not like interruptions. The Chilite settled himself a bit more comfortably. Leaving an ear open to the noises of the swamp, he gave the rest of his mind to Nifft's words, smiling slightly to himself.

'But it goes further – much further than this, Barnar. For if you meet the Guide's minion in combat – if you grapple with the Soul-taker, and pin him – then the Guide will bring you with him on his journey below. He will bring you to any soul you seek, wherever it lies in death's domain. And he'll bring you out again too if you're lucky . . .'

II

We were crossing the great steppes when the night caught us short, Haldar and me – just as it's done us tonight. In case you don't know it, that's wolf country, and I'm not talking about your carrion-eating skulkers of the foothills, but big, red-jawed man-eaters as high at the shoulder as a two-year colt.

Our mounts were bone-tired with staying ahead of them all day long. We'd drawn no steady pursuit, but the price of that was holding a pace that would kill our horses if we kept it up the next day. Even so, we rode long past sunset, encouraged by the full moon that rose at dusk. It bought us nothing – there are no safe camps on those plains – and we finally had to take what offered. We wound our way into a boulderfall on the flank of a ridge. We settled into a narrow clearing well-overhung by the big moon-pale rocks, and we hobbled the mounts at its mouth. The rocks were polished granite, and were something to set your back against if it came to swordwork against wolves. But they had none of the friendly feel of something that gives you shelter. The very gravel we crouched on had a nastiness to it – a kind of sick smell. You know such spots; a fear inhabits them over and above any fear you may be feeling for this reason or that. We made a small fire, broke out a loaf and cheese. We didn't talk.

The mean little prairie towns we'd just come through, and the ill luck we'd had in them had left us bruised and black of spirit. All our tricks had been small and mean, our purses were flat, our bellies vacant and our skins unwashed. Lurkna Downs, on the shore of the Great Cleft Lake, was little more than a day distant – a city large and rich and old. Assuming we survived the night, we had an even or better chance of reaching it. But we took no consolation in this. Our gloom had gotten to the philosophical stage, you see. Or rather Haldar's had first, and I'd caught it from him, as usual. The upshot was we felt so leaden that it was damned unlikely we ever *would* reach Lurkna. We sat chewing slowly and glaring resentfully at the plains that fell away below the ridge.

The land itself there is wolfish. The boulders, pale and smooth, were like earth's bones jutting from her starved soil. Out on the prairie the moon-silvered grass grew lank and patchy, like a great mangy hide. And if you want to stretch the comparison, the wolves themselves were the lice moving through the patches of silver, or merging with the moon-shadows. We saw more than a few such, too, though at the time no comic view of them suggested itself.

At length, Haldar sighed bitterly and threw down the crust he'd been gnawing. He glared at me, then at the fire.

'You know, we're not a jot different from those wolves,' he snarled. 'We walk on our hind paws, and pull leggin's on over our arses, but that's all.'

To one who'd shared Haldar's thoughts for years, this said much in little. I must tell you my friend was terribly idealistic. I loved him as a brother, and tried to cure him of it, but I never did. And when I say *terribly*, I mean it.

22

You want an instance? We once turned a trick in Bagág Marsh. It was a fine and nimble-witted piece of work, I promise you. We galloped out of town on the night of our take with near a hundredweight each of wrought gold. We were galloping out of sheer exuberance, you understand. Our canniness had guaranteed a delayed pursuit.

Well, we came to a bridge crossing a very fast-moving river to the north of the city. Suddenly Haldar reined up at mid-bridge, and stood in his stirrups. He was a light man – wiry like me, but middling short. He had a hatchet face – his nose and chin formed a ridge-line which his black eyes and black beard crowded up to. It was a fierce little face, hawkish, and as he stood there in his stirrups he thrust it up greedily against the starlight. He seemed to want to breathe the whole night into himself, and you almost believed he could fit it all in, so intent and still he was. Suddenly he dismounted, pulled his saddlebag off the pommel, and dumped his hundredweight of gold into the river. I died a little at that moment, Barnar. No! I died a great deal! Thanks be to the Crack, I was professional enough to hold my tongue about what a partner does with his own share of a take. But I nearly had to bite it through to hold it.

Yet even in my shock, I understood. The only fitting celebration of his pride in his work was to show that beside it, the gold was nothing. Oh, he was a craftsman too, every bit as fine as we are, Barnar, and I honored him truly for the passion of his gesture. But couldn't he have made some poetic statement, such as: 'Beside the wealth of my art, this gold is but dross to me!' – and then squandered it on lowly things – flesh and feasts – to show his contempt for it?

Well of course the point is that for Haldar, there was no substitute for the absolute. If he got pessimistic, as he did not seldom, he might not just talk about it. He was capable of jumping up and striding out onto the plain and fraternizing with the wolves, just to express his sarcasm and disgust with a thief's way of living.

The cold and sickly feeling of our camp hadn't left it. The lure of Haldar's furious despair was strong.

'Roast you!' I growled. 'Will you eat? Blast and damn you, Haldar, you've got no right to go sour. If you sink I'm almost surely gone. *I'm* not a wolf! If I were, I'm sure I'd like my life that way just as much as I like the one I've got, and I mean to keep the one I've got.'

Sadly, easily, he waved away my words. 'You're fooling yourself, Nifft. The great tricks are gone now, don't you see? Those feats of deep cunning and brave flair – we're all alloted a few of them, and we get no more, no matter what our longing is. And you know, you're lucky if you even recognize when you're *having* your best moments. Half the time your soul is looking the other way when they come. And you never grow wise enough to know what they were until you have passed the hope of having more. Then, the rest of life is this – ' he waved at the moonlit plain ' – greedy, four-legged scavenging through a desolation.'

Well normally I can turn a sharp retort to such elegiac horse-flop, and so too, surely, could Haldar himself at another time. But just then I hadn't the spit for it. I felt such a freezing, putrid sadness! And all at once I understood that it was – still – the place we were camped. For the feeling was seeping *into* me. These boulders and this gravel were giving it off the way ice gives off cold. There was something here, and its presence was getting stronger moment by moment.

Haldar, it was clear, was reacting to it without realizing its source. He sat jabbing a stick into the fire, as if trying to stab it to death. I tried to speak but my throat caught, and it seemed for a moment I couldn't find even the simplest words. My friend threw down his stick, rubbed his forehead, and then jumped up and shook his fist at the sky.

'By the Crack,' he shouted. 'I'd give my life to work just

24

one great feat more – one greater than any I've yet accomplished. My life! I swear it by the Wizard's Key!'

Well his words shocked me. Even though my dread of this place hung heavier and heavier from my heart, like a poison fruit that would fall and break and cause something foul and dark to be born – I still had the wit to be both alarmed and startled. I was alarmed because Haldar wasn't a man to bandy oaths, and if he spoke one he was dead serious about it. And I was startled by the oddity of the oath itself. Have you ever heard anyone but some Kairnish outlander swear by the Wizard's Key? It certainly wasn't Haldar's custom. We stared at each other and he looked as surprised as I was. And then I got a feeling.

'There's something here,' I said. 'Do you feel it? Not far. *Under* us maybe . . . but approaching.'

Haldar looked around, nodding grimly, scowling at the shadows. 'Mark me!' he cried aloud, 'who- or what-ever you are that stand near us now. You have put a thought in my mind, and a word in my mouth. But I defy you! I claim my oath as my own. I stand by it as mine. So stand forth now, if you mean to offer what I ask!'

That was the man all over, Barnar. No one spoke straighter to the point. Let nameless things skulk, if he heard them in the woodwork he'd call them out to state their business.

We waited in silence. The ugly weight still dragged on my heart. I was so absorbed I didn't realize my hand was on my swordhilt until I had the blade half out of the sheath. I remember hearing, as I listened, a sound of toenails on stone, and thinking to myself, *No, that's only a wolf.*

So in a way I wasn't surprised when Haldar's mount screamed and we turned to see its legs buckling as two huge wolves dragged it down by the throat. Two more swarmed onto it while my mount rose and stove in the skull of a fifth with its forehoof. I was already launched

25

toward it when I saw the wolf above and behind us on the rock overhanging our fire. I shouted to Haldar and as I completed my spring, I had a last sight of the wolf leaping down on him: a giant silver dog that hung above him on the firelit air.

Then there was only the work at hand. After that cold, festering dread, the bloody uproar was like fresh air. I brought down a two-handed stroke on one of the beasts, and no more than half clove its neck, though I had my broad-blade then, and a full swing. That's how big those brutes were. Its spine held my blade almost too long as a new wolf plunged in from the dark, but I got my point up to its throat and its own leap killed it, though both my shoulders were nearly unsocketed. I slashed my mount's hobble and it stood its ground unhindered. Haldar's already had four beasts sunk to their shoulders in its opened belly, while it still screamed. My friend shouted.

That leaping wolf had taken his blade in its open jaws, but the thing was so big that its heart wasn't cleft till its jaws had reached the hilt, and Haldar had had to drop the sword or lose his hand. The animal lay twitching now, the sword-pommel between its teeth, and Haldar had only a brand from the fire in one hand, and a knife in the other, with which to face a new attacker up on the rock. I swear, this wolf was two-thirds as big as a horse. It had shoulders like a northron bear. Its ribs showed as distinctly as so many peals of a death-knell – ours. Its eyes were as yellow as honey and insane with hunger and from the dark behind it, in the intervals between the horse's screams, came the sound of other paws scrabbling on stone.

Then the giant, instead of springing, scrambled desperately backward from the edge of the rock. The bush of its tail glinted in the firelight as it turned, and it was gone. A noise of many hard, fleet paws scattered away through the dark around us, and the ones that were feeding plucked their drenched heads from the horse's ribs and fled away, their sticky ears flattened in fear. The horse still screamed, but with less strength. I almost clung to the sound, in my fear of the silence it covered, but pity won and I split its skull.

'It's coming,' Haldar said in the silence. 'But from where?' He sounded hushed, fascinated. There was no mistaking the terrible nearness of something. The air swarmed with ticklish sensation. The very stones were crawling with premonitions like a million invisible ants. I felt fascinated too; but far more strongly I felt loathing. I could not wish to leave – you can't, you know, if you come as near as we were, and if you have any enterprise or fire of soul in you. But I could not bear to wait in stillness. Like some housekeeper in a frenzy, I began, insanely, to tidy up. I freed Haldar's blade and wiped it on the beast's coat. I began to drag wolf corpses out of our clearing. I cursed and snarled and hauled on them with furious strength and with each instant I felt the air swarming and breathing more intensely. Haldar shouted: 'Nifft! Look at the rock!'

Even as I turned, one of the big boulders near our fire bulged. It swelled out sharply, just as pliant as a mother's belly where a child, impatient to be born, gives a kick and a shove. It settled back. Then it bulged a second, and a third time. Then it peaked out again, and this time, did not return to shape. The thing within stretched it unrelentingly now, with all its force. A crack appeared in the apex of the bulge and with it, as if pouring out of the crack, a charnel stink entered the air. The crack widened with a snap, and a skeleton hand thrust out.

It had just enough yellow gristle and tendon on it to keep the bones together. It clutched and plucked at the air like some nightmare crab feeding on a kelp-leaf. Then the rock heaved again, split farther, and the entire forearm sprouted out with its one straight and one curving bone. Arm and hand flailed and scooped at the air, and the stone

27

tore again – mightily this time. Our knees buckled in the reeking gust that hit us. The other hand and arm thrust out – this hand grasping a large golden key. A being of bone and parched ligament dragged itself out onto the gravel. Its skull was patched with swatches of black, rotten hair that looked wet and flattened like the womb-licked hair of babes just born.

The boulder lay in halves now, and the thing writhed toward us, its ribs leaving scalloped furrows in the earth. It moved like a spent swimmer hauling himself from a punishing surf – from an icy, stinking sea. The chill those bones gave off was as powerful as their stench. When the thing collapsed near the fire, the flames turned red and shrank, as if crushed by the cold.

But have I talked of stench? By the Crack, I did not yet know the meaning of the word. For as it lay, weakly stirring, the thing began to change, and as it changed, it seemed our noses and throats were being crammed with grave-dirt, so fiercely did the thing reek. We leaned against the rocks and stared, our wills not our own. Flesh had begun to web and drape the bones.

Not flesh, mind you – but just such gluey rags as comes before it's utterly gone. This foul paste spread. Lumps of it rose within the ribs' cage like loaves in an oven, and the festoons on the rest of the skeleton thickened, and wove, and knit into skin. And that skin began to stir, and then to crawl, and then to boil – with worms.

In my heart I thanked the fire's weakness, for I had no power to look away. Both of us had our hands covering nose and mouth, but the stench came through mine as though they weren't there. The thing rolled onto its back.

The twisting maggots covered it so thick that it shed clumps of them as the swimmer might shed the foam he's crawled from. The worms dripped, and then drained down. Here and there they fell away completely, and left patches of fresh, pale skin. Over the ribs they rose in a pair of squirming domes, and then avalanched away and left behind two fat, rose-nippled breasts as luminous as full moons. And at the same time, luscious thighs and loins shed their foulness and glowed, and her skull sockets spilled out their contents as great black eyes filled them.

A woman had been born, nude and whole. The earth she lay on was clean, and the air was pure again, though when she moved she still gave off a gust of cold like wind off a glacier. She touched her cheek with one hand. With the other, the one that held the key, she touched one of her nipples. She smiled up at the sky. Her teeth were clenched and there was a bitter joy in her eyes. She began to run her fingertips all over her body. Her hands were swift and trembly, like those of a miser searching over a treasure he had thought lost. Two great tears slid out of her eyes, and drenched the black hair at her temples. She rolled her head to stare at us across the fire. For several heartbeats she only stared at us, smiling that clench-jawed smile, her breasts surging softly. Then she said: 'Raise me, mortals. My strength is nearly spent with climbing up to you. There will be little time.'

Her voice, Barnar! It entered your thoughts like cold silk scarves being pulled through your ears – one sounds mad describing it! I moved to obey her, but leadenly, and I'd hardly stirred before Haldar was at her side. He reached his hands down to her, this woman of the living dead, just as promptly as a thirsty man might reach to pluck his flagon from the counter.

But he had to bite back a cry as she took his hands. Heroically, he held on as she rose, and in the end fell to one knee so that she could steady herself, totteringly, by putting her hands on his shoulders. He was hard-put to mask the pain of her touch. And she – her body was full, smooth, and sturdy as a woman's in her twenties. But it seemed she could only hold it upright with the greatest concentration. She kept one hand on the boulder beside

29

her to steady her, once she had gained her feet. Haldar, still kneeling, bowed his head and said shamefacedly: 'Forgive my outcry, Lady. It was . . .'

'It was cold, Haldar Dirkniss,' she said, looking down at him as a spirited queen might look down on one of her favored young earls. 'It was the cold, and the sorcery of the key, which you touched. But you must stand away now, little hawk-faced mortal. I must speak quickly.'

Oh well-beloved Haldar! He never lost the power to astonish me, Barnar! He was always correct, but seldom courtly with women. The way he was acting could only mean that he had been . . . *smitten* by this grave-delivered ghost. There could be no mistaking. The way he jumped up at the word 'little' and drew himself up to full height, and stared at her with deep reproach and bitterness – and the way he had called her 'Lady.' He was no hypocrite with terms. He would have called her Darkling, as is generally prescribed, but for some sudden, special passion.

Not that she wasn't harrowingly female. She was fine, ample and free, even in her tired stance. Her face was small and square, with animal-black eyes and strong teeth. The eyes were wide-set and she had the planed-back cheekbones of a Sargalese peasant, or a Green Plains woman. Her lips were full, restless. She smiled ironically at Haldar's eyes. 'Dear mortal, it is deadly, unendingly hard to rise. It is a long way up and a long way back through the paths of decay. Merely to stand and speak in the living air is a titan's work. The moonlight scorches me. Sweet thief, don't balk at trifles. Stand away and hear me.' Haldar stepped back, bowing his contrition.

She nodded to me. 'Hail to you, northron Nifft, called also Nifft the Lean. You and Haldar both are known to me – your qualities of craft and soul. It is your luck that you chose this camp, and mine that I reached you in it. Know, gentle thieves, that your fortune has turned. I am your gate to fame, to wealth and power past the tongue's telling.

If you go through me you will go, at first, through terrible darkness, but at the last you will go in brightest daylight, amid pomp and acclamation. I am Dalissem. I was a temple-child of Lurkna Downs. I have been dead these seven years.'

It seemed that I heard each thing she said one instant before her lips finished forming it. I felt her voice twice with each word – a double echo of no sound at all. Haldar made a half step toward her, meaning to swear unconditional fealty then and there, no doubt. She thrust out her hand warningly and shook her head, causing her black hair to move in snakes upon her shoulders.

'Listen only! I cannot stand up long against the pull of the Underground. It is true I put a thought in your mind, Haldar – but you were not betrayed. I caused you to swear by the Key, because I *have* the Key, the Key itself of the Marmian Wizard's Manse. It is this one. Now I come to you to offer what you seek. I'll give you your life's transcendent feat – your greatest exploit – and I will not ask your life in fee, though you have sworn it. Instead, I shall fee you – I'll give you the Wizard's Key. For this, you must bring down to me one living man, one man still living down to me in the Winds of Warr, down where I dwell in the Place of the Raging Dead.'

She pointed again and again to the ground as she spoke. Haldar and I exchanged a look. It cost him something, I believe, to tear his eyes off her, and his face held no doubts of this exploit. His look said simply: *What fortune, eh Nifft? What colossal luck*!

And I confess I was no more than a shade off feeling the same. Imagine being presented with Sark's Wand, say, or the Sandals of Speedy Flight. You don't really believe that they must exist in one particular place or another. It's dumbfounding to consider that some one person actually possesses the Key of the Marmian Wizard's Manse – let alone that he might be standing before you, holding it in

31

his hand! She brandished it to us now, the way you hold a sword up in anger and challenge to someone who stands far off. The head of it was a quincunx of wrought-gold roses – just as the tales have it. It was so massive that the holding of it etched little lines of strain in Dalissem's forearm. Of course there was only one good test of the key, lacking the door of the Manse to fit it into, I said, courteously.

'May I touch it, Darkling, to be sure?' I forced myself not to say 'Lady' which, once spoken, seemed so right for what she was. I wanted to irk her slightly, interrupt her, to loose the trance she was weaving in my mind. This you must remember to do when you talk with the more-than-mortal. Dalissem chuckled. It felt like being grinned at by a big mountain cat – delightful for the beauty of the animal, disturbing for the possible sequel. Her face now was showing the wear of a continued effort, along with its bitterness and black delight. She said: 'Dear Nifft, your insolence is what this work requires. I honor your impudence, for you'll need it all. Come here and touch it, then. Come and feel the power in it.'

I approached her, sinking deeper into her cold with each step. The cold drenched you – even through the bone – but it did not freeze your movement. As I stood near her I feared to smell the grave, and smelt instead a rainstorm, the smell of wet wind, chill and lightning-purged. By the Crack, her eyes were dark and deep. I looked at the key, and gently, gently, put my finger to it.

Though prepared, I almost cried out in my turn at the fierce charge humming and grinding within the gold. I pulled my hand back, but the briefest contact sent towering hallucinations skidding across vast polished floors in my mind. I nodded and stepped back.

Dalissem now swayed slightly on her legs. She'd locked her knees, the way a strongman at a fair will do when he's holding a weight aloft. She pressed the Key against her

32

belly and it vanished within her substance. She put both hands to the boulder for support, and smiled at us haggardly.

'You're just men. It will matter to you that the life of him I seek stands forfeit by the oldest laws of every land and subworld. It is Defalk of Lurkna Downs I want. He swore away his life in pledge to me, as I did mine to him. I paid my debt to death, swiftly on the promised hour. He has these seven years turned his back upon his oath, and cherished his flesh, and walked in the light of the world. You may ask any of that city for my story, and know my truth.

'My mother is a Purgatrix, one of the chief seven of Lurkna's temple. She still lives. She swore me to the white tunic at my first blood. Because she hated me. Because I told her that I wished to know the love of men. I found Defalk, Defalk and I found ways. And we had much together.

'Until I was followed, and we were taken at a trysting. Upon that bed, as they were breaking in the door, we swore our deaths. Their ways and hour. For we were sure not to meet again. He would be freed, with reprimand. I, who had stained the Tunic, stood liable to death at my mother's hand on the next Purgation's eve. I meant to forestall her.'

Dalissem had begun to sweat. To see the drops snake down her flanks reminded me of horrible earlier sights. She hugged the boulder now, rested her head against it, while her back registered the earth's pull with shadow-lines of strain. She grinned with an exquisite, almost savored hate.

'But my mother did not mean I should escape her in Death. She condemned me to grow old and die in a small room that had one window too high to reach. But I . . . escaped.'

She let her legs go. Her bare knees hit the gravel with a

33

painful sound. She still hugged the rock with arms too small by far to encompass it.

'My guard, still raw. I killed her on her second day of duty, a Post she'd thought . . . she'd have for life . . . Indeed, she did. That morning of my escape. The world seemed almost in my arms.

'I got a mount. I rounded Lurkna's walls to reach Defalk. I did not keep well off. I was sighted. A patrol set on me. I rode all day. I could not circle back. They contained me though they could not close my lead. My mount was strong, but he must die at last. Near here. It was near the hour of my vow. I had time to strip, to bind my hair, to raise the knife, and cry my lover hail and farewell. The captain was so close I read his eyes. He saw his death in mine. Behind him I saw, with joy, my mother's rage. I must lie down, I cannot choose, I must lie down.'

She fell from the rock then. 'Come near me, Haldar Dirkniss.' She looked up at him from the gravel, and smiled at his haste. Though she lay on her back her body seemed still tensed against the earth. Her head she rested there, but the rest fought back.

'The door to my world lies through the death of another.' She spoke more easily now, glancing at me as well as Haldar. 'There is a man in Lurkna sure to die soon. Arrangements would be easier, of course, if you caught and killed some alley-trash. With the spell I shall give you, you will have passage through the death of anyone at all.'

'We are not butchers,' cried Haldar, pained. He needed no backward glance to know he spoke for me as well. 'We relish difficulty. We'll come to you through the door that offers.'

Dalissem nodded with slow, harsh-eyed approval. 'Well spoken little mortal. You know, Haldar Dirkniss, that you are not a little man.' She said this sharply as my friend was bridling again. 'Others have passed this way through even these few years. I have let them pass. Sent up no feelers of my thought. Would I have cast my nets entire, and climbed this infinite, high climb for little men? Come nearer, and I will put in your memory the manner of your coming, and the spell.'

My friend put his ear to her lips. She whispered for a long while, and my friend looked outward as he listened, but you could see from the dazed shifts of his eyes, strange spaces opening in his mind.

She let her head roll to the side when she had done. Her body gave an exhausted shudder, and just barely regained its tension. 'Stand away,' she hissed. 'Turn your backs, I must return the way I came. In the face of horror, keep your thoughts on the Key. It will be yours.'

We turned away. The reeking cold washed over us. The foaming sound of ten thousand little maggot jaws got louder and louder. Two fat tears jumped out of my friend's eyes and sank into his beard. That night we slept without guard. Death's presence was so strong in the place no wolf would come near it for many days.

My horse had stayed within the boulderfall, its nose having quickly told it of the wolves' departure. We rose before the sun and saddled up, having decided to run and ride in shifts. I took the first turn running. As we started out in the first light of day, Haldar said musingly: 'You know, Nifft. She told me far more than the spell, and the information about Defalk and Shamblor. There were a thousand other things too, endless they seemed.'

'Well what were they?' I asked.

'I don't know! She left them all there inside me, just past the reach of my thought.'

He rode and I trotted on. I left it to him to call the time. I ran all morning long, so far away his mind was. I didn't object to it for three or four hours, greyhound though I am. But at length I had to rouse him. He swore he had not thought an hour gone.

III

Defalk of Lurkna Downs went to many inns and taverns in the course of a day. He went to the fashionable ones in the Exchange district, which stands on giant floats upon the lake, just off shore; he went to the more colorful ones in the wharfside district ashore; he went to the ones in the old center of the city where the chambers of law stood. Where he went depended on whether he was talking to a broker, or negotiating the sale of a haul of his father-in-law's fishing fleet, or cajoling a judge in Maritime Equity to smile upon a renewed charter to fish some particularly rich zone of the vast Great Cleft Lake. I promise you the pair of us learned Lurkna Downs well in the course of dogging the fellow and marking his ways and times. We worked with an ear always pricked to the news of Fleetmaster Shamblor's progress. He didn't command a fleet, you understand, he owned one – one of the city's largest. Gossip about his condition was abundant and we sifted it carefully, for his death was to be the door through which we took our quarry. The Fleetmaster rallied briefly shortly after our arrival, and gave us a week that we did not waste.

The upshot was that on our chosen afternoon, I crouched in an alley alongside the Quill and Scroll Inn. This is in the center of the city and the narrowness of the streets there decided our choice, for it compels passersby, if they wish to ride, to use one of the runner-drawn chariots that are the district's only feasible form of taxi. Defalk never walked when he could ride, and he lunched here almost every day.

On the previous night I had been inside the inn – after hours, you understand – and improved a crack high in the wall through which I could command the side of the inn our quarry almost always sat on. Empty crates in the alley screened me from any who glanced into it as they passed. I mounted a barrel and applied myself to the opening. I meant to watch for his entry, but he was already inside, at the table nearest my vantage. He had only a flagon before him, and seemed to be waiting for someone.

He was a tall, blond man. His wide shoulders recalled an active youth, but his belly and hips now matched the shoulders' girth. His face still had the habit of handsomeness, though soft living had already blurred its lines. But after all, the habit of beauty is the essential thing. He would still be a favorite among the women in his world. His world was that of the no-longer-young, would-be rich. His father-in-law was middling wealthy, but we knew he kept Defalk on a short leash. Our quarry was a man who could expect to be comfortably off eventually, after his youth was well past, and he had served a decade or so as a go-between and adjutant in the world of finance. And you could see at a glance that Defalk was a simple man who wanted no more than to be brilliantly rich, admired, and unencumbered with work. His face said it so plainly: 'I'm an excellent fellow. Isn't such a life no more than my proper portion?' I assure you, I half agreed with him, his conviction was so uncomplicated and sincere. At one point in our observation of him, Haldar had turned to me and said with strange bitterness: 'By the Crack, even the best women love just such men in their inexperience. A brainless complacency must be one of the great secrets of winning women's hearts!'

A burly man, black-bearded and doubleted in burgundy silk, came into the inn, and Defalk signaled to him. The man was Defalk's age, but his movement had verve and his eyes flashed a swinish vitality. Both men wore the insignia of wealth – most notably the fur-trimmed short-capes then in vogue – but when you looked at Defalk's lax shoulders and slightly vague blue eyes, and then at the other's energy, you knew at once that the bearded man was born to the world which the other was still scrambling to enter.

The man strode to Defalk's table and dealt him a hearty shoulder-clap whose familiarity bordered on offense in that relatively staid little tavern. He stood for quite a while, bantering boisterously, drawing lots of eyes, which he enjoyed and Defalk obviously didn't. At last he sat down, still gusty and hail-fellow in all he said. There was some small talk. Defalk kept his voice pointedly low and at the same time tried to return a toned-down version of his guest's conviviality. His awkward insincerity was painful to watch. Kramlod, his friend, drank it in greedily.

At length Defalk set his flagon aside and leaned toward Kramlod. 'We've known each other long enough for me to be blunt,' he said. 'Bespeak what you'll have, and I'll come out with what's on my mind.' He signaled the keep. Kramlod smiled.

'Ah, Defalk, you're just the man to speak out what's on your mind! I remember you as a young man, chasing temple skirts, no less, for your pleasure. We all thought you such a daring romantic then, and so outspoken about all us more conventional souls! Remember what you used to say about the world of business? All toadying and chicanery, lean purses fawning on fat ones for favors? Were those not the days? How far we wander from our youthful views!'

He made only the thinnest pretense of speaking at large. He sat grinning in Defalk's face as the latter chuckled – a sickly and unpleasant little cackle, I judged it, but obviously music to Kramlod. The keep appeared and Kramlod made a stridently jovial affair out of ordering – prodding recommendations from Defalk, echoing them, rallying the keep for his reactions. At last he ordered a small glass of punch. Defalk ordered a double firewater and I didn't blame him.

'Favor-seeking you mentioned,' Defalk said when the keep was gone. 'By coincidence, Kramlod, that's precisely my own role now! Perhaps you guessed it! There's no dimming your eyes, old buck! In a word then, noble fellow, you must ask us to this evening of yours! It would help us greatly and harm you not at all. Lurissil sends her pleas with mine – very pretty ones, I promise you, they'd charm you in a minute. Come then, I know you simply overlooked us!'

Kramlod smiled with childlike wonder. 'I'm baffled!' he said. 'I'm nonplussed. I'm robbed of speech. You and Lurissil, music lovers! For surely it's the orchestra on the raft – the prospect of waterborn music under the stars – that starts your saliva regarding our little evening! There you have it – one thinks one knows someone, only to have them reveal utterly unsuspected traits of character!'

The drinks came. Kramlod took up his and looked blandly about the inn, as if the topic had been disposed of. Defalk smiled wryly and took a pull on his firewater, no doubt to take a certain taste out of his mouth. 'You're like one's elder brother,' he chuckled, shaking his head as if Kramlod indeed recalled to him some affectionate memory. 'You hold the candy out of one's reach, just for the joy of being taller! Look here, this is really unconscionable, old man. And you know very well I'm no music lover! You rogue!' He smiled in relish of Kramlod's roguishness. The crinkles round his eyes looked more like pain than mirth, and Kramlod studied them avidly.

'But really, Defalk. I'm absolutely adrift. What but the music could make you beg so hotly for an invitation to my little evening? I'm forced to think you're teasing, that you don't *really* want to come at all.'

Slowly Defalk shook his head, displaying further relish for his friend's humor. 'Well, well, I see you'll insist on playing the fox, Kramlod. I don't hide my motive. It will give Lurissil the opportunity of inviting the Lady Squamash to her afternoon next week. Lord Squamash's fleets have the charter for the waters adjoining my father-in-law's. We have a negotiation in view. There. A man can't be plainer. You see I don't seek to minimize the indebtedness we'd feel for this little favor from you.'

'By the Crack I understand. I'm terribly thick, Defalk – ludicrously so. To make a mystery of a thing I might have seen in an instant if I'd put my mind to it. Lord Squamash! Of course! Darla swears I'm far too dim for public duties. I deny it, but in my heart I confess I think her right! This was delicious, Defalk. What was the name of it again?'

'Red-posset punch.'

'Indeed. Well, I've had great amusement here, dear friend. I must get away now – Darla is hiring the music all day today and wants my help. Convey my heartiest kisses to Lurissil.'

Kramlod stood up, beaming. Defalk looked up at him blankly – getting his gorge down, I suppose, so he could speak. Kramlod waited in obliging silence, giving him the time he needed. At last Defalk said: 'And your evening, Kramlod – will you invite us to it?' His voice was flat, and he didn't manage or bother to get all the hate out of it. This apparently was the last treat Kramlod was waiting for. He smiled with a pleasure which it must have felt downright obscene to have given him. He gave a brightening start of recollection and thrust his hand into his doublet.

'Now see the decay of this noble memory! Here we've been talking on and on about it, and all the time I had this for you from Darla! Here! Spare my dignity, Defalk – don't tell anyone else of this humiliating display . . . of my forgetfulness!' He tossed a little beribboned scroll on the table and left with a cheery wave.

Defalk sat still for a while, looking blank – looking like a man who was busy not thinking or feeling anything. I felt as embarrassed for him as if I'd been sharing the table with him during the brown-nosing. I was so ashamed of him I wanted to hit him. An odd thing that. I'd never have felt it, of course, if I hadn't known that Dalissem had died for this man. He picked up his drink and drained it, and sat still again. His eyes got meditative. He took on a rapt look of vengeful fantasy, and his lips stirred, with triumphant rebukes, I guessed. At length he sighed, and ordered another drink. He never touched the invitation till he had finished his second drink and gotten up. Then he pocketed it quick and strode out.

I knew his route from the inn to the main thoroughfare, and I got ahead of him on it, glancing back to be sure of his following. Haldar waited just past the first turning I took. As you've guessed, he stood by a chariot. He was barebacked and oiled against the cold – all in the mode of a Lurkna taximan. He stood far nearer the Quill and Scroll than Defalk could usually hope to find a vehicle, as the tavern was in a commercially dead zone. We could be sure of his taking our accommodations.

'He's a minute back,' I told Haldar. My friend threw me a leather sack. I sprinted ahead to the next lane, and turned down it. I ran, light and fast, to a cul-de-sac between two abandoned dwellings. It was deep enough to look like a through-way when you first turned into it, but after a slight veer you saw it was blind. I passed this turn and crouched down.

After a few moments I heard the chariot coming, and then Defalk's voice: 'Is this a through way? I think not.'

'It is, my lord, and dodges the snarl of the carts on Vertig lane.'

'I don't want to lose time . . .'

The chariot whirled past me. I jumped out to stand behind it while Haldar stopped short and heaved upward on the traces. Defalk spilled headfirst and backwards out of the cart. I brought up my sack's mouth to catch him and he tucked himself into it all the way to the waist, just

41

as neat as your foot thrusts into your boot of a morning. Then Haldar was by me. We got the bagmouth to Defalk's ankles and knotted the heavy drawstrings. He was bellowing to bring the walls down. We righted him, and I punched him in the center of the ribs' arch, just enough to knock his breath out. He sagged, and we put him in the cart, folding him to fit the bottom. I got in the seat. Haldar turned the chariot and trotted us off to our lodgings in the wharfside district.

Hitting him had been a relief – it felt like revenge. How could he be what he was, when he had had Dalissem before him, beckoning him to all he could have been? I found I was as angry with him as Haldar was.

But, not being an idealist like Haldar, I couldn't help seeing it in a saner way too. The man had only been vain and weak. Cold-blood killing is bad enough, is it not? But to drag a living man down there . . . he was an oathbreaker. He'd sworn his life away, and it stood forfeit by all laws known in this world and the subworlds alike. I kept a firm grip on this fact in my heart, you may be sure. And wouldn't you have done the same, gritted your teeth and dragged away – for the Key of the Marmian Wizard's Mansion?

IV

Two days after taking Defalk, we lay in readiness for our descent. Our captive lay between us, tied hands and feet, with Haldar's dirk-point in the hollow of his throat.

I've said a great deal in saying we lay in readiness. Here's what it meant: We lay on top of a great velvet canopy that overhung the bed of Shamblor. The Fleetmaster himself was below us, in the bed, busy dying. Half a dozen other people were in the room. We were invisible to them all, due to the canopy's height, so long as we did not sit up, but the room was so quiet that even the growl of a man's stomach was clearly audible. I knew from some carefully stolen peeks, and from following their conversation, how they were situated.

Two of them were druggists, and wore their sable cowls up in sign of professional engagement. They did not sit down, as their guild rules forbade this at a deathbed. Of the other four, two were seated. One was a dried-out woman, Gladda, the magnate's spinster daughter and only child. The other was her nurse-companion, a burly, short-haired woman with an oddly beautiful face. The remaining two were a cousin of Shamblor and his wife. They might have found chairs, for the room was full of opulent furniture, but they stood with a stoicism that conveyed a fitting sense of humility and gratitude in advance. The man, a long rickety fellow, insisted on being the one who ministered Shamblor's medication when his breathing got rough. This was a posset in a gold cup that stood on a table by the bed.

We had got Defalk into the house the day before by delivering him, drugged, inside a gaudy funerary memento sent to the house with the condolences of a fictitious earl. It was a great ceramic tombstone, all bewreathed with black-dyed plumes. Defalk, folded, just fit within the 'stone.'

The memento was accepted with perplexity by the daughter. Within the hour I followed it, properly garbed, as the said earl, I spoke to Gladda with moist intensity, wringing her unwilling hand. When I had been a mere fopling, before the days of my family's increased fortunes (we were a great house latterly decayed) a jovial old gentleman had once given me a copper for some sweets. He clapped my little shoulder, and spoke words of encouragement and good cheer which had lit a little blaze that had warmed me ever since.

But one always forgets precisely these small yet precious

43

debts. The march of time, the whirl of events, the flow of circumstance! I had long known the kindly old man's name – Fleetmaster Shamblor – and still had never called, never squeezed that gruff but giving hand. And now I came too late! I had learned of the great man's death. And so I had sent that poor token she had already received, and had come myself with a plaque of graven silver commemorating his good deed to me.

What? He still lived?! There was still a chance to meet those eyes, still a moment in which to – you get the drift. Within five minutes Gladda was leading me up to Shamblor's chamber, and with a fairly good grace too, considering the dry and suspicious woman that she was. She was no fool, either. People will sometimes lose sight of the most fundamental truths merely through the long habit of them. I'd tinctured my tale with circumstantialities, I'd done my research, but Gladda momentarily forgot what she'd never have doubted an instant if you'd asked her about it directly. Namely, that Fleetmaster Shamblor wouldn't give a fly a swat without something in return. The plaque was a costly thing – the silversmith we got it from was paying for it himself, though he didn't know it – and perhaps the spinster was persuaded by its value. Mind you, I gave her a perfect version of the rich man who had nothing better to do than go around making himself look soulful.

At the magnate's bed, I laid the plaque tenderly beside him, sprinkled some more drivel on it, and wrung his suety hand. Shamblor peered up at me like a fish through ice. While all this went on, I did the one thing I'd come for. I let a rat pellet fall from my codpiece, and as I rose from the bed, much affected, I crushed the pellet with my heel.

I asked for the conveniences. Gladda blushed and directed me, remaining in the room. But out in the hall, I went no farther than the next bedroom door. This room was the only suitable place for lodging the sick man, once

44

the other became unbearable, and the other room would become unbearable some time near midnight. I pulled some light, strong climbing cord from my doublet, anchored it to a window mullion, and let it fall outside. We had dyed it the color of the stone of Shamblor's walls. I reclosed the window but left it unlatched. I returned to the sickroom and took my wordy leave.

Our plan was loose and chancy. In such a big house, they might choose another room. Or the rats might come too soon, and Shamblor be moved before we could get ourselves into it.

Well, every big house, however fine, has plenty of rats in it, especially in damp waterside towns like Lurkna. But the staff was well paid and hard-driven by Gladda, and the bait was as slow as we'd hoped in bringing the invasion. Haldar and I limbed in just after dark. We chose our hiding place and lay listening till we had a good sense of how many servants were about, and what was the frequency of their movements.

As soon as activities appeared to be tapering off for the night, we stole out. Without trouble we slipped downstairs, got Defalk out of the mock tombstone, and brought him back to the bedroom. Once we were all settled on top of the canopy, there was time left for a half hour's sleep apiece. Then we brought Defalk round with a restorative herb. He must not suddenly awake in the midst of things. He had been prepared for his situation, but given no explanation of any kind. He knew only that we meant to ransom him, and that he would emerge unharmed, providing he did nothing, no matter how bizarre the circumstances he found himself in. So when he woke, he only glared at us both, and said nothing. Haldar and I lay listening.

Sometime near midnight we heard the first hasty footsteps and shouts of disgust in the corridor. Soon after, we heard the skittering little feet of drug-maddened rats charging past. The rat-sounds got even thicker and never wavered, not even when several pairs of feet hammered up and down the hall. Ripe concussions, the squalls and coughs of slaughtered rats, reached us. The reaction was as we'd hoped. The passionate fixation of the rats on that one door alone was observed. Two wheezing grooms burst into our room with the sick man on his mattress between them, and the burly nurse like a harpy from hell on their heels. Rats, after all, are a groom's business.

Down the hall the storm raged, and would till the pellet faded. The apothecaries and the relatives quickly left the battle and cleanup to the servants and resettled in our chamber. Strong beverages were brought which, by the sound of it, none of the watchers refused. Conversation was attempted several times, but it did not thrive.

And thus we'd lain in our readiness for two hours and more, when I decided we'd have to take a hand in things. Shamblor had settled into a snore that sounded like restorative sleep. He'd gurgle now and then and some posset would be dribbled into him, and he would sleep on. It began to seem he'd rally again. I was not about to meet the Taker of Souls with my nerves worn and raw from a grueling wait. I reached across Defalk to warn Haldar with a touch, but before I'd moved farther, Gladda broke the long silence. Quietly she asked: 'Do you suppose they came . . . *for* father?'

'No,' said the nurse crisply. You felt, hearing them, that they'd forgotten everyone else. 'They haven't followed him, have they? There's your answer,' she concluded. There was a pause.

'So many of them . . .' Gladda said.

Thus was a ploy pointed out to me. I eased a copper out of my breeches, the room's carpet being dark brown. I flipped it through the air so it struck the farthest wall. At the sound, the old cousin screeched and someone jumped up from her chair so fast it fell over backwards. The

Druggists were made to inspect the other side of the room, and everyone else gathered at their backs. I sat up and flicked a pellet of poison at the goblet on the stand. It was as adept a move as I've ever brought off in a tight spot. It landed with a plurk in the posset – the noise raised more gasps, but no one could fix its source. They didn't find my copper either. They returned nervously to their positions. We had only to wait for the magnate to gurgle again.

Poisoning the cup made it all realer. The man would now die, sure and soon. Which meant the door to that world would open, sure and soon. None in the room but ourselves would see it open, and only we would see what entered. And roast me if I didn't nearly throw a fit then and there, Barnar. I was taken so fiercely with a shout of laughter that the canopy quivered with my holding it in.

It was Defalk, you see. The grimness of what stood now so near him, coupled with the ridiculousness of all he had just been through! How grotesque his puzzled theories must be, and how far off! I remembered the last thing I'd heard him say before we took him: *I don't want to lose any time.* Alas, Defalk! Haldar, at that very instant, was wheeling you to Eternity! I know you'll not think that because I laughed I did not pity him. Pity was half the reason of that laugh. I barely managed to wrestle it down – a bad omen, considering the bout I'd have to fight shortly.

The sick man wheezed and there followed the sound of a dram administered. Hearing the sound was like having a key turned in the pit of the stomach, letting in dread. Haldar touched my shoulder to sign his readiness. We clasped hands over Defalk's chest, and Haldar began to whisper the spell. The breathing noise of the magnate suddenly grew spastic and harsh. The nurse said: 'Your father! Look!' Her voice was crisp and alert, a sensuous tremor in it, as if the moment of passage were a physical pleasure to her. And I felt her voice as if it had slithered across me. My skin was unnaturally alive. I was feeling

47

everyone in the room, as if they were moving through my nerves. I felt the quiver in the nurse's loins, and in Gladda's cry of 'Father!' I felt the doubt mixed equally with hope. Everyone was gathering toward the bed murmuring . . .

And then the room was absolutely soundless except for the dying man's breath. Nothing moved. So strong was the sense of the chamber's emptiness that I sat bolt-upright on the canopy, and got a bad shock to find everyone still there, frozen mute in postures of approach to the bed. Gladda faced us directly, but her face had stiffened in a look of heavenly appeal, and her eyes registered nothing. And then there was a sound outside the door. A progression of sounds. Footsteps.

Oddly, the steps seemed to scuff on stone, not carpet, and to echo in a cavern, not a corridor. The door of the chamber drifted open – inward, against the way it was hinged. A naked manlizard six feet high and a yard wide, stalked in, shoulders swinging. Since it grasped a leather sack in one hand, it would be the Soul-taker, my opponent. I shuddered at the leverage in that cold, leathery frame. Its tail was short and massive, better than a third leg with its flexibility. The Taker would have tremendous stability in a tussle.

But when the Guide of Ghosts followed his servant into the room, I breathed a prayer of gratitude that it was only the henchman I had to fight. The Guide was a wild-haired barbarian. He had to stoop through the door – more than seven feet I'd put him. He wore a ragged and muddy kilt, and battle-sandals, also muddy, whose thongs wrapped his calves. He wore nothing else but a travelers cape, under which his trunk bristled as hairy as an ape's. His eyes were black slots, his cheeks like glacier slopes, flat and cold. His mouth was a restless chasm deep in the brambles of his beard. All he carried was a staff, but its crook was a living serpent as thick as my arm.

The two of them stood looking up at us, pausing without

surprise in their approach to the deathbed, waiting. I cleared my throat.

'Hail, Guide of Ghosts,' I said. 'We beg you to take us with you, alive, on your journey back down with the life of Shamblor Castertaster.'

Slowly, the Guide said, 'Come down.' He had the voice to give those two words their ultimate expression. His tones seemed to fall endlessly – his speech echoed and fell away within him, and it drew you after it, into him. I jumped down onto legs that almost buckled under me, what with our long lying. Haldar handed Defalk down – he'd started to struggle when he heard our aim, and Haldar had stunned him with a blow to the neck. Haldar jumped down in his turn. We were in the midst of the watchers. Gladda still looked heavenward, the nurse hung poised nearest the bed like a hunting dog, the apothecaries exchanged an endless grave expression, the old couple wrung their hands, making paralyzed haste to their benefactor's side.

Alone among them, Shamblor was awake to us. His eyes moved with dismay from one to another of us, and real sweat shone on his face. He knew his moment, and was alive in it.

The giant stared at us; I believed I saw him smile, noting Defalk's bonds. As he stared, the serpent that sprouted from his staff leaned near us, and its tongue flickered with inquiry near my face. Its impudent obsidian eyes scanned us as a toad scans flies. Shamblor Castertaster spoke, it was the first time I had heard his voice. It was scratchy, and thin as a mosquito's whine: '*What? Now?*'

The Guide turned his eyeslots on the manlizard. He gestured at Shamblor. The Taker of Souls marched to the deathbed with its wrestler's waddle. It climbed onto the bed and crawled over the magnate's legs. Shamblor thrashed weakly amid his sheets. The lizard demon lowered its head and butted the sick man's belly – at least I thought

49

it only butted. But in fact its blunt scaly snout, and then its whole head, sank right through the blanket. Then the whole damned squamous beast crawled through the belly-bulge of the old man, leather sack and all. For a moment it was gone, Shamblor gaped, and a bizarre, liquid convulsion moved through him. Then his face split assunder like a rent fig, and the bulky reptile poured out of the wound.

The Taker jumped off the bed where Shamblor now lay whole and untorn, but stone dead. The manlizard now held his leather bag down near the base, trapping something in a tiny bulge, while most of the sack hung slack. The Guide of Ghosts nodded at the sack. 'Observe, mortals,' he said. 'He hardly had a spirit at all – just that little clot of ectoplasm. He'll hardly make a ripple when he's dumped in the sewers of the world beneath.'

What could one reply? I bowed. 'Great Guide, what is your answer? Will you bring us down to the place of the Raging Dead and bring us, or two of us at least, back again?'

'You must fight for passage,' said the Guide. His words fell with a dire resonance into his emptiness. 'One of you must wrestle my Taker of Souls to a standstill.'

'I am prepared to do that, Great One,' I answered. 'I would forgo it willingly, should you decide it was not really necessary.'

'It is necessary,' said the Guide.

V

It was indeed necessary to wrestle the Soul-taker without delay, because it handed its sack to the Guide – who grasped it in the same place – threw itself at my middle, and drove me to the floor.

It was like fighting a wave. The only way to survive the

assault was to roll with the surge, to twist and scramble to stay out of its holds. Forget attacking! The thing had not only a third leg in its tail, but a third hand in its jaws. They were toothless, but bone-edged, and could crush muscle. Look here at my forearm – these two marks. The Taker made them. Yes, see the breadth of his bite? To this day I don't know how I got my other arm free to throat-punch the beast, for all the rest of me was writhing across the floor, one heartbeat ahead of a chestlock that could have staved in my ribs like a rotten cask. I flattened its gullet and just as I freed my arm we piled up against the legs of Gladda. It was like colliding with stone-planted bronze. It knocked me half silly, but I got both hands up to one of her arms and hauled myself free of the manlizard, whose head had taken more of the impact of collision.

The thing shook off its daze in a blink, but I had time to find my feet and as it came curving round the statue-woman I threw a side kick to its chest. Full force, mind you, with all my leg and all my weight behind it. The thing reeled back to its three-point stance. I hit my feet again and skipped back and fired another kick to its sex.

Now my target was problematical. Lizard's privates lie under one of many identical slat-like scales on their bellies. I chose the broadest slat and hoped for the best.

With my greater experience, I can now advise against this tactic with large reptiles or quasi-reptiles. The Taker rocked with the blow and then exploded forward, as if I'd fired it with new power. For an instant I thought I'd outwitted it when I leaned aside from its dive, and threw a neck-lock on it from behind with my arm. Then I was just holding on as the Taker stormed through the room, hammering the floor and walls and time-frozen people with my body.

I had such desperate work keeping my body tight against the crushing and the blows, that I had no strength to strangle it with, the best I could manage being to keep its head and jaws out of action against me. We crashed into the old woman – her abundant skirts were like cement – and careened from her to a great oaken wardrobe. The Taker rammed me into it dead on to break my hold on its throat. We smashed right through and into the wardrobe – through an inch of solid oak! Wait. Look here on the back of my shoulder where I took the blow. That's where it cut me as it broke.

And then it was like fighting underwater, drowning and blinded in the heavy coats and cloaks. The Taker worked its head halfway around and its jaws gaped right under my face. I thought I would suffocate in its swampy breath. Meanwhile it had twisted up the length of its body and was pounding at my head with its tail. It had me pinned in the box, and could well hope to pound me senseless, given time. I was forced to keep one arm up to protect my head, and my shoulder was being beaten numb.

Then, the next time his tail came up, I grabbed it with my blocking-hand and shoved it down the Soul-taker's own gaping throat. That freed my hands for an instant, which I used to get a double strangle-grip of its throat, locking its tail in its gullet. Its body was bent in a hoop around me, now, and I kept it pinned with my weight.

If the Taker had a weak point, it was its hands. They were as big as a man's, but only three-fingered, and had the scaly delicacy of a reptile's. Plucking a soul off its rack of meat takes dexterity and finesse, I suppose. The Taker couldn't break my grip on its throat, and in its extremity for air, it at last lay still, conceding the match.

I staggered back to the Guide. My opponent got up swiftly and moved to a position by the door, showing no slightest sign of fatigue or pain. He could have fought again, at this instant, I realized, and annihilated me in a moment. The Guide said to me: 'It is Dalissem, the temple child of Lurkna Downs, who has called you.'

Haldar and I assented. Defalk stared at the Guide

fixedly, but without shock. Surely he had guessed who had sent for him. One could not be as close to such a woman as he had been, and come away without a feeling of her power to work her will.

'Come then, mortals,' the Guide said. 'We will seek her soul.' He handed the leather sack to the manlizard. The servant preceded the giant out the door. The three of us followed, after slashing Defalk's ankle-bonds. The wardrobe, I saw, stood whole and undamaged. The people, it seemed, began to soften, and to stir. We stepped out the door, and into a spacious gloom. The torch-lit corridor was gone. We'd entered a vast, rawly stinking sewer.

It was arch-vaulted, hundreds of yards across, and its only light was a kind of glow from the scummy river that filled it wall to wall. We were on a rickety wooden staircase that led down to a tiny pier. There was a raft of tarred logs moored at the pier.

The Taker and the Guide stepped onto the raft. We forced Defalk after, and got on ourselves. The Guide said:

'You may unbind your captive. You are within the realm of Death. If any of you leave my protection, you are forfeit unto Death, forever.'

We freed Defalk's wrists. Up at the head of the stairs the ornately carved bedroom door of Shamblor Castertaster swung shut and, with the stairs, vanished from the muddy sewer wall. Our raft was afloat, riding the hideous flood. The manlizard had taken up a pole and was pushing us out to center stream.

Those waters teemed, Barnar. They glowed, patchily, with a rotten orange light, and in those swirls of light you could see them by the score: the little bug-faced ectoplasms that lifted wet, blind eyes against the gloom, and twiddled their feelers imploringly; and others like tattered snakes of leper's-flesh with single human eyes and lamprey mouths. And there were bigger things too, much bigger, which swam oily curves through the light-blotched soup. One of these lifted a complete human head from the waters on a neck like a polyp's stalk. It drooled and worked its mouth furiously, but could only babble at us. All these things feared the raft, but you could *feel* the boil and squirm of their thousands, right through your feet. The heavy logs of the raft seemed as taut and ticklish as a drumskin to the movement of the dead below.

The Guide said: 'Defalk. This is a journey you should have taken in another form, and long ago.'

'You know our companion then, Great One?' I asked. Defalk looked away from the Guide and said nothing.

'Whose name do I not know, northron Nifft? I learn every living being's name as it is given. When the mother first speaks her infant's name, she's whispering it in my ear too. She is saying, though she does not know it, "Here, O Guide, is my Defalk, another job for you someday."' The giant chuckled gently. There was silence for a while. The stink of the place was so entire and all-enveloping I found I could ignore it – like a waterfall's roar when you're near it long enough. It seemed to me that the current of the turgid flood was moving a bit faster.

'But even if I had not known him early,' the Guide said abruptly, 'I would have learned of him later. Did I not carry down Dalissem? Oh, that stroke she gave herself meant business, mortals. No hesitation in that thrust – between the ribs and through the heart. She split it sharp and firm as a kitchen maid will cleave an apple. There was a woman! Her soul filled this whole sack! It bulged with her spirit! That's rare enough, I promise you. Most of what we take is a dwindled-down and wretched little clot of greed and complacency and fear – like this! We let such slugs worm their own way down to the floor of hell. Thus!' The Guide shook out the bag over the side of the raft. Something rat-sized clawed the air and splashed into the flood. Shortly, a whiskered snout without eyes surfaced and squeaked lugubriously at us. The Soul-taker drove the pole against it and it swam off.

'But Dalissem,' said the Guide. 'Dalissem was one of those who won a place. Souls that burn hot enough, you see, stay lit in death, and win eternal being in this kingdom – being you can *call* being, I mean, not buglife in scum. Rage was the fire she endured by. Therefore her place of endurance is with the Raging Dead, amid the Winds of Warr.'

'Rage?' burst out Defalk. His speaking surprised us all. He looked at the Guide. 'Why in a place of Rage? She died for love – for our love!' I caught in his voice both his guilt, and his more terrible secret vanity.

'To your own shame you speak it!' – it was Haldar who said this, seizing Defalk's arm and shaking it. 'But it was rage much more than love. Could you have known her so little? I knew her entirely with one glance – such is her fineness! She would have killed her enemies with her own hands, she would far rather have wreaked her rage than died! But she was powerless except against herself. So she struck there, scorning a life in chains.'

Quietly, tenderly, the Guide asked, 'She is beautiful, is she not, Haldar Dirkniss?'

'She is, Lord Guide.'

'You Defalk,' said the Guide, 'you should have seen her journey down. You should have seen her birth from the Soul-taker's bag. Such splendor out of the foul, dark thing. True souls emerge with the shapes they had. She lay here on this deck, seven years ago, and she barely stirred when she understood where she was. Her first movement was to stretch her arm beside her, as a sleeping woman will do in the early morning, to be sure of her man in the bed by her. Dalissem found no one to her right, nor to her left. Then she sat up slowly and looked about her. I looked away to spare her shame in her disillusionment.

'She never said anything. After a while she stood up and

55

watched what passed. Through all her journey, she stood by me and watched, and her expression scarcely changed. At the very last, when we stood by the chasm of the Winds of Warr, I pointed to the staircase that lead down their brim. She stepped from the chariot gravely. She turned back to me and gave me a deep reverence, dropping to one knee. She did it like a queen! Then she strode down those steps, elegant and grim. But at the bottom, on the brink of the pit, hauteur alone was not enough to express her wrath. She stopped and raised both fists above her head and shook them. Throwing back her head, she howled. Then she dove from the steps, head-first into the black hurricane.'

While the giant spoke, Defalk sat down on the deck and rested his head in his hands. How much can you hate weakness? I felt sorry for him. But then the first thing he said was:

'What does she want with me now? Is she going to take my life?'

'We don't know,' said Haldar. Strictly speaking, we didn't. But could there be any doubt?

After a moment Defalk, still not looking up, asked: 'What has she paid you for this service?'

Haldar gave a disgusted snort. The reaction was odd – after all, we *were* working for hire, weren't we? I answered:

'She is giving us the Key to the Marmian Wizard's Mansion. It is, somehow, in her possession. She showed it to us.' I looked hopefully toward the Guide as I said this. He volunteered nothing about how one of the dead might obtain the Key. After a silence, barely audibly, Defalk said: 'I see.'

VI

The soul-sewer branched and veered and branched. We steered through the reeking maze for an endless time. Defalk sat hunched, no doubt remembering things. Haldar stood rapt at the Guide's side, his eyes straining with an avid light at the semi-dark.

I could not share his calm rapture. It seemed to me the current had begun to quicken, and that the gloom was thinning . . . and somewhere ahead there was a sound, too faint to read, but growing. I was not at ease. It made me realize how separate our thoughts had really been in the days just past, even during our closest planning. For my friend this exploit was, from its first proposing, a feat of devotion, a chivalrous quest. He loved me well, and made a point of gloating over the prize we would win – but he did this out of concern for my feelings, lest he should seem to scorn the baseness of my motive by proclaiming the disinterest of his. Splendid Haldar! He was transparent to me. I saw then that when the moment came he would, on oath, renounce his share in the Key, and would demand that Dalissem bestow it formally on me alone. Thus did he mean to declare his love to that queenly ghost. For him, Defalk was a cur, and Dalissem nearly a divinity.

But I was in it for the Key. For me, Defalk's suffering was an ugly necessity, and Dalissem was a splendid but utterly self-willed spirit. And most important, nothing was to be taken for granted in that place. In Death's world, any covenant, no matter how mighty, can fall null – any spell, however cogent, can be abrogated. The only certain law in that place is Death itself.

Just then my uneasiness was getting a lot of encouragement. The current was unmistakably increasing, for the

57

ectoplasmic sewage had begun to seethe with alarm and resistance. At the same time it was getting lighter – a yellowish light that thickened like mist. The ribbed vaults above us showed clearer. I discovered, with horror, that the Guide had no eyes. His sockets were wrinkled craters filled with grey smoke.

I was sure he had eyes in the death room – or had he? I can't explain why it unnerved me so – I gaped at him. He looked back at me, waiting.

'What is that noise, Lord Guide?' I stammered.

'It is the entrance to Death's domain,' he said. That it well might be. It was a holocaust of cottony sound – a mumbling roar of waters. The Taker shipped his pole. All around us, the soul-trash – all the bugfaces and rotten monocular snouts and desperate feelers – made a mindless noise of woe, and churned up the speeding scum with their struggles. The sewer fell abruptly to a steeper pitch, and took a turn.

As we slid out of that turn we saw the terminal arch of the tunnel far ahead, framing a burst of yellow light. We knew the hugeness of the smutty gulf beyond the arch by the way it swallowed up the howl of the falls. The giant reverberations fled away to unguessable distances beyond. At that point I knew – *knew* that we had been tricked, and all three of us were being abducted into the land of death forever. It was my blessed luck to be too stunned by the thought of the falls ahead to make any move at all. Therefore I did not draw my blade and assault the Guide of Ghosts. Woe if I had! Down that last slope the raft seemed hardly to rest upon the leaping, jostling waters, so smooth and fast we went. Then we plunged into the dreadful jaundiced sky that yawned out and down.

We sledded out upon the empty air, and saw that we had issued from the face of a wall stretching past vision, with a hundred tunnelmouths to either side, puking and groaning their currents down. These waters braided in a vast feculent tapestry, whose lower reaches hung hidden in boiling fog. Into that fog we ourselves settled, the raft spinning, tilting, swooping – descending with the crazy zigzag of revelers staggering down a street, and falling no faster than a wind-buoyed leaf. The fog wrapped us close.

We spun through the mist so long I thanked its being there to hide the drop from us as we first went over. Then we broke down into clean air, and found under us a huge black lake. We knew by the sound that we had moved far out from the falls, but even here the laketop danced and jittered like a tubful of shaken slops. As we dropped to the water it stirred my nape to see, under the surface below us, a blurred eye half as big as the raft. It blinked and submerged. The waters were alive.

The shore was not far – a line of crags against the sky – but we saw much getting there. We moved steadily, by what means did not appear, and the water's denizens, as they saw us, all dodged our course. Some were rooted and could not: men whose legs fused and tapered to a stem and whose bodies hung just under the surface with every vein and nerve sprouting out of them, like fan-corals red and grey, and with their brains branching out above like little trees. Crabs with human lips scuttled up and down these nerve-festoons. And everywhere in the water were shoals of armless, bald homunculi, fat as sausages, kicking through the darkness. Scores more of these same creatures were to be seen bandaged in silk and trailed in wriggling, staring bunches by water-skating spiders big as dogs – though not spiders entirely, for men's faces were set in their flat forebodies, just behind the fangs.

So many combats broke the surface, what must those depths have been like? Men backed with great limpet shells emerged here and there in a grisly wrestling that entangled their limbs and their slithersome, ropy innards as well, everted for the fight. Off to port something as big as a whale heaved up, foaming. All along its length ranks of spindly limbs flailed pitifully – they were human arms. We shortly understood their panic when that island of skin was over-swarmed by scorpion men and pinchers like flensing knives. With these they busily lopped the waving arms.

Some shacks stood at the foot of the crag we drifted toward. Beyond that ridgeline which marched with the shore, was empty yellow sky, promising that the land fell away past the lake's brim. The Taker of Souls jumped out and beached us. We stepped onto the soil of Death's domain. It had an ugly resilience to the foot, a bruised and sweaty texture. The manlizard waddled toward the shacks, and disappeared between two of them. The Guide stood by the water, turning the smoky nothingness of his gaze on each of us in turn.

'Mortals, to pass through this place, you must meet one hard condition. The Master's lieutenants dwell everywhere. To pass those places where they have the Right of Toll, you must pay them a morsel of your flesh.'

I asked him, 'Does the Master have ... many Lieutenants?'

'As many,' he said, 'as there are ways to enter this world. But no man must pay toll more than once. Nor may the toll be lethal in its nature.'

Having come through what we had, we couldn't let this ghoulish necessity be an obstacle. We nodded – Defalk said nothing, knowing that consent was not required of him. There was a banging from behind the shacks, and a noise of wheels and harness. The Taker reappeared, leading a pair of shrouded beasts hitched to a giant black chariot.

The wheels were high as a man, the body like the prow of a fighting sloop, black as obsidian but ribbed inside with ivory. Of the team we could see two hairy tails and eight massive paws with nails as long as my fingers. The beasts' heavy shrouds of black canvas were bound snug with leather straps.

The Guide mounted the car, took up the reins and drew them tight.

'Mount,' he said, 'and grip the rail. You must hold fast before we loose the team.'

We got up into the chariot – but Defalk stayed on the ground. 'It is unfair!' he shouted. 'How many oaths are made and broken by how many thousands of young lovers?' None of us answered, only waited, for we all knew he had to come – he too knew it. We couldn't grudge him the thin comfort of making his moan before descending to his fate. 'I loved her well – I loved her greatly – none of your sneering can alter that. But love is life, not swords in the heart! How could I know she would *do* what she swore?'

'Oh yes,' Haldar said. 'I'm sure you thought her as trifling as yourself, you had to save your pride. So you missed your sworn hour. What about *after*, when you knew what she had done? You had seven years to make it good.'

'Kill myself! Cleave my bowels with a dirk! Oh yes, thief – what easier done? She was *dead*. Her pain was past. With or without me she faced her mother's hate and imprisonment. She'd have loved any man she had the chance to, just to spite her mother, and she'd have died for the same spite whoever had been her man.'

'Climb aboard, courtier,' said the Guide. 'Our way is hard, and we must start.'

Defalk let his shoulders hang, and looked at the ground. Then he got aboard. The Guide tightened the reins and grasped his staff near the butt, stretching it out over the shrouded pair. The serpent coiled restlessly, and its tongue flickered. The Taker of Souls unbelted the shrouds, and leapt away as he pulled them off.

Two immense black hounds sprang up against the light, and howled. Then they fell on each other like famished sharks. Their knotted, lean-strung bodies were not of living flesh, but something more like clay, for their red jaws tore great clots of it from one another, and there was no blood.

61

Only a giant's strength could have held them within the traces. The chariot rocked and swayed. The serpent began to strike down upon the beasts.

With a hammer's power and a whip's speed it sank its fangs into their heads and shoulders. The hounds wailed with pain and raised their fangs against the snake's, always too slow. With flicks of his wrist, the Guide administered pain to the beasts, till their fighting ceased, and they cringed apart. Then he shook the reins, and the dogs bounded to his will. The Taker of Souls bowed his farewell to the Guide, but we did not see him rise from his salute, so swiftly were we whirled away.

We thundered up the lakeside ridge, and poured across it. All hell spread out before us, far below. A score of rivers foamed down into those black badlands, which were all tunneled and canyoned and chasmed with the branching waters, till the terrain looked like the worm-gnawed wood you find on beaches. Then we were plunging down into it.

Ye powers dark and light! What a ride, Barnar! There was no road – there needed none. Though we favored high ground, following ridgelines, we cut just as readily across the flanks of hills, or dove down the steepest canyon walls and charged through fordings with our great wheels tearing the water to spray.

And one had no wish to linger down in those gulfs either. From above you saw only forests of branched things that stirred slowly, or the roofs of bizarre dwellings. But within the valleys you could see the victims splayed upon what had looked like trees, feeding their foul, slow appetites – and you could see that those roofs were thatched with bones, and caulked with black blood. I was glad of every hamlet, every thicket of rooted shapes, which we steered clear of. At the same time, it was impossible not to exult – even to rejoice – in the power of our passage through a place of such infinite, endless captivities. To surge through league on league of darkness, where a whole world is doomed to endure forever, and be yourself exempt, on fire with life! I caught Haldar's eye; he smiled and nodded. Drinking the dead air like wine, we rocked and soared behind those dead titans which the viper scourged on.

But our glorious detachment was not to last. We crested yet another ridge and saw that it broadened to a wide field which ended, far ahead, at a chasm. This field bore a crop of big, tough bramble-vines, and in each of the vines was entangled a man or a woman. The feet of these sufferers merged with the dry roots, while their bodies were pinned and pierced in a hundred places. Little buckets hung from the vines to catch the rivulets of unexhausted blood that twisted through the thorns. Three hags moved among these plants – pruning, or tying the vines, or guzzling from the buckets. As we drew near they sighted us, and dropped their work. They began to race for the chasm, toward the point we seemed to head for ourselves.

They moved their crooked limbs with ghastly speed, shrieking like daws as they went, and waving. The dogs pounded past the bleeding thousands – our spokes hummed in the dead air. But the hags came before us to our goal: a bridgehead at the chasm's edge.

They blocked the bridge, bobbing and leering as the hounds were reined up in a scramble of paws. Stooped as these crones were, their height matched the Guide's. They were huge in their stench too, charnel house mixed with the smell of a brothel's slop room. Their eyes were flat and opaque, like glazed snot in the wrinkled cups of their sockets. They all had torn-out patches in their hair, and what showed was not scalp, but yellowed skullbone. Yet their faces were fleshed – wenned and warted. They wore grave-rags cinched with gallows rope at the waist. A glimpse through the robe of one, where a cancered breast showed a tumor-pit you could get your fist into, was enough to tell us that their rags were a mercy to our eyes. The fiercest of the three came forward, grinning. One of the hounds leaped on her with a roar. She gave it a clout to the skull with her fist that sprawled it shivering in the traces.

'Skin, Guide!' she shrilled. 'Manskin with blood in it, *living* blood. We want a piece or you can't cross. We want a piece now!'

'Hail, Famine-sisters,' the Guide said. 'We shall pay your toll.' He turned to us. Haldar and I traded a look, and turned to Defalk. He saw our intent to make him pay first. His hopeless expression gave me a twinge of guilt, and so I said:

'I'll pay it, Lord Guide.' I'd have to settle up sooner or later, after all. The Guide nodded, and motioned me to jump down.

'What piece of this man do you want, starving ones?' he asked. They flew into a raucous discussion. They squawked, hissed, cursed and counter-cursed with a force that sent out gusts of their vampire-breath. They named every part you might think of and there were moments when I blanched and promised myself to draw my sword and be damned. Then at last the chief one came forward again.

'We want an ear,' she shouted. 'A nice, fat red ear hot and juicy with blood we want. A *left* ear.'

'No!' shrieked a sister behind her. 'A *right* ear. We want a *right* ear, you scabby sack of tombslime!'

'A *left* ear,' insisted the first. She snatched some rusty shears from her waist. The blades were furred with mold where the blood was crusted, but I took the tool almost gratefully. It was only an ear, you understand, and the hole would still be there for hearing. Look. Here's my work – I spared myself a bit, you see, but I had to give them all the lobe, for that's where the blood is, and they'd have noticed a cheat there. Seeing through a bright red haze, I tossed them the shears, and then the morsel. Instantly they were a screeching heap, fighting for the prize. Hair was rent, and strips of flesh torn from lean flanks. They fought like famished gulls, while I remounted, and the Guide lashed the dogs. Haldar bound my head with a strip from my sleeve as we whirled across the bridge. It seemed endlessly long. The gulf beneath was a dreadful one. A groaning of deep waters filled its darkness.

Even before my brain had swum clear of nausea and pain, I discovered I was hearing things most deep and hidden and distant – hearing, impossibly clear, the secretest sounds of this world. The smallest whispers from the gulf floor entered my brain as if little rat-mouths were murmuring directly through the ruined gate in the side of my head. Pleadings in a mindless speech of moans; torturing giggles and chuckles from dry throats of bone; babbles of devil-confession; the liquid noise of strange stews; the scuff of hooves, claws clicking – even the silken sweep of deep fins. That gulf and all the canyons beyond said much to me as we pounded through them, and hinted countless things I did not wish to know.

VII

I think that Haldar caught my cue of pity. For after a while, he said, 'I will pay next, Lord Guide.'

'Then you will pay soon,' said the Guide.

We had run for some time through a deep canyon whose walls overhung and whose course was branched and mazy. The light on the river and the wide banks was dim and shadow-crossed. The hounds raged forward, tireless, like a destroying wave that comes pushing through miles of ocean. But the grey chasm mocked our speed by seeming endlessly the same.

We watched for changes at the Guide's hint, but at first

saw only familiar things. There were huts with door-curtains of strung teeth still chattering from the denizens' quick hiding. (I alone heard also their rank breathing within, and the groans of their tightly muffled victims.) There were ghoulish smithies too, where toad-bodied giants hammered smoking limbs onto struggling souls stretched on anvils, and other shops as well where similar giants with pipes blew screaming dwarves into being from cauldrons ˊf molten flesh. There were rat-men struggling in thickets of tarantula weed, and there were groves of dung-bearing trees with twisted trunks, translucent like gut. Soulcreeps such as Shamblor inhabited these groves, grazing endlessly. Their drear whining said it was not by choice.

I was the first to sense the new thing ahead. I began to hear the guzzlings and growls of ten thousand carrion-eating throats. It was the noise of a great host, tearing and gulping.

My companions were alerted shortly after by the sooty cloud of birds swooping and wheeling beyond the next bend in the river. We flew through the curve. Before us a mammoth dyke stretched to the river from either wall of the canyon. It was a little mountain range of the freshly killed – fifty feet high and a hundred wide, they were piled. Jackals tugged and shouldered and fought all along the fringes of that wall, while its upper slopes were glittery black with birds. Necrophage insects hung thick as coal dust in the air, and I heard with intolerable distinctness the wet working of their mandibles.

On our bank there was a gateway through the heap. It was overlooked by a guard-tower made of bones. As we neared, something big could be seen moving in the tower. We could also see that most of the corpses in that wall were those of women and children. Their torn faces looked out everywhere from the black swarming of wings and jaws and pincers.

The tower was an insane jumble of the reknit skeletons

66

of everything you could think of. In fact it was more a monkey's perch than a tower, and the giant that came swinging down from it moved more like an ape than a man. He bellowed as he came, with thick, fang-hindered speech:

'Skin! You've got *living* manskin, Guide! I want some!'

The guide reined up, crying. 'Hail, War-father. We shall pay your toll.'

The ape wore as a helmet the top half of a man's skull – a giant's, you understand, for the ape was as big as the hags and yet the skull's sockets came all the way down over its red eyes. The immortal also wore epaulets of braided human hair, but nothing else. It carried a battle axe with a bit as wide as an infantry shield. It rolled up to us, enlisting its free fist as a foot. Both of the hounds instantly leapt upon it. It pummeled them with vigor, but it seemed a long time before they lay still in their harness.

Haldar leapt down from the chariot. The Guide said: 'What piece do you want, starving one?'

The immortal answered decisively. 'I want an index finger.' It shifted its stance restlessly, poised on feet and knuckles. Haldar held out his left arm, the finger extended. The ape began an incredible preliminary dance of strokes and feints and flourishes. It hopped and postured in a great, dust-raising circle around Haldar, whooping with every loop it cut in the air. It dodged and ducked and parried and, at the climactic moment, took a soaring bound at Haldar, and brought the axe in an heroic arc down upon his finger.

Haldar was jolted through by the shock, but stood firm. The finger was clipped off as neat as a daisy at the base, the other knuckles not even grazed.

The ape rolled the finger thoroughly on the ground. 'Best with dust,' it growled companionably. It popped the treat in its jaws and crunched it with gusto for a long time. I helped Haldar bind his hand. He was drenched with the sweat of pain, as was I. Regretfully, the War-father swallowed the last of the finger and sighed.

'I wish I could take more,' the immortal rumbled wistfully. 'What do you say, fellow? Let me have one more finger, hey?' It poked Haldar cajolingly in the shoulder.

'No more, beast!' snapped Haldar. 'Damn your greed!' The ape stamped furiously, and smote the ground so hard with its axe that the chariot rattled. I helped Haldar back aboard. The Guide stung the hounds, and we surged through the gateway. Our passage sent up a cloud of panicked birds and insects. For a time they hung seething above the dyke, like the black smoke of some great city's sack. Then they settled back down on the hill of torn faces. Soon we were driving for high ground.

VIII

I heard the nearness of our goal before the Guide said anything. I heard wind, wind and fire in measureless, empty places, yet nothing was as dead as the air of this world. Haldar too knew something – he said only that he sensed a chill, but I had seen his shudderings since paying the toll. He had a way of rubbing the skin on his arms as if to erase grotesque sensations, and sometimes he looked with amazement at his hands, as if he expected to find something in them, or crawling over them. I guessed his skin's premonitions matched those my ears received. Then the Guide pointed to a region of rocky outcrops which thrust up from a clay mesa to form a higher and more ragged mesa of stone. 'Up there,' he said, 'are the gates of the Winds of Warr.'

It appeared Defalk would be spared the payment of Toll, and it heartened him, I think. He began to stare ironically at the two of us. I said: 'You look amused. What sunny ray has pierced your horizon?'

'I was only thinking, friend assassin,' he said. I let this pass. 'I was thinking how very like Dalissem it would be to show me her contempt by spurning my life. I mean once she'd proven it to be in her hand, for a nature like hers, the mere killing of me would seem too puny a conclusion. She would need a more exquisite gesture of scorn. To spit in my face, perhaps, and then to send me back to my little life – as she would call it . . .' I thought I saw as much self-disgust as amusement in his smile, but my friend got growling mad. It was easy to understand because Defalk's guess sounded so likely. Indeed, the man was not far off the mark, as things ended.

'How can you bear your own miserable littleness?' Haldar asked him. His body shuddered with a sick wave of sensation that his aroused mind seemed not to notice. 'You bank so smugly on her heroism! How gratefully you'd creep away with your face only spat in! If it saved your rat's hide, you'd wear her contempt with joy.'

'You're a life-stealing, sneaking dog!' Defalk raged. He was beside himself, and did not even notice that the Guide gave him a dreadful look. 'You've practiced skulking and back-stabbing all your scummy life. You swagger and beat your chest about heroism and nobility – ' His voice was shrill, and words failed him. It was plain to me that he was as badly infected with high-mindedness as the man who taunted him. Poor Defalk agreed with Haldar in his heart. To my friend's credit, he contained himself. He did not even answer. Perhaps he glimpsed the same truth.

Now, just as the mesa towered quite near, we saw that a last canyon lay between us and them. We were nearly upon it before it appeared. As we spun down into it, we found a road beneath us, and saw a small city down on the canyon floor. Our road dove down the chasm wall and through the city's heart. Black smoke hung over the roof-tops, and there were towers here and there in the streets supporting the braziers that produced it. Even from on high we breathed a reek like a druggist's shop afire. We noticed beyond the city a field of great square pits, where the smoke hung even denser, but our descent was swift, and we only had a moment's vantage of this. Defalk murmured, as to himself, 'A pestilence . . .?'

It was indeed a place of pestilence, but different from all plague-struck cities that I have heard of in being thronged and active. The Guide did not rein up as we tore into the streets, but our team at once began colliding with the citizens of that place.

All went thickly muffled – double hooded, with even hands and face wrapped. At a glance it seemed a drowsy place, for people sat or sprawled in doorways, and on the cobblestones with their backs to the walls. We even saw them lying in the raingutters under upper-story casement windows. The foot traffic usurped even the middle of the lane, for everyone walked quickly and gave everyone else a wide berth. The hounds snarled and bit, and the Guide plied his serpent on the heads of the people who blocked us. The drivers of other vehicles treated obstruction just as high-handedly, but our dire team made the other carters and wainsmen rein up. The wains were full of the dead, tied up in their sheets.

So we moved in surges through the streets, parts of which were narrowed by improvised spitals which were scarcely more than cots under canopies. The doctors who sat in these were coweled, and the limbs that poked from their sleeves were like barbed and jointed sticks. They did nothing, and seemed to watch eagerly while things like crablice, but big as cats, crawled from cot to cot laying eggs in the patients' open sores.

More than one man, in the extremity of sickness, ran raving through the crowd, trailing bedclothes. One such seized a mother who was hastening her child along; he tore her scarves aside and kissed her wetly. He did the same to the child, not relaxing his grip even as the woman hammered him to his knees with a stone. Another man who ran in delirium was chased by several apothecaries. He was nude, straight from his bed, and as he fled, huge swellings in his groin and neck split open. Wet young wasps the size of doves crawled out of them and clung to his body, waving their wings to dry them.

Meanwhile, above the street level, women in boarded-up houses conducted business from upper windows. Some used broomsticks to roll the night's dead off their eaves and down into the waiting wains. Others traded with cart-men below. We saw one lower a bucket to a man with a covered grocery cart. As she fished in her purse for coins, the man thrust his hand into his doublet and pulled out a handful of struggling cockroaches. He threw these into the milk he'd filled her bucket with, winked at me, and covered it.

For Defalk, the worst spectacle came as we put the town behind us. It was the gate that stood before the field of smoldering pits outside the city. Our road lay through this gate, and a giant figure, all wound with foul bandages, sat in our way. It was weeping, and cradling a swaddled object. Past the gate, a second bandaged figure emptied a wain into a smoking pit, using a pitchfork that speared up three men at a stroke. The mourning giant sprang up. Its voice told the female sex which its pus-stained wrappings hid.

'Guide!' she sobbed. 'He is so hungry and ill, our poor babe! Manflesh is what he needs. Give our starving babykins manflesh, please!' The worker – her husband by his greater size – was already out of the wain and running toward us. 'Yes!' he shouted. 'Manskin for our little sweetling, Guide!'

'Hail, Parents of Plague!' the Guide said. 'Step down to

71

them, courtier. What piece of him will you have, great ones?'

The parents fell into a doting conference with their precious one. They teased aside the swaddling rags, and questioned their child with twiddlings of their fingers: 'What does he want then? What does Babekin wants at all, at all?' – until the mother raised her head, and crowed: 'An eye! Sweetkins wants an eye, he does he does he does!'

Defalk had stepped down and stood forth, and steady enough, too. But at this he reeled back. Faster than he moved, the Plague-father shot forth his hand. His black, gnarled fingers seemed to fumble against Defalk's face. Defalk shouted and his knees gave, and then the Plague-father held something teasingly above the swaddled bundle. 'See? See? Does he wants it, hmmm? Does he wants it?'

The mother opened the swaddling wider, revealing not a face, but a boil of bugs, teeming and scrambling in the fetid caul.

'See? See? Does little lord love-kins wants it at all at all?'

Then the black fingers opened, and an eye fell, trailing red strings, into the anthill turmoil. As if floating on some liquid it bobbed there a moment. Defalk clutched his face and bellowed. The insects foamed over the bright ball, and it sank amid them. Defalk howled again. He held his face less in pain, it seemed, than in the way of one who tries not to see something.

IX

When we'd topped the first mesa, and reached the foot of the smaller one, the Guide reined up. He drove his staff in the earth and hitched the hounds to it, under the Snake's guard. With a gesture, he told us to follow him, and began to climb the rocks.

Defalk's worst agony had barely subsided. He no longer raved aloud, but he kept wiping his hand across his face and jabbering rapidly, in the barest whisper, like a man speaking spells he doesn't want overheard. He scarcely had his legs under him, and the rockface was hundreds of feet high and not far off vertical. There were deep seams and chimneys to climb in, and we kept him between us, but I thought a dozen times he'd topple out, and waste all our toils in a single plunge.

But I'm damned if his giddiness came of fear or a slack will. The man was fighting off the drunkenness of pain and shock. He was in a fierce hurry to clear his head, and soon he was shaking off our hands when we reached to help him. He got steadier as he struggled. Hate and remorse drove him, I suppose. Rack me, Barnar, if I didn't admire poor Defalk then. I even stopped feeling sorry for what I'd had to do to him – I'd brought him his finest hour, you see. He meant not to be dragged before Dalissem. He meant to walk up to her like a man. So he clawed and clutched his way upwards like a daw with a torn wing fighting its way into the sky. I suppose actually he was like a draggled jag, with his fine clothes all rumpled. As for his face, it was something very different now. The soft, self-loving man was gone. What was left was a gaunter face, a vision-troubled face, a bit like a prophet's or a seer's. A smudgy line of blood ran from his puckered lids down to his jaw.

Visions no doubt he was having, images of the place we were now so close to. For I know I was hearing it as we climbed. The cleanness and simplicity of that sound! – the sound of fire and wind. And there was something else, fleeing through that roar, obscured within it, but recognizable. It was a multitude of voices. Voices, I say, not the croaks and chuckles of soultrash, but bursts of thought and passion. I was hearing speech from entire and vital souls celebrating some cryptic, furious triumph. The space and clarity in that sound was intoxicating here in this world of foul, drear pain. I saw Haldar rub his arms and smile with a kind of recognition. Defalk climbed with growing vigor. When we reached the top, and stepped out onto the plateau, he was as firm on his legs as we.

I mean to say we expected to step out onto a plateau. In fact, what we'd had premonitions of was closer than we knew. It's a rare shock to put a gulf behind you, rise up, stride forward, and find a gulf a thousand times as deep before you, and you on its very edge. Plateau there was none. We'd mounted the rim of a giant crater.

Just for a moment, as you looked down into it, you thought that the crater's bottom was covered by a glittering black lake. But the wind that came dodging out of it, and the roll of echoes through chambers past measuring, taught you to see better. The lake was a hole broken in the crater's bowl. Beneath was a dark cavern system, endlessly deep, where powerful winds drove clots of fire like a blizzard underground.

A flight of stairs cut from the stone descended the wall of the crater – it was a long flat-arching flight, and the steps were narrow. The Guide was halfway down it already, and he waved us after him impatiently. We started down.

There's no conveying how light and breakable you feel, stepping into a dim cauldron of gales like that, and on such a slender track. It was like following an icy goat path crossing the Imau Mountains in a winter storm. But here the winds wrestled and surged and blew in constant contradictions. You scarcely dared brace yourself against them for fear of leaping off with the next shift.

Our downward progress did not reveal much within the gulf. The infinite traffic of fire there showed you flashes of ragged vaulting, or tunnelmouths. The fire itself seemed like a fabric. It flew in mighty banners or was caught in crosswinds and torn to tatters, and we had glimpses of the pit's inhabitants whenever their flight was entangled with the flames. They were too swift and deep to be more than wheeling shapes, smaller than moths to the eye.

Some half-dozen of the last steps marched past the brink and formed a ramp down into the void. The Guide stopped well above this point, and bade us pass him.

'It is for you to call her – stand down.'

We eased past the immortal – Haldar was first, Defalk between us. My friend stepped down the last steps, and I thought he moved with an uncanny assurance, a steadiness that did not dread this depth.

'Dalissem!' he shouted. His voice was as nothing in the wind. 'Dalissem of Lurkna Downs. Approach. Defalk is delivered to your hands!'

The puny words were erased even as they left his lips, but a freezing updraft followed them like a response, an icy column of wind that pushed against our faces without wavering. Very deep, but directly below the last step's broken edge, there was a small and constant movement. It grew. It was a figure swimming upward.

And that's how she came to us, Barnar, clawing upward out of the dark, her eyes stark, raving bright, her hair twisting in snakes upon her shoulders, her nakedness like a torch in the pit.

Here, movement was no labor to her. She sprang upon the foot of the stairs as light and lithe as a winged cat. She stood arms akimbo, and after nodding to the Guide, she grinned at Haldar and me, and seemed not even to see the man we had brought her. He called to her – his voice had a crack in it: 'Dalissem! Forgive me, and take me!'

Even Haldar was surprised enough to tear his eyes off her and look back at Defalk. For my part, when I'd grasped what he'd said, I gaped at him. But Dalissem spoke as if nothing had been said.

'You have brought him then! I chose my men well. Truly, you two are among the greatest of your brotherhood, to have accomplished this!' (I promise you, Barnar, those

75

were her words to the letter.) 'Alas, good henchmen, who will ever believe you, if you tell them of this exploit?'

Haldar answered her with a tremor of feeling:

'Lady, for myself, the payment of the exploit is this second sight of you. And I here renounce the Key – let it be wholly Nifft's. Please deign to receive this tender of my chaste and absolute love.'

She laughed. 'Chaste and otherwise, Haldar Dirkniss. Oh, I'll receive this tender, and far more! As for the Key, there is none to renounce. You were deceived with a simulacrum.' She laughed again, with ravenous long looks in Haldar's face, and gleeful looks in mine. She was a beauty in truth, with her fat paps, and her loins' black patch, as charged with energy as a cat's hackles. Defalk made a drunken movement but said nothing. I think he was dazed a bit, with the shame of her ignoring him. I was fairly fuddled myself with a shock that was half recognition – the fulfillment of a suspicion I hadn't known I had.

Dalissem raised her arms triumphantly above her and grinned skywards: 'Oh, how I've outwitted you, King Death! Great Thief, you are not half so sly as poor Dalissem, poor Dalissem dead these seven years, cheated of love she paid her life for. For look now what she's done! She sneaked *back*, Your Majesty, and stole the love she had a right to. Oh dear little hawk-faced mortal. Your life on earth is at an end. I chose you instantly I sensed you through the portal of my dying-place, and instantly I knew how much you'd love me. You're mine now – admit the truth!'

'Yes!' cried Haldar, and his voice rang like the harbor bell of Karkmahn-Ra.

Then Defalk cried out in his turn:

'Dalissem! Will you speak to me? Will you take me? I was less than you thought – you were more than I understood! But take me now. This man is nothing to you. Remember how we were!'

He looked quite fine then, Barnar, with his one red teartrack, and a new uprightness in his body. He put me in mind of an aging dolphin I once saw sporting, making clumsy leaps out of the water. Defalk's soul was just such a fat old fish, yet here this fleshly fop was managing, with supreme feeling, to heave himself up, and catch a flash of sun upon his back. Dalissem looked at him then. Perhaps she had meant not to, and now gave him this much tribute.

'Well, it is you Defalk! This is pleasant luck, to find you here. I am as you see me.'

Defalk hung his head. 'I was a little man who assumed he was great. I learned better!'

'But what is this, Defalk. You ask me to take you? You ask me to receive you to my love-in-death? Can it be your spirit does not thrive? Can it be you've weighed your life of kissing arse and crouching before fat purses, and have found it wanting? Can it be that your lady's paintpots and her witless rodent's chatter oppress you?'

'She is a small woman, Dalissem. I am small, and I have not helped her to be more. I ask you to forgive – '

She cut him off: 'I readily forgive what is forgotten. You are forgotten, Defalk, now that I have the two minor things I wanted from you: your self-contempt and your jealousy. Thus I am released from the shame of having loved you. Now, Haldar Dirkniss, stand nearer, for I mean to take you to me.'

My friend nodded, and stepped down. He wore leather and stout wool, but she put her hands to his chest, and tore away his clothes, and they rent to tatters as easily as dead leaves. She stripped him babe-naked and looked on him with smiling lust and pride. My friend was in a manly state. So, indeed, was I. She gave off desire that pressed physically against you, fierce and steady as the wind. She clasped her hands behind his neck and sprang backwards.

Her leap carried them both far – impossibly far out over the blizzards of fire. They didn't fall, but drifted out, as if gliding on ice – and he mounted her. Then, coupling, they fell in wide, smooth sweeps, wheeling as they slid, then banking, diving, gone.

There was a shout as deep as a bull's. Defalk slowly raised his fists overhead. He roared again, wordless, as if merely trying to break the instrument of his voice. Then he jumped out into the gulf.

Surely the rage of that last cry should have gained him entry into that furious place. But the firestorm did not receive him. As he sprawled out upon the void he did not drift, but hung there, bouncing and jolting and skidding horribly upon the invisible surface of the wind. He could not enter it – the gale's cold, speeding mass erased his substance as he jounced atop it. His hands vanished in a smooth smear of white; his face was rubbed to nothing in an instant; he was gone.

I turned to face the Guide. Slowly but firmly, I climbed to stand before him.

'Lord Guide,' I said, looking up into the smoky craters of his eyes, 'a great swindle has been worked upon two of the age's foremost thieves. One of them is cheated of his life, though he would not describe it so. But as for me, my lord, I believe some further time up in the sunlight still belongs to me, before I must see your face, and your servant's, a second time. Let this much faith be kept, at least: take me back *now* to the world of living men.'

Part 2

Shag Margold's *Preface to*
The Pearls of the Vampire Queen

This account is the work of Ellen Errin (known perhaps equally well as Greymalkin Mary) – something I flatter myself I would know even were the manuscript not written in her unmistakable script, which is both exceedingly minuscule and almost preternaturally legible. For just as distinctive to me as her hand, is her subtle, incessant parody of Nifft's voice. That the two were lovers for many years need not be concealed. Ellen herself certainly regards the fact with outspoken pride, and Nifft always did likewise. It is probably best understood, then, as a lover's liberty that she takes when she invariably, in adopting Nifft's voice, makes him sound twice the boaster that he ever really was. It is never his tone she distorts, but only the measure of his bragging. In the present instance she was sharing the jest with Taramat Light-Touch, who did indeed receive it as a missive from Chilia, where Ellen had been staying with Nifft and Barnar for more than six months before she relayed his adventure to their mutual friend in Karkmahn-Ra. In sum, I find I must confess that these gentle parodies of hers always make me smile, for truly, Nifft was never *over* modest.

Fregor Ingens, where this chapter of Nifft's career has its setting, is still referred to by certain intransigent members of the cartographic guild as the 'fourth continent'. It is scarcely a sixth the size of Lúlumë, and it is clearly part of an island system, namely the Ingens Cluster, which lies halfway between Kolodria's southern tip and the Glacial Maelstroms of the southern Pole. But because it is the largest island known, it seems there will always be some contentious souls ambitious to promote it to continental

81

status. In my view these commentators could toil more fruitfully on other ground, such as the amplification of our extremely sparse information on the geography and inhabitants of Fregor's central highlands, which are spectacularly mountainous – thought indeed to contain several of the earth's highest peaks – and shrouded in perpetual clouds.

The lowlands of Fregor's northern coast are at least rather better known and it is here, some hundred leagues inland of Cuneate Bay, that the swamplands of the vampire Queen lie. Indeed, the bay's cities owe their modestly active shipping trade largely to the proximity of Queen Vulvula's pearl-rich domains, which are productive of little else and in consequence draw heavily on the resources of the teeming Kolodrian continent. The swamp pearls – like a ceaseless, glittering black rivulet – trickle northward overland in heavily armed caravans: the Kolodrian merchant argosies river southward from the Great Shallows; the two streams meet in the ports of Cuneate Bay, mingle turbulently in clearing houses and brokerage halls, and resume their flow, the pearls northward overseas, the goods southward overland to the royal vampire's hungry fens and tarns.

But to speak of hunger is to raise the issue that must be foremost in the mind of anyone who has perused this record of Nifft's Fregorian exploit: can a vampire's rule be a just rule? I confess that the question is still so 'alive' for me – that is to say, unconcluded – that more than eleven years of diligent inquiry have left me as destitute of any certain answer as I was when Taramat first showed me the manuscript. Perhaps as close as I have come to any such thing is in considering the case of a realm near Vulvula's which is just as trade-dependent as her own, that of Gelidor Ingens. Gelidor is the second-largest (it is the size of Chilia) and southernmost island of the Ingens Chain. During the season of the sirikons it is only five days' sail from Samá-drios, the western-most isle of my native Ephesion Chain. Whether Samádrios' need nourished an infant industry in Gelidor, or Gelidor's natural abundance of the resource in question nurtured Samádrios' inclination to rely on it must rank as one of the most venerable controversies in Ephesion academic tradition. (That it has been so since the Aboriginal Trade Wars suggests – to me at least – that the answer lies either beyond the reach of formal inquiry, or beneath its notice.) But past any dispute is Gelidor's preeminence as a nursery of arms, especially since the decline of Anvil Pastures (elsewhere detailed), and Samádrios' centuries-long dependence on those arms for the prosecution of her interminable bid for empire in the islands of the Kolodrian Tail. And Samádrios is far from being Gelidor's only customer. Her mercenaries are the highest paid in the world. The skill and bellicosity of her army and navy have not only made her mistress of half the islands of the dense and disparate Ingens cluster, they have also caused war to become her prime export. The Hipparch of Gelidor subjects his teeming island to a painful diminution of prosperity – always swiftly and vigorously deplored by the populace – whenever he fails to dispense at least two-thirds of his annual crop of academy-trained officers among the globe's annual crop of red and rampant battlefields. And so we might fairly ask: Who drinks more blood – the Hipparch, or Queen Vulvula?

Shag Margold

The Pearls of the Vampire Queen

I

To Taramat Light-Touch
Sow-and-Farrow Inn
Karkmahn-Ra

Warmest salutations, O Prince of Scoundrels! Dear deft-fingered felon, Paragon of Pilferers, Nabob of Knaves – good morrow, good day or good night, whichever suits the hour this finds you! Do you guess who I am that greets you thus? Eh? Of course you do. Who else but your own nimble, narrow-built, never-baffled Nifft – inimitable Nifft of the knife-keen wits!

Has it been two years since we've been out of touch? That much and more, by the Black Crack! I'm sure you thought me dead or something like it, and I promise you, Taramat, I came close to it, for the haul that Barnar and I made in Fregor Ingens has taken us all of twenty-six months of breakneck squandering to dissipate, and if it had been just a jot richer, we would certainly have died of our vices before we'd wasted it all.

Haul? In Fregor? But of course – you don't know about it yet! Stupid of me . . . suppose I write you a nice long letter telling you all about it? It's raining here in Chilia where we're visiting Barnar's family. I've got lots of time on my hands, and we won't be getting back down your way till late this Spring. So it's agreed then, and I assure you it's no trouble at all, for I love to reminisce about exploits, especially remarkable ones. Just be sure to share this with Ellen if you see her – you know how she dotes on me and relishes keeping abreast of what I'm doing.

Well, it was swamp pearls, Taramat – *five hundred apiece*. Yes. You may well gape (as I know you're doing). You know their value, I'm sure, but have you ever seen one? Black as obsidian, twelve-faceted (the runts have six) and big as your thumb. They are dazzling to behold – nothing less – and we never doubted that obtaining some was worth risking the vampire queen's wrath.

Now we knew that Queen Vulvula's divers go down after them in threes – one pearl-picker and two stranglers. But this is because they are anxious not to kill the pearl-bearing polyps. With a pair of heavies, the thing's palps can be pinned and the picker left free to take its pearls. They attack the polyp's strangling-node only as a last resort, to free one of their team from a lethal grip of one of the palps. But a diver can get sufficient diversion from just one strangler if the man is strong enough and goes straight for the strangling-node and squeezes to kill. You try to be quick and not leave the thing dead, as their corpses make a good trail for the archer-boats, but to get by with one strangler, he can't be shy about damaging the things. You know Barnar's strength. I was content to risk the picking with him strangling solo, and he was willing to try it if I was. So we signed up as men-at-arms on a Chilite skirmisher to get passage to Cuneate Bay, and spent three days there in Draar Harbor getting provisions. Then we headed south.

With good mounts the swamps are about ten days' journey inland. It's bad country, but our luck was good right up through the eighth day. Then, on the eighth night, it went bad. We were in the salt marshes near the mountains that flank the swamps when three huge salt beetles attacked us. Luckily, though wood is scarce there, we'd kept enough of a fire going to give us a little light to fight by. We killed them all, but not before they'd killed our mounts. Worse, their caustic blood destroyed both our spear shafts. We still had our bows and blades, but we would rather have lost these than the spears, which would be the only really useful weapons in the swamps. When you're swimming you can't use a bow, so it's no help against lurks, and it's scant help against ghuls because they're so tough-bodied in all but a few places. And swords bring you far closer than you ever want to be, either to a lurk or a ghul.

The swamps begin to the south of the Salt Tooth Mountains. As soon as we reached the upper passes of this range, we were looking across a plain of clouds that seemed to have no end. The range forms a wall the clouds can't pass, and the plains below have been a sump of rains for thousands of years.

Descending the range's swamp side, we were deep in cottony fog most of the way down, but just as we neared the plain we entered a zone of clear air between the clouds and the swamp. In the cold grey light between the cloud ceiling and the watery floor, we could see for miles across the pools and thickly grown mudbars that concealed our illicit fortune-to-be. The bars and ridges of silt are mazelike, turning the waters, which look jet black from a distance, into a puzzle of crazy-shaped lagoons. But the growth on these bars, though thick, is not as lush as you'd expect. It's mainly shrubs and flowers; big trees are rare. The question of cover would be tricky as a result. The place offered many avenues of vision down which a man standing on a flatboat could overlook a dozen lagoons at a glance.

But when we stood on the bog's very rim, pausing before we entered the waters, Barnar snuffed softly, and said to me: 'It's got that smell, Nifft. There could be a great prize waiting for us here.' He was right, too. It had that peculiar stink of threat about it. You looked at that low-riding cloudcover, looking torn and dirty as a stable-floor, and then at those endless unclean waters, and you knew that obscene riches lay ripening out there, riches so encumbered with danger that their guards had ceased to believe that they could ever be stolen, not in any big way.

II

The waters only looked unclean. Once you were in them you were amazed to be able to see all the way down to your feet – and down to the bottom of most of the pools, none of which, even of the broader ones, was very deep. The reason is the soil of the swamps. If you dive for a handful of bottom silt, and squeeze the water out, you'll find it hefts like iron, and if you kick at the bottom you set up a low boil of mud that sinks down very fast. I've been told since that the polyps need this dense earth to nourish the growth of their pearls. While the light was still at its strongest, grey and bleached though that was, we made haste to cut our teeth in this business.

In half an hour we were swimming, nudging our packs before us with one hand and holding our drawn swords before us underwater with the other. We had put cork inside our packs and wrapped them in oilskin, and our swordblades were heavily greased. The best way to survive in the swamps is to turn into a water-rat and stay in the water for the whole of your working day, and to crawl out onto the bars only to sleep. For one thing it keeps your water-adjusted reflexes in top readiness. The clarity gives you a few seconds warning when a lurk comes off the bottom at you, but if you're in and out your underwater eye will get fuddled and you'll be too slow to take one of those warnings. For another thing the lagoons are so interconnected that if you swim a mazy path you can go anywhere and almost never risk the visibility of crossing a bar of land.

The first polyp we found grew alone in a small pool. It stood as tall as a man, its palp tips almost touching the surface. Neither of us knew if this was big or average. It would have been beautiful, standing there in the pool, its blurred redness seeming to burn, if we hadn't had to fight the thing. The palps began to writhe with exploring gestures the minute we paddled into the pool. Keeping out of range we sank underwater to view it. Down at the base of its anchor-stalk, right below where the bouquet of its arms began, was the small cluster of exposed fibres that is called the strangling-node, from the use men put it to. At the same point on the stalk, but on the other side of it, were two large lumps – pearl blisters for sure.

We surfaced. 'Get well breathed, Ox,' I said. 'I'll hit the blisters the instant you touch the node and draw its arms out of the way. Breathe up.'

Barnar nodded. He tied his sword to his floating pack. I wore mine for lurks, but Barnar was going to have both hands full. He emptied his lungs and filled them, each time more deeply. I did the same. We nodded our readiness, and went under.

We swam toward the polyp, dividing to hit it from opposite sides. I had to hang back till Barnar had drawn all its palps, and I watched as he swam in low and seized the node. All those bloodred palps whipped together and grabbed for him, faster than you'd believe anything could move under water. It bent like a bush that's suddenly lashed by a storm wind, and it had him by the neck, trunk and leg so suddenly that he could keep only one hand on the node and had to use the other to free his throat.

I went in. My contact with the thing was brief but still it made my skin crawl – for the thing was like stone that lived and moved. This toughness is what makes one's work so hard, for the things are unpierceable by any weapon. I pressed on either side of one of the blisters and the pearl popped out into the water like a seed squeezed from the ripe fruit. I tried to grasp it, but it kept squirting out of my fingers. Something hit me like a hammer between the shoulders. Catching the pearl with a lucky grab I crawfished madly through the mud, took two more bone-cracking blows on the shoulder, and was clear. I came up starving for air.

Barnar was still down there, a huge blur in the silt where the red arms were still striking like thresher's flails. I pocketed the pearl, took air, and went down. The two of them were deadlocked, because Barnar's one-hand grip on the node distracted just enough palps that he could bear, for a few moments, the assault of the rest. In the steppes he had taken a piece of rock-salt and crushed it in one hand – it was as big as a road-apple. But his lungs were surely fit to crack by now, while the polyp was not weakening. I swam in beside him and added both my hands to the node. It was just enough pain to loosen the rest of the thing's grip on my friend. We scrambled backwards. Something tore flesh from my face, and then I was free. Barnar boomed like a whale as he broke back into the air. We swam weakly to the mud bar and rested our upper bodies on it. I showed him the pearl. His face was torn in two places, the kind of raw, nasty wound one gets from rocks. My left cheek was a ruin. You see the scar of it here?

'Well,' said Barnar, 'high pay, hard work.'

'True,' I said. 'Still, friend, this may be the hardest work I've ever done.' And then we heard a movement, distinct, but perhaps a lagoon or two distant. We drew our swords and towed our bundles round into the adjoining pool. Some bushes atop the farther bar were still shaking. From the lagoon beyond came a flat striking sound, the tearing of water, and the grunts and panting of a man.

We swam to the bar and looked over. A smallish man was thrashing on the surface of the water, driving a spear beneath him against the bottom. Even as we watched his thrusts grew more methodical, and he calmed down. A thick fluid, denser than the water and green in color, was boiling up around him, mixed with bubbles.

I began to think I knew the man. He turned his spear round to prod something down there with its butt – the head showed green above his shoulder. Then he cursed, spat, and swam to the bar, where some bundles lay on the mud, and a sword hung in the bushes. I then remembered he had been at the trade fair at Shapur, where I had first learned of the pearl swamps. He had been in the room where a small group of friends of mine had been talking about poaching. He seemed not to have learned more of the matter than was spoken there, to judge by his spread-out gear. Your goods on a bank are like a promise to any archer squad that happens on them that you yourself are somewhere nearby, and they'll hound you out even if you've managed to duck them first. As for the sword, even in the dull swamplight its sheath of chased bronze was as good as a signpost.

'I think I know him,' I told Barnar. 'Best join with him, eh? The work would be easier for three, and if he's not instructed he'll draw patrols into the area.'

'All right,' my friend said. 'But he gets only a quarter share till he shapes up. Obvious amateur. I think he's just lost a partner.'

He had indeed, as we saw as soon as we swam into his lagoon. We made gestures of peace. He turned his spearhead towards us and waited warily. Then we had eyes only for what lay under the water.

First, we saw that our polyp had been a small one. This pool was dominated by a nine-footer. Held in its palps was the body of another man, a big one. It was not the polyp, though, that had killed the man – and it was probably not his or his partner's inexperience either, but just bad luck. For a lurk as big as a mastiff also lay on the bottom, its fangs still hooked into the man's leg, its flat, eye-knobbed head broken and giving off a green cloud of body fluids.

Lurks look just like spiders except the rear part of them isn't a fat, smooth sac – it's plated and ribbed, instead, like a beetle's body. Their poison balloons a man up a good one and a half times his size. Even allowing for that, the pale sausage of a man down there must have been big enough in life to make Barnar look normal.

Of the three things down there, only the polyp lived, and we learned something further in watching it as we swam past: the things have, amidst their palps, mouth parts for animal prey, and if left with a sufficiently inert body in their grip, they will devour it, though with a disgusting slowness. The polyp had the dead man's arm hugged tight in its arms and was working on the flesh with a slow rasping and plucking movement.

The little man's name was Kerkin. He remembered our meeting, and knew my name without being told, be it said with due modesty. He was no less impressed with the difficulties of this task than we were, and we reached partnership promptly. Kerkin's hopes would have been defeated without us, and he accepted a quarter share with humility. We gave him some cork and helped him remake his bundle.

'Look there!' he cried. The great polyp was thrashing convulsively. It had more purple in it to begin with than ours had – we were to learn that that was generally the color of the big ones. But now it was amazingly pale, almost white, and its rhythmic stiffening had a helpless, purposeless quality, as of sheer pain. In a short time, it slowed, and ceased to move at all.

'The lurk poison!' said Barnar. Of course that was it. The polyp's toughness would have laughed at the biggest lurk's direct assault. But the poison entered the creature handily through its tainted meal. The thing had four blisters, three of which had full sized pearls in them, the fourth a runt.

For a while we had a perfect poaching implement. We

dragged the body of Kerkin's friend – his name had been Hasp – to several more lagoons. We found that if a polyp was jabbed forcibly in the node, it would attack and ultimately feed on the corpse we thrust into its arms. We took more than a dozen pearls this way, and then Hasp began to come to pieces – due not to the nibblings of the polyps, but to the lurk poison. The skeleton began to fragment and the skin to dissolve with terrible suddenness, filling the water with unwholesome, stringy clouds of corroded flesh. In a few moments the whole lagoon was transformed into a disgusting broth from which we swam with desperate haste, keeping our faces clear of the water. It killed two small polyps growing there, but we did not dive for their pearls.

The real labor re-commenced. While the takings were so easy Kerkin had begun to whine after all; Hasp was *his* partner, and we should share even thirds. Now that it was again a wrestling game he dropped this theme readily. We took three more pearls in the same time we had taken to make our first dozen. We climbed up onto a broad bar in the evening, too tired to eat the jerky in our packs. We worked our way into the bushes and lay like the dead – that is, Barnar and I. Kerkin had the first watch and in his excitement over the wealth we had already made, sleep was far from him. He would not even let me take mine. He showed his eagerness like an amateur, but I couldn't help seeing him with a friendly eye – he might have been a stupider version of myself at that age. So I talked with him awhile.

'Not a single flatboat did we see all day,' he crowed. 'So few people realize, Nifft, how clear it gets here for poaching at this season – of course if it got around they'd get poached so hard in the fall that they'd take action and the easy times would be over. But we are here now, that's the great thing!'

'You said its the Year King ceremony that caused it,' I said. 'So what's that all about then, friend Kerkin?'

Kerkin was eager to talk of this. In matters of the Queen's government his information far exceeded ours, and every man likes to be expert in something.

'The ceremony's called the god-making of the Year King. It means that the Queen ends his year's reign by immortalizing him, as they say.' He paused, and chuckled, and so I played along and asked:

'And how does she do that for him?'

'How else? She drains his body of every last drop of his blood, before the eyes of her assembled people. She's very thorough too, for she has to get all of it. If even a cup is lost to her, the charm of the blood is imperfect, and its magic fails.'

'And what is its magic for her, Kerkin?'

'It erases from her body the entire year's aging! Of course like all great magic it carries a terrible penalty for failure in its execution. Starting from the sacred night, for every single night that she is in default of the Year King's blood, she will age an entire year. And this aging, if subsequently she repairs the charm, can never be erased; thereafter, the Year King's blood will restore her only to the age to which she advanced while in default. A month's default, you see, would then make a hag of her, and a hag she would stay ever after, with the charm reinstated.'

Kerkin was a river of information, and I encouraged him to flow on – it does not hurt to gather what one can, when it's being offered free. The queen's feeding was not confined to this yearly rite alone, though this was the bare minimum essential to her needs. She fed sporadically on random subjects – seldom fatally, to encourage her citizen's toleration. The natives of the swamp had received her as their ruler for over three hundred years now, because she had provided the necessary sorcery to expel the ghul, who are also originals of the swamp, and with whom the swampfolk have been immemorially at war.

Kerkin grew warm with his tale. We should kill a ghul, or take the lurk he'd killed, and go to Vulvula's palace to collect the bounty, he said. The great pyramid at the swamp's heart would be alive with folk. Think of the spectacle, and of the jest of being there with a fortune in poached pearls under our doublets! We could sneak a look at the doomed Year King in his chamber before the god-making, for the guards routinely granted a peek for a small bribe – it was almost a tradition. He rattled on, describing the labyrinthine interior of Vulvula's palace as if he knew it at first hand.

Poor Kerkin didn't live past noon of the next day. He fell behind us as we were seeking the day's second polyp. The first had taken all morning, nearly tired us to death and yielded only a runt. Kerkin didn't have our stamina, and swam in a tired daze. Having lost sight of us, he took a side-channel by mistake, and drifted off his guard into a pool he thought we had crossed ahead of him. The violent splashing he made in his misfortune brought us back. We were stunned by what we found. He had blundered into a very deep pool where grew a grandfather polyp so big it raised the hair of my nape – at least fifteen feet from root to palp-tips. And seemingly it hadn't waited provocation, but had seized Kerkin's dangling leg in palps thicker than his body. We got there just as it pulled him under. It enfolded his head between two immense palps and wrenched violently.

Kerkin's whole body spasmed as if lightning was going through it, then he hung from the thing's grip like a sodden log, and the polyp began to feed with a tearing and grinding that bared his armbone in a sickening few seconds. We did not even try to get the pearls off his body. We swam to a silt bar and crawled onto the mud.

We felt glum as a northern winter. Now our labors must

94

increase, and we'd begun to appreciate the full range of accidents that could befall a man here. We counted our pearls again. We had enough to live well on for a year – enough to buy expensive magic from the best sorcerers; enough to buy women of the rarest accomplishments. But there was so much *more* all around us. You know the feeling. I was racked by it once before. I had just robbed the Earl of Manxlaw, and was passing through his seraglio on my way out of his villa, in the dead of night. I was beckoned by a lovely thing. Reckless with success, I paused to serve her with a will. But as soon as I rose a half-dozen others had wakened, and they hotly persuaded me in whispers. I was profoundly moved. I felt filled with the power to stay there and serve them all. But I had a king's ransom in my bag, and left with a wrenching of the heart.

This was worse. The pearls are worth far more than gold by weight – a fortune of them is so marvelously portable for a man who lives on the move! Still, we stared at the dirty clouds and each of us waited for the other to be the first to suggest that we rest content with what we had.

'Well,' I sighed, just to be saying something, 'we have to thank the queen for making this place as safe as it is. Think if we had ghuls here too!'

'At least they breathe air and have blood,' Barnar growled. 'They're not this nasty, mud-crawling kind of thing. Polyps, lurks, *pah*!' I was only half seeing him as he spoke, for at that moment a plan was being born in my mind. This plan was a thing of unspeakable beauty and finesse I was almost awed by my own ingenuity.

'By the Black Crack,' I said quietly. 'Barnar. I have an idea that will make us staggeringly rich. We must get that lurk Kerkin killed, and we must kill a ghul as well, and take them both to the pyramid of the queen in time for the god-making of the Year King. Kerkin said that would be in five days. We can get there two days early at the least, and that will be perfect!'

III

You might pay me high and press me hard, but I couldn't say which was worse – killing a lurk in a lagoon with a seven-foot spear, or hunting a ghul in the black hills west of the swamps. We had to do both.

What? you'll say, we couldn't find that lagoon again? No, we found it fast enough. Our polyp had turned black, with half its palps fallen off. The lurk was there too. Unfortunately, its whole hind section had been eaten away. We were saved the trouble at least of hunting out another lurk, because it *was* another lurk that had eaten the dead one's body away, and it was still right there. I hope my fate never again puts such a sight as that before my eyes, black as the mud it crouched on, and looking half as big as the whole pond bottom. I was swimming lead because I was quicker with the spear, and that thing came straight up off its meal at me.

Now as to the spear, it was luck we'd met Kerkin and had it all, but two feet should have been sawn off its haft and the thing should have been rebalanced for aquatic use. The thing was too unwieldy, what with the water's drag. If I hadn't been carrying it head down under water, despite the way it slowed my swimming, I would have died right there. That lurk's fangs were as long as my forearms and before I could even react they were close enough to my thighs for me to count the thorny hairs they were covered with. I had time only to brace my arms – the lurk's own thrust carried him up and pushed the spearhead through the flat part of his body, amongst all those black, knobby eyes. I clung to that spearhaft like an ant to straw in a hurricane, and the buck of that big hell-spider lifted me so far out of the water that I was standing on top of it for an instant.

A handy thing about lurks is that all their hard parts are outside, and these by themselves are not very heavy. They will even moult like snakes, and when they do they leave entire perfect shells of themselves, light as straw. This lurk was a monster, big as a pony, but when we'd bled it we reduced it to half its weight. We milked the bulk of its poison out too – the bushes where it splattered yellowed and died before our eyes.

We towed the carcass out of the swamps to the foothills we had entered from the day before. We scrounged enough dead scrub to make a fire in an arroyo. We found that by slitting the abdomen and shoving coals and heated rocks inside, the rest of its guts could be liquefied and drained out. We worked over it the rest of the day and finally had reduced both parts of the body to a bare husk, mere shells of a tough, flexible stuff that was too dark to reveal its hollowness. The whole thing now weighed no more than a small man, though it was unwieldy. We lashed it to the spear and carried it between us like game. We carried it all night, moving toward the hills in the west.

By dawn we had reached them. Here the ghuls have retreated, to lurk near the swamp, just outside the reach of Vulvula's sorcery. We hid the lurk in a gully and covered it with stones, even though nothing will eat a lurk but another lurk, and they seldom leave the water. We found a place to sleep nearby, well hidden though ghuls never come out in the day. They hunt at night, and we slept till then, for that's the time they must be hunted too.

The things can only be pierced through the sternum, which is narrow, while their backward-folding knees give them the quickness and dodging power of hares. You know me as a man who'll take your money at any kind of a javelin match, but for ghuls I ask a good clear set and a chance to launch before it knows I'm there.

We tried an unusual approach. It was Barnar's plan, and a lovely piece of wit it was. He spun it out of the well-known melancholy of ghuls. They frequently commit suicide by flinging themselves against Vulvula's barriers – one finds them, it's said, hanging dead in mid-air, snared by the queen's invisible nets of power, and crawling with the blue worms which her spell engenders in its victims. Barnar reasoned that given this sad temperament, a ghul would believe a man claiming to have come to him seeking death.

We found one high in the hills by the light of its cookfire. We studied it carefully from among the rocks. It had a man's leg and haunch on a spit – the skin was flaking away in ash, and the thigh-muscle swollen with its juices. The rest of the man lay in pieces by its side, limbs and head pulled from the trunk like a torn fowl's – for ghuls use neither steel nor stone. The huge hands that had done the tearing were crusted with black blood.

Let's say you were to take our friend Grimmlat. Leave his arms the same length but start his hands at his mid-forearms, and crowd all his muscles into the shortened arm that's left. Give him feet of the same proportions with toes like fingers and knees jutting backward. Double the size of his poppy eyes, undersling his jaw an inch and give him haggle teeth as long as your thumb, and you've got a ghul.

I picked my position in the shadows. Barnar heaved a loud sigh and called out: 'Hail there! Is that a ghul?' He trudged noisily into the ghul's camp and under the cover of his noise I moved up into the spot I'd picked. The ghul sprang up at Barnar's entry.

'May I sit down, friend ghul?' my friend asked. 'I want you to do me the service of ending my life.'

The ghul, for all its ugliness, had a profoundly sad expression due to the way its great eyes droop at the corners, and you rather feel for them when you're not involved. This one was in a defensive crouch, otherwise I would have had my shot at once. In almost all postures the things keep their shoulders folded forward, with their breastbone sunk in between their chest-muscles. They're only vulnerable at the moment of attack. That was the point of Barnar's scheme. He sat down crosslegged, like a man who means to stay. Anger began to replace weariness in the ghul's face.

'Are you deaf?' snapped Barnar. 'Why do you hang drooling like an idiot? Kill me!'

The ghul didn't like this. It snorted and sat down again, and resumed turning the spit with a stubborn glare.

'Why should I?' it said. They have small, spidery voices, like a hag's.

'Why not?' boomed Barnar. 'You could eat me! Are you so stupid you can't see that I'm a man like the one you're cooking there?' He gestured indignantly at the head that lay on its side by the ghul. The man had had an enviable black moustache. 'You'd kill me quick enough if I didn't ask – you make no sense!' Barnar complained.

'I'm no idiot, you're one,' the ghul quivered bitterly. 'You'd rot before I got hungry again. Don't you know anything? And anyway I'll do whatever I please and I won't take any orders from you, you big sack of horse-flop!' And it licked its ragged teeth loudly to drive the insult home.

'Insults!' cried Barnar, 'and I thought I'd be doing you service for service.' He heaved a great sigh, and rested his forehead on his hands. The ghul looked interested now.

'Why do you want to die?' it asked grudgingly.

'Why?' Barnar's head came up in disbelief. 'The world so grey and spongy and futile and cold as it is – life so short and nasty and poor and hemmed in on all sides by destruction – and you ask why? I've had enough of it all, that's why!'

The ghul looked musingly. It stood up slowly and took its supper's head in its hand – the hand was big enough for the head to roll several times over from the blood-black claws to the heel of the shovel-wide palm. It rolled the head thoughtfully for a moment and then drew back its arm to throw. That was my shot.

I pinned it so solid that half the haft re-emerged from its spine, but ghul vitality is terrible, and it actually finished the throw with my spear in it. Barnar moved in time, and the head struck the rock behind him so hard that it flew into pieces like a burst earthen jar.

We took the ghul back to where we had cached the lurk, getting there by dawn. Now we had to build up the lurk's body. We were sure it could be considerably collapsed, and with some experimenting we found how to fold back the legs over the head part, and flatten and fold the back part. We tied it snugly into this reduced position with thongs, and wrapped the whole thing in oilskin. The finished bundle was about the size of a small man who has folded himself up to sleep. We bled the ghul, too, but didn't prepare it any more than by tying the wrists and ankles together. Barnar slung it crosswise over his shoulder and back, and we entered the swamp again. We walked the mudbars openly now, hustling the lurk through the water where we had to, making fairly quick time.

We soon struck one of the marked routes to the pyramid, a series of yellow poles that followed an almost continuous system of mudbars. We stayed with this and late in the evening, we came in sight of the pyramid. It is truly immense, tall enough to join the flat, dark waters with the ragged cloud ceiling. We laid ourselves down atop a broad bar amidst the bushes. We found it easy to sleep.

IV

In the morning we weighted the bundled lurk and sank it in a pool by the sixth route marker out from the palace – more than a mile out. Then we headed for the palace.

I've taken these eyes of mine to many places, and have been no Jack-out-of-the-way, but I'll tell you I had sense enough to be impressed by that pyramid. It had to be a good three hundred feet high to thrust it's upper tiers into the clouds as it did. It was a mighty, terraced hill of a palace. It had quays and docking berths all around its skirts, for it stood in the center of a lake, and water unbroken by solid ground spread half a mile around it on all şides. The lower two-thirds were all of stone, but its upper tiers were built of wood. Those great beams were as massive-looking as the monumental stone under them, and could have come from no nearer than the Arbalest Forest, on the fringe of the Iron Hills. One could read the wet of the fog up at the summit from the wood's deep blackness.

By the time we got to the fringe of the palace's great lake, we'd been passed by several inbound boats. The lake was alive with taxi rafts, for it's quickest to get from one side to another of the palace by sailing round it. The interior is a master maze of corridors and chambers. We saw only one archer-squad going out to patrol. They gave us a wave. Bountymen are liked there, and to be traveling palaceward with a dead ghul over one's shoulder, is to go with as much guarantee of welcome as a stranger may expect. At our signal a taxicraft came promptly away from the palace's bustling perimeter.

Our pilot liked bountymen but seemed to think they were a bit stupid for taking on such a hard job. A man never gives away more than when he speaks in friendly contempt. We wore no teeth or fangs and thus had to be beginners, and this gave countenance to very particular questions about the pyramid's interior, and the god-making rite. The answers confirmed Kerkin's tale.

'We hear the whole top of it is made of big beams,' Barnar said with yokelish awe. We were drawing near. Light leaked down the sides of the pyramid from rifts in the cloud, but it was weak light that was itself just leakage from higher clouds. Still, anything so huge, and alive, and old, raised by the hands of man, must fill you with awe – that's my view. The pilot spat in the water to say it all wasn't that wonderous if you knew it like he did.

'You should see the beams in the vaulted ceilings at the top, where the King begins his pilgrimage,' he said. 'Some of them weigh a ton each, yet are groined and dovetailed just as neat as a fly's whiskers.'

The pilot was most reassuring on every important point. From his description a man could move through the entire top level among the ceiling beams, and never touch or be seen from the floor. And the guard on the King's door was two spearmen, no more – for the King was administered a paralytic beverage in his preparation for the pre-ritual vigil. He sat, immobile and awake, in his windowless cell. And even though the level just below would be sealed off on the night before the rite, barring access to the top, the guard up there would not be added to. For it is part of the ceremonial assumption that the King awaits his god-making eagerly, and that his guard is just an honor guard.

We got off at the west quay, by far the most public one. The Queen's Cabinet uses the entire east quay for military and economic business, while the terraces on the north and south sides are interrupted by several water-level exits – channels let into the palace's foundation, to permit the launching of craft directly from its interior. On the west are all the major markets and bazaars, and more than half of the inns and wineshops.

We loitered in the plazas, browsed at the scarfmakers and swordsmith's stalls, and had wine at several different places. We got ourselves seen and made chat with merchants – fitting in. Feeling the mood of the place, and establishing our role, you see. The ghul on Barnar's shoulder was an excellent introduction. Most showed us the condescending warmth the pilot had. Bounty hunting is a common way for the rustic youths of the northern hills to get their first look at the metropolis, and folk are used to finding them sufficiently simple. A man whose eye is awake would have been alerted by our mature age, but as we know, most people don't look at things very closely. At one winestall the tapster overcharged us for the amusement of the other customers, then stopped me as I paid up, smiling, and revealed the joke. We all had a good laugh and when we left I was able to steal the lidded goblet I'd had my wine in. It was just what we would need.

Next we bought rope and bowstrings. We needed quite a few yards of each; we split up to make the purchases and both of us went to several different places to make up our halves of the quota. Less professional men would have been lulled by the holiday extravagances all around them, and the amazing number of people. It seemed the whole northern swamp – the drier part where most of the population lived – had joined the already large resident population in the palace. We knew that all you need is to raise a few doubts in a few chance souls to have your best-laid plans buggered and blasted.

At noon we went to the Audiences, held in the central chamber of the pyramid's water-level. The Queen presided here, tirelessly, most of the year. She was now in her seven days' retirement in the catacombs under the foundations, below even the swampwaters. There she communed with the mummies of Year Kings past. She would ceremonially rise from thence on the eve of the god-making, and at the same time the King would be brought down from his cell

103

on the pinnacle which was called the 'heaven' station of his ritual 'pilgrimage'. The pair would meet in the same Chamber of Audiences which we now entered. After their meeting, the King's body would be taken down to the catacombs – the 'night' station of his pilgrimage – there to join the other Year Kings. There they stand in the dark, all gods together – gods of Night, you understand.

Now take an inn the size of this one, friends – you could have put five or six of them in that chamber. Three of the Queen's priestesses were hearing the representations of the people – it's a job Vulvula handles alone, such is her wit and memory – and dozens of under-judges occupied tribunals throughout the hall. There must have been a thousand litigants there, which did not begin to fill the palace. Let it be said here: no one we talked with ever denied the Queen's justice is thorough and scrupulous, treating the great as strictly as the small. True, in her domain some dozens of people each year wake sick and groggy after horrible dreams, and must keep their beds a month after, and a dozen or so others each year do not wake at all one morning. Still, fair rule is only had at a cost, eh?

Routine matters like tax payments had their own designated tribunals, and we found the one for bounty payments. The clerk there assigned us a skinner. The man rose from a bench where he sat with two other dirty-aproned men. He led us out of the chamber and through a good half mile of corridors. The building is fascinating. You get no sense of pattern at all, even after moving through it for a quarter of an hour. The ceiling heights vary and some halls are short with many rooms, while others are long with doorways that are few and large. Residents here – and the halls thronged with them – rarely know more than their immediate 'neighborhoods' very well. We came out of the municipal quay on the east side.

The man brought the whole skin off in one piece, so fast

104

I couldn't follow his moves. They make parchment from it, and clothiers use it for rich men's slippers and ladies' dagger-sheaths. The guts and bones he threw in a bin on a raft, to be used for baiting the lurk-traps around the lake's perimeter. The head he threw in also, after breaking the jaws with a sledge and removing the teeth for us. It had ten – big grinders with cutting edges. He gave us a runt-pearl in payment.

On the same quay an old coppersmith sat on a stool. He offered to bind our teeth with wire for wearing round the neck. His work was cheap and quick, and we came away wearing our trophies – a five-tooth row apiece. This established our role, with a small disadvantage. Accomplished bountymen wear 'jaws' – ten-tooth strings, row under row. They tend to be rough with novices of their own guild – they give them the treatment that greenness gets everywhere, and a bit more besides, if you see my meaning. There were surely some ace bountymen in this convocation. It would just have to be taken as it came.

We did next precisely what a pair of bumpkins *would* have: we went up to the peak of the pyramid to bribe the guards for a gawk at the Year King in his cell.

V

As I've said, the pyramid's top is in the clouds. From its outer terraces you can't see anything but sweating-cold whiteness – above, below, all around. Standing there gave you a desperately lonely feeling. That blind whiteness made it a place without time, a kind of Death. You felt as if you might have been dead without realizing it, that all your busy actions had been grave-dreams, and you yourself a skeleton, a rack of hard white bones that had stood there without moving for a thousand years. We went inside and ascended to the last and highest level, which can only be reached from inside the second-to-last.

There were others coming and going, but the custom of peeking at the King still had enough of the illicit about it to keep people brisk and quiet up here. As rustics turned bountymen we had some countenance for moving slower and staring around us.

The place was perfect – it alone of all the levels was simple in plan: a hollow square of halls with three doors to a side. A Year King must not have his vigil in a predecessor's cell before twelve years of purification have passed. Each year therefore the King waits in a different room. The halls were gloomy. They had very deeply vaulted ceilings because the tier is built to adorn the pyramid with an elegantly roofed crown, though it's never clear enough for this to be seen from below.

Our greatest encouragement was to see the two guards posted at the end room of a corridor, near a corner. Barnar muttered to me:

'I can do it. I'll want a catwalk of ropes from just over the door and running round the corner and sixty feet up that next hall.'

'I'll string it tonight then,' I said.

We looked the guards over as we waited our turn at the door's barred window. They were scarred veterans – blank, observant-eyed, and ready of movement underneath their practiced immobility. They would be good men. The post was lucrative and the palace guard had elimination bouts just before the rite to determine who would get the King's Watch. I paid one of them and we took our turn at the window – we'd already noted the door had no lock.

The cell was windowless, the plainest little box of bare wood you could imagine. By the far wall was a heap of cushions. A young man sat on the floor with his upper body leaned back on them. His legs were sprawled loosely on the floor with his lower body. He wore only a breech-clout and moccasins. The garments were silver, signifying moonlight and Night, of which he was soon to be a deity. He was well made, muscled like a runner. It was eerie to see a body so moulded, ridged and knotted with the habit of life and activity, yet lying so unstrung and strengthless. He seemed powerless even to sit upright. His eyes moved slowly and without aim, but for some reason he suddenly fixed them on our faces at the bars. He knit his brow, and his hand stirred from the cushions as if to reach up and touch his own face, but fell back before it could. I wonder now what kind of dreams or portents we were to him. If he had known the truth, he would have known that we would neither harm nor help him.

We came back down to the lake level without directions. It cost us two extra hours of blundering around, but it sharpened our wits to the place and it taught us a fairly direct route in a way that guaranteed our remembering it. I didn't come out onto the quay with Barnar. In a dark turning I transferred to his pack all my share of the bowstring we'd bought, and all my gear except for my rope. He gave me all the rope he had. We had already chosen the wine shop where we would meet later that night. He went off to find an apothecary. I retraced the route we had just figured out, and returned to the upper levels.

I found an inn and killed an hour with wine and smoked eel. It was full dark when I reentered the dim halls of the Year King's vigil. They call me Nifft the Lean nowadays, but when I first earned myself a name – it was not in these parts, friend, and it was some time ago – I was called Nifft the Nimble. I did the hardest work of this whole glorious nab right there in the next two hours. Right at the door where I entered, I slung up a line I had weighted with my dagger, and hauled myself up among the ceiling beams. I did it with a gaggle of revelers climbing the stairs just behind me, and several others, to judge by the footfalls, just about to round the next corner of the hallway. I was up in a blink, and my line after me.

I moved through the beams to within fifty yards of the guarded door, perfecting my movements and learning the pattern of the joists and rafters. Then I sat down to prepare my ropes. I suited them to the beam intervals where I was, which of course would be the same everywhere. I tripled the ropes, braided them loosely, and knotted them, three knots per interval. The finished hundred feet of catwalk, when I had it coiled round my shoulder, was half my own bulk. Now came the true feat. I proceeded towards the King's door and coming directly over the guards, I began to anchor the catwalk.

I strung it high, with two levels of beams between me and them. Though the regular spacing of the beams made me visible enough to anyone who was looking, I was well in the shadow and being seen was not the danger. The risk was in the fact that a mere fifteen feet of empty air separated me from the ears of those guards. I worked slower than a miser's hand moving to his purse to pay. Gawkers at the King came steadily and I managed to coincide the loudest part of my work with the advent and the murmurs of these. This was the knot tightening, for the catwalk must not sag and creak when Barnar used it, as then the halls would be barred to visitors, and the silence complete. But rope noise being sharp, and the noises of the visitors subdued, it took agonizingly long to get even one knot firm.

The pressure eased as I got round the corner and down the next hall, but I was soon sweating so hard I was amazed it didn't drizzle down into the corridor and give me away. By the Black Crack, there's no work like hanging frozen for indefinite periods, again and again, unpredictably. It's lizard's work, to tell the truth. But when I had done, I'd left a catwalk up there neatly paralleling one of the longitudinal beams, such that with one foot on that beam and the other on the ropes, Barnar could move along a good broad-stance support with both hands free for his special task.

The palace is mortal cold, and drenched as I was I nearly took a chill on my way down. A noisy fit of rheum would have ruined our next night's work. I hurried to stay warm, and at the wine shop out on the quay, where I found Barnar sitting, I ordered a hot posset.

Barnar gave me his afternoon's purchase: a healing gum used by pearl divers to seal wounds that might draw lurks to them. It was twisted in a scrap of ghul skin. I pocketed it, and ordered a second posset, feeling much better. I began to observe that our table was getting respectful clearance from other customers, and interested looks. Barnar explained in a murmur:

'When I've gone you may inherit a quarrel. A pair of bountymen, with two jaws apiece. Biggish men – the one with a pair of lurk fangs over his jaws is the troubleseeker. I didn't quite break his right arm, thought it would bring too much notice if the man had to be carried off. People will tell them you're with me, and if they underestimate you, you'll be getting trouble.'

'All right,' I said, 'any hints for procedure?'

'He's on the strong side, but very slow. His friend plays the jackal, follows him up.'

Barnar's mention of leaving told me that he had not yet accomplished the most important errand that fell to his share today. We had rather expected that it would have to be done tonight, as sorcerers are a nocturnal breed.

'You found no one to consult, then?' I asked.

'Just getting a name was much,' he rumbled. 'It takes a lot of drinking around and rumor-gathering to begin to get a fix on someone reliable. There seems to be a consensus about a certain swamp-witch. I'm going to her now – she lives in the northern swamp. I've hired my guide and he's standing ready with his raft.'

'Then you'll go from her to get the lurk?'

'Yes. I'll see you just after dawn at the dock we landed at this morning.'

'Good luck, Ox. Bargain hard. If you offer more than one pearl she'll take you for green and pass you off with nonsense.'

I sought out an inn almost as soon as he left, meaning to be out of trouble's way. I was spotted and followed even so, it seems. They were the truest kind of cutthroat, waiting for the dead of night, so at least I had a couple of hours' sleep – it was in a great barracks of an inn, with more than thirty pallets – before I was awakened. A heavy boot-toe kicked me hard against the soles of my feet.

I had laid the spear, which Barnar had returned to me before leaving, along my right side under the blanket, with the head at my heel. This is the way you should do it, so you can lift it straight into action against anyone attacking from your bed's foot, which they must do if you've lain with your head to the wall, as I did. After the kick it took me one second to sort out the two shapes in the darkness, and another to be sure of the rattle and gleam of teeth at their chests.

Then one further second passed during which the man who kicked me said the word '*Get*' in a fierce whisper, very distinct. He probably meant to say more than just '*Get*', but the passage of my spearhead through his heart supervened.

I used just enough thrust to strike heart-deep and no more, because I knew I'd have to have my spear free again quick; a man doesn't get to be a two-jaw bountyman by being slow on his feet. Sure enough the other bolted quick as a rat. I used one and the same jerk to free my spear and pull myself to my feet. That man was fast. It took all my force to cock and throw before he got to the door, and I pinned him through the side of his ribcage below his arm just as he was sprinting through it. My spear was just sinking into him before the first man I'd stabbed hit the floor – I swear I was just in time to catch him and kill the noise. I laid him on my pallet, and went quietly after the second one. Some people were awake but feigning sleep, seeing that the scuffle was already settled. I carried the second bountyman back to my pallet, laid him by his colleague and covered them both with my blanket. I took up my things, wiped my spearhead, and left. At another inn I caught three more hours' sleep.

VI

Early morning is a graveyard kind of hour in the swamps – there's no clear air under the clouds then, because the mist is rising from the waters. It moves in slow, torn columns across the quays, and if you're standing at the waterside, you can't even see the pyramid. I found Barnar at the dock. We carried the bundled lurk across the terrace, and into the palace.

Inside there was some activity – here and there a tavern door opened, and you could see the tapster inside kindling the public-room fire. We went as quickly as we could without running, and feared no questions. Since the Audience Chamber would be closed now until the god-making, bountymen arriving with a catch would be expected to wrap it up and take it to an inn for the duration.

But at the highest levels there were neither inns nor taverns, and outlanders ascending here with a large burden would draw scrutiny from any guardsman. Here we went even quicker, prepared to kill, counting on the hour to spare us the necessity. We met no one, and gained the outside staircase leading up to the second level from the top.

From the head of these stairs I crept to the door. Inside there was a guard strolling down the corridor, at the end of which was the staircase to the King's level. He passed the door and turned the corner. He was followed by another walking the same way about twenty seconds later. So it went – I watched five more minutes, but there was no gap in their circuit long enough for us to get to that staircase unseen. We would have to kill one.

I conferred with Barnar, then memorized the face of the next guard who passed. We took the one who followed. Barnar seized him from behind as he turned the corner and broke his neck. We hauled him back out to the staircase. We were going to tie his body to its underside but I found a flask on him so we chose a less mystery-creating plan. We drenched his beard and doublet with the liquor, replaced the flask in his belt, and Barnar lifted him high overhead. There was a gardened terrace about six levels down – invisible now, but I remembered its location and directed my friend. He heaved, grunting softly. The guard arched outward, seeming to hang sprawled in the fog, staring upward open-mouthed, and then was swallowed in the whiteness. After a moment there was a soft crash of broken shrubbery. Barnar, as a last touch, wrenched the staircase's heavy banister loose and left it hanging. When the guard whose face I had memorized passed, we entered and dashed down the hall with our load.

I got into the rafters and Barnar threw up the lurk so that it landed across a beam. He came up and we pulled our line after us. The level below would be sealed off by a full guard at mid-morning, to begin the King's two-day pre-ritual isolation, and just after the breakfast hour there would be a last-minute rush of gawkers. We rested, saving our work for that noisy hour.

When the folk began arriving, we carried the lurk within fifty yards of the King's door, and unwrapped it. I inserted crossed sticks into its body through the slit in its abdomen

112

and this swelled it out perfectly. Barnar prepared three thirty-foot lengths of bowstring and hooked one end of each into the body – one to the rear part, and one to either side of the flat, head part, amid the base joints of the legs. Then, with as little left to do as possible, we carried it to just above the King's cell. We stretched it lengthwise atop a beam, tying its forelegs and rear body to two daggers pushed into the wood. It would have a whole day to lose the last of its creases. We laid the coiled bowstrings on top of it, and got out of there.

I have the trick of sleeping to kill time, and Barnar had been up all night. We found perches two full corridors away, in case we made sleep-noises.

When we woke my time sense told me we had an hour or so to wait until our chosen time, the pit of night. The guards were under oaths of silence during this part of the vigil, but they ignored them. We listened to the small shapeless sounds that were all that was left of their conversation by the time it reached us. Their talk wavered feebly, like the flame of an ill-made candle in a gusty room. You could read their oppression of spirit in the way their voices blurred, ceased, and then, doggedly, started again. Barnar and I traded our thoughts with a look: they would be jumpy all right.

It was a man like themselves they guarded, and he lay at the threshold of a grisly journey. When humankind make covenants with the more-than-human, or the less-than-human, you may buttress them with traditions and rites as you will, but there remains an unacknowledged horror that is never quieted in men's hearts. At last we moved, and as we came closer, our movements got as deft and still as the creeping of rats, minus even their tiny noise of nails. We entered the perilous silence above the King's door, and looked down upon the two polished domes of the guards' helmets. Their talk had stopped again. You could almost feel their gloom. They were ripe for our game.

We undid the lurk from the daggers – it had straightened nicely. Barnar took the coils of bowstring and tucked them under his arms, then picked up the lurk by the three lines, holding them near the hooks. I crouched on one side of the gap in the beams and fastened a line to a rafter. Barnar stood on the other side of the gap, one foot on the catwalk and the other on the beam, and poised the lurk over the opening. Remember the weight of the thing, my friends! He looked to me and I nodded that I was ready. He began to pay out line through his fingers, letting the legs drop foremost and bringing the whole thing almost flush with the wall, so that it looked like it was crawling down it. It looked real enough to stir your hair, its black legs flung out in their six-foot spread, its jointed barrel of a body taut and poised behind. If I had been standing twelve hours in the empty half-dark gnawed at by unhealthy thoughts, and had turned to see such a thing a foot above my shoulder, I would have done just what the guards did.

This is not to detract from Barnar's masterful handling. When he had the thing positioned, he let it drop a good four feet and scuff the wall as it did so. This brought their faces up at just the right instant to see the monster lurch to a murderous, poised halt an arm's length above them. They peeled themselves from the doorway and spilled across the corridor, one man losing his spear as he sprawled. Barnar was already hauling the lurk back upwards with a marvelous smooth speed that made it seem to be scuttling in reverse motion up the wall.

Holding the lurk straight-armed before him, he danced along the beam and catwalk to the next large gap in the rafters, and cast it down through. The throw was perfect. The skeleton struck with a rattling splash right next to the men, who were just struggling to their feet. He was playing dangerously near them, for the bowstrings were far from invisible, but his speed and timing were such that they kept the maximum panic alive in the men. The second throw sent them stumbling round the corner. I had dropped my line, slid down and entered the King's cell before I heard the sound of Barnar's third cast down the next hallway. Things couldn't be better – they had only one spear and so they wouldn't risk a cast with it, and Barnar could play them several moments more while they gathered their wits and the puppet's reality was put to a test.

I moved as quick as a dodging, darting fly. I had cup, salve, and poniard out, and the King by the ankle in an instant. I cut him under the bump of the ankle, where you'll get a good half-cup of blood and the bleeding will then peter out. I pocketed the goblet, wiped the wound clean, and sealed it with the salve. I scarcely spared a glance for the King's face – he was staring at me with strange sad intensity, as if he knew me and I had somehow disappointed him. Then I was shutting the door, shinning up the rope, and drawing it after me.

I rushed along the catwalk past the corner and signaled through the beams. Barnar was just drawing up the lurk. He unhooked the lines and set the great spider-thing on a beam so that its forelegs hung down into the guards' range of vision. Then Barnar was with me and we were dancing through those beams almost as fast as a man can jog on level ground, going the opposite way round the square of halls from the point where the reinforcements would be entering. Our two guards had been shouting for them for some time – for it was death for them to leave their post on this floor – and we heard boots thundering on the stairs already.

We had left our plans vague at this point, counting on turmoil, but unable to foresee its precise form. We had included the possibility of revealing ourselves as practical jokers, since there would be enough guards there who were jealous of our two victims' special post to raise a laugh and some sympathy for our game. But this being the eve of the god-making, and the swampfolks' prime night of revel out of the whole year, when the pyramid was alive with drinkers and singers from top to bottom, we'd seen at least a good chance for a cleaner escape. This we got. The downstairs guard flooded up into the hall where their colleagues were, and after a brief interval a stampede of more miscellaneous footfalls came pounding up the stairs. We got down from rafters in time to be in the hall as the red-faced citizenry rushed in. They eddied at the head of the stairs, prevented from entering the hall where the action was by the crowd of guards there. We jumped from round the corner and waved excitedly.

'This way! We can get through over here!' I shouted. Threescore of men and women cried out and pounded after us. We let the crowd overtake and surround us, falling back into it as we all rushed round the other way. As they rounded the last corner before the King's cell we dropped out of the rear of the rout and ran back to the stairs.

VII

On the next night we stood by this dais in the center of the Audience Chamber. It had cost us our runt pearl from the ghul to buy this place from one of the chamber guards. Those near us had paid as much. The whole vast hall was packed with folk, hot and close, from wall to wall. We had taken our place hours early, and heard the tale of the 'puppet-show upstairs' passed among the folk around us, variously distorted. People enjoyed it hugely. A new jocose tradition might have gotten started, had we not spoiled the humor of the idea for the Queen a short time later.

She appeared in the great doorway at midnight. Lines of guards held clear a broad aisle from the doorway to the dais, where the altar stood, and she remained in the doorway at the end of the aisle, not moving for a long time.

She wore a coarse white robe that covered her entire body. Her long black hair was unbound, and her face had a terrible beauty, meaning both those words. It was a northron face – nose large and strong, eyes set both shadowy deep and wide apart, a marvelous wide mouth with lips of infinite expression.

There was a weight and power in the way she stood, a *realness* that made that whole human multitude seem a shadowy and passing thing. She stood in her straightness and silence and six hundred years of life – for she was ancient when she came to this place – and all of our thousands surrounding her seemed brief, fugitive, whispering – like a host of dead leaves. Truly my friends, aren't our lives as quick in their passing as a thief's shadow across a wall? Queen Vulvula's hand moved to her throat, and her robe fell from her nakedness. She moved forth down the aisle.

She had a body to stir and stiffen you: big guava breasts, hanging-ripe; thighs round and strong; hips like a bulging vase for milk or scented oil. But as she drew near the dais, we saw it was an autumnal body. The breasts were frost-nipped, beginning to dwindle from within as apples will. Her thighs moved with a chilled slowness, and the veins were beginning to map themselves out on the backs of her hands. And as she mounted toward the altar we saw that at the corners of her plump and flexible mouth dark nets of wintery erosion were spreading out across her jaw.

As she stood on the dais I felt her presence fully, like a gust from the icy gulf of her heart. She looked over us as a harvester looks over a great stubborn field which he has made to yield him fruit. She knew her alienness in her people's minds; their unspoken horror and the danger she lived in because of it. And she relished it. The risk and care of empire gratified her centuries-deep mind. She smiled very slightly. Looking at her mouth, you knew that it would have a small, frosty atmosphere all its own around

it, and that its kiss would suck your soul out in the fire.
She moved to the head of the altar.

Literally its head, for the altar was a big statue of a man
in a wrestler's bridge, that is, supporting himself on his feet
and hands but face upwards, so that his thighs, stomach
and chest formed a long level surface. The Queen spoke
some words in a language I have never heard. Her voice
was mellower than you expected, soft at the edges. Effort-
lessly it filled the whole hall. As she spoke she pointed
overhead, then to the altar, and then floorward, meaning
the catacombs below, no doubt. Then she spoke for our
understanding:

> 'Your sons have fattened in my rule.
> Your rafts go laden with peaceful trade.
> There's no man's wife need fear the ghul.
>
> Your pearls are spared the poacher's raid –
> They're farmed by laws that spread their worth,
> And keep ensheathed war's wasteful blade.
>
> You've had what Good men get on earth –
> Now grant your Queen does nothing cruel
> Who, dead with craving, ends her dearth.
>
> Her year-long lord, with year-long Heaven paid,
> Comes now to her to see her thirst allayed.'

The King appeared in the doorway, borne on a litter by
two bearers. He slouched, still strengthless, in the seat, but
the set of his head showed his wits more awake than before.
He wore a sacrificial fillet of graven bronze round his brow,
and as they carried him forward, you could see his eyes
moving restlessly under its line.

The bearers set the litter before the altar. They were
powerful men, of Barnar's type. One grasped the King's
wrists and the other his ankles. The Queen spoke again,
and there was a tenderness in her voice:

118

'Rise to me now, my love, a king,
And descend from me as a God.

You will sit in Eternity with your line,
And rule the ever-after-living hosts.
You will wield the scepter of the shadow-kind,
You will be judge and shepherd of the ghosts.

Rise to me, now, my love, a king,
And descend from me as a God.'

When she had said this they lifted the King onto the
altar. He looked to this side and that as they pressed his
legs against the stone legs, his back against the stone chest,
his arms and shoulders against the arms and shoulders of
stone. And as he looked here and there, I thought for a
moment that he looked at me, and smiled, ever so faintly. I
don't insist on this – I half think it was a dream myself –
the air was so charged, and the silence crawled all over the
skin of the multitude like a swarm of ants. But do you
suppose he understood what had been done, and took
some last small comfort, some revenge in the thought?

She knelt beside him, and her face was taut, refined by a
tension of icy love, made younger before our eyes by her
passionate anticipation. She lowered her face – worship-
fully, kissing – to the muscled juncture of his neck and
shoulder. And then there was a crisp, liquid sound of
horrible distinctness, her hands clutched his shoulders, and
the King's body rose and convulsed upon the stone with
the raw, coiling power of a speared eel.

The two giants holding him grunted with strain, and the
Queen's head rode with the youth's surging body as if it
were a part of it. He hammered the rock like a beached
dolphin pounds the wet sand, slowing with suffocation,
and as he stilled, the Queen clutched and nuzzled with a
weasel's self-forgetting lust. Her shoulders worked like
pumps as she sucked and her hands kneaded his torso as if

it were a great udder of blood. She almost drowned herself in her hunger, and had to tear her face up from its feeding to breathe with all the desperate speed of a diver breaking the surface. She reared her crazed, glass-eyed face before the crowd – her lips smeared, her chin drizzling red. Her breasts were actually fuller now – they jutted youthfully, and I saw a thin thread of blood-red leakage from both her nipples. She leaned and drank again. The King barely moved. His skin tightened over the muscles, while the muscles themselves seemed to be slowly dissolving.

She grew calmer, methodical. She drank from both his wrists next, and then from inside of both his thighs, to empty him efficiently. She licked her mouth clean, then cupped and lifted her breasts and licked her nipples clean. A priestess ascended the dais with a silver laver in which she washed herself a second time, and then drank off the water. Another priestess brought her a robe of scarlet. She put it on and, flanked by the priestess, stepped down. It was done.

When she had exited the littermen laid the King's husk on the litter and bore it from the hall. The Queen would spend the night above, in the King's cell where the priestesses would install for her a large mirror framed in gold. The king would go to the catacombs, where other priestesses waited with the sacred taxidermy tools.

VIII

The next morning, on the western quay, we waited for the expected to befall. We had hired a taxicraft, and had it standing by. Then the commotion came boiling out of the palace, born by scores of hurrying folk. The Queen had been heard to waken, rise and, a moment later, scream.

We boarded at once. An hour later we had reached a

certain great mudbar near the fringe of the swamp – one so large it amounted to an island. Here we waited, sending the pilot back well paid and at double speed with a small scroll for the Queen. We'd chosen a shrewd man who would have the savvy to get himself into the Queen's hearing in an uproar like the one you would expect in the pyramid. The scroll's marking would help. We had written on the outside: 'Concerning the Year King's Missing Blood.' A glance at this added vigor to his plying of the stern oar, and he was soon out of sight.

This was the most ticklish step of all. Having two thousand prime swamp pearls put into our hands was going to be a simple matter now. But remaining alive for even an instant after the King's blood was back in the Queen's control – this was going to strain both wit and nerve to accomplish.

Barnar's interview with the swamp-witch was made with this difficulty in mind. If you're going to guarantee your safety with sorcerers – and the vampire queen was a very great one – you've got to get them to protect you with their own thaumaturgy. The trick is to make them give you magic which they cannot themselves afterward over-pass. You've got to ask for the best thing in their repertory.

The swamp-witch was no Vulvula. But it was worthwhile having her professional opinion as to what is the fastest thing that wizardry can call to the aid of man. I would have guessed, all by myself and without paying a pearl, the answer that she gave my friend. Still, it was something to have a confirmation. She told Barnar that the fastest being, in the upper world and the subworlds alike, is a basiliscus. I see you nodding wisely, Taramat. Read on a bit.

So we demanded, along with the pearls, a ring charmed to command the service of a basiliscus. Then we sat down, had a bit of jerky and wine, and waited.

The priestess of the Queen came almost impossibly soon.

When we saw she had two archers on the raft with her, I quickly waded into the water. The King's blood had dried into a greyish biscuit, full of little holes like lava-rock. I held it up and called out:

'Throw your bows in the water – double quick! Otherwise the Queen is going to have to drink this whole swamp to save her youth!'

The bows went overboard. The men kept their spears but this was fair, as we had one, and we couldn't expect them to risk our robbing them. The raft came up to the islet. We gestured the soldiers back. The priestess stepped ashore with two leathern bags, and stood staring at us, rage in her eyes, her mouth impassive. I stayed in the water, as the soldiers were so near. Barnar said:

'Time is short, woman. Give us the ring. We'll make the exchange when we're on the creature's back.' She nodded wordlessly, and tossed him a small silver ring. Barnar put it on his smallest finger and raised his hands. The spell the witch had taught him was brief. He intoned it with great verve and authority. First there was a long silence.

Then the earth began to wrinkle and crack, like pottery glaze, along a thirty-foot seam that crossed the width of the islet. The cracks darkened and grew, the fragmented clay began to buckle, and even I, standing in the water, felt a giant mass jerking and slithering underfoot. A lizard-foot that could have held me like a doll reached out of the tormented mire. A second followed, as a polished, scaly snout appeared. The seam bulged and gaped and the vast reptile heaved clear, hurling blocks of clay to all sides, and raising waves from which I was barely quick enough to save the blood-cake. With imperial self-absorption the basiliscus hauled itself into the water on the other side of the islet, and unfolded its wings to bathe them. They were no bigger, fanned out, than the raft the soldiers stood on – curiously stunted-looking given the body's bulk. In its own good time it crawled back into the islet and aimed its obsidian eye, big as a target-shield, attentively at Barnar.

The basiliscus isn't a true demon because it can barely use speech at all, but it falls under the compulsions of the Great Age of Thaumaturgy, and is part of our inheritance of power from our forebears. You tell it where you want to go. It takes you there and you feed it the ring in payment, allowing it to return to the subworlds. And you'd better feed it the ring, and ask for no further trips. Magic compels it just so far, and then its nature asserts itself. Into its ragged pit of an earhole, Barnar whispered the name of our destination, then mounted its back. I jumped from the water and vaulted on behind him, keeping the blood-cake poised for a throw at the lagoon.

The priestess approached and opened the mouths of both bags for our inspection. I don't know which felt more unreal, to be sitting on the back of that lizard or to be looking at the oily lustre of two thousand perfect swamp pearls. The priestess stepped nearer, the bags in one hand, the other extended for the blood. I made the exchange with pickpocket deftness, hugged the bags to me, and Barnar shouted: 'Away!'

A slow gale of breath entered the cavelike chest under us. For a moment nothing happened, and fleetingly it bothered me that in that time, neither the priestess nor the soldiers stirred. They didn't make a move, and yet had time enough, if they were good, to spear us both from our mount. Then we were fifty yards away.

The basiliscus's scales were big as flagstones and smooth as wax. Luckily there was room in their interstices for you to sink half your hand in, because its back was far too broad to grip with your legs. It took exactly three running leaps, crossing lakelets like puddles and using big mudbars as stepping-stones. Its wings hammered once, twice, and then suddenly they were winnowing cottony fog, and there was no swamp to be seen.

We swam thundering up through clouds and mist for several moments, knuckles cracking with the strain of our climbing speed, and then we were in clear sky, with the clouds a level white broth below, hemmed in a bowl-like rim of ragged peaks. Beyond the hills, where we were headed, the salt steppes lay parching under the hot blue emptiness. Then, through the rush of wind and the creaking, leathery toil of the vast wings, we heard a whine far to our rear.

We looked back, and learned in one glance that there *is* something faster than a basiliscus. Whatever its name is – for that we never learned – there was one of them bursting from the cloud-broth just where we had exited. It had one human rider. Even at that moment I marveled that any man should venture to sit astride the spiny neck of such a thing.

I have seen its kind in little – stiltlegged bugs with long bodies and two forelegs it uses as arms, barbed along their insides for piercing what they snatch. Their flat, triangular heads have two globelike eyes and dainty greedy mouths, whose hunger the barbed arms must constantly serve. This one's head was big enough for a man to dance on, and it was dead white all over. Only the furious power of its wings – two shining blurs at its sides – set off its form against the white background of clouds. The thing was big enough to kill our basiliscus, though it probably wouldn't be able to eat more than two thirds of him. Of course it would start with us.

There was no hurrying our mount, which sped its maximum as a matter of course. Meanwhile, the Queen's rider guided the huge, pale insect into a long, sloping climb which would intersect our course, for we had leveled off. I remembered seeing the lightning deftness of the little cousins of this thing – they can snatch a spider out of its web without leaving a tremor among the silk threads. This thing would have a fifteen-foot reach if an inch, and to cap the mess, I could only defend our rear with one hand; it was imperative for both of us to keep one hand dug into the lizard's scales, or the wind of our passage would sweep us off.

We were over the steppes now. Hopelessly I chose a stabbing-grip on our spear with my free hand. The look of the hell-bug as it rose behind us was all fragility and grace. Its two lower pairs of legs hung trailing in dainty curves under its long body, which looked as smooth and balanced as the war-canoes of the southeastern savages. It was getting so near you could make out the faceting of its eye-globes, a taunting reminder of the pearls in our bags. I could even see the face of the soldier guiding the thing.

It's strange to see a man's face through the screaming wind of that speed, with the whole sky around you and the whole world beneath, a barren floor, and still to get as clear a feel for his past and his character as if the two of you were sitting at mugs in a cozy tavern. But I did feel I knew the man in that glance – plain sense said that it would be a tough and tried soldier, for an important mission like this. The face said that and more – the scars above and below the steady bright eyes, squinted against the wind, the mouth shut and thoughtful. It added up to a sturdy, cool professional who thinks ahead and then kills you without slip-ups when it's his job to do so and he has the edge.

Good soldiers stay alive by being unsentimental and having a quick eye for the main chance. There was no time to chew it over. That quirky peep into the man's nature showed me our only longshot hope, and without a pause for thought I did the hardest thing I've ever done. I grabbed a bag by the bottom, and with a snap of the arm that forced open its drawstrings, I flung its whole contents into the air behind us. I groaned as I did it, looking back. The pearls sped earthward in a glistening black clot, scattering slowly, seeming to swarm as they fell like bees do before hive-making. Our speed and theirs made the jewels flee the faster from sight, and I still see them sometimes in memory, a thousand black stars, tumbling down through the wide blaze of noon.

If betrayal of his Queen was on the soldier's mind before, I do not know. Perhaps if he'd caught us and had the whole two thousand, the habit of loyalty would have stayed firm and he would have smoothly completed his mission. But seeing the pearls there, stark and dazzling in the sky, and knowing that they could be his or they could be who knew whose – it shocked him into realizing the wealth he was pursuing. If he did not follow them down, and finished the chase, they would be leagues behind, and he might never find them. Almost without hesitation, he reined his mount into a dive.

It had to be a whole thousand, you see, for some would be lost, and there must be enough even so to purchase swift escape and a new life. The Queen would eventually work a spell of recall on the mount he rode, and in the meantime he could use it to his advantage. Luck go with the man, I bear him no grudge! Still, as I say I see them tumbling, tumbling, those thousand dazzling, jetblack pearls, sometimes in memory.

Ah well! Having a share of a full thousand would simply have meant more squandering to do. The soldier was a career man, a maker of plans and investments, and is probably cherishing his coffers right now, and dreading thieves. For me, it was work enough to rid myself of the five hundred I came away with. Think – I did it in two years! Surely, that's a feat as great as any involved in the winning of those black beauties!

Part 3

Shag Margold's *Preface to*
The Fishing of the Demon-Sea

Kairnheim, whence Nifft's and Barnar's ill luck led them down to the primary subworld, is as remarkable for its ethnic homogeneity as the other two continents are for their diversity. It does not lack all racial variety. The perimeter of Shormuth – the huge bay in its eastern coast – is host to a miscellany of folk. But the bulk of the continent is inhabited by Kairns, a cattle-raising people originating from the southern limb of Lúlumë, across the Sea of Catástor.

The Kairns came to Kairnheim in two major waves of migration separated by an interval of about four hundred years. It was the southeast half of the continent that received both influxes, for east of the Ikon Mountains luxuriant grasslands stretch practically unbroken for three hundred leagues to the coast. This gently rolling land, thickly braided with rivers, is the realm called Prior Kairnlaw. It is superlative grazing land. The Kairns who held it first were loathe to share it with their late-coming cousins, and indeed, did not do so, for their cousins – more numerous and hungrier than they – drove them out of it, and into the northwestern plateaus, the colder, rockier, more arid half of the continent known today as Latter Kairnlaw.

Kine Gather lies in Latter Kairnlaw not far from the Bone Axe Mountains, a northern branching of the Ikons. Like its sister-cities of this area – White Lick, Crossgulch, Bailey's Yards – it grew from a cattle market on a river, a rough-and-ready sort of place where stock could be auctioned and shipped by enterprising men unwilling to endure tedious inquiries into their herd's provenance or prior ownership. And, again like their neighbors, Kine Gather's citizens retain even in the moderate prosperity they currently enjoy all the predilections of their city's founders: raiding, cattle-rustling, passionate quarrels over boundaries, and blood-feuds.

Most Latter-Kairns share these traits and this is understandable. Their sparse-grown, harsh-wintered terrain compels their herdsmen to arduous seasonal pilgrimages to keep their animals in pasture. Only the hostility of that land to any other economy – combined with what might be called a very stubborn cultural spirit – keeps them at their historic trade. And yet, for all their pains, they can expect to raise only maculate hornbow and dwarf-ox with any success, while in Prior Kairnlaw both these breeds thrive and four others besides: palomino hornbow, crucicorn, plodd and jabóbo (of which last, more presently). If scarcity alone had not made cattle thieves of the Latter-Kairns, their enduringly bitter sense of dispossession would have done it. Inevitably they have robbed one another, but they have always preferred the richer plunder and the prestige among their fellows to be won by raiding their homeland's usurpers.

One aspect of this historic conflict – the jabóbo question – has proven particularly fateful for both Kairnish nations by leading them, indirectly, to a dangerously frequent contact with the demon realms. Wimfort's folly and consequent abduction – which compelled Nifft and Barnar to their dire expedition – are perfectly symptomatic of this trend, and so its cause deserves some amplification.

Jabóbos flourish in Prior Kairnlaw as they do nowhere else on earth. The beasts are big quasi-bipeds, about twice the size of a man. They are cleanly (they wash themselves in the manner of cats), short-muzzled, small-eared and, except for their thick, stubbish tails and huge thighs, have a rather anthropoid aspect. They are valued for their milk, not their flesh, and no more males than are needed for breeding are ever raised. The females have remarkably pronounced mammary developments which are, if I may so phrase it, directly and immediately exploitable by men. The herdsman's feeling of communion with such a breed is – imaginably – great. Not to put too fine a point on it, jabóbo cults – originating in various fertility-promoting rituals informally practiced by herdsmen – now abound in Prior Kairnlaw. Sacred herds are designated and the rituals centered on them are reported – probably reliably – to have both dionysiac and priapic features. (The herds are often called, by local cynics, 'sacred seraglios.') Whether the ancestors of the Latter-Kairns, when they possessed that bovine Eden, ran to similar extremes is a moot question. A primitive purity of both rite and tenet is hotly alleged by them today, and it may have been so. Certainly they too in their day had sacred herds, and their doctrine holds the descendants of these beasts to be sacred still, and still their own religious property. Hence Prior Kairnlaw cult activities are felt by Latter-Kairns as an intolerably flagrant profanation of their lactescent icons, a heinous sacrilege daily renewed. On this question the Latter-Kairns focus all the rage and anguish of their dispossession. And it was during the First Jabóbo Wars that they – athirst for a vengeance beyond the scope of torch and sword – began buying sorcery in the cities of Shormuth. The Prior-Kairns armed themselves in haste from the same dubious arsenal, and three centuries of necromantic skirmishing, not yet abated, were begun.

More than one observer has remarked on the great number of subworld portals to be found in Kairnheim. Some – like Stalwart's Quarry – resemble Darkvent in having been opened by human inadvertence, but far more have appeared with ominous spontaneity, unlocked by earthquake, erosion and even lightning. The speculation that a zone of extraordinary demon vitality underlies the continent, while doubtless correct, misses the heart of the matter. For surely, centuries of haphazard and indiscriminate invocations of demonic power by the Kairns have had the effect of *concentrating* the ever-alert malevolence of the subworlds beneath their land. The Kairns lack any coherent thaumaturgical tradition, oral or written. Impetuous and ill-informed, they offer a ready market for the services of third-rate mages and unscrupulous spell-brokers, such as are now to be found in great numbers in the Shormuth region. Such 'wizardlets' command powers sufficient to tap demonic forces, but inadequate to ensure the mastery of them. In essence, the true demon highways to man's world lie through man's spirit; to yearn for destructive power is to open a gate to the subworlds, and from this we must conclude that the very foundation stone of Kairnheim is by now vermiculate with the hellish traffic that her people have kept so steadily aflowing.

The manuscript of this narrative is in Nifft's own hand. He himself told me he felt a particular responsibility to undertake the labor of writing it, as an act of homage to Gildmirth, for whom he conceived an abiding affection and regard. The Privateer surely merits some particular comment. His birthplace – Sordon Head, on Kolodria's southern coast – is as rich and empire-inclined a city now as it was when he swindled it three hundred years ago to finance his journey to the Demon Sea. Indeed, Gildmirth's ploy proves him a native son, both in his cunning and his venturesome greed, for Sordonite policy has always leaned as heavily on deception to gain its ends as on the strength of its navy. Many writers have held its people's ruthless duplicity to be a shade more (or less) than human, and subscribed to the legend that there is demon blood in the population. There is little more than the city's proximity to Taarg Vortex – the subworld marine portal down which Gildmirth escaped his enraged fellow citizens – to support this tradition. More probable is the rumor that many Sordonite families have close ties with the formidable

132

wizards of the Astrygal Chain southwest of the Great Shallows. Gildmirth, at least, almost certainly enjoyed such connections, for it is unlikely he could have obtained his shape-shifting powers in any other place.

– Shag Margold

The Fishing of the Demon-Sea

I

Just after dawn, they buckled us into the strappadoes. The mechanism is fairly simple. Your wrists and ankles are pulled toward the four corners of the upright frame, and you're splayed in the center like a moth in a web. Each machine has three executioners. Two work the winches until all the joints in your body are pulled apart. The third has a long-handled pruning scissors for starting the cuts around your separated joints. Then the winchmen go to work again, to tear you apart at the cuts. They alternate. It's considered good winch-and-scissor work when your trunk falls all at once out of the splayed rack of your limbs. They don't like thieves in Kine Gather.

The strappadoes were set up in the courtyard of the Rod-Master of Kine Gather. This was a place as big as a town square, for the Rod-Master was a man of vast wealth. In this he was like his city, which was why we had come there. As for the foundation of that wealth, it was obvious to anyone with a nose. Even within those mosaicked walls, among those flagstoned promenades with their potted cedars and urns of flowers, you could smell the dung and horses' stale that laced the morning air. The aroma might have come from any of the corrals and stockyards around the city, or it might have come from the thousands of citizens themselves who waited in the courtyard, chatting pleasantly, to see us die.

Frankly, I was in a rotten mood. I saw no way out of this. The order would be given at the first rays of sun that entered the courtyard, and the east was already well ablaze.

The bailiff climbed onto the platform we were strung up on. He undid a scroll, and read aloud from it in a mellow voice, which the crowd fell silent to hear:

'The good and great lord Kamin, Rod-Master of Kine Gather, conveys herewith his judgment to Nifft the Northron, known also as Nifft the Lean and Nifft the Nimble, and to Barnar the Chilite, called Barnar Ox-back and Barnar Hammer-hand. This is the judgment of lord Kamin: that you are both egregious felons, remorseless reprobates, and sneaking thieves; that you have entered the city of Kine Gather, and moved through the bailiwicks thereof, in pursuit of criminal aims; that you were taken in possession of a tool of criminal thaumaturgy; that you have merited death. You are permitted final remarks. Do you wish to say something?'

'I wish to say three things,' I answered.

'Speak them,' said the bailiff.

'First,' I cried, 'I wish to express my regret that I did not have more than a week in this city, for then I could have given all you Kine-men bigger horns than your cattle have. Alas, I have cuckolded scarcely more than a dozen of you. I would have worked faster, but you Kine-women smell so much like stockyards that I could only stand to serve two or three of you a day.'

Nobody in the audience seemed to like this much, but on the other hand, they didn't get very excited either. Justice is harsh there, and they're probably old hands at hearing last remarks.

'Secondly,' I said, 'I want to share with you all my conviction that the good and great lord Kamin is a wart-peckered, dung-munching cretin whose great wealth is a ludicrous accident, whose only talent is for vigorous self-abuse (with either hand), and all of whose living relatives resemble toads so strongly that I wonder they can look at each other with straight faces.'

They seemed to enjoy this somewhat more. Here and

there, amplifications were gleefully shouted. They are a tough folk, law-abiding, but not overawed by authority. In fact, they're not hard to like – for somebody in freer circumstances, that is.

'Thirdly,' I said, 'let me convey my fascination with Kine Gather as a whole. I would not have believed so large a city could be built up from nothing more than cow-flop and clods!'

This made some of them mad. The town has great municipal spirit. I had the sour satisfaction of rasping some of them, however slightly. It was small comfort but I made the most of it. Barnar said he wished to make two last remarks. The bailiff told him to proceed. My friend produced an epic flatulence, after which he spat on the stage voluminously, making the bailiff hop to save his boots. The edge of the sun topped the courtyard wall, and flung its rays like lances in our faces. The bailiff raised his hand. At just that moment a herald burst from the big two-valved door in Kamin's manse at the farthest end of the courtyard.

The timing told me the whole tale in a heartbeat. That the herald should burst out at *precisely* the last instant, crying, 'Hold! Kamin bids their death be stayed!' – it was just too stagy. It was theatrics, and for whose benefit but our own? Kamin required some service, hard and dangerous, which we were intended to welcome in prefer-ence to this harrowing alternative.

II

Rod-Master Kamin was a big, florid man. He surely did like theatrics. He was sitting on the chair of office in his receiving chamber, wearing a brocade robe and several fillets of braided gold whose ends, trailing on his shoulders, made me think of the relaxed ruff on a fighting cock. He sat, grand and awful, till enough of the townsfolk had filtered in to provide an audience sufficient to witness the majesty of his rising up. Then Kamin, Rod-Master of Kine Gather, stood.

When this imposing spectacle had transpired, and a suitable pause had been allowed for a hush to fall on the assembly, Kamin spoke to Barnar and me – or rather, spoke down upon us in a ringing voice that addressed everyone: 'Outlanders, hear me! Your guilt remains, and yet your lives are spared. This decision is not motivated by spinsterish sentiment. Your treacherous skills, your skulking cunning are needed to save a life far worthier than both of yours combined. Are you prepared to purchase your lives with your daring?'

Oh, he mouthed us roundly indeed! I wondered if my remarks about him had been conveyed to his sanctum. Surely not, I decided. Underlings are not so frank with a self-loving master. I made him an impeccable bow, which caused my chains to rattle.

'As for daring, Rod-Master, we dare such things as poor, foolish mortals must to make their way in the world. Concerning purchases, a man may ask to hear the price before he says yes or no – whatever he may be buying.'

Oddly, Kamin seemed caught off guard by this demand. Could he have expected anyone to be so cowed by his dramatics that they'd take his deal without hearing it? A man too ignorant to know that there are many things in the world worse than death on the strappadoe is not likely to be a very useful man on a difficult exploit.

But Kamin's jaw made a brief, dazed movement when he heard my answer, and I read a quick, unmistakable fear in his eyes that he was going to fail to enlist us. He recovered himself by scowling.

'You will be instructed in this tragedy by one whose hands are red with the guilt of it. He is one who will pay a dreadful price if . . . if this is not made well. Go to Charnall now! You will be brought back to Council to give your answer.'

As we were marched down a corridor that led to a staircase, Barnar murmured to me:

'He was afraid we'd turn him down. It's an ugly job he wants done, Nifft.'

There seemed little doubt of that. We were led into a wing of the manse. We mounted to the third floor, and were passed through a stout door with a double guard outside and another inside. A gaunt, balding man nodded at us from a table where he sat devouring breakfast. This was surely he of the guilt-red hands, though all he had on them at the moment was fish grease and breadcrumbs. There were a lot of these on the table too. Charnall was narrow all the way down, and ate like two men. The type is not uncommon. He had on a costly but untidy and very well worn tunic. His short beard, and the grey hair on the back of his head, had a tattered, plucked-at look. His eyes were intelligent, but with a tendency to go out of focus. He struck me as bookish, somehow.

The leader of our guard told Charnall to stop eating.

'Just finishing!' he gasped. He swept the rest of the bread and fish into his face. Then he stood up licking his lips, dusting his hands. The thin comfort of breakfast was behind him now, and regretfully he focussed on his situation, and us. He was a man profoundly depressed by his situation – you could see it in the way his shoulders sank as his mind ran over the information he was commanded to give us. Withal, he had the self-possession to recall what our morning had been. He pulled out his stool from the table for me, and motioned Barnar to sit on his cot. He dusted off his table and sat on this, his long legs almost reaching the floor. He folded his hands on his lap and scowled at them for a moment. Then he looked up and said: 'You are Nifft the Lean, of Karkmahn-Ra. You are

Barnar Ox-back, a Chilite. I am Charnall of Farther Kornuvia.

'You are men at the top of your profession, and in all natural skills of wit and hand you are known masters throughout the Sea of Agon, and even in the western waters. I am a man mediocre in his profession, though it is a greater one. I am a student of the lore of Power. I have encompassed certain tracts of dark knowledge. I know enough to buy wisely from true sorcerers. So much for our resources, gentlemen. They would be considerable for any sane task. Our task is not sane. Our task is impossible. And yet, I will tell you that I have conceived a glimmering of hope. Can you believe it? So intractable is human folly, so . . .'

'I beg your pardon, Lore-Master Charnall,' my friend said. 'You've had a chance to get used to the facts of the case, and we'd like to get past the shock of them too. It's been a racking morning. Can't you begin with the gist?'

Charnall bowed ironically to Barnar. 'You're right of course. You two will be bearing the brunt of it, after all. My life will ride on yours, so our risk is equal, but you will be the ones below – ah! Forgive me. The task is this: to bring a demon's captive back from where he lies, down in the primary subworld. The captive is a youth, Wimfort. He is the Rod-Master's only son, and my own erstwhile . . . employer. It happens we know, very generally, where the boy lies. We are lucky in the certainty, but unlucky in the place. You see, Wimfort summoned a bonshad. That's what took him. Bonshads are aquatic entities you see . . .'

Charnall looked at us with raised brows. Barnar nodded slowly.

'I think I do see. The boy lies somewhere in the Demon Sea.'

139

III

Charnall showed us a miniature portrait of Wimfort which belonged to his father. The Rod-Master's son was a handsome lad of sixteen. The artist's rendering of his bright, scornful eyes, and saucy tilt of chin, harmonized with the story Charnall gave us of him. The box of wrought gold that contained the picture supported another part of the tale – discreetly touched on, since Kamin's men were in the room – namely, the doting indulgence of the father toward the son.

For the past three years, young Wimfort had enjoyed so ample a competence from his parent, that he'd been able to buy his way deep into the mysteries of the arts of Power. He purchased no real understanding, of course, for that's bought by the coin of toil and thought. But he hired Charnall, and read smatteringly such texts as the scholar directed him to. He also employed his 'tutor' in obtaining texts which he knew of from other sources. Many of these Charnall would not have recommended to one so young and light of will, but he was as compliant as his principles allowed him to be. He couldn't have earned half so much in the Kornuvian academy where Wimfort's agents had found him. Nonetheless, he had repeatedly to throw the boy into a tantrum by flat refusals of his aid in various dangerous directions.

Wimfort always yielded the point after such clashes. He would tolerate no program or plan of study, but he had gained some sense of the endless interlinkages connecting all aspects of the wizardly art. He was stubborn. Charnall guessed that when he gave in, he made an inward vow to find his way back to his goals by some other route. In the meanwhile he lived with his mentor's scruples because he had to.

His debut performance was a compromise that Charnall had agreed to as the least perilous of several projects. The boy was ambitious to awe the populace, and this he did. His head was steeped in cheap ballads of the wild old days of Kine Gather when boisterous herds stormed through a town of mud streets and corrals, and his thaumaturgy was meant to be a commemoration of this era. With Charnall, therefore, he went to the slaughter-house district of the city on a night of the full moon. He intoned a very potent spell of regathered vitalities. They raised, in an endless surging forth from the bloody earth, the spirit of every animal that had ever died in those precincts. And as they raised them, they sent them stampeding into the streets of the town.

All night long the shadow-cattle with their blazing eyes panicked through the streets, raising a boil of dust and thunder with their shadow-hooves. The boy had flair, all right. The people woke. In their first horror, some dozen or so died in the poorer quarters, falling downstairs, or trampled by their tenement neighbors. But as the stampede thickened, and people understood its immateriality, more and more of them dressed and came into the streets. Kamin ordered the streetlamps relighted, and several of the city's magnates were persuaded to open their cellars. An eerie, impromptu festival was the result, with knots of staggering revelers run through by the endless bellowing herds. At dawn the spirit horde poured streaming back into the slaughtering yards. There the beasts plunged back into the earth, each reiterating its death cry as it dove.

The success intoxicated the youth. Moderation vanished from his schemes; he proposed one heroic folly after another and fought Charnall bitterly. Then he stopped proposing schemes altogether, and settled down to mining Charnall for texts, references, and instruction in the pronunciation of various tongues. The scholar could guess the direction but not the specifics of his charge's intentions. As he feared, the boy finally sprang his next miracle on the city all by himself. It was a dreadful fiasco. Its only lasting result was that it left an entire pasturing slope to the west infested with vampire grass. The incident was four months old when Barnar and I came to town, but the hillside decorated with bleached skeletons of stock were still a landmark for travelers approaching Kine Gather.

The boy was formally reprimanded by his father in the presence of the full council. This was a wrist-slap in the popular opinion. Many of the council men wanted other parts of the boy's anatomy involved in the rebuke. Yet still Wimfort was mortally affronted. At that age you invent extravagant compensations for bruises to your dignity.

The scheme he turned to was one of long-standing in his dreams, but he now put a really coordinated effort into the realizing of it, and Charnall did not guess his direction in time. He was determined to obtain some of the Elixir of Sazmazm from the primary subworld.

'Imagine it,' Charnall said to us with a kind of awe. 'A callow, headstrong boy in possession of the powers of a being from the *tertiary* subworld! May Almighty Chance prevent anyone from ever retrieving that elixir . . . But for that boy to have it? Imagination boggles and averts its eyes from the prospect!

'He worked harder than I'd ever have thought was in him, I'll credit him for that. He spaced and mixed the sequence of his requests. He wormed out of me some of the intonation patterns for High Archaic, and only after a long interval, asked for Undle Ninefingers' *Thaumaturgicon*. Only after the disaster did I realize that Undle's work includes a selection from the Kairnish *Aguademoniad*. These are spells for water-demons, and Undle provides a key for transliteration using High Archaic.

'The short of it is he had me summoned to our study in the basement of this house, and he was well prepared for

142

whatever I might do. He said he was giving me a last chance to share in his glory, which meant he would have been glad of my guidance in the actual speaking of the spell he had uncovered. He did well to wish guidance, and ill to go on without it!

'He described the spell of incorporation, which was now active within his body, and which would allow him, with a swallow, to make himself the vessel of the elixir. Indeed this is the securest way of holding something like the elixir, whose aura of potency must be so strong as to attract incessant theft spells from other wizards. He had also determined the probable truth of the belief that bonshads are unique among the marine demons in being able to obtain the elixir, whose source lies outside the sea, and thus out of their sphere of power. I urged him to consider why the water-demons are never called, though the spells for it are quickly come by. It's because no one *wants* to call them. Not even the greatest mages report the fruitful employment of these entities. The limit had been reached. I commanded him to come with me to his father and render a report of his intentions. The lad – that . . . *pup* – threw a paralytic powder in my face. I was a powerless witness of the very brief sequel.

'He made the classic error of the amateur; he barely managed the summoning spell adequately, and he made a grave mispronunciation in the spell of control that is woven into the formula of summons. The control spells are always by far the most difficult portion of the whole. It is even said that many entities will overlook slight errors in the summons if they sense that there are also flaws in the control. These latter mistakes they do not overlook. The boy stood forth boldly and spoke out loudly, and the thing came.

'The slurring of the intonations must have confused its course, for it came up within the wall. The masonry is twelve feet thick down there, and it wrenched itself out of the rock like a drenched cat clawing its way out of water. It was a thing of fur and hooks – tarantula's fur, and hooks to hold you with. Its head was a bouquet of three great spikes, all beaded with the knobs of its eyes. It boomed out of the wall, spraying gravel and dust. Wimfort's jaw dropped and swung like a tavern sign in the breeze.' Here one of our guards made a choking sound, and coughed at some length. Charnall looked demurely at his hands for a moment. Then he went on evenly:

'The lad didn't produce another syllable. The thing sprang on him. By the Crack, gentlemen – it had the quickness of a . . . a stupendous *flea*. It seized him, spun him, sank its spikes into his back, neck and skull, and sank through the floor with him. They're still shoring up the hole it left in the wall, but the floor shows not the smallest chip or crack.'

IV

There was silence for a moment. 'You mentioned hope,' I said. Charnall looked at me, and acknowledged the irony with a thin smile. Slowly he rubbed his palms together.

'It sounds unlikely, does it not? As for getting down there we have, as you surely know, our own little hellmouth not twelve leagues distant, near the ruins of Westforge in the foothills of the Smelt Mountain range. But once down there, you will be without maps of that terrain, and no one knows the size or whereabouts of that sea. And yet, hope we do undeniably have, however slight.' As he turned to this topic, he brightened considerably. His gaunt body trembled, I thought, with a scholar's suppressed glee over a rare discovery. He looked at us, probably gauging what we could understand of literary matters.

'I'll spare you details,' he went on. 'But I began with a

faint recollection of a figure generally called the Privateer who had done some exploit, or suffered something, in the Demon Sea long ago.'

'But that's – ' Barnar said. Charnall begged silence with a gesture. 'Patience, good thief – legends, I know, but still relevant. Luckily, so far I have been the most advanced mage that Kamin has found available, as well as being the most intimately acquainted with the boy's plight. For a month now Kamin's funded my efforts to find a solution. Last week I found a poem written about a century ago. Listen to these lines, gentlemen.'

He dragged a chest out from under the table he'd been sitting on, and took a parchment from it. What he read us was nothing more nor less than a garbled version of the third and fourth quatrains of Parple's 'Meditation'. His mention of the Privateer had half prepared us for this. When he was done I said to Barnar, 'Do you recall the rest of it, my friend. He's just read us the middle of it, hasn't he?'

Occasionally Barnar can be brought to display his reading. Soon after joining with him, I knew he was fluent in three tongues, but even I was long in learning that he could read High Archaic every bit as well as I. And it's always a treat at such exhibitions to watch his hearer's bewilderment at the erudition flowing from the mouth of that gruff, battered giant.

Barnar cocked an eyebrow and bowed slightly. '"Meditation on Man and Demon," by Curtus Parple,' he intoned. Then he recited it:

> Man, for the million million years
> He's shared the earth with demonkind,
> Has asked why they, in their ageless lairs
> So lust for his frail soul and mind.
>
> Whatever hands set the clock of stars
> Wheeling and wheeling down through time

145

Also sundered those two empires
With barriers both now over-climb.

That men should go down to those sunless moors
Where Horror and Harm breed deathless forms,
Or to the Demon Sea's littered shores,
Or its depths, where riches breed like worms –

That men do this (as the Privateer
Gildmirth of Sordon did in his pride)
Is no surprise, save that they *dare*
To sail that shape-tormented tide.

But why are netherworld nets flung here,
And men snagged out of their mortal terms –
Trawled kicking down from life in the air
To immortal drowning in monstrous arms?

Early on in the recitation, Charnall had stopped grim-
acing and started correcting his text to Barnar's version.
Now he looked at us ruefully. 'Courage, Charnall,' I said.
'No one can read everything. Parple's work is highly
esteemed in Karkmahn-Ra. Moreover, Gildmirth's name
is prominent in children's tales thereabouts.'

'No doubt you know all I've dug up and more,' he said.
'Still I won't believe that I've followed a fool's trail, no
matter what you may have heard of the legend.'

'I won't try to tell you that you *have* been wrong,' I
answered. 'For all we know, it's one of those tales with a
true core. The tradition is not highly specific, after all.
Gildmirth is depicted as a master entrepreneur and swindler. His exploits are variously reported, but all the stories
agree as to his last feat. He swindled the city of Sordon
Head – his home town – out of a fortune, which he used to
finance an expedition down to the Dead Sea. He did not
return. Some sources say he endures in bondage, like so
many thousands of lesser souls in that place.'

Charnall was much consoled by this. 'Splendid! This
chimes with my further discovery, and it seems I can tell

you something after all. For no more than three generations ago, a man descended to the sea and returned alive, and he returned with gold which Gildmirth the Privateer had gathered for him from the depths. The Swindler of Sordon Head does indeed endure, gentlemen. He lives, and moves freely in those waters, and yet bound he surely is – time without end. He's held by a ghoulish disease of the will that some being, slipping through his ingenious spells, infected him with. But as he was a man of powers, so he continues to be in his captivity.'

Barnar nodded. 'It's said he was a shape-shifter, and that he had five metamorphoses – one for fire, ice, earth, air, and water.'

'He has far more than five now,' Charnall answered grimly. 'I will tell you of that. The source of the information is the merchant Shalla-hedron of Lower Adelfi. It was he who went down to the sea and retrieved some of its wealth. His son recorded Shalla-hedron's experiences in this.'

Charnall showed us a massive leather-bound book entitled: 'The Life and Personal Recollections, as well as Many pointed Observations, of Grahna-Shalla, son of Shalla-hedron of Lower Adelfi, who Fished in the Demon-sea and Returned with Booty Marvelous to Tell.'

The scholar threw the book on the table. 'Almost every line is about him – the *son* , an intolerable, vapid ninny with a turgid and interminable style. But there are among the rest two brief pages of priceless information. The essential thing is that the Privateer's aid can be purchased. What the price is, Shalla-hedron did not report, or his sprout did not remember. All we learn is that "it is a price easy of the paying, and not missed after."

'Well now – I didn't say a great hope, did I? It is something at least, to have such an ally, if once you can find him in that place . . .'

V

We talked a good deal longer before we told our guards that we were ready with our answer. It was one of the most discouraging conversations I've ever had.

It had seemed unavoidable that we should make the descent to the subworld. But there are, of course, a number of portals, and we'd heard one of them was in Torvaal Canyon, scarcely forty leagues from Darkvent in the Smelt Mountains, where we'd be going down. So there had been some hope that, while we couldn't evade entering that hell, we could at least spare ourselves the soak in the Demon Sea, and make straight for the nearest way out.

But it turned out that Charnall wasn't so mediocre in his craft that he couldn't command Undle Ninefingers' Life-Hook. The spell was the great bibliophile's only original creation in thaumaturgy – he used it to secure the loyalty of the slaves who worked in his vast archives. It puts your life in the spellcaster's hand, and until it's removed he can jerk the heart out of you at any time. It also lets him visualize where you are – quite vaguely, but enough to distinguish between sunlight and the subworld's lurid sky. Charnall told us regretfully that he must guard his own life by governing ours very strictly through this means.

It was mortifying! We'd come to the city intending a theft, of course, but were guilty of no more than a week's general reconnoitering when we were taken. It was clear to us now that the order to plant goods in our inn-chamber, and ambush us by night, had come straight from Kamin. The man, after desperate efforts, had faced the fact that wizards great enough to retrieve his son by spells alone were rare; the few he'd managed to approach made it clear what the attitude of the rest would be – that amateurs played with Power at their own risk. Thus we were such things as the stones a soldier flings at some enemy who'd just shattered his lance and sword. We were scarcely likely to make a dent on the problem, but Kamin seized us and used us because we lay to hand, and he had nothing else. There was a certain pathos in this, I suppose, but my eyes remained dry. The ignominy! That Nifft the Lean, and Barnar Hammer-hand should be snared like a pair of wood-hens, trussed with magic, and booted below to fight demons with swords! As we were marched to the council-room, Barnar and I needed only a few murmurs to agree on our course. Our dignity was going to be salved with Rod-Master Kamin's gold.

That impressive individual was on his feet when we were brought into the chamber, and he turned an august scowl on us that was supposed to strike us like a wintry blast. The man had wide cheeks and small no-nonsense eyes, but he didn't scowl well. It made his neck bunch up on the collar of his gold-brocade tunic, and made you think of a pig's head on a plate in a grocer's stall.

The councillors were mostly older men, and their silence reflected not Kamin's power, but their own neutrality. We'd gleaned enough of the political picture during our week in town, to know that they were all powerful property-holders. Because Kamin was the son of the city's most beloved Rod-Master, he could usually count on a vital minimum of popular acceptance, and was, within limits, deferred to by the magnates. They would not follow him into disgrace, however, and some of them were said to dislike the prospect of a three-generation dynasty in a post that was traditionally elective. Wimfort's past and his predicament were thus queasy ground for the Rod-Master, and his arrogance with us showed he knew this. He wanted the business done, without protracted discussions aggravating the council's sense of what a burden the boy had recently been on the community. Kamin meant to ram it down our throats and trundle us off quick.

'Now you understand the terms,' he said. 'If you bring the boy back, your sentences are transmuted. The council has affirmed this measure. Give us your answer: Death, or the journey.'

I bowed. 'I assure you, my lord, Barnar and I are agreed on one thing: You are very tall and impressive the way you tower and glower and glare like that. I promise you it does make a man shake to look at you. But if you think Barnar and I will tramp through the prime subworld, and wade in the infernal lake itself, for no more pay than a kiss-my-arse-and-fare-thee-well, then you can go hump your hat. We'll go all right – for the terms I state and not a jot less. If you don't like our bid you can put us back on the rack. We'd rather die than demean our reputations by accepting the swindle you're offering.'

Kamin was one of those men who are strong mainly through the habit of success. He had no real toughness or resilience of spirit. A dab of insolence had him red and sputtering:

'You impudent, skulking dog!' he said. 'You arrogant gutter-sneak. I'm going to have them . . . I'll have you . . .'

'Oh yes, your eminence,' I said, '*have* it done. What would you not *have* done to us? You're wiser than to risk the doing yourself. But mark me. You took us for fools once with your false arrest. Once is all. We'll go down there all right, and you have your luck to thank that you trapped us rather than others. We have high reputations to maintain. We dislike to turn aside even from such a thing as this once the challenge is down. But we'll be paid what we dictate, and heroes are expensive. And that, you jowly sack of slops, you sagbellied sodomite, you puffed and strutting human pimple, is that.'

In these last remarks, I was mixing business with my

pleasure. He had to be roughly handled to feel our seriousness. Otherwise he would be trying to wear us down or
torture us into compliance.

He took it hard. The council was dead still, eating up
every word for their friends afterwards. Kamin blazed like a
signal fire, and glared at the guards. They came uncertainly
forward, but Kamin could bring out neither a word or
gesture of command.

He must now either kill us or ask our terms. We all
knew which he would do. Still, he took a long time to
swallow what I'd put on his plate. At last he did it with a
certain grace. He sat down. He looked at the floor a
moment, then turned to me a blank face.

'What are your terms?' he asked.

'Let your scribe set them down as I speak them, and
then article yourself to them in full legal form.'

'It will be done. I will article myself if the terms are . . .
acceptable.'

So I gave our terms. If we emerged from Darkvent with
his son, we were to receive mounts, a full set of new arms
each, an oath of non-pursuit, the freedom of Charnall, who
was to be liberated on the spot to accompany us, and four
packbeasts.

I rather liked Charnall, but our main motive here was to
ensure our freeing from the Life-Hook and any other
ensorcellments that might be slipped into us along with the
protective spells we were going to have to submit to before
descending. As for the packbeasts, I didn't explain them
until I'd given specifications for all the other things. This
took some time, and the scribe's quill squawked and
chuckled on the parchment, keeping up with me. At last I
said: 'And, divided equally on the four packbeasts, four
hundredweight of pure gold, securely lashed in saddlebags
of stout leather.'

Kamin had been waiting, eyes on his hands, for the real
price to be named. Now he shook slightly, but kept silence

151

and didn't look up. From what one heard of the man, the price probably represented about a third of his personal worth – and he could be sure he'd get none of it from the municipal pocket. I'd have liked to take two thirds, but it's a fool who takes so much that he guarantees pursuit while making fast flight impossible. The quill scratched. Wax and taper were brought. Kamin didn't move, and I thought the wax would harden before he did. Then, with a grunt, he jammed his signet against it, seized the quill and slashed his signature across the vellum. Then he sat glaring at me, as if I were some species of pestilence his fate forced him to endure. It made my gorge rise, and I shook my fist at him.

'By the Black Crack, Rod-Master,' I snarled. 'I'd love to take you with us. You'd think the wage a small one then.'

VI

The subworld portal called Darkvent is an abandoned mine shaft in the Smelt Hills. The Smelts are a bouldery, bony-looking range bordering a desert, and we reached them in the afternoon of a windy, sun-drenched day. As our mounts climbed the switch-backs toward the hilltops, Barnar and I let our eyes linger on the limitless sky with a feeling that none of our escort could have shared. Around us the wind muttered as it does among rocks in a dry country – a sad, confiding sound I've always liked.

We had neared the summits when Charnall, riding behind, nudged me and pointed down to the desert floor. I could now see the ruins of a town there on the range's footslopes. It had been a big town, but built mostly of wood, and such bleached shards of its walls as remained standing – shaggy with dead brambles – recalled those cracked husks of insects that hang in dusty winter spiderwebs. For the rest, the townsite was marked mostly by weed-lines, where crumbled planks and posts had fattened the stingy soil.

'Westforge,' he said. He got all the life the place must have had into the way he said it – the shanty-taverns, the sharpers, the whores, the nights of fierce music and lightly drawn blades. In twenty years a town doesn't take deep root, but it can get big and lively. And then had come the day when, up here in the hills, the miners had pushed their shaft that last yard too far. The very mountain core which it pierced had trembled, fractured, and plunged into the unsuspected abyss underlying it. The luckier of the miners, who were working higher up the shaft, made it back into the light of day, and saw the sun once more before they were taken. And then the outwelling horror had plunged like an avalanche out of the hills and down upon Westforge, where no warning had reached. And then human voices raised up a new and dreadful music from the streets of that city, and many danced there for long days and nights, clasped irresistibly in alien arms. Much of darkness and catastrophe was vomited up from Darkvent in those days, before one of the Elder League perceived the leakage, bestrode his winged slave, and came to seal the breach.

And now we approached the shaft. The sight of it was indefinably loathsome – it carried a crude shock, as if its raw stone had literally touched my naked eyeballs. Darkvent. A bottomless hole filled to the brim with shadow. A diseased mouth forever spewing its one black syllable of obscenity at the sunlight. Barnar and I dismounted and walked to its threshold.

It was like looking through a loophole in Time itself, for inside the shaft, all the handiwork of the Westforge miners lay untarnished, bright and whole despite its three generations of sleep. We looked disbelieving back down at the splintered bones of the city, and again at what lay within the shaft's ensorcellment, annexed therewith to the agelessness of the subworlds. There Westforge's craft and ingenuity survived, and testified to the vigor and hope it had once enjoyed.

I have heard of nothing resembling their methods of mining elsewhere. They had been great smiths, and had made their ore-carts of iron, with iron wheels. The wheels ran in a pair of steel troughs laid perfectly parallel and affixed to thousands of short wooden beams set into the earth, all lying crosswise to the parallel troughs. Heavy cables hauled the carts by means of big windlasses, one of which stood in clear view within. The tremendous weight this system could haul – swiftly and with scarcely any drag – was instantly obvious.

All that gleaming wrought steel, paralyzed and silent, all swallowed and sepulchred by forces against which the rarest works of human enterprise are like sand-forts on a stormy beach. How keenly we felt, at that portal, the lunatic futility of our own enterprise! Compared to all this impotent iron, what were our own poor tools? Two short-swords, two broad-swords, two slings, two lances, two javelins, two shields. Granted this was not all we had – heavens no! Charnall had also laid three spells on our bodies. One, the Wayfarer's Blessing, we felt only as a kind of blankness in gut and throat – we would need neither food nor drink while subject to it. The second was the Charm of Brisk Blood. This felt like a large dose of tonic weed. My muscles were as taut and jumpy as a pack of hungry rats, and my veins were so fat my arms felt like they were wrapped with snakes. In situations where mere fleetness and stamina mattered, this would be an undeniable asset. The third spell was the Life-Hook. This I experienced as a little sore spot in my heart, the kind of pang a large, old scar sometimes gives you – a flesh-memory of pain. The asset here was entirely our captors'.

A sensation of absolute aloneness touched both of us, in the same instant, it seemed, for we both turned to look behind us. And I almost laughed to see how alone we actually were, how far off from the shaft-mouth Kamin, Charnall, and the fifty soldiers, who were going to have to bivouac here to await our return, held even their eyes averted from Darkvent. Kamin sat tall in his saddle, his unease masked with disdain. Charnall sat slumped, avoiding our eyes.

Barnar grinned bitterly. 'Are you all so modest?' he cried. 'You stand so removed, gentlemen! Perhaps it's delicacy? You fear we'll snub you if you come forward to wish us luck?'

At this, Charnall dismounted and came forward with guilty haste, stumbling slightly. He was able to imagine our destination in far greater detail than the others and felt, I think, a generous dread for us, beyond his sense of his own danger. As he neared us it was his right hand he held extended, but then he faltered, and it was his left he ended by giving us, for on his right he wore the graven ring to which he had anchored the control of the Life-Hooks and the other two spells he had put on us. I could not forbear letting my gaze rest ironically an instant on the ring. He shrugged, smiling sadly, and I found I had to smile back.

'What clowns we are, Charnall,' I told him, 'with all our supposed wits. Do *you* believe we are actually doing this? I mean, if *I'm* not dreaming the whole thing, maybe *you* are.'

'And if you are,' Barnar put in, 'feel free to take a break any time. Why overdo? You could just summarize the rest of the plot for us over a cozy breakfast.'

'Nifft. Barnar. You *do* know that this whole idea . . . I mean that this whole approach to the problem was the farthest thing from my remotest . . . I mean let alone my even knowing who you were or that you were in town, or ever planning your – '

I clapped him on the shoulder saying, 'Peace, good wizardlet.' The epithet made him smile ruefully. 'You're too well aware, good Charnall, of what it means to enter

155

the subworlds, even to have hatched this scheme. Only an arrogant ignoramus like Kamin could seriously entertain it.'

Charnall nodded, moodily, twisting the control ring on his finger. 'It's ridiculous,' he said, 'even callous perhaps, but I keep thinking that if only I could find more to like in the boy, all this wouldn't seem quite such an insane *waste* of . . .' He checked himself, mortified.

'Our lives,' Barnar finished gently. Charnall nodded, but then angrily shook his head.

'*No*. There's Gildmirth. He *is* there. There's something about this legend – from the first I heard of it it struck me as truth, and even more than that, I could feel the man himself in it, feel a rare and vital personality behind the deeds reported of Gildmirth. I mean, for some reason, when I think about it, I actually feel *hope*, and if only you can *find* him, *reach* him . . .'

His own words had brought back to him the utter vagueness and improbability of the entire project. His shoulders sagged. I squeezed his arm consolingly and looked at Barnar, who nodded. Raising my arm in salute, I hailed Kamin: 'So down we go after your brat, cattle-king! Go home and reflect that if you have any hope at all, it lies with two men whose freedom you have stolen, and whose fealty you have coerced. If you find any comfort in such an arrangement, you're welcome to it.'

A soldier came forward with two lit torches and a bundle of several dozen more. As he neared the shaft, he made a sign against evil over his eyes, which he tried to hold downcast, sparing them the least glimpse of our destination.

Thrusting our two ridiculous little flames ahead of us, we stepped inside Darkvent. We felt a light shock of immersion, as in a very tenuous, oily medium. Being men, we felt no more of a transition than that, and received no hint of the hell of pain which the barrier-spell opposed to any of demon-kind who strove to pass through it in the other direction.

VII

The main shaft, with its steady downward pitch and its triple course of cart-tracks, remained unmistakable through a multitude of intersections with branch-shafts. It was a warm, gingery darkness that we walked through, with an elusive, sickish spice to it that you not only smelled and tasted, but also felt with your skin, like a breath of fever. And I could have sworn that in that darkness, the torchlight didn't fan out and attenuate – it stopped short, enveloping us in two eerily distinct bubbles of light outside of which the perfect blackness teemed with all the shadows the torches had not yet summoned into form. Meanwhile, within the light, the shadow-play made it seem that our passage called back the long-dead will of the Westforge miners to fugitive, fretful life. Crazily leaning carts appeared to lurch, struggle against the puddled gloom their wheels were mired in, craving to roll again and bear ore. And, in the little maintenance-smithies inset at intervals in the shaft walls, the dropped sledges and toppled anvils twitched restively in the elastic nets of darkness constraining them, as if we'd set them dreaming of the meddlesome, relentless hands of the men who had made them. All this lay in a huge silence that our footfalls hacked at feebly, but could not break. It was an infested silence, wormy with almost-sounds – a great, black throat with the noise of an anguished multitude locked inside it.

An endless time passed, which nevertheless could not have been more than two hours. Just as our second pair of torches was burning out, we reached a broad gallery. It had served primarily as a switching-yard for ore-carts, dozens of which stood in the central maze of track, sidelined long ago for recoupling to new cart-trains that had never rolled. These carts were unusual in being of two sizes. Among those of the by now familiar dimensions, there stood an equal number of more than twice this capacity. These giants were concentrated toward the gallery's farther side, where the shaft we had been following resumed its descent – resumed it at a markedly steeper angle, and with a bigger gauge of track, from which it was clear that the larger design of cart had been devoted strictly to working this more swiftly plunging segment of the shaft. In the gallery the giants had transferred their greedily heaped plunder to more manageable vessels for the long climb to the sunlight.

This place had been described to us. Here the mother vein had taken a sudden, steep downturn, while simultaneously thickening and complexifying to a fabulous richness. The Westforge engineers had hesitated only fractionally, then rushed down to pursue the vein at full gallop.

Boom times ensued. Several years of smooth progress and serene profits unrolled before the city, just as (if we'd been told rightly) four unflawed miles of this more cyclopean tunnelwork would now flow easily under our footsoles before we reached the next turning of the mine's fortunes, which was also a turning – a wrenching, really – of the shaft's course. We were told that it continued past this rupture for one more tortured mile, to end in a ragged edge above the subworld gulf. We crossed the gallery's switchyard and continued downward.

The riskier slope, the new giantism of carts and other equipment – this combination was subtly frightening, for in it you could read the city's state of spirit at that period. They were luck-drunk. The headlong grade revealed the dangerous exhilaration to which initial incredulity had yielded, while the unwieldy presumption of the machinery's

158

new scale betrayed the tipsy acceleration of Westforge's appetite to possess its inordinate good fortune. Poor, luckless wretches! What haste they made to feast on the mountain's bowels, thereby, with precisely equal haste, delivering to demon-kind a very different feast – themselves.

The crossbeams of the tracks started to get slippery before we had pushed even a half mile beyond the gallery. Barnar took a nasty fall that snuffed his torch. As he got to his feet I interrupted his muttered blasphemies: 'Look down ahead. Is it getting light?'

It was. At first it was scarcely light we saw – an oily pallor veining the dark, no more. But soon the features of the shaft before us began, unmistakably, to emerge, varnished with a glossy, jaundiced fulgor. Barnar took another fall, and then I took one worse than either of his, and suffered truly amazing pain when forced to use my elbow for an emergency anchor against the track's slimy beams.

'Barnar,' I said between gasps, 'beyond the collapse . . . It's *bound* to get steeper . . . So we should just simply *string out* . . . a simple, stinking, putrid, slime-kissing, thrice-buggered *cable* . . . to go *down* along . . .'

I was proposing more toil than I knew. Even though we could all but count on finding supplemental lengths of cable on our way down, which our line could incorporate as we descended, still we gathered, cut, coiled and packed over two miles of it before proceeding, if only because we did not yet imagine how we could reach the subworld floor from the shaft, and for all we knew a simple line might serve the need. From our supply, and what we foraged, we pieced out our safety line behind us as we stepped – steady and methodical – deeper into the sulphuric haze in which tracks, crossties, timbers and walls were manifested with gradually increasing detail, all of them like objects emerging from smoke. Four torches later – for we kept them past our need of them, for the sake of their earthly familiarity – we reached the shaft's mortal wound, the catastrophic rupture

Charnall had called 'the buckling.' Here commenced the shaft's terminal phase, for past this point its stony matrix had partially subsided into the subworld chasm, though it had stopped just short of following the rest of the mountain's core down to the demon-infected plains. The megalith still clung to its place in the architecture of the upper world, though it hung askew of its former placement. The discontinuity this produced in the shaft was dramatic. The tunnel was brutally torqued, its rocky walls having splintered while its shoring, though wrenched, had held. The tracks had also held together, though their bending had divorced them at some points from their crossbeams. They arched gracefully through a half spiral, then plummeted down the nearly vertical drop that followed. Hereafter we fervently rejoiced in my foresight regarding the cable, for the shaft's terminal segment often opposed slopes of sixty and seventy degrees to our progress, while the febrile subworld light, which now filled the tunnel, seemed more than ever to have the property of lubricating whatever it lit.

And yet we all but forgot the hardship of the tricky path once we had seen a certain thing awaiting us below – or more exactly, once we had suddenly *understood*, and rightly interpreted, something we had been seeing for some time. It was at the center of our vision's limit, a ragged patch of yellow, criss-crossed with grey lines. And when, all at once, it became obvious that this was a patch of subworld sky framed by our tunnel's end, our rapt scrutiny had a new puzzle to pick at – the meaning of that disorderly grey network. Down we came, planting our feet with absent-minded care while our eyes strained ahead to untangle this perplexing image.

But we had drawn quite near it before we comprehended its spatiality. At last it was clear that all the strands of the meshwork hung outside of the shaft, that somehow the whole crazy rigging was strung up in the open air just beyond our tunnel's ragged issue.

And then a warning was murmured to me. I was ahead of Barnar on the cable, and I heard from behind me that one fleet syllable of premonition, a throaty hum like that of a loosed bowstring. This touched my ears, and in scarcely the time it takes a hand to clench – which my rope-hand did – it was followed by a crushing blow laid across the backs of my knees. My legs shot out from under me as neat as ninepins. My grip on the cable held – it was my shoulder that nearly came apart while, for an instant, my body was stretched out on the air like a banner in a brisk wind. Well before I hit the ground, I understood that it would be far better for me if I did *not* hit the ground, and that if I must perforce do so, the less I tarried thereon the better, since it was clearly upon the ground that this trap was designed to throw me.

Actually, the line had robbed the trap of its full effectiveness. The blow I'd taken would have flung an unanchored victim right out to the shaft's ragged lip and left him sprawled on its dizziest salience above the webbed abyss. Instinctively I riveted my eyes on that menacing spot even while – finding I had no real alternative – I gave gravity her due and yielded to my body's stubborn determination to hit the ground, will-I nill-I.

Starbursts blotted my vision, yet still I held my eyes to their target. And while my stunned frame wallowed to get its legs beneath it; while returning vision dispelled the white obscurity that filled my eyeballs; while my right hand groped for its dropped lance – throughout all the harrowing micropulses of precious time which these accomplishments consumed, still I fought to see, exclusive of all else, that shaft-lip and any least thing that happened there. Unmonitored by me, my palm found the haft of my spear. Precisely then, as if the touch had summoned it, a scorpion as big as a battle-chariot swarmed into the shaft-mouth, and came avalanching towards us on a great splashing racket of rattly legs. My own legs weren't quite under me yet, but Barnar's lance came plunging past my shoulder and planted its razor-edged steel a half-yard deep in the junction of her soft throat with the first of her glossy black thoracic plates.

For of course this thing was not pure scorpion. Most demons, having something of man in them, are just such hybrids as this which leered at us with an old woman's face obscenely socketed in the huge ribbed and jointed body. The shot had stopped her, by which I mean made her pause, no more. For she crouched perfectly poised, the dreadful, limber power of her legs undiminished. Cautiously, delicately, her bulky pincers nibbled at the shaft sprouting from her gorge. And though this brought tears of pain in thick streams from her eyes, it was a look of the purest lunatic glee that her face beamed on us. It was a jowled, flabby-mouthed face, the brow fantastically gnarled – nightmare-knotted – above her crazed red eyes. Her mouth gaped – displaying not teeth but black barbs – and she paid out an endless red tongue that dangled to her wounded throat and licked it caressingly. Then, in a gurgling whisper, she said: 'I'm going to lick your face clean off your skull. Slowly, thoroughly, lick it entirely off. I'm going to sting you and bind you and scoop your loins hollow and lap out your brains. And then I'm going to make you again and start over.'

It was just as she finished speaking that I made my cast. Almost casually her pincers rose, their movement perfectly timed to shield her face. Unluckily for her, I wasn't aiming at her face. Crouched for attack as she was, with her tail advanced in a strike-ready arc over her body, my target was positioned several feet above her head, and I didn't miss it. Skewered, her stinger's poison bulb dropped a black bucketful of her venom onto her face.

Her agony was volcanic. She surged and crashed against the shaft walls like a stormy sea, her pincers tearing at the sizzling mess whence her howls erupted and her simmering eyes leaked out in red rivulets. We stood with broadswords drawn waiting for a safe moment to move in, but in the end we were spared that task, for after a few moments the poison seemed to reach some central nerve in her. She rose in the air, folding and unfolding spasmodically, crashed down on her back and writhed so mightily that the movement propelled her like a snake straight backward and launched her from the shaft-lip. We rushed to the lip and looked out. We learned then the obstacles that opposed our entry of this vast prison where the key to our freedom lay.

The tunnel issued from a stupendous wall of ragged bluffs, scarred by great landslides and stretching past vision to either side. The cliffs dropped sheer below us for nearly half a mile down to a zone of swampland, and all across the face of them the grey webbing spread, like a shroud crawling with grave-lice. For everywhere big multilegged shapes crouched in that dingy rigging, or ran along it with the incredible speed ants have on their own tiny scale. And other forms decorated the nasty weave – dangling bundles of webbing which stirred and twisted impotently against their anchorages. Vague though they were in their wrappings, we could see that many of these were winged things of a stature about twice that of a man, but the commonest food of the scorpion demons was themselves. Their cannibal struggles raged everywhere, including at a point not far beneath our feet, where our recent adversary, snagged in the web by her tail, offered little effective resistance to the greedy pincers of two of her confreres.

As for the swamp below us, it was apparently a kind of backwater off a river which, far to our right, flowed out from the foot of the cliffs, and divided the plain with a shallow valley. Across the valley, perhaps two leagues distant from us, a city of giant towers stood, stilt-supported platforms crowned with buildings. And, looking small as flies above a faroff corpse, things numerous and fleet flew among the titanic structures.

But we gave most of our attention to the cliff that we had to descend. We could see that any rope we dropped would hang in striking range of a score of places in the webbing. We'd be picked off within ten minutes of our starting down. And when we'd brooded on this for a while, we discovered an added unpleasantness; the swamps we must cross once down were astir everywhere with the movement of submerged shapes. None broke the surface. All we could be sure of was that they were big – very big.

We sat down and rested. We were so discouraged, we couldn't speak a word. I discovered that my spear had fallen free from the demon's stinger, and that her venom had only slightly corroded its ironwood haft. I was about to exult in this luck, but then only smiled bitterly. We had so little to work with! Barnar spat vigorously out into the yellow air.

'I'd like to sweep that foulness off the rock, like cobwebs with a broom,' he snarled.

'Too bad we didn't bring a broom,' I sighed. 'Do you think we could drop rocks big enough to break a path through the web?'

'How many do you think we could manage that were even as heavy as that demon, let alone heavier?'

This had already occurred to me. I sighed again. Then I had an idea.

When Barnar had heard me out, he sat meditating for a moment. 'You know,' he said, 'its wildness may be the thing about it that will make it work. I mean, I don't think you can ease and creep your way into a realm like this. If you try, the first little entity will smell your uncertainty and hesitation. Horror and bad luck will converge on you. But if you barge in with all possible force, storm the gate

. . . then maybe luck might just give way a few inches for you, and let you pass.'

And so we started back up the shaft.

VIII

A long time after ascending – how can I know *how* long? – I counted off the first hundred paces of our second descent, measuring from the switching-yard gallery and down the main shaft's penultimate steepening. I found my mark and looked back toward the gallery. It was suddenly eerie that the sections of its walls and ceiling I could see should be stained with the lurid wash of the forge's light, braziers and many torches.

'All right!' I shouted. 'Send it down!'

My voice woke the noise of the mighty windlass above, and it all felt even more like some ghostly resurrection of the mine's great, toilsome soul, so long in its grave. Dusty and smoke-stained as I was, it was not hard to feel like some reanimated Westforger – certainly, I was as far from the world of men as any ghost is.

But when the thing I had summoned rumbled into view and came easing down the tracks, my little whimsicality was badly jarred. No such conveyance as this had ever ridden these rails in the doomed city's heyday. Though one soon saw the two giant ore-carts that were its substructure, its embellishments made it look far more like some monstrous weapon than any kind of mining equipment, and of course it *was* a weapon.

We'd welded on a prow – an unswept scimitar forged from the smithy's stocks of sheet-iron and sharp as a well-honed axe-bit. We'd also welded two long horizontal vanes to the sides of both carts – these were shaped rather like an arrow's fletches and were also sharpened. Lastly, both carts had a pair of broad vanes that pivoted on pins set in the frontal segments of their boxes' rims. At present they resembled a beetle's wings half-folded over its back, but they could be pushed out to a much broader lateral spread, and locked in this position, from inside the carts.

When this huge, haftless spearhead had nosed down to my mark, I shouted: 'Hold!' Barnar locked the windlass and appeared in the mouth of the shaft. When he reached me, he found me staring down the shaft ahead – rather glumly, I suppose.

'The buckling?' he asked after a moment.

'Yes,' I said. It didn't bear much dwelling on. We had spent hours there fine-measuring by every trick we could think of, and the tracks at that point certainly *seemed* – throughout their contorted stretch – to have been bent perfectly in phase. At the speed we would be going when we got there, they had better be. Barnar nodded, sadly, gazing where I did. He sighed.

'Oh well,' he said.

I nodded. 'Well put.'

We went to our vehicle. I climbed into the fore-cart, and Barnar into the rear. We spent a moment adjusting ourselves in the shredded cable with which we had packed both carts for cushioning, and checking the operation of our folding vanes. Then we poked our heads up and looked at each other. Barnar had his shortsword in one hand.

'Well, old Ox,' I smiled, 'all I can say is, I just wish it was *you* riding up front. I still think it's *nose*-weight we should have.'

'Tail-weight. But be comforted, Nifft. Either we'll enter that place safely, or we'll ram ourselves so far up its arse you won't even notice the difference.'

'Well that's true enough. Yes indeed. You realize of course, Barnar, that it is simply not possible that we're actually doing this?'

'I've come to the same comforting conclusion, old friend.

166

Therefore let's away – an impossibility can only do us an unreal sort of harm, after all.'

I nodded. He reached his sword over the cable holding us by the stern, and the blade whickered through it.

The slope plucked us down. The great iron mass seemed to ride a ramp of ice, so dreadfully smooth was its acceleration. The fetid gloom of the tunnel surged up against us like a foul throat swallowing us ravenously.

The racketing of the tracks rose to a howl, and in moments it had grown light enough to see the shoring's main beams, at their thirty-foot intervals, merging into one blurred, continuous wall.

All that lay in our power to do, in the way of navigational control, we had already done when we cut the cable, and nothing remained for us to do but – when it came time – to spread our vanes as we exited the shaft. The assumption that we would ever be called upon to perform this second task now appeared quite clearly to me as the most extravagant folly, based on a wild delusion conceived by a raving idiot. We would never reach the shaft-mouth! How could we have dreamed that we would attain this velocity? When we hit the buckling, we would quite simply be thrown up against the roof of the shaft with enough force to wed carts with stone – and ourselves between – in an eternally indissoluble bond. Already we were leaving the tracks and resettling on them in long, giddy surges. The feeble subworld light seemed to be igniting, coming on like a flare, so swiftly did we drive towards its source. I saw the buckling just below. I pulled my head back in and lay down. I could not forbear shouting farewell to Barnar, though he could not have heard me over the shriek of the wheels. Then my body, in its cushiony coffin, was seized, lifted up, pulled down, and torqued into a tight spiral – all in the same fraction of an instant. For another half-instant I was floating, and then the wheels were roaring again, our speed unabated.

167

I sat back up. Before I had succeeded in believing what I saw – that we still swept down the track – I saw ahead the webbed tunnelmouth. It seemed to howl as it yawned at us, though its voice was actually the din of our own white-hot, fire-spitting wheels combined with the thunderstorm of echoes we trailed behind us. I lay back. As the carts erupted from the roaring corridor, and into the stunning silence of that sunken sky, I slammed open my top-vanes.

Then whips murdered the air all around us – the webbing, through which, despite its toughness, our plunge was as smooth as the arrow's first leap from the bow. We punched through something that made a horrible, wet cough, but did not slow us, and three scorpion legs flopped over the nose of my cart and hung there lifelessly. Then we were falling clear, and I raised my head again.

It gave me a kick in the pit of the stomach to see how steeply we plunged. The vanes had given us even less lift than the little we had projected. Though we would clear the heaps of landslide – rubble strewn along the base of the crag, I found it easy to form a vivid image of being driven like a tent stake thirty yards deep in the swamp muck. And then a vast hand seized us from behind, and slowed us in midair.

This was how it felt, and as I looked back it was no more than I expected to see, in such a world as this. What I saw, and Barnar too in the same moment, made us shout and cheer like madmen.

We trailed an immense, twisting banner of tangled silk, and a score of hell-shapes struggled in the undulating acres of this train of ours. It flapped and bellied, and let fall a many-legged thing which plummeted, scrambling for purchase on the oily air.

In the lurch and sway of our hobbled fall, we argued over which part of the black-scummed waters we were likeliest to hit, but in reality the particular spot seemed to matter little. Systems of grassy silt-bars made escape afoot possible from most points. Meanwhile the waters looked uniformly threatening. Almost everywhere they bulged and folded with sunken movements of a fearfully large scale.

But now our fall took on a frightening wobble, and a sudden burst of speed. The windstream had compacted the webbing behind us, twisting it in a knotted skein that offered far less drag against the air. Our plunge got fearfully steep, and the unclean waters swelled toward us. Scant hundreds of feet from impact, we saw an immense leech – it resembled nothing else so much – thrust sixty feet of its slime-smeared body-tube out of the swamp brew, open a round mouth-hole with a haggle-fanged rim, and chew – blindly, kissingly – at the sky. Others of its ilk sprouted almost simultaneously, concentrated in the immediate vicinity of our now imminent crash.

One of them in particular towered at what appeared to be our inevitable point of collision. It seemed to be tracking us, by what sense I don't know. Its mouth's groping centered ever more sharply on our line of approach. I couldn't determine whether or not its mouth could swallow us whole until the last instant, when I saw that it wouldn't quite manage it. Then we hit our greedy welcomer.

Perhaps these things had a single predatory response for all airborne entities because they were unacquainted with any especially massive ones – I can't say. Whatever the reason, this leech was the victim of a serious miscalculation. We clove his mouth and the first sixteen feet of him asunder before snagging with sufficient firmness in his blubbery plasticity to wrench his eighty-foot bulk clean out of the water, like a plucked root. We hit the swamp, laying the whole floundering length of him out across the bog behind us. He had greatly cushioned our impact. We swarmed out, snatching our bundled weapons, and thrashed thru shallow waters to a cluster of sodden hummocks that offered a broken path out to dry land.

As we fled, we heard behind us a vast threshing of waters, and shrill, agonized voices. The leeches were gathering round the tasty entanglement of web-demons that we had strung across the lagoons, and feeding on them with gusto.

So we fled inland, and at length we found a zone of dry ravines where we could crouch in safety. Here we took our first period of rest in this world – this world so hard merely to enter, let alone survive in. Our venture was begun, at least, and ourselves still both alive and free, no slight feat in itself.

But ah! what a drear hell it was we now had to venture through! What a maelstrom of relentless gorging, one creature upon another! The claws and jaws of the upper world are red enough – who denies it? – but the carnage has intermissions, periods of amiable association, zones of green peace and fructification. In the subworlds, the merciless seethe of appetites never simmers down. Even while the leeches still fed on the web-demons, squads of the winged beings we had distantly glimpsed round the city of platforms swept into view. Their bodies were manlike, though scaly and of thrice human stature, and their temperaments were, as it proved, playful. Flying in vast and flawlessly coordinated formations, they dropped lassoes on several of the leeches and hauled them ashore, where armies of their fellows assembled mountainous heaps of brush. On these the winged things, twittering volubly together, incinerated their huge, vermiform prey alive. Cooking was not the object. The leeches were burnt to ashes while the beings swarmed in the air above their pyres, clearly intoxicated by the greasy smoke to which the worms were transmuted by the flames. And as for the smell of this smoke, I earnestly beg whatever gods may be that my fate may never again set my nose athwart such a stench.

Dismal, eternal, remorseless gluttony. We came to see

the hideous vitality of that place as a single obscene shape, its multiform jaws forever rooting in its own bleeding entrails – guzzling and growing strong upon itself.

We knew that by following the nearby river we should eventually find the sea. As the light is never truly full there, so the darkness rarely completely falls. We paused an indefinite time under the changeless sky, and then rose and made our way toward the river by the best-concealed route we could discern.

IX

We found the Demon-Sea. We *reached* it. At the time, though it was merely the threshold of our journey, we gaped at it as if it were the unimaginable peak of all Exploit simply to have attained its shores. Once we had come to ourselves somewhat, and recalled that next these waters must be entered, and plumbed, we were yet further awed. It was a moment for taking stock of ourselves.

The personal inventory this led us to was a sobering one. We had set out wearing light body-mail over heavy jerkins and doublets of leather. All three of these layers were now scorched in many places, and as ragged as old curtains in a house full of cats. We had one spear between us, and the head of this was half-melted. Barnar's sword lacked two feet of blade. He kept the remnant because one throws away not even the least asset down there. He still had his target-shield, but mine was now a fused and corroded lump under the carcass of a thing I had killed. Our bones were stark against our skins, our eyes were those of almost-ghosts, and our beards told us we had been at least a month en route. This was our only clue to a sane reckoning of time, in a world where horror, harm, and long, eerie calms flow past the traveler in endlessly unpredictable succession.

We sat down – fell, really, as if our legs had done their limit, and now forever renounced their task. The feeling of futility we had then was the heaviest weight I have ever felt upon my back. For a simple fact which we had known all along was now striking us with its full dreadfulness: having reached the sea, we must now turn either right or left, with no way of knowing which was the correct direction.

If, indeed, there *was* a correct direction – if even Gildmirth the Privateer could have survived till now on the shore of this subearthly deep. The wrong turn meant a grim eternity of plodding, another of retracing our steps. Gildmirth's present nonexistence meant the same. And the Demon-Sea spread before us like the very image of infernal eternity to either side.

We had first sensed its nearness while still deep in the dunes of salt. When we got a tang of brine, we identified a deep susurration we had been hearing for some time as the big-breathing sound an ocean makes. The dunes steepened, and we kept to their crests, trampling their ridgelines into crumbling staircases, winding always higher. And then there was before us a narrow plateau of rock salt ending in white cliffs and, beyond these, crashing against their pallid feet, the subworld waters.

The essential horror of its aspect you could not at first identify. The sounds of it had an awesome musicality, and the prospect a barbarously rich coloration, which conspired to exalt and bewilder your senses. The shingle footing the cliffs was jet-black, seemingly composed of something like broken obsidian, and when the cream-and-jade surf pounced up it varnished their contrast to an ever-renewed brilliance. Moreover a wealth of gaudy flotsam littered the beaches, so that the breakers made them flash every other color as well. The sea itself was bizarrely dappled, for though a gloomy cloud-cover vaulted it over to the limits of vision, this was abundantly rifted, and wherever it was broken it permitted avalanches of the reddish-gold light of sunset to pour onto the water. The clouds themselves were in many places caved in, and lay in foggy islands and ghostly ziggurats upon the green-black waves, and these misty monoliths had a bluish luminescence of their own lurking within them. Meanwhile the winds on those waters were strangely various, and everywhere wrenched them into a crazy-quilt of local turbulences.

It did truly ravish the senses, and so it was only belatedly you felt the horror of the *enclosure* of so huge a sea. For though the light that broke through the clouds might suggest earthly sunset colors, it was quickly recognizable as a demonic imitation – more garish less subtly shaded than the dying sun's true radiance. Such subearthly luminosity, in varying hues, had been our sky for weeks now – never a real sky, of course, never a transparent revelation of endless space, but always a kind of bright paint masking the universal ceiling of stone imprisoning this world. Now a true ocean is the sky's open floor – that's the feeling men love in it, the reason they venture upon it, apart from gain or exploration. But this bottled sea, for all its terrible vastness, gave you not the awe of liberation, but its black opposite, the awe of drear imprisonment's infinitude.

We sat staring at this vista for a long time. We meant to discuss our situation, but simply failed to muster the effort of speech. At last Barnar drew a long breath. In a voice utterly blank of feeling he said: 'To hell with everything. Let's just go right for luck.'

And so we did, both secretly grateful that we had managed even this minimal act of decision, for neither of us had believed it impossible that we might just sit forever on that impossible lookout. As it was, we set out sharing the glum, unvoiced conviction that we *knew* where the manse of Gildmirth was to be found: nowhere. And we would take forever getting there, except, of course, that we would not survive nearly that long.

Though we marched atop the salt bluffs, we found our eyes and minds constantly entangled with the vivid jetsam cluttering the beach below. And what we saw there had soon roused us from our despairing stupor, for though our spirits were jaded with terrors and atrocities, those sights revealed to us new dimensions of demonic activity. Some of that bright tangle on the black strand was merely the detritus of lower life forms indigenous to the sea: broken coral branches thick with budding rubies, sapphires, and emeralds, or uprooted crinoids whose torn husks were purest gold. Such common objects bespoke nothing beyond the ocean's grotesque fecundity. But equally numerous were products of art, of active – and surely malign – intelligence: wrought chalices of gold with elaborate silver inlay, tiaras of gem-studded everbright shaped and sized to crown no human skull, shattered triptychs whose fragmented images were vivid as hallucination. There was a broken chair, elaborately hinged and barbed, designed to hold unimaginable shapes in unconjecturable postures, and we saw several battle helmets with triads of opalescent eyes inset in the visors tumbling empty in the foam. All such evidences of active artifice serving unguessable aims proclaimed the sea's hidden cunning, its vast, unbreathing population aboil with a million malefic purposes.

Yet this was only the inanimate portion of what lay scrambled on the dark gravel. Shorelife abounded. The human form was so much a part of its makeup that we could not always tell whether we were looking at demon hybrids native to the place, or at the deformed thralls of demonkind. If even half of them were captives, then truly, our race has fed multitudes to the subworld's endless appetite for our woe. The lifeless wealth on the beaches – clearly a slight fraction of what the depths contained – showed plainly enough the bait that has drawn so many luckless souls within the subworld's grip, most commonly thru ambitious and uninformed spell-dabbling. And surely it is dangerously easy nowadays – most especially in Kairnheim – to buy the power to call up entities which can only be dominated and put down again by a degree of power not even generally understood, let alone purchasable, by any overweening dilettante.

Some of those we saw, of course, were unmistakably of the latter group: the sea's human 'catch,' spoils of its malignant enterprise, its fishing among men. Some grottoes, for example, were densely carpeted with victims whose faces alone retained their human form. The rest of their bodies – everted and structurally transformed – now radiated from each face's perimeter in wormy coronas. They resembled giant sea-anemones. The souls within those faces still – all too eloquently – lived, while every vermiculous grotto of them had its demonic gardener: an obese, vermillion starfish shape, all scabbed and barnacled with eyes, and which inched the slathering mucosae of its undersides across the quasi-human meadow. Each threatened face expected its embrace with a piteous look of loathing and foreknowledge.

And there were others of our species who lay in nude clusters resembling the snarls of kelp which a northern sea will disgorge on the sand in storm season. Their legs and hips merged in central, fleshy stalks, while their arms and upper-bodies they endlessly and intricately writhed and interlaced. These were the very image of promiscuous lust, but the multiple voice they raised made a hospital groan, a sick-house dirge of bitter weariness. Crablike giants, hugely genitaled like human hermaphrodites, scuttled over them with proprietary briskness – pausing, probing, nibbling everywhere.

But how were we to interpret the huge terrapin forms we saw plodding ashore to lay clutches of eggs on the black gravel? Their hatchlings, which erupted instantly, were scaly homunculi with frighteningly individualized human faces. We saw more than once their cannibal assault on the parent beast, as well as their launching of the dead mother's hollowed, meat-tattered shell – a swarming nursery-barque – through the surf, and out into the open sea.

It should be understood that I don't imply that the open waters themselves were barren of vital signs. Everywhere the waves suffered swift, grotesque distortions, and the shifting architectures of mist and fog that cluttered them everywhere pulsed unpredictably with movement, as of shadowy things in their depths. Once we saw what was surely a combat of invisible entities, which occurred about half a mile offshore. The waves there dented and sagged under massive, dancing pressures. It appeared that a pair of feet or paws were involved on one side – each as big as a large ship – and that a dimpling multitude of claws or tentacles were involved on the other. At length, something huge hammered a hollow in the water. The waves calmed, and an immense volume of saffron fluid gurgled onto the sea from what looked like a seam in the air, and sank coiling roots into the deeps.

Such spectacles as these, always accompanied by the incessant, soft, mind-seducing antiphonies of the ocean's vast noise, beguiled our sense of time just as completely as an interval of ease and merriment might have done. For the most insidious aspect of that place was the subtle, instantaneous *comprehensibility* of what we saw and heard. It was already halfway to madness just to realize that at the very first note, you understood those choruses of mangled rapture, those arrogant boomings of idiot Murder triumphing over defenseless Life. In short, slowly though we progressed, we were swept along by all we witnessed. Days had surely passed, though how many we could not know, when Barnar first opened my eyes to something he had been aware of for some time.

For out of a seemingly endless silence that had settled on

us, he cried: 'I can't help it! I've got to ask you.' He laid one of his great paws – all cracked and scorched with our trials – on my shoulder. The other he aimed up the coast where we were headed. The shoreline there was an endless white serpent of cliff and surf, diminishing to a wisp of smoky pallor near the horizon. Barnar's eyes, which the squareness of his face has led some to call bovine, but which are in truth alive with acuity, he aimed at mine. He had a haunted look. '*Am* I seeing a little blackish spur, which *might* be a headland, about three-fourths of the way to the horizon?'

It was a long time before I answered, my voice a hollow strangeness in my own ears: 'Yes. I think you are.'

The sinuosities of the shore protracted our approach to the apparition almost unendurably. We were still far from it once it had resolved itself sufficiently in our vision to become a source of hope to us, and thence of new energy. For what had appeared as a large landspit proved to be a small one, densely crowned with structures, opposed by a crescent of breakwater and pilings, which also supported numerous buildings, and whose arc mirrored the headland's, so that the two formed a pair of pincers which enclosed a broad, shallow lagoon shaped like a teardrop. If this landmark proved to be of human construction, it was certainly on a scale attributable only to an entrepreneur of Gildmirth's legendary stature, and in that class, his was the only name we or Charnall had been able to discover. We began to toy with the belief – pretty stupefying to ourselves – that we were going to find our man. Still the twisted coast interminably multiplied the hours of our drawing near, and through them all, the vivid, ersatz light never changed, and it was always sunset that poured from the broken iron-grey of stormwrack and fog.

But, long though we had studied the place on our approach, when we finally crouched above it – as low in a fissure of the salt cliffs as we could get without abandoning

177

the land's protection from the sea's powers – it was long again that we stared at it from near at hand. There was an indescribable poignance in it – in the combination of its splendor and its damage.

For the whole architectural sweep of the place was marred at the base; the headland had been riven, and half its length was subsided several fathoms into the sea. An imposing pyramidal structure that crowned the spit – by its grandeur the Manse itself, if Gildmirth's place this was – was sunk with it, and its lowest terrace was half-inundated by the swell. The sea's weirdly spasmodic surf climbed triumphantly up the sculpted pediments flanking its doorways, and went rummaging inside through its gaping windowframes.

Yet the rest – the bulk of the establishment – looked remarkably intact. The jetty and rank of pilings that opposed the headland's curve supported an elegant and various procession of architecture that didn't look in the least derelict or decayed. It was a splendid defiance, this parabola of human workmanship that pierced – stood kneedeep *in* – the Demon Sea itself. Such a flamboyant trespass upon so deep a universe of malignant power! That fragile ring of earthly art was a lunatic declaration of empire, a flagrant challenge to all that swam there. And yet, withal, there was this half-drowning of the manse. Seeing this, we no longer truly doubted that we had found – if not Gildmirth – at least his fortress, for the spectacle tallied with the report. If, in his bondage, the Privateer indeed lived freely here, his outpost's general soundness reflected it; while, if it were equally true that he *suffered* bondage, his broken manse proclaimed that just as clearly.

That a man should choose to come to such a place, and to abide in it, astonished us. That he should have done so for so long on his own terms moved us to awe. That he should endure here now on demonic terms made us grieve for him – for whatever kind of man he was, he had dared much, and alone.

'What impudence!' Barnar rumbled, smiling softly.

'And a hundred years of freedom and power before he was taken.'

'So you accept that part, then?'

I nodded. 'I *feel* it. If men do age here, it's far more slowly than they do under the sun.'

'For everyone, captive or not,' Barnar muttered, nodding in his turn. 'I confess I feel it too. Somehow it's part of the ... *weariness* of being here. So I suppose, if we assume thralls are protected by their possessors, we can also assume he still survives.'

'I think so. After all, who else could be maintaining that ... that zoo down there.'

'If it is a zoo. If those aren't invaders of the place, new tenants.'

The notion startled me. For some time we had been studying the water enclosed by the headland and pier. This was shallow and quite clear, and its floor was a sunken labyrinth of scarps, reefs and grottoes. And in each pit and den of that maze shapes crouched, or restively stirred. And despite the irregularity of the maze's structure, it gave an impression of design which made me still incline to see it as a menagerie, and not an enclave of demon usurpers.

'They're too various,' I pointed out. 'Demons don't usually form coalitions. One species might have invaded him, but not a mob, surely. It looks much more like a sampling, a specimen collection.'

Truly, a collection of more infernal rarities than those would be hard to imagine. It was like looking in a fair booth through a Glass of Piercing Sight at a drop of pond-scum. Many of those beings are now a merciful blur in my mind's eye, but others I am doomed to remember. There was a globular explosion of spikes and spines, like an

179

immense sea-urchin, and from the tip of each of its spines oozed a yellow human tongue like a drop of poison. Another of them was a crystalline blob of veined but otherwise transparent material in which hung a constellation of anguished human faces. And there was one demon that resembled nothing so much as a huge lurk. Just as I was studying this one, I made an unnerving discovery.

'Look up there,' I said to Barnar, 'on the pier about half-way out.'

'By the Crack. Is it a lurk?'

'It's a twin of that demon down there in the water, in the grotto just below where it's crouching.'

X

The shape on the pier clarified for us the murkier features of its submerged counterpart. These demons differed most strikingly from lurks in that their flat forebodies were studded, not with the onyx eye-buttons of lurk-kind, but with a freckling of human eyes. Their feeding-legs too – that shortest and foremost pair that cleanse or hold prey to their bristly fangs – were tipped, not with hook-and-barb feet, but with clawed hands on the human model. Their color was a phosphorescent green marbled with scarlet. Their movement – for both were restive with mutual awareness – *was* lurkish, both in its steel-spring quickness and its overall liquidity.

Then the monster on the pier – it appeared to be somewhat smaller than that in the water – heaved itself up onto the balustrade, its hairy bulb of a body teetering as its legs bunched to spring. It launched itself into the air. Its dive seemed sensuous, floating, and its multitude of eyes closed dreamily as it plunged. Its counterpart reared and tore the water with its forelegs, and met the leaper's impact with a frenzied counterassault.

Bubbles thick as smoke masked their struggle, but when at length the water stilled and cleared, we saw the attacker had mastered the larger demon. Locking the latter's forelegs in a cross-grip with its own, it pushed upward. This hoisted the other's forward half off the sea floor, keeping its fangs out of striking range while its hind legs scrabbled impotently for counter-leverage. From the attacker's underside a brilliant red coil extruded. Its twisting length touched a slot in its pinioned opponent's underside and slid into it. For several seconds the linkage was maintained, the coil pulsing with the transmission of unimaginable essences. Then the coil was retracted. The attacker released the other, which had grown oddly quiet, and began to swim toward the manse just below us. During its progress all the monstrosities it overswam, including many far larger than itself, shrank down and cowered in their craggy cells. It accelerated, gathered itself tight, and rode a swell through one of the manse's gaping doors.

Barnar and I exchanged a long look, each waiting for the other to say something that would clarify his own excited thoughts.

'He was renowned as a shifter of shapes even before his expedition here,' my friend said at last. That enabled me to take the next step.

'Yes. And maybe, in all this time, he has gone over.'

It was some relief to have spoken what we both feared, but not much. Without much hope Barnar countered after a moment: 'Yet Charnall did say that half his passion to come here was for exploration, for knowledge of the ocean's demon forms.'

'Knowledge,' I snorted. We looked at the lagoon and Barnar shuddered.

'Let's hail him,' he said, 'from here. We're still technically outside the sea's zone of influence.'

I agreed. Barnar cupped his hand to his mouth and cried down upon the manse: 'Gildmirth! Privateer! Gildmirth of Sordon Head! Two men of upper earth ask your hospitality!' The words rolled down and broke in echoes that reverberated in the empty, tilted terraces of the great ruin. It felt exceedingly strange to shout a summons here. The human voice, human speech – they were tools that were utterly unavailing in this world, and for long weeks we had struggled through it without using them, mute invaders who simply fought or fled whatever they encountered. So it almost made my flesh crawl to hear an unmistakable response to Barnar's words: a small, watery commotion within the manse's sea-level tier. From the door through which the lurkish demon had swum, a naked man swam out.

He had a squat frame, and moved with quick intensity – ferocity almost. He whipped round in the water, seized the luxuriant bas-reliefs framing the doorway, and – monkey-deft – hauled himself up to the next higher tier. Here he stood scanning the sky, as if he thought Barnar's voice had literally penetrated to him through the eternal cloud-ceiling, direct from the world of the sun. I looked at Barnar, hefting my spear. He gave me his target shield and I gave him my sword, thus wordlessly agreeing to what had been our armed strategy of recent days – I would be advance harrier, and my friend, with his one-and-a-half blades, my back-up. We stood up and hailed the small, solitary shape on the terrace.

He turned in our direction then, and dispelled our last doubt that he was Gildmirth, for the eyes with which he met ours were – both pupil and ball – a lush red. The purplish red of summer plums splitting with ripeness. 'Bloody-eyed' was an epithet two textual references had applied to the Privateer in describing his post-capture condition. For the rest, he had a full-lipped, goatish face, was fleece-haired and fleece-bearded. Though his stature was small he had the feet, sex, and hands of a larger man, and his knotted limbs, chest, and stomach bespoke an unusual vigor. He grinned when his eyes had targeted ours, and we caught the flash of a second demon detail that set our own teeth on edge, for *his* teeth were large and splendid, and made of the brightest steel.

He laughed. 'Are you real? Come down! Make me believe it!'

We climbed down the bluffs to a point from which we could leap to the tier of the manse next above the one where Gildmirth stood. Still grinning, he motioned us down. We jumped. By the time we reached the railing, the Privateer was clambering over it.

We both made him a reverence when we greeted him. It was instinctive; the heart will honor excellence where it meets it. Sardonically, he bowed in return.

'Do I merit such a salute? If so, you merit the same, my friends. For it seems you have walked here. If so, you are the fourth and fifth to have done so this hundred years and more. Believe me, if I could feel amazement at all any more, my jaw would be dropping off my face at the sight of you.'

In fact, his jaw – a powerful one, fit to drive the dreadnaught teeth that filled it – scarcely stirred with his speech. 'Do you know what you are to me?' he concluded, as if in afterthought.

'What are we to you?' Barnar asked obligingly.

'You are two brief escapes from here. You are two lives in whose light I can live for a while, before returning to this.' He gestured at large. 'I refer to the payment I will ask for any service you may be seeking from me. Unless, of course, you've just come down to clasp my hand. That service is free.'

I took the hand he mockingly extended. This wasn't a simple act, for I had not yet decided that he was still on the human side of the line he had drawn here in the days of his freedom and expeditionary pride. His hand was as cold as a month on a Jarkeladd glacier, but innocent of any malevolent aura. I said: 'I am honored. I am Nifft of Karkmahn-Ra, a master thief. It is likewise with my friend Barnar Hammer-hand, who is a Chilite.'

He took Barnar's hand. 'Your honor honors me. I smell no great sorcery about you. In reaching me, you have done much with little.'

'We are here,' Barnar said, 'to buy our lives out of mortgage by retrieving a certain lad from your puddle out there. It took us all we had just to get here, and we have neither hook, nor line, nor rod.'

The Privateer smiled pleasantly. 'You seem to have little of anything at all besides determination. Yet still you carry with you the price of my services. I don't promise success, mind you, but once I have made my best effort, if I survive that effort, pay me you must – which is to say, you must admit me to the treasury of your personal memories. It is done in a moment, but afterward I will possess every jot of your lives as intimately as I do my own, including many things you might yourselves not even recall, in the riot and variety of your freedom. For an absolute lover of privacy, it is much to pay, but a trifle otherwise, while for me it is a blessed mental oasis in the desert of my bondage. Can you accept the terms?' We nodded. 'Then what was it that took the youth you're looking for?'

'A bonshad,' I told him. He nodded slowly.

'Heavy work, both the finding and the killing. But feasible. We'll cross over to my armory. Kindly bear in back, gentlemen, that henceforth your safety lies solely in your nearness to my protection. You already stand within the surf-line, and are now fair game to all the wet half of hell.'

He gestured slightly with one hand. From the swamped doorway two tiers below a coracle – made of hide stretched on a bone frame – drifted out. We climbed down after

184

Gildmirth, waded to this craft, and boarded it. It seemed to propel itself, and as we crossed the enclosed waters we watched the pier we approached, not to be looking at the monstrosities crouched so near below us.

'Gildmirth,' Barnar said abruptly. 'That was you, just now, swimming here?'

The Privateer smiled a thin, cold smile, and answered without turning to face us. 'Swimming. Indeed I was, and more than that, though I don't think you'd really care to hear about it. I'll tell you what you do want to hear, though it's for you to decide if you trust my word or not. But no. I have not altered. I am still a man in my essence and allegiance.'

Barnar nodded. There was much more we wished to know about him, but we held our tongues. We felt ashamed to have doubted him in his adversity, thereby discovering that we *did* trust him. But presently, in concession to our unvoiced perplexity, Gildmirth added: 'You must understand that I am not bound here by an external compulsion. It is my own will that has been captured . . . infected. I may not leave because certain of my own appetites will not permit it. They have been exaggerated, distorted, rendered insatiable. And only here can I even begin to feed them. One of my appetites earned me a title in Sordon Head. *Curator*, they called me. A subject of jest. It was my larceny I grew famous for among them, especially my great swindle of the city itself – not a subject of jest. They never knew that I robbed them for the Curator. Lesser, periodic thefts would have sated my mere cupidity – I was never impatient. It was only the Curator's secret ambition, long-cherished, that needed so huge a grubstake. That quaint old Curator. Is it really three hundred years and more since he came here? He had the zoographer's passion for living form, its precarious and infinite complexity, its stupendous diversity. And these seas teem as none above

185

ground with unmined marvels. This is an empire of discovery such as no savant ever hoarded to buy posterity's undying thanks . . .'

He fell silent, and brought the coracle to a ladder up one of the pier's pilings. He climbed this, his movement forgetful, that of a man who thinks himself alone. We followed in silence.

We set out atop the pier, flanked either side by the imposing facades of his handiwork. These reflected the catholicity of his tastes, for they presented every variety of architectural style – high-arched temples of the Aristoz school, monolithic shrines in the Jarkeladd mode, triple-columned stoai with the austere grace of Ephesion public building – an encyclopedia of traditions passed in review on either hand, and yet their endless contrasts were so cunningly orchestrated that the whole medley of styles flowed pleasingly. Meanwhile we walked on an equally various succession of pavements, and often looked down to find ornate tiles or lavish mosaics underfoot which snagged our eyes and made us stumble. From Gildmirth's terse indications of this or that building's function it appeared that most were repositories for artifacts, specimens, or texts, and that their builder still made regular use of them.

And they looked anything but derelict, were all in excellent repair. And yet after a while I noticed that they all shared a certain unobtrusive mark of decay – or perhaps vandalism – in common. For wherever their facades bore friezework, intaglio, sculpted cornices, cartouches of bas-relief, you could see – by bright tatters of metal still lodged in the deeper angles and convolutions – that these features had once been richly inlaid with gold foil. Catching Gildmirth's eye on me, I saw he had observed my notice of this detail.

His look discouraged questions, and he said nothing till he had brought us inside the armory that was our destination. I had taken this building for a shrine or mausoleum from the severe grandeur of its design. It was a pleasing shock to see its huge, unpartitioned interior thronged with weapon racks. Its ceiling was just as crowded – with boats. Small craft of every description dangled in chain harnesses. Each harness was anchored in a system of slotted ceiling tracks, which converged at a steepening pitch toward a huge bayed door in the armory's seaward wall.

While we were gaping at everything, Gildmirth found some steel-bossed leather breeches and a corselet of light mail, and pulled them on. 'Arm yourselves, gentlemen,' he said when he was done. His tone parodied an ostler's convivial welcome. 'You see what there is – we have everything. Equip yourselves as suits your tastes. Mail and body-armor are here, and there is another rack yonder, just beyond the spears and harpoons. Blades of all types there, helms and casques there, greaves and the like here, clubs, maces, axes as you see them. Now for myself, I find that today I'm taken with a fancy for yon cuirass.'

He gave an odd stress to this last remark, and though I was greedily pawing some fine ironwood lances I kept half an eye on him as he went to a rack of body-armor. The cuirass he took down was a marvel, of everbright lavishly filigreed with gold. He carried it to a rack of knives, plucked down a poniard, and started prying the filigree off the breastplate.

We stood staring, understanding that this was something he wanted us to watch. He grasped the filaments he had worked free and ripped the golden skein off the everbright. Letting the cuirass drop, he stared at us with his wound-colored eyes as his thick fingers wadded the network into a lump as big as an apple. He held this up, not ceasing to stare at us.

'Forgive me for taking my customary refreshment, which your arrival forestalled. The exertion of my zoological studies always leaves me feeling peckish.' His jaws gaped, and sank their great, inhuman teeth into the nugget.

Ravenously he chawed, crushing the buttery, pliant meal, bolting it down. We watched him dine while he watched us watch him, his eyes bright with sharp hunger and sharper misery. When he was done he just stood there before us for a time, as if in simple presentation of himself, his diseased captivity. We struggled for something to say and found nothing. Smiling slightly, the Privateer nodded, agreeing with our silence.

'But I want you to understand, my friends' – he spoke casually, as if we had been conversing all along – 'that it has been my *choice* to despoil my own works. The open sea offers infinite pasture to this hunger of mine, but pride demanded that I deface what I'd wrought. Its beauty was a boast I was no longer entitled to make. Gilt walls are for conquerors, not prisoners. Well then. Shall we proceed? Take what pleases you, but I must ask you both to take one of those full-visored helmets there, and two heavy harpoons as well. Is either of you skilled with a spear?'

Barnar rubbed his mouth to hide a smile. I confined myself to assuring Gildmirth that any harpoon work our mission required could with reasonable confidence be left in my hands.

'Then choose two that please you,' he said, 'and kindly make any last additions to your equipage now, for it only remains to unsling our craft and pick up a few needfuls at my quarters.'

At the room's center a platform towered amid the legioned weaponry. This he mounted, and started working an arrangement of winches that crowned it. The boat slings began to move along the maze of ceiling track from which they hung and, to a music of groaning chains and grinding gears the dangling armada commenced a slow aerial quadrille.

While Barnar meditated on a case of battleaxes – his favorite weapon – I hefted harpoons till I found two that felt promising. Then I tried on one of the helmets Gildmirth had prescribed for us. It resembled the antique Aristoz casque-and-vizard, a slot-eyed brazen mask with a wolf-muzzle shape. As I buckled the neckstrap tight, my lungs turned to stone. The slightest breath – in or out – was impossible. I clawed at the strap in panic, but then discovered I had ceased to crave breath and – after a moment's anxious experiment – that my strength and mental clarity were unaffected by this suffocation. When I had taken it off I called to Barnar: 'By the Crack, Ox! These helmets here – they exempt a man from breathing! What a wealth of exemptions we're getting lately! We needn't eat, we needn't drink, we needn't sleep – and now we needn't even breathe. But you know, somehow it's not making my life feel any more secure. In fact, it's beginning to make me feel less and less sure that I'm still alive at all.'

'I still feel one need,' he rumbled, 'and that's to get my arse utterly and forever out of this filthy, infested basement of a world. And from this I conclude that I am not yet dead. It isn't much to go on, but it'll have to do.'

The Privateer laughed. It was a shocking sound – a bark of feral glee whose echoes rang like yelps of pain. 'Ah, you are wise indeed, dear Chilite. Though a man here might in time lose the entire self he started with, lose mind's and heart's identity, so long as he still feels that need, he lives, and in that simple need the germ of him survives.' Perhaps Gildmirth thought he had sounded self-pitying, for after a pause he snorted, spat on the platform, and cranked the gears more fiercely. In a more offhand voice he added: 'Will you come up now, gentlemen, and board?'

We complied, though dubiously; the vessel just then gliding into position over the platform, shaped like a war-canoe, was made of scaly hide stretched on a riblike rack of bones. Its prow was a huge skull with long, fang-jammed jaws that snapped and gnashed furiously at the air, while its stern was a skeletal tail that whipped with futile, metronomic force.

189

But when we reached the platform this had overpassed it and Gildmirth had docked the vessel just behind it. This looked oddly normal to belong to so grotesque a fleet: a slender little sloop with one mast and one gracefully tapered outrigger pontoon on its port side. We got aboard. There was no cabin, just a bare deck built a scant two feet below the gunwales, and some rowers' benches. The mast was bare of sail, and there was no tiller. Gildmirth shifted some levers which moved all the boats in our path to side-tracks, then set both hands to a crank. As he worked it, the big steel door down to which our trackline plunged purred open, spreading to receive us that blue quilt where blurred nightmares were bedded, Gildmirth's watery stableyard. The Privateer got aboard, motioning us to take the rowers' benches. He sat himself in the stern, and took hold of a handring attached to a steel pin that knit the chains of our boatsling together.

'That wire,' he told me – 'dangling just off the bow from the ceiling. Reach out and give it a sharp pull. Tell me, was this boy you're after looking for the Elixir of Sazmazm?'

My hand stopped halfway to its task. 'You *know* of him?' Gildmirth laughed and gestured at the wire. I pulled it. This freed the ball-joint from which we hung, and our boat in its little steel basket began the plunge.

'I know of his type, no more,' Gildmirth said. 'Almost all of those whom bonshads bring here have themselves summoned the things to procure them the Elixir.'

The whisper of the track grew steely and shrill. We swooped through the door and out along a boom projecting some sixty feet above the lagoon. Gildmirth pulled the ringbolt when we had almost reached the boom's end. The bottom fell out of our sling, the chains racketed free of our hull. We skated out upon the golden air, and down to the bright, infested waters.

XI

We had to row the boat across to the manse. 'Our sail,' Gildmirth explained, 'is one of the things we must pick up from my quarters. You'll forgive my resting now when you understand the labor I have undertaken for you.'

'We are delighted to help,' I grunted. 'And so? Please go on. What can you tell us about Wimfort?'

'Wimfort?'

'The boy we're after.'

'Oh. Little more than *why* he made his mistake about bonshads. You see, Balder Xolot's *Thaumaturge's Pocket Pandect* has a mistake in it. And in the hundred and twelve years since he published it, it's been disastrous to all that class of people who study not at all, and yet buy serious spells by the lot. For all such go-to-market magi are quite correctly informed that of all abridgers and condensers of Power Lore, Xolot is unquestionably the best. Alas, he was human. In his transcription of the Paleo-Archaic texts concerning Sazmazm, he misread the word *parn-shtadha*. This is a rare variant of the more usual *sh't-parndha*, which one need have no Paleo-Archaic to recognize as meaning *no one*, so close is it to High Archaic's *hesha't pa-harnda*. But Xolot decided it was a scribal error for *parnsht'ada*, which is to say, bonshad. What a crop of ruin from so small a seed! One little sentence. "And no one" – it says – "hath power to bring it" – meaning the Elixir – "from where it lieth up into the sun." Give one more pull please, gentlemen, and ship your oars.'

We obeyed. The boat's momentum carried it across the terrace and through the flooded doorway.

Till now we had only glimpsed the pain of the Privateer's imprisonment. But here, inside his manse, the ruin of his

191

spirit was starkly visible in the ruin he inhabited. You could see that formerly, this great chamber had been the throne room of his pride, both the showroom of his past achievements and the workroom where he shaped new projects. At present it was an indoor lagoon which the low swell filled with echoes, and everything in it was the sea's. Even the canvases arrayed along the walls to either side of us, though only the bottoms of their ornate frames hung in the water, had all been invaded and colonized by sea growth. The bright imagery was spotted with leprous mosses; shell life scabbed and sea-grass whiskered it. Gildmirth figured in all these pictures and in them it seemed he had recorded – with great artistry – key events in his history here. Now you saw his face everywhere – crusted, bearded, or grotesquely blurred, like a drowned corpse.

Much more in there was literally drowned, of course. The ceiling was hung with luminous globes whose light sifted down to the sunken floor, and we could see that this – which we crossed so smoothly now – had been a crowded place to weave your way across before the waters had possessed it. Low platforms and daises stood everywhere. Many of them supported taxidermic displays, various demon forms arranged in tableaux – surrounded by simulations of their environment – which illustrated their feeding habits, modes of combat, nesting techniques, and the like. Amid these was a larger dais supporting a multitude of architectural models. In this beautiful micro-metropolis of the Privateer's ambitious designs were many structures we recognized – dreams fulfilled and standing large as life out on the pier – and many others which would doubtless never exist on any larger scale than this.

But the largest of all these platforms, near the hall's center, testified to an even broader ambition than the little sunken city did. What it held was a topographic map sculpted from stone, a landscape of wildly various terrain where mountains bordered chasms and volcanic cones thrust up from gullied plains. This lay between us and a large table standing just clear of the water near the hall's far end and toward which Gildmirth, using one oar as a stern-paddle, seemed to be heading us. Crossing it gave us a queer shudder, for we quickly understood what it was: at one edge of it was a tiny, perfect model of the manse and pier. The irony of its now being under water had a disturbing savor of conscious malevolence about it, and the wavelets rolling over it had an eerie, triumphing quality in their movement.

'That is a model of the ocean floor?' Barnar asked. Gildmirth back-paddled and our prow nudged up against the tabletop.

'Of a little piece of it. Let's take some wine, and I'll show you where we're going to start our search.'

We disembarked. A hundred men could have stepped out onto that massive board and milled around quite comfortably. It stood clear because the pitch of the broken manse left this end of the hall shallower, so that by the time the little surf reached the great fireplace in its inmost wall, the water was barely deep enough to overleap the fender. In his bitterness, his self-punishing pride, the Privateer had done no more than place the table's downslope legs on blocks, and encamp on it. He had a bed there, a larder-cabinet, a chair and writing desk, a drawing table, a rack for writing materials, some bookshelves, and no more.

It had been weeks since we had swallowed anything but our own spit. The first draught I took from the flask Gildmirth brought us was a shock close to pain. Sweet sensation raged like flame in my fossilized mouth and gullet. The second draught was uncompounded bliss. All in my vision wore new radiance, as if the wine had bathed my horror-scorched eyes. Speaking of the first thing I fixed on, I marveled inanely: 'What beautiful instruments! Do you play them all?'

The wall to the left of the fireplace was hung with a

great variety of them, their lacquered wood, silver strings, brazen keys all gleaming with magic in my eyes. The Privateer's glance at them was odd, perhaps ironic.

'Some of them. Not all are mine. Please finish that my friends, here is another – I know how pleasant it must taste. Shall we view our destination? We can see it from the end of the table. May I borrow a harpoon, Nifft?'

He led us to the edge of his island. 'It's not too distant from here,' he said, sinking the steel barb toward a point not quite half the map's length from the model of the manse. Barnar and I marveled anew at the little landscape as we shared the second flask. It seemed a wonderland, and ourselves lucky titans whom some enchantment would shortly enable to shrink and enter it, and there disport ourselves by probing the crests and gulfs of its barbaric grandeur. The bright barb hovered near a cluster of very sharply rising peaks.

'These four steep-sided mountains that you see here,' Gildmirth said, 'overtop the water. Their peaks form the islands that we'll be anchoring near. And this chasm half-circling the base of the mountain-cluster. The only feature of this map that is not to scale is the depth of this gulf. It's the Great Black Rifft, and its depth cannot be ascertained, for it goes all the way down to the secondary subworld. Its perimeter is a scene of intense demonic activity. And here, quite near, is a major bonshad territory, in fact the only large aggregation of them I've ever found.'

We had drained the second flask. The factitious lustre and charm which the wine had shed on the whole grim project was so far from having worn off that it seemed to me I heard a faint, delicious music as my eyes roamed the miniature ocean floor.

'What light will we search by?' I heard Barnar ask. I still heard the music – a minute sound, it seemed properly scaled to belong to the miniature realm I was still peering into.

194

'Near the Rifft there is light in plenty. Few parts of the sea floor lack some kind of a poison glow to work by, but *there* – well, it is as you will see. We must prepare.'

Gildmirth returned me my harpoon and turned away with an abruptness that would have startled me had not an unmistakably audible fragment of music already done so – one isolated, silvery arpeggio. It came from inside the manse, somewhere on this level, though from what point was hard to tell amid the hollow, many-chambered grieving of the sea against the walls.

Gildmirth jumped off the table's shallow end and waded toward the wall on the side of the fireplace opposite that on which the instruments hung. From the miscellany of gear displayed here he took down what looked like some fishing net tied in a bundle. This he tossed onto the table. 'Gildmirth!' I cried. 'Do you hear the music? Strings?'

The Privateer turned back to the wall and took down from it a monstrous broadsword – nine feet long at least, pommel to point. This too he laid on the table, ignoring me still.

By now I heard the music much less brokenly, finding its melodic line engraved more sharply now in the shapeless oceanic echoes. Lute music ... no, *shamadka*. On each plangent string of it I could now discriminate individually the clustered notes sweetly ripening under the musician's provocative dexterity. Wanderingly, it wove nearer, meandering through lush elaborations while yet never lacking elan, a backbone of stark and resonant melancholy. Such music! With the shock you might feel to discover that one of your limbs – long unnoticed by yourself in any context – suppurates transfixed by a dirk already rusting in its lodgment, I realized that music's utter absence up till now had been a sharp and crippling part of the subworld's tormenting ugliness, a wound I'd lacked the mental leisure to note that I had, and bled from.

It was now clear Gildmirth heard the music, and willfully

ignored both it and us. We watched him as impassively as we could, loath to seem we felt entitlement to anything he did not choose to offer. He approached the wall a third time, and took down a very small, dishlike craft, no more than one man might stand knee-deep in. It had no more than a slight flattening for a stern, and the gentlest tapering for a prow. On either side of the latter two indentations marked the vessel's rim. A moment's looking identified these as the edges of two eye-sockets, and the craft as a whole as a cranial dome sawn from some huge skull. Setting this on the water, Gildmirth made a shooing gesture; the skull-skiff slid round the table and nudged itself against the stern of our boat.

The music had grown distinct, directional; it poured – long rills of it now – into the hall through a wide doorway in the left-hand wall. Gildmirth remounted the table, his eyes blank to ours. Taking the bundle onto our boat he unbound and began anchoring it to the boom. It *was* a net. Through the left-hand doorway, a shamadka came gliding like a tiny ship – the polished bowl its bows, the silver strings its rigging – full to overflowing with its cargo of music.

The instrument was strangely festooned with what at first seemed a sea vine, shaggy purplish stalks draping both bowl and fretboard. But almost at once we realized their supple muscularity, and that it was their caress extracting these limpid euphonies from the shamadka. A voice began to sing, a soprano that was icy-sweet like children's temple choirs:

> What man in wealth excels my lover's state?
> He hath no cause to dread lest others find
> Where all his mountained spoil doth fecundate,
> His breeding gold that spawneth its own kind
> And sprawleth uncomputed, unconfined!

The Privateer was still anchoring the netting to the boom, his eyes remotely overseeing his patient fingers. As the singing continued the shamadka coasted through a dreamy curve toward the table, disgorging treasures of polyphony under the intricate coercion of the things embracing it, tough, snake-muscled things despite their looking nerveless as drenched plumes, with the water swirling and billowing their silky shag.

> For what argosies of argosies,
> Though numberless they churned the seas,
> And endlessly did gorge their holds
> With loot from his lockless vaults of gold,
> Could make him rue their paltry decrement?
> *His* eyes these dunes of splendors desolate –
> They've scorched his palate for emolument,
> And they make him call 'a tomb' his vast estate.

Gildmirth was methodically lashing the great broadsword and its harness beneath the portside gunwale. His eyes, still fixed on his task, looked as red as fresh blood. The water chuckled. We turned and looked our minstrel in the face.

It trailed astern of the instrument, where a flabby, tapered sack of skin ballooned along just under the surface. Near its peak this bruise-colored bag of flesh – bald as bone and blubber-soft – was puckered into a jagged-rimmed crater. Half cupped in this and half leaking into a maze of bays and channels branching from it, was the being's eye – a viscous, saffron puddle all starred within by black, pupillary nodes that burgeoned, coalesced, diminished or multiplied by fissure into smaller wholes, their evolution as incessant as the whole eye's melting flux within its mazy orbit.

A mouth the thing had as well, down near the juncture of the skin-sack with the tentacular fronds. It was an obese blossom of multiple lips like concentrically packed petals. All of them moved, and you couldn't pinpoint among them the exact source of their utterance.

A face you had to call it, though the stomach rebelled, and, for all the ambiguity of the features, it was a poison-ously expressive face, always conveying something search-ing and sardonic in the way its pupillaries constellated. A veritable chorus of derisive smiles rippled across its lips as it sang on.

> In beauties what man is my lover's peer?
> For, as in gold, so is he rich in graces.
> None hath a form so various and rare,
> Nor charm that shineth from so many faces.

Gildmirth, still sedate and unattending had stepped into the skull-bone skiff floating alongside the boat. He stood serenely as this bore him toward the wall of instruments. His whole manner had the absolute concentration of a veteran gladiator's moves in a close fight, and certainly this was a duel he had been fighting for many scores of years, his own sanity always the prize at stake. The little cyclops pursued its song, giving it an ever more voluptuous prolongation of tempo and articulation:

> Mayhap another's eyes are stars – both clear
> as diamonds are – still they are but a pair!
> My love's as constellations blaze
> Wherefrom a host of figures gaze
> Whose features are so manifold
> That tongue must leave them unextolled . . .

But past this point, where the voice's honeyed languor deepened, mellowed toward diapason, the verses were lost to us, for a tenor squallpipe which Gildmirth had musingly taken from the wall here commenced a traditional South-Kolodrian jump-up. It was a vigorously impudent piece, even brisker than most of its ilk, the melody overlaid with irresistibly nimble and saucy fugal embellishments. The Privateer's fingering was consummate and his coloration, in a hundred different shades of irresponsible levity, was unerring. He had keyed his tune to the demon's, and while the phrasing of the two pieces was entirely incongruous, Gildmirth's had an accent whose stresses erratically coincided with the demon's, to produce a variety of emphatic discordances. Between these points of energetic collision, the jump-up's busy note-swarms ran amok in the roomy, pompous resonances of the demon's lyrics, trampling his words past comprehension. They thronged through the shamadka's extravagant architecture of moods like a convivial mob of ne'er-do-wells who heedlessly affront refined environs by engaging in a perfect orgy of gaffes, crass conversation, accidental vase-breaking and crude personal habits.

Neither duellist faltered for an instant; each wove his half of the mismatch with unflawed continuity. Gildmirth seamlessly grafted a medley of other jump-ups onto his tune's conclusion as the demon prolonged the coda of its piece. The tumult of impacting notes was like swordplay, their relentless profusion chilling me with the thought that such a combat could be protracted to inhuman lengths, while we must wait however long it took the Privateer to fight his way out of danger.

And just then the music stopped. First the demon, and then Gildmirth swerved into ingeniously improvised resolutions, and stilled their instruments. For a moment none of us moved. We listened to the surfnoise as it repossessed the huge building. Slick as snail-bellies, the tentacles unwove from the shamadka till one plume only touched it. With this the demon pushed it underwater till its bowl filled, and it sank.

Then the demon lay almost inert. Its lax fronds, floating frontally extended, made slight, teasing undulations in Gildmirth's direction. At length it cocked its peak more upright. Its optic jelly regarded the Privateer, the honey-colored corpulence sagging and beginning to branch through its ragged socket. The steady sloth of this process

199

put me in mind of a sand-clock's drainage. Pupillary buds began multiplying in the jelly's central depths, converging like glittery, dark hornets to torment the man with their scrutiny. Smiles and smirks of coquettish reprimand rippled out over the multifoliate mouth like water-rings fleeing a dropped stone.

'My precious pet!' it fluted. 'Still so untidy? Oh gentlemen!' – the eye now swung to us, pupillaries scattering to read us separately – 'My stubborn little plum-eyed poppet here, he *will* not tidy up! I tell him if he's going to *stay* somewhere, he *ought* to tidy up. He's supposed to be a man of consequence, or was long ago at least. He's told *me* so at any rate. Just listen. What's your name? Are you still who you said yesterday you were?' The pupil-swarm recondensed, gnawed busily at the Privateer's impassive face.

'I am, oh Spaalgish weft, the man you well know me to be. I am Gildmirth of Sordon Head in southern Kolodria, also called the Privateer.'

'*Still* this Gildmirth, today as well? What about tomorrow?'

'I am who I have been, and I'll remain so, while I live.'

The Spaalg abandoned this seemingly ritual banter as abruptly as it had opened it. Plumes swirling, it whipped round in the water, and traveled squidlike, in head-first zig-zags to hang above the map of the seafloor. From here it resumed its fretful confidings to Barnar and myself:

'This exquisite map for instance, see how he leaves it sunken. How are all his guests and visitors to read it there? As it is, only he himself, when he swims out to play in other shapes, can consult it conveniently. And he has no need to do so. When the gorging lust has been on him he's gotten as intimately familiar with the seafloor as the well-known louse in the proverb got with the bumps on the drunkard's arse. I'm sure that in sum my precious pet has spent more years groping on alien feet across these hills and plains' – it let the tip of one languid plume sink, and

200

drew it tickingly across the facsimile terrain – 'than any alleged Gildmirth ever spent in any such a place as this so-called Sordon Head that he clings to in his stubborn fantasy. My goodness though . . .' Its voice deepened with musing to the sound of a well-seasoned old wood-horn, and the caressing plume scribbled graceful whimsies on the map. 'Whatever the name of the man who made this map, what a swaggering little pup he must have been, don't you think? I mean, did he expect to *finish* it? And fit it all in this room? How callow! What a dwarfish conception! This is not genuine scholarship! Real research is a coming-to-grips with phenomena. This, as a transcription of the ocean's infinitely various text, is a fraud, an egregious counterfeit, which patly reduces the Primary Sea's endless-ness to a cozy finitude, such as it pleased this puny entity to regard it, for he must have had but a feeble stomach for enterprise of a dark or difficult kind. Why indeed, behold! It *was* some dwarf, for is not this little city over here his former habitation?'

The Spaalg flashed through another turn, and hung buoyed above the Privateer's architectural micropolis. The fact that the creature was a Spaalg, when I learned it, had meant little to me beyond the fact that the breed was relatively insignificant in terms of the threat they posed as predators on humankind. The conventional expression 'dimwebbers, meeps, and ropy spaalgs,' connoting the whole class of minor demonry, told me this much. But now, watching that plumed slug – swift and graceful as a fine-muscled cloud of oil – pour one lithe tickler down into a little agora, and tease with its membranously tufted tip the minutely fluted columns of a colonnade no higher than a gold Kairnish half-nilling set on edge – watching the Spaalg doing this, I recalled another jot of information. Undle Ninefingers refers to them somewhere as being 'vermicles,' which, in his nomenclature, designates the class of demons that are internally parasitic upon their

201

prey. A cold squirming, originating from some point in the back of my head, made a fast, nasty trip down my back. Gildmirth's body was so solid – square and hale. Did his composure mask the deep gall of worm-work, neat, lethal tunnelings serving somehow as the pathways of this Spaalg's influence within him?

The Spaalg, keying up now to melodious contempt, continued: 'How touching, in a way! Such diminutive presumption, such minuscule pomp! Such an imperious fellow too, this titbit tyrant. Things would be thus and so, done this way, that way, and this other way' – the plume flicked silkily among the toy rooftops – 'in precisely that order, and immediately! How could such a proud-ling *fail* to deem his ambitious appetite too large for less than empire to sate? So innocent he was of the endless, orgiastic feast of exploration and discovery he was proposing for himself. The poor tot! He elbowed his way up to the table, and now he is surely gorging still, willy-nilly, on that stupendous repast. I'll wager his sides are splitting with the meal's abundance. And surely by now, through the ages of his engorgement with this – to him – alien universe, the bubble of whatever self he formerly had – so briefly and so long before – has burst, and is less to him now than the idlest imagining. Oh dear! Look! Oh, most horrible! Defacement unspeakable!'

The Spaalg's body-sausage folded, thrusting its eye from the water, the pupillaries cohering toward a painting across the room, one of Gildmirth's rather grandiose self-chroniclings in oils. 'What has befallen my babekin now?' Its voice had a grieving crack in it. 'His face! What obscene infections have obliterated it?'

The demon sped to the picture. Lifting and fanning out its plumes upon the canvas, it slid caressingly up its surface, holding its body arched upward to gaze pityingly at the encrusted canvas it climbed.

It might have chosen any of the other pictures, for in all

of them the Privateer's face showed the same staining, erosion and motley overgrowth as marked the rest of the imagery. The scene the Spaalg unctuously ascended appeared to involve some wizardly ceremony of subjugation performed by Gildmirth upon a shadowy knot of manacled demons. A large, metallic gladiator's net enveloped the subworlders. There was a chain attached to the drawstring closing the net's mouth, and the figure of Gildmirth held its free end firmly with several bights wrapped round the wrist for surer purchase. It was all crazily dappled and blurred with tidal growths, but their obscuration didn't quite look like an impartial vegetable proliferation. To some extent it seemed to edit, to revise the painted forms. You could just make out how Gildmirth had made his face sternly judicial, brows threatening storm, while the netted crew had a crouched and huddled posture as a whole. But now, bright lichens highlighted and contorted his cheeks and brow while a diffuse smokiness of fine black moss darkened mouth, eyes and throat-hollow to a necrotic black. On his arms the oils themselves, crumbling and damp, suggested tomb-flesh. No longer the solemn arbiter, he now stood in horror and recoil, a mortally damaged moribund. The hand that had been painted as reaching magisterially toward a table stocked with some kind of instruments, or texts perhaps, was now plunged into a plane of indecipherable dark shapes, and shadow had erased his hand along with what it sought. Meanwhile the demons' net was half-dissolved and their postures, due to subtle re-emphases and re-delineations, glowered, and crouched more as if to spring than cringe. In the revised work, the chain seemed more Gildmirth's fetter than a leash he held.

'Oh my little treasure-ling, my little toy-let! Who has treated you this way?' The voice was all wine and honey again. Two tremulous plume-tips grievingly caressed the painted Privateer's fungus-whiskered temples.

I felt a pang of rage that twisted like a sword in me. I'd watched the Spaalg feeding on its nobler prey, probing for the taste of despair with its tongue, long enough for the shock of comprehension to pass, and all at once I felt myself its prey as well, my soul as much the object of its defilements as Gildmirth's was. Looking round I saw the Privateer's face looking tormentedly from a dozen masks of putrefaction and blight. The Demon-Sea's revision of his self-image was galleried around us like a chorus of jeers. That he had been arrogant the paintings themselves, so huge and bravely framed, proved plainly. But it was an arrogance he more than redeemed by the straightness of his back now, surrounded by his enemies' vandalisms of his spirit. He unremittingly met the Spaalg's eye, clearly meaning to endure it till he died, or was free.

Yes! Still he waited to be free, defying the centuries of multiform turmoil that had rolled across him to erase that ever-receding little span of his independent existence – that comparative pittance of years containing all he had been, and all he had resolved to be. It was too much. It overflowed my capacity for outrage. The Spaalg had begun to speak again, and I roared:

'Silence!' Among my new gear was a battle-axe. I pulled this from my belt, not so much with intent to attack as a pure expression of feeling. 'You feather-legged maggot,' I hissed. 'Is it that your pin-head simply lacks the circumference to contain the truth? We surface-folk are easy enough to kill the bodies of, but as for our wills, the heart-and-mind of us, we can be harder to kill than ghosts. Because we *are* ghosts. Believe it, Privateer.' I turned to face that impassive prisoner of his own ambition's ruin. 'You know I speak the truth. You in your sunless bondage, though starved of your world and glutted with this cosmic cloacum, remain no whit less real than any man free to walk under the sun. For we're none of us more than wisps of desire and imagining! What man is not, at the center of his mind, a ghostly *wish-to-be* haunting the jerry-built habitation of his imperfect acts? Haunting the maze of *what-has-been*?"

The Privateer answered nothing. He stared back at me, his pain-colored eyes huge with all the things he knew about what I spoke of – things I could not know, and hopefully never will. I suddenly felt foolish, useless to help him. I found I had been waving my axe as I harangued, and still held it brandished. The Spaalg gave a buttery little chuckle and said: 'He has from me prolonged vitality. No man's memory is made of so tough a fabric that sufficient – '

I only knew I was going to throw the axe in the instant that I let it fly. The Spaalg, unflustered, dropped like a stone. The axe sank half its bit into the demon's late position on the canvas, while the creature turned its plunge into a neat, splashless dive, and surfaced smiling. It began – at once – to sing:

> I once was a man with a heart and a face,
> And while this heart and face were mine –

Even as it sang Gildmirth stretched forth his hand, and the Spaalg was plucked from the water by its plumes, as a turnip is uprooted by its top. The process did not disturb the demon's singing:

> I had two eyes that I lived behind
> In a place for hoarding the things I'd seen,
> And I had two ears that I lived between –

Gildmirth made a second gesture and, still hanging inverted, the Spaalg moved through the air toward the doorway by which our boat had entered. Throughout its aerial progress it continued its song, nor had it ceased when its exit from the manse made the verses inaudible:

> Where the things I heard could be brought to mind.
> But now, where my heart stood is empty space

Where sights lack anything to mean,
And my ears' reportings echo to waste,
All lacking a place for taking . . .

'What did you do with it?' Barnar asked vaguely, his
eyes still watching its form dwindle against the clouds
framed by the distant doorway.

'I'm having it dropped in the Fenkrakken Mangles, a
coastal zone disturbed by tidal torments, winds, and water-
avalanches, about two thousand leagues downshore. It'll
be back tomorrow.'

'I'm sorry about your canvas,' I told him, finding nothing
else to say. This drew his eyes to it and he started slightly,
as if he'd not remembered that the axe had struck there.
His mouth, as though not quite yet ready to smile, made a
little rictus, and the plentiful irony-wrinkles around his
eyes deepened a shade. His eyes were not blood now, but a
murky carnelian.

'Who knows?' he asked with a slight shrug. He turned
and went to his larder chest, from which he started filling a
provision-sack. I didn't understand, and looked to Barnar.
He, with one blunt digit, mutely redirected my eyes to the
canvas.

I saw it this time. It was the axe's accidental pertinence
to the image my throw had attached it to. Its scale and
angle of lodgment were such that if you squinted a bit it
looked painted in with the rest. And it was the chain that
the axe lodged in, shearing it through at a point just below
Gildmirth's hand.

I said to Barnar – quietly, not to torment Gildmirth
with it – 'Let it be so, then, by every power that stands
higher than this hell.' Barnar solemnly nodded.

'Gentlemen,' our guide called, 'please get aboard. I must
move now if I'm to take this on at all. There is a painful
blackness on my mood just now.'

We boarded. Gildmirth raised the sail, lashing a corner

to the mast's top. It bulged and bellied out. The Privateer, though sitting in the stern, didn't visibly steer us as we slid away from the table and smoothly recrossed the windless, chambered pool with the skull-skiff tagging after us.

We surged breasting through the doorway. The cloudy vaulting of Gildmirth's prison-cosmos felt like freedom after the entombment of his private cell. Our sail swelled dead against the on-shore wind and we skated onto the field of Gildmirth's living plunder in their sunken oubliettes, aimed for a gate sealing the gap between the pier's tip and the headland's. Inside the manse it had seemed impossible to probe Gildmirth's pain with questions, but in the invigoration of this setting-forth it seemed less cruel. Still, I spoke from the bow, not quite turning back sternwards to meet his eyes.

'You cannot kill the Spaalg then, Privateer?'

'No. And would not if I could. It alone could ever free me.'

'It occurred to me that Undle says somewhere that Spaalgs are vernicles . . .'

Barnar glanced at me. He too looked forwards out of compassion. We stood watching the gate to the open sea draw nearer as the Privateer replied, his voice remote, carefully even, as if the recitation were a duty he had set himself always to perform without shirking:

'Spaalgs have a technique for infecting shape-shifters. Their larvae lies integrated in the body of a larger demon. If a man, or any creature, would acquire another being's shape, he or it must enter a specimen and become congruent with its form, to learn it. If a Spaalg infects the study-specimen, it can transfer to the shape-shifter, and infect him by any means it devises. Some of the Spaalg's nerves it engrafted onto mine, at places where they were naturally suited to receive the amplification of its own passions. Now, raving lunacy would follow my loss of either the sea's gold, or its sorceries and the infinity of shapes it offers me

207

on which to practice them. Here my spirit dies at length, by attrition. Above, insane hungers would tear it to pieces within days.'

XII

We were sprawled on the deck amidships, backs propped against opposite gunwales. Barnar reached into the provisions sack near him, and withdrew another jack of wine. He smiled at it, hefting it lovingly, then snorted: '*Elixir*. Huh! The only real elixir is right here, as far as I'm concerned.'

'I don't know. The stuff the boy was after must be pretty potent. He didn't even touch it, and it transported him all the way down here.' I had quite a good laugh at the wit of this, though my own. Barnar shook his head gravely.

'Potent. Maybe so. This, on the other hand, is miraculous. It transports *me* all the way *out* of here without even moving me an inch.' Barnar repaid my favor, and laughed for me, but I joined him anyway. 'Plain truth, oh canny Chilite, and that's a miracle worth having. Toss. Thank you.'

'Don't mention it. Merely permit me to reiterate: henceforth, as regards this Sazmazm matter, kindly elixir me no elixirs. It's only what you're guzzling there that deserves the name, and that's all I'll say of the matter. Toss. Thank you.'

'Certainly. By the Crack, the aftertaste is splendid!'

'Mmmm. Yes. Almost as splendid as the taste itself.'

'Not to mention the bouquet. Toss.'

'Indeed. Because, to get to the heart of the matter, the wine itself is splendid, as was Gildmirth's forethought in providing it.'

'You've put your finger on it. And you know, while

208

we're on the subject, when you really see the matter in perspective, this is really a rather splendid exploit we're on. It has a noble, undeniable splendidness about it. Toss.'

'You're quite right, really. A hapless young lad, abducted by demons, lying in torment, all that. And two reckless dare-devils trekking after him, only their wits and their swords against all the might of the primary subworld. There *is* something splendid about it. Toss.'

There was a mellow pause as we savored all this newly discovered splendor. I gazed about us, suddenly groping toward a kind of inspiration. 'Hang it, Barnar, you know what else? Toss. Thanks . . .'

'*What* else, Nifft?'

'Even this . . . this vast pool of sewage — even this festering corpse of an ocean is splendid . . . is rather splendid, in a way?'

'. . . Yes?. . . Yes, in a way I suppose . . .'

We looked uncertainly toward Gildmirth, who had sat brooding in the bow for so many hours we had almost forgotten him. If he'd been following our talk he didn't show it, nor withdraw his sullen gaze from the sea's crazy-quilt of surface patterns whereon, just ahead, yet another collapse of the cloud-ceiling had dumped smoky avalanches of fog.

Barnar sighed. I tossed him the jack and he drained it. The winds in their ceaseless, tormented shifting whipped round and cut a chill keen as a poniard across my back. Even as Barnar pointed behind me and said – 'Watch out! Another howler!' – I heard the careening approach of a furious noise, and looked behind. A track of town water snaked toward us. An instant later it ripped across our decks, a little cyclone of pandemonium. Our minds were blotted out by a thousand voices whose desperate unison compounded their words into one stupefying roar of gibberish. For an eternal instant it obliterated our thoughts and sensations alike, and left only their torn edges in our minds in the silence after it veered away over the sea to spread its urgent, indecipherable alarms.

It may convey some sense of its impact to say that, though it surrounded us for less than two seconds, it was an absolutely sobering experience. The radiance which wine had almost given the ocean was killed, if it had lived at all. The waters we were left gaping at remained what they had seemed from the first – wormy with an infinite, multiform anguish. Jittery zones, all spikes and fangs of chop, were sharply bordered by areas of perfectly smooth water in greasy bulges seamed and puckered here and there as with the deep maneuvers of large masses, while adjoining both we saw tracts where great galactic sprawls of scum wheeled sluggishly, all overswarmed by bug-sized multitudes at war, slaying and dying with cries like cricketsong. And above all the fever and convulsion of the maggoty main, the livid clouds dispread their slow decay, their many fissures bloody-rimmed with the demon light that streamed from them, while everywhere their bloated substance was sloughing off to lie in clammy heaps upon the waves, like those we now began to thread among. Gildmirth had told us that our sail snared other currents than those of the wind – rivers of subworld force impalpably tangling through the air which it netted according to its master's will. For all his mastery of this method, which kept us smoothly centered in the twisting corridors of clear water, it sank my spirit a notch deeper to remember that the very atmosphere was worm-holed with demonic disease.

Barnar was feeling the same oppression, for he burst out with a question which his compassion would have spared our guide, but which his weary loathing could not bite back: 'What is it in us that *feeds* them, Privateer? Can't they be sated on each other's flesh?'

His eyes apologized when Gildmirth met them, but he waited for the answer, as did I. Though the Privateer's eyes were blood-bright again with the pain of his long introspection, his voice was gentle:

'Who more than they, Barnar, are their hungers' slaves? Whatever it is their natures arise from, they are absolute and unalloyed with any purpose but the predation their breed assigns them. Their essence is an eternal, joyless toil of feeding.'

(As I listened I watched a small crack opening in the nearest fogbank's wall. Its opening revealed a little, crooked shaftway ascending from the misty deeps.)

'And what beings more than human kind have a will that far outreaches their given nature? A willful dream of Self that can contradict, or defy outright, their actual circumstances, and past performances?'

(A small, shadowy something was toiling frantically up the crooked tunnel – a blur just visible through the mist's opacity.)

'It's just this the demons crave to taste, this unique faculty of superordinate desire that sheds lustre and significance on the brute machinery of uncontested reality. In the violation and destruction of a man's will, a demon tastes a rare drug, gets one delirium-inducing whiff of the unimaginably rich world of human experience.'

(A tiny homunculus, naked and sweaty-bright, came plunging up the shaft. It dove for the opening and had actually thrust its clutching hands into the open air, when a scaly paw shot from the tunnel, closed round its waist, and hauled it back within, the fissure closing behind it.)

The longer my footsoles felt it through the deck – those waters panting and shivering in their vast sickbed – the more obsessed I grew with Gildmirth's extravagant rashness in ever choosing this realm as a challenge to his powers of mastery. I held my tongue until a certain glimpse of what teemed below us loosened it. Most such hints of the deeps had been in the way of flotsam, or brief eruptions of conflicts that quickly sank again, but this was a trio of structures, gallows standing sixty feet above the surface. Two men and a woman dangled from them, nude, with that idle, dejected posture the hanged have. In the course of our approach, a huge, coffin-jawed reptile set all three swinging with the wing-work of banking its dive to throw a short swerve that grazed the nearest gallows. It encoffined the corpse on the wing, pulled up, and was yanked short and hammered back-first on the water. The corpse in its jaws was genuine, but had been endowed with bizarre plasticity and adhesiveness. The dead man's fang-broken shape was stretched to a breadth of seven or eight feet by the reptile's efforts to separate its jaws. The rumble of massive chains sounded underwater. The gallows smoothly sank, as did the reptile, though less smoothly.

As this place fell astern, I burst out: 'Most noble Privateer. By the Crack, by all that falls in or crawls *out* of the Crack, why *here*? Why must *this* place be your chosen ground of exploit? For me, with all respect, it's a question beyond the reach of the most delirious conjecture.'

Gildmirth smiled, something he hadn't done for quite a while. 'Can you really not imagine? Perhaps you know the lines – is Quibl still read these days? – the lines:

"For all who may will seek to know
Whence they've grown, or whither grow."'

I was a shade slower to understand than Barnar, who nodded and quoted in his turn:

'"Are we their ancestors or heirs?
. . . Are they our children, or we theirs?" – And have you got an answer then, Privateer?'

Gildmirth shook his head. 'I have an opinion. As for firm proof, or even clear evidence – '

I had touched his arm. 'Look there – the water's seething.'

Gildmirth reefed the net and we stood off the turbulence. Shapes popped out of it, jostling furiously in the boil.

Before we could make anything out the Privateer said: 'Ah! Surely a grove of sessiles has been attacked, probably by a big Dandábulon. We won't see the combatants, just the wreckage. Look there now! Do you see?'

We saw. The boil of battle drifted erratically away, and the wreckage that choked it began dispersing through the calmer waters. Shards of giant fan-corals they seemed at first – trellises of fiber red and green and tar-black. And then we made out the torn parts of men and women woven into these shards. Here a hand, there a man from the diaphragm up – they spun bleeding on their attachments of trellis-work. The half-man ejected one loud fragment of voice from his mouth – an incomprehensibility, the last thing in him – and died. Gildmirth let out a little sail and brought us slowly around the widening patch of breakage and blood.

'A survivor! A whole one!' said Barnar. 'Over there.'

It was a woman. The great fan she was splayed against was unbroken, and we could see how it originated from her flesh. Her extended spine was its center-rib. From her sides the grey of nerves and red-and-blue map of veins entered the fan's weave. So did her long black hair, spreading out on it like a vine on a wall. Nerve-threads from her nipples, and the abundant dark fern-curls of her loins, complicated her bondage above and below. The fan spun slowly, trailing a torn-out root stalk. Her eyes knew and clung to us as she turned. She had been very beautiful. We looked at Gildmirth. He shook his head. 'She cannot be remade, nor even kept alive for long. The 'dábulon will eat her, or the Hurdok whose flock this is will replant her.'

The woman said, 'Travelers.' The air seared her lungs – her voice was as if made of pain. She took more breath. 'You are men, as you see? Not thralls? Sailing freely here?'

'Yes, unhappy one,' I answered.

'Free me!' she cried. Her glistening corona of nerve and vein wrinkled and writhed as she cried again: 'Free me!'

Gently, the Privateer said: 'You are past re-transformation. Your growth shows you many, many centuries a thrall.'

'Do I not know this?' said the woman. She smiled, and tears slid down her temples. 'How goes the world, travelers?'

Softly, the Privateer snorted. 'What would you know, my lady?' I asked her. Her slow turning on the waters had brought her round so I could look her in the face. She said, still smiling and weeping:

'One thing I would know, gaunt one – does Radak still rule in Bidna-Meton? Do his catacombs of dark experiment still swallow men and women down from the light of day?'

'Radak,' I said after her. The trellis of her nerves shuddered again to receive the word. 'That name, sweet thrall, is now a proverb. I have heard the expression "to keep a house like Radak" used of innkeeps and ostlers with bad establishments. The name of Bidna-Meton I have never heard.'

'So great a city . . .' she said. 'What of the nation of Agon, mother of mighty navies, where my father was a shiplaw in the capital? And what of the second moon, foretold in the heavens by fire and holocaust?'

'Unhappy one, I know of no land called Agon. There is a great ocean of that name, between Kolodria and Lúlumë. As for the moon, there is one in the heavens, sweet lady, and ever has been, so far as I have heard.'

'My world has been, gaunt traveler. So free me now. Free me!'

I started to speak. Gildmirth touched my arm and turned his eyes on one of the harpoons.

It was a short cast – I have never made one with greater care. I waited till a wave lifted and turned her, so that she no longer faced me, and was on the crest. I said, 'Dear Lady – ' as if beginning a speech, to distract her from any expectation of the cast. I threw with a great downpull, giving it a fast, flat trajectory, and pinned her below her splayed left arm. It was a smooth entry, between the third and fourth ribs, with no grating on the bone. Her eyes showed white, and the nerve-fan crumpled and writhed about her, but she did not die with the hit. Her hand came up and caressed the shaft, and only when we came alongside and I leaned over and pulled out the spear did the life leave her.

The boat rode at half-sail, in which state its only motion was a slight, incessant counter-action against the tides, which here seemed to want to bring us toward the cluster of islands before us. Thus we hung at a fixed half-mile offshore of the quincunx's largest member. A man in a meditative mood, as Gildmirth seemed to be, found much for his eye to muse on there. Apart from the five main isles – dense with verdure wherein movement swarmed, and over which clouds of winged things hovered and sketched an endless turmoil – there were many reefs and craggy ridges, and these lesser saliences of the drowned mountains also swarmed with life. The waves rushed in – oddly erratic in terms of timing and direction, but always violent – and smashed in palisades of white foam everywhere against the islands' green fringes. In particular, waves seemed to come with special force from a huge crescent of unusually dark water which lay perhaps a mile off the cluster's right as we faced it. The curve of this smoky zone paralleled that of the cluster's perimeter, and the entire zone was subject to sudden, deep puckerings which sent towering pairs of waves out in opposite directions, one of each pair always came exploding against the islands.

'I suppose,' Gildmirth said, 'you surmise what that dark zone overlies?'

'The Rifft,' Barnar said softly. Gildmirth nodded, smiling bitterly.

'The Great Black Rifft. Ten times as strictly guarded *and*

furiously assaulted by the denizens of this world as this world is by the ambitious beings of our own.'

'And below that,' Barnar muttered, 'the Tertiary sub-world. Deeper and deeper. Ever greater power. Ever greater evil.'

Again Gildmirth nodded. 'And so on, down to what? How do you read the dreadful map of this world, my friends? It seems that an evil past name and conception must lie at its core. Was this the yolk of the egg of life? Are men the highest-climbing descendants of that deep, ultimate germ of darkness and horror? Are we the last, the frailest, and yet the least-dark, highest-soaring, of all that grim line?'

I smiled back at his bitter, sword-bright grin. 'Go on,' I said, 'give us the rest of the question, and then tell us what *you* think.'

Gildmirth got up and went to the great sword he had lashed under the gunwale. He unbound it, sat on one of the rowers' benches, and laid it across his knees. Almost tenderly, he ran his finger along one edge of it. 'As perhaps you guess, it's the other theory I hold with – though I have not a whit more grounds for certainty than you, despite all I have experienced. Do you realize how long man has prevailed on Earth? There is no word for the number of his millennia of sowing and sailing, of building and battling, of seeking and striving and slaying, of learning and losing. In that eternity man's wielded and then utterly forgotten powers we couldn't even dream of. He's lived whole histories, garnered troves of miracles, built marvels, and then has fallen and buried all his works in the dust of his own disintegrating bones, and begun all again, and again, and again.

'Spirit, soul – it doesn't die, you know. The strenuous, fierce flames endure. The great in Evil and the great in Good – both leave an immortal residue. That's why I favor the other view. The demons are not our ancestors – we are

216

theirs. The greeds and lusts, the wealth of horrors here, are not the archetypes of our own – they are the derivatives, the dreadful perfectings of all the evil that men have spawned and nourished. Call Man a great, roasting beast, spitted and turning above the fire of his own unending cruelty. The things of this world then, and of those yet farther down, are the drippings of the tortured giant, Man.'

There was a long pause, and then Barnar ended it by asking: 'Then where are the Great in Good? Where are the other half of Man's residue?'

'Ah yes!' cried Gildmirth triumphantly. 'Where else but – ' He had started to sweep his hand above us. He checked the gesture, and gaped up at the plains of ragged smoke, cloven here and there with shafts of unreal light. 'Three hundred years,' he said after a moment, shaking his head, 'and still I forgot, and thought to point to the sky.'

I waited a moment, then prodded gently: 'The sky, great Privateer?'

'The stars, Nifft. Perhaps man's other spawn has reached them. Perhaps, somewhere past memory, we have peopled them.'

'One wishes some of them had stayed here, to even the odds,' Barnar mumbled.

'How do we know they have not?' cried Gildmirth. 'Our greatest wizards, our noblest kings, who knows what unseen influences prop their powers, and keep them just enough ahead of the legions of chaos?'

We didn't answer him. There was no telling how sweet the world might look to him in memory by contrast to his prison. I felt that, as things go, the legions of chaos do all right for themselves. Gildmirth stood up.

'So. We will go down together. If you sight the lad, I'll bring you back up and go down for the bonshad. 'Shads keep the nerve-bundles of their flocks in their jaws, and even wounding them before prying them loose means destroying the flock. Once I've pried it loose I'll be hanging on for dear life with all four of my paws. It will be all I can do to bring it up. You must be ready in the skiff to kill it with the harpoons when I maneuver it in range. The skiff's operation is simple – it obeys your will. Practice with it while you wait for me to resurface. Please remember that the 'shad will be more than a match for my water-shape. If at any moment it should break my body-lock on it, I am dead.

'The greatest powers in the sea are concentrated near the Rifft, my friends, and yet it may even be safer there than elsewhere, given their absorption in the frontier. You'll see much activity at the chasm's brink. One league of very mighty demons has even succeeded in hauling something up from the Rifft. The entire sea is alive with the rumor and fear of it. But do not be distracted. 'Shads keep their flocks in the seams and gullies of these islands' footslopes, and we will not be far from the doings at the chasm's edge, but concentrate on scanning for the boy's face. You will see many faces to scan.'

Gildmirth set down the sword, stripped off his clothes, and leapt overboard. The waters began to roil where he had sunk, and huge, silvery limbs sprouted beneath the masking effervescence. We pulled on our helmets, and doffed all our weapons save a harpoon each. A huge saurian head thrust from the water and laid its jaw upon our prow. The beast reached a webbed-and-taloned paw into the boat and took up the sword, whose scale at last was appropriate to its wielder's size, for the water-lizard was almost thirty feet long. When Gildmirth spoke to us it was with a huge red tongue that labored between sawlike teeth, steel-bright as before though savagely reshaped. His words came out as whispery, half-crushed things which the tongue's unwieldiness had maimed:

'Cleave to my belt, good thievesss. Carry those lances couched. Hassste! Let's be down and doing!'

We leapt in. It was hard to swim up to the giant, for all

218

our knowing who it was. Hard also to grasp the swordbelt that girt its middle and feel its scales, rough as stone, against my knuckles. But hardest of all was holding while it did a whipping dive and hauled us underwater with the terrible speed of falling through empty air. And then another world yawned under us, and as I was snatched down into the limitless swarm of it, I became eyes, and awe, and nothing more.

XIII

Sometimes, when I am in Karkmahn-Ra, I will climb at nightfall into the hills that stand behind the city. Wolves haunt them, and an occasional stalking vampire, but the sight's worth the risk. A great city sprawled in the night – it wakes up the heart in you, stirs your ambition, reminds you of the glory that can be man's and your own, for toil and daring can produce accomplishments that shine back at the stars like those million lamps and torches do.

But now I have seen – deep in a place itself deep under this world – a dazzling sprawl that's vaster than a thousand cities. Its drowned lights dot and streak the flanks of the sunken mountains and crawl like fire-ants over reefs and knolls and gullies out to the brink of an utter blackness that is fenced with flames.

The titanic blaze banners and flaps and buckles, as earth-flame does, but slower, as if weighted down by the tons of ocean on it. It rims the gulf of the Black Rifft, and masks its depths with the volumes of slow, black smoke it vomits up, like the ink of an immense squid. Meanwhile those flames dispense a poisonous luminosity for miles across the ocean floor, a ruddy fog that roils across the multicolored phosphorescences of the deep-dwelling hosts.

All the most formidable encampments of those hosts are

concentrated near the fiery wall, their fortressed bivouacs often encompassing some huge machinery for siege or assault. Misshapen crews drive ensorcelled battering rams against the unyielding palisades of fire, or swing great booms from derricks to reach across the flame crests.

One such encampment dwarfs all the others – or it did, at any rate, when I went down. There is reason to think its aspect might have changed since that time. But then it was such that I could make out its form from afar while many nearer works, though huge, were still vague to me: lying quite near the brink-fire were two stupendous ovoids; these had been netted over with scaffolding, and were flanked by mammoth cranes.

Gildmirth pulled us down to search the intermediate terrain. In the manner of a hawk working a range of foothills, we swooped along the sea floor, rolling with its roll, at a fixed distance above it. At first our cruising itself was as horrible as the things it manifested to us. The saurian's speed was astonishing, absolutely unslowed by the water's crushing weight, but in eery contrast to this my spirit felt all the heaviness of nightmare, where a dreadful pressure murders the will, makes it an unheeded voice exhorting a body that is infinitely slow to move.

Our leveling off brought us first above a field of waxen cells, like a giant honeycomb laid flat. Blurred within the cells were men and women folded tight, eyes and mouths gaping. The workers on these fields were like great, slender wasps. They moved with a dancing, finicking daintiness, stopping here and there to dip their stingers into a cell and, with a shudder, squirt a black polyhedron into it. I began to notice, here and there, the fat, black, joint-legged things sharing the cells with their human occupants, tunneling gradually into their bodies burgeoning as those bodies writhed and dwindled.

Glowing rivulets of lava bordered this infernal nursery, molten leakage that threaded downslope in all directions from a volcanic cone that pierced the surface up to our left toward the island peaks. Within this magmatic mazeway a second zone of demon enterprise began. Here lurking monsters of the breed our guide had so lately grappled with plied trowels to mold the lava into smoking walls. These demons were of the class whose use of man is artistic rather than anthropophagous, for these steaming ramparts were the matrix for human bas-reliefs, wherein the living material, variously amputated, were cemented to compose a writhing mural. The innards of these sufferers were grafted to a system of blood-pipes set in the scalding masonry so that, once troweled and tamped into place, they lived rooted, sustained by that vascular network of boiling blood. At least our guide's plunging speed, indifferent to any sight irrelevant to our goal, abbreviated our witnessing of these things.

Yet he surprised us shortly after our leaving this last zone by making a sharp detour. We had just made out what we thought must be a Bonshad not far ahead, when Gildmirth swept down into a dive upon a huge polypous growth directly beneath us. It lifted huge menacing pseudo-pods, each fully half as thick as the great lizard himself, to meet the latter's plunge. The Privateer brought his blade – all asmoke with bubbles from the murderous energy of the stroke – athwart the nearest pair of these scabby extrusions, and sheared them cleanly through. One of the sundered members flew, heaving and shuddering past me, giving my shoulder a glancing blow that was like being jostled by a warhorse at full gallop. Two more strokes and Gildmirth had barbered the monster clean of its last protectors. Amid their bleeding stumps were the creature's massive, five-lobed jaws – made of purest gold and crusted over with rubies as big as apples. Those hideous beaks mouthed impotent appetite as Gildmirth plunged his sword into its throat. The jaws gaped and froze. The lizard sheathed his blade, reached down, and ripped the jaws apart.

The rubies he ate greedily, crushing them like sugar-candies swiftly in its jaws. The gold he relished more, with a humiliating hunger that could not mask its own trembling. His steel fangs tore the honeybright metal, and his big, scaly gullet throbbed with the meal. When he had done he drew his sword again, planted his hindlegs against the sand, and surged up toward the 'shad that hovered over a coral knoll just beyond us.

It was huge, hanging there over its flock of naked humans. Their veins and nerve-wires all sprouted from their backs and ran up like puppet-wires to join in a ball of fibers which the shaggy, hook-bellied thing was applying to its abdominal mouthparts.

The flock was grazing – after a manner – for the 'shad had them all sprawling and crawling over a system of reefs which were forested with giant anemones that bristled with man-large tongues and antennae. The waxen-fleshed, horror-eyed folk wriggled through those rippling, squeezing pastures of outrage while the Bonshad floated over them, nursing on the anguish coursing through their nerves.

It was a flock of about thirty. We had studied the miniature of Wimfort until our eyes rebelled at the sight, and we quickly made sure that he was not one of that lewdly palpated, trembling little herd. Gildmirth turned me his right eye and Barnar his left. We shook our heads. His great paws clawed us back up to our cruising speed and we plunged on, breasting out over another falling-away of the seafloor, and curving toward the right, where lay a larger stretch of anemone-carpeted terrain. Over this hung numerous 'shads, all territorially spaced, hideous, hairy little balloons in the distance, sucking each on its tether of nerve.

Our course brought us closer to the Black Rifft's brink and as we swept toward the 'shad-meadows we coasted past a clearer view than previous of some of the siegeworks there, particularly of a thicket of derricks which thrust

222

great lateral arms through the gapped crest of the flame-wall. From these wrought-steel arms huge hooks were lowered on the ends of massive chains. Enormous windlasses drove the movement of the booms themselves as well as paying out the fishing chain off its immense spools. Stumbling human gangs, vast in numbers, provided the power that turned those windlasses. Similar gangs powered the vehicles of the demon-bosses who oversaw the work. These were brawny toads as big as houses. They lolled in the sodden hulks of galleons – storm-taken ships all bearded and furred with bottom-life, some of their hulls half stove in. Each of these had hundreds of slave haulers dragging its keel over the ocean floor. Their eyes had been taken, their hair was longer than the ever-springing hair in graves. Their skin floated up from their arms in brine-fat tatters. Their tread was sottish, their feet hidden in clouds of sand.

But we quickly ceased attending to anything except that greatest of the works which bordered the Rifft farther down its perimeter. Though still more than a mile distant, it was now revealed to us in greater detail. Each of the ovoids – of a pale rose tint, and minutely faceted – was as big as a mountain. Near them, small hills of iron bar were being forged, amid geysering sparks, into an irregular construction that looked like the beginnings of a cage – a cage big enough to *hold* a mountain. Meanwhile, beneath the web of scaffolding that had been thrown over the nearer of the two titanic shapes, a large hole had been broken in its substance, which appeared to be little more than a relatively thin shell. And we had drawn just near enough to find that something was visible within that hole, a small part of what the shell contained. It was a three-taloned foot as big as a city. Gildmirth pulled us away from the Rifft , working in an upslope path that would skirt the 'shad-meadows.

We found the boy in the fourth flock we surveyed. Almost in the first instant of my scanning, the victim my eye had lit on wrenched his head around in some access of suffering, and the face of Wimfort was flashed at me. I tugged Gildmirth's belt and pointed. He looked at Barnar, who confirmed our quarry. The Privateer bucked and heaved and plunged straight for the water's ceiling.

I felt each instant of that swift climb as a distinct and individual joy. We surfaced to find the boat awaiting us at a spot halfway around the island-cluster from our starting point. We were not far from the crest of the volcano we had seen. The cone's steaming rim, which barely over-topped the waves, swarmed with activity. Gildmirth laid his jaw on the boat's stern and we climbed aboard along his body, joyfully shucking our helmets, eager more for the act of breathing than the air itself, such that it felt sweet to draw in even that tomblike atmosphere.

'Practisss the ssskiff!' the lizard enjoined me. Its squam-ous head glittered and ducked under. The waters bulged with the force of his dive.

Taking both harpoons, I stepped into the little bone coracle. I willed it twenty yards to starboard of the boat. I sped so swiftly thither I was toppled, and clung aboard only with undignified difficulty. Barnar's braying followed me as I thought the skiff through several other maneuvers, standing better braced now, more fluid at the hips.

'You might well laugh,' I shouted to my friend as I zig-zagged ever more skillfully over the swell. 'See how far we've come! Impossibly far. We've *found* the young idiot – actually reached him and ferreted out his squirming-place in this infernal stew!'

Barnar merely whooped and waved his arms for a reply, and I myself felt giddy and nonsensical enough with our continuing good luck. I made a quick excursion toward the crater-top to view the siege in process there. Rafts of batrachian demons, reminiscent of the larger breed I had seen being charioted below by human gangs, were beached on the crater's flanks and mining at it furiously, using battering-irons or huge hammers and steel wedges. Their assault was countered by fire-elementals within the magmatic cauldron they sought to inundate and conquer. These shapeless, smoldering beings catapulted avalanches of lava on their besiegers, driving them by the score to quench their sizzling skin in the sea. Meanwhile with this same material the elementals ceaselessly caulked and re-knit the breaches broken by their enemies' tools.

I heard Barnar shout, and sped back toward the boat. Not far from it there was a milky spot in the water, like a cataract in an old dog's eye. I swung near just in time to be drenched by the explosion of Gildmirth in battle with the Bonshad.

I should actually say 'Gildmirth hanging onto the Bonshad,' for he gripped its back with all four paws and his locked jaws, and by wrestling mightily *steered* his opponent to some degree, but all the rest of the motive power of that struggle came from the 'shad. Its hook-rimmed mouth-hole gaped from its underside, which the lizard's grip on its inhooking legs exposed uncharacteristically to view. Such a wad of muscle was its lumpish body that you could clearly see the freeing of just one of its pinioned legs would enable it to compact itself with a power that must surely break the reptile's desperate grip. The speed with which it would then be able to sink its mouthparts into the Privateer's flank was amply attested to now by the monster's volcanic convulsions, which sent the pair of them cartwheeling insanely over the waves.

I began gathering speed with a series of quick swings into their zone of combat and then sharply out again, after each such approach pulling immediately round to make a new and more driving interception. My nearest glimpses of the Privateer told me that he was bone-tired – his paws showed their tendons stark as an oak's roots against rocky ground. His snakish neck bulged so full with strain that its scales jutted out, like wind-lifted shingles in a storm. I swung out to my widest retreat thus far, then pulled in, driving for a peak speed from which to make my cast.

The saurian made a mighty effort, and so far controlled the 'shad's tumble as to keep it belly-out in my direction. I balanced the harpoon by my ear, taking the skiff's buffets with loose knees, for now we sheared, half-flying, straight through the crests of the chop. I saw, some moments ahead of me, the spot and instant of my cast, which I would make at the apex of the skiff's turn, so that the cast would have a sling's momentum behind it, augmenting the strength of my arm. I saw too just where that haggle-rim mouth-hole would be, and my spirit welled up in me with that prescient certainty that precedes many of the greatest feats of weaponry.

I drew back to full cock for the throw, then hit my turn. Obediently, the mouth-hole tumbled precisely to its foreseen spot and I pumped that shaft dead into it, not even grazing the hooks that twisted so furiously round its border. The shaft sprouted full half its length out of the demon's back, and grazed Gildmirth's flank, for he was not quick enough in letting go. The 'shad flopped and churned across the swell for a full minute of storm-wild, crazy force before it realized it was dead, and settled, and sank.

We had to dive again with the Privateer, and be quick in pulling on our gear for it. The abandoned flock below was a free confection for any drifting entities that scented it. Being pulled under again felt like a burial-alive – no part of me desired it, and I scarcely kept my grip.

We swooped upon the meadow in time to drive off a many-mouthed, ray-shaped demon, which for all its mouths had no stomach to face the lizard's sword. The nerve-ball still hung above the little herd it tethered, just where its savorer had hung, and the flock remained as powerless as if the demon still hovered over them.

The saurian took the wadded skein of tissue and began

to bounce and jiggle it in his paws, the way you have to do to untangle snarled rope. The fibers began to open out. We helped, teasing strands apart. Toward the end it became a gossamer-light labor. We had to swim more than fifty feet above the pasture to make room for the endless unraveling, which we accomplished with gentle upward sweeps of our arms. Our work caused the flock to lurch and spasm in the lubricious embrace of their pasture.

But suddenly, just when the ball was entirely combed apart, the slick web of innards snapped simultaneously back down to its flock of donors and vanished inside their spines, which sealed up like sprung traps. Then the truly terrible dances began, as they awakened to their freedom in that grisly place. We came down quick on Wimfort. Gildmirth began plunging his sword into the things that held the boy – cloven tongues and shattered antennae recoiled from their prey. Barnar and I plucked him up, and I helped my friend get him tucked securely under his left arm. We cleaved to the Privateer and he sprang skyward with us all.

When we were settled with our unconscious charge in the boat, the Privateer took time to bind the wound which crossed half the left side of his ribs, a more considerable wound in his human stature than it had appeared on the lizard's huge bulk. Smiling with a sudden, strange cordiality, Gildmirth told me:

'That was a remarkable cast, Nifft.'

In temperate language I replied, as candor compelled me to do, that it had indeed been one of the finest feats of spear-work that it had ever been my fortune to witness.

XIV

For much of our voyage back the lad lay in the bow, his glazed eyes aimed at the clouds, or stirring mindlessly at sudden lurches of the craft. We had emptied the provision sack to make him a blanket, and had fallen to sharing the wine this had brought to light. Gildmirth, after musing on the boy's face awhile, said, 'He's a handsome lad. What are his chances of growing to a good man?'

Barnar sighed, and spat gently into the sea. I looked cheerlessly at the boy. My friend and I had had much time to reflect that all our toil was for a resurrection which, while it might not turn out to do the world great harm, wasn't likely to do it any good either. Wimfort's features had the fine symmetry that adolescence can show right up to the brink of adulthood's emergent emphases and distortions. A certain heaviness of cheek and jaw was already just beginning to suggest the sire.

'I'm afraid, good Privateer, that the signs are discouraging,' I answered. 'He's here, of course, strictly through his own ambitious carelessness.'

'Prime flaws of youth, of course – but also its strengths, this carelessness and ambition.'

I nodded. 'He has imagination and boldness. You wouldn't expect him to temper a rich boy's arrogance with much thought of others. He's the Rod-Master's son, as I've told you. But maybe with this – ' I gestured at the sea ' – and all he'll have to endure going back, he might get that needed awakening to the world around him.'

'If you get him back it will be your business to hope he *has* been wakened. Ambitious dabblers in sorcery add much to the hell that is on earth. In my origins of course I am just such a go-to-market meddler in the arts as I speak of.

228

But at least for every spell I purchased I bought the best tutors in its use and meaning, and I sought no new spell until I had faithfully learned all lore foundational to the last I had bought, or anywise tangent to it. Nor have I ever, to get to the essence of it, brought accidental doom upon my fellows through the casual practice of arts for which my wits were premature.'

I did not want him to fall silent on this topic. 'It is indeed a part of your legend, Privateer, that many of your . . . sharp practices were aimed at financing your thaumaturgic studies.'

Gildmirth regarded us blandly for some moments. 'Is that indeed a part of my legend? I am touched that my swindles are remembered at all. Toss. Thank you. It *was* an expensive education; I was never, before now, a glutton for mere gold itself. All my major larcenies were devoted to scholarly ends, in fact.'

'I understand,' Barnar said, 'that just before your coming here you worked an extremely lucrative deception on your native city.'

Gildmirth let a bitter eye roll across the cloud-vaults before allowing himself to sink into the obvious pleasure of boastful reminiscence. He drank, and handed me the jack with a pleased sigh. 'That one bought me this boat and sail. It was a good piece of work. Sordon Head was gearing up for yet another trade war. A major competitor of hers, the Klostermain League of Cities, had just lost half its navy in a storm, while we were just nearing completion of an admirable new navy. Our High Council suddenly recalled a gross defamation of one of our outlying shrines by a drunken Klostermain sailor. It had happened several months before that storm so disastrous for the League, if I recall rightly. We began applying diplomatic pressure on the League for trade concessions, while hinting ever more strongly of war. Our High Council was ripe for anything that might create assurance enough for us to go the last inch to candid armed aggression for profit.

'I came to them with the proposal of constructing a spear-head fleet of superlative fighting frigates, and demonstrated how such a tactical weapon could penetrate harbors and destroy ships in the docks, sparing us many chancier engagements on the high seas. I was an object of guarded civic pride for my exploits abroad, and I had always kept my in-town dealings well masked. They heaped my lap with gold. Their dreams of empire, of Klostermain plunder made them practically force on me the sum of eleven million gold lictors.'

Wimfort screeched, gull-voiced. He twisted, as if ants covered him, and under the sack we'd covered him with we could see his hands moving to rub some nameless memory off his skin. Barnar pressed a huge hand onto the boy's forehead. The boy's eyes closed again, as if that slight pressure crushed down the ugly dream behind them.

'Conceive the sum,' the Privateer said after a moment. 'Still it astonishes me, though I have often seen that sum quadrupled on a few hectares of the ocean's floor. Of course, it was spent a fortnight from my getting it – on this craft. It was a purchase I had studied and planned for more than a decade.

'You should have seen my shipyards in Sordon Head. Giant, covered buildings, windowless – the danger of Klostermain spies stealing some forewarning of their fate, you see – we couldn't risk it. And in those great empty warehouses a fleet was indeed a-building. A brace of towering frigates, made of leather, paper, and feather-wood. While my crews toiled on these, I had another crew working, a crew of musicians. Their instruments were mallets, saws, augers, rusty winches. Their oratorio was woven of shouted curses, and gusty dockworker's cries: "Lower away there, easy now! Down with it – a bit more, another arse-hair – hold! Maul here, and quarter-inch

230

spikes, prompt now!" Whenever the great men of the council passed my yards they drank in these melodies and passed on smiling.

'There was a grand harbor-side assembly to witness the launching of our raiding-frigates, as they had come to be called. The docks on all sides were crowned with walls of expectant citizens. The day was a glory – a steel-blue sky and a sweet, steady offshore wind. The council had a tiered platform at the tip of our major pier. When my flotilla came past them they would set afire a huge, wooden mock-up of the city's seal.

'I was in the shipyard. All the craft had been blocked on ramps and set to slide down by themselves to a launching in fair order. There were six of them, and I was in this boat, ramped to slide out in their midst, and so be masked by them at first. I pulled the block-pins. The great doors opened and our convoy skidded like so many fat swans onto the water.

'And they were light as swans too, at first. They were very proud ladies, my paper frigates, in the first moments of their promenading out onto the sea. They drew gasps from the crowd. But almost at once you could hear everyone saying "Eh?" "What?" Because the six of them wandered out giddily, like so many drunks reeling through the town square on their way to dance at the carnival. They bumped each other, some turned stern-first, and rocked till their masts looked like metronomes. The council buzzed. The seal was already proudly blazing, but the town orchestra was already faltering in mid-bar. The breeze jumbled the boats out to the center of the harbor. And then they began soaking up water in earnest. Here and there a sodden hull caved in like pastry left in the rain. Now a great noise arose from the multitude. The first of my ladies drank the limit. She went down so straight her masts looked like a weed being yanked under by a gopher.

'I was lying just here, in the stern. I would be unveiled

on center-stage, so to speak, when the last frigate sank. Now this was the riskiest part of my venture, because for the whole five minutes it took all of them to go under, I was fighting for my life with an attack of laughter that almost killed me. That's how I was revealed to my fellow-citizens, despite my best attempts at self-command. But when the populace gave a . . . what shall I call it? A *surge* of comprehension, I struggled to the mast and pulled myself onto my feet. The rest of the fleet had at last begun to weigh anchor, and undertake my capture. Gasping and clinging to the mast, I shouted: "Citizens!"

'That set me laughing again – the thought of them all. "Citizens!!" I croaked again. "I can't understand it! I'm . . . *appalled*! I used . . . the *best* . . . paper!" Getting that said nearly finished me. The fleet's lead ship was less than a hundred yards off now, and archers were forming up on its quarterdeck. I unfurled the sail. I'd researched the demon currents and they're quite strong near Sordon Head. I departed then from the bay of my native city, and as I left I noted with satisfaction how the hard-taxed multitudes were swarming off the docks and onto the main pier, and how the entire council – at pier's end – had risen to its feet in what looked like alarm.

'It took some ingenuity to stay slow enough for the fleet to follow me. It was a point of pride, I suppose, but perhaps something less personal than that as well. At any rate I wanted my destination known, my descent witnessed. One doesn't want to leave the world of one's kind without some moment of farewell, some acknowledgment by your fellows of your kinship and your departure. I came down by the Taarg Vortex, which is a maelstrom in the Yellow Reefs. I did not think that any would come down with me, but the captain of the flagship was a zealous man and did not pull up and bring a line in time. He was pulled down after me. Those I could manage, in that raging hurricane of water, I killed with arrows, but many were taken instantly by demons, and I could do nothing for them. Wheeling in anguish, they went where I did, through the Dark Rapids, down where the whirlpool's root feeds into a subworld river which none have given a name, and which empties in the sea some thousand leagues in that direction.'

At some point Gildmirth's voice must have entered Wimfort's dream-webbed brain, because when the Privateer stopped, the boy snapped open his eyes. They were large and dark, not piggy like his father's, and they now registered the clouds they stared at. With Barnar's help, he sat up. He looked at us, the boat, and us again. Seeing such astonishment as his, I couldn't think of what to tell him. It was Barnar who gave him the necessaries:

'We are men, Wimfort, not demons. This man has helped us fish you out, rescue you. Your father sent Nifft and me for you. We're taking you back up to the world of mankind.'

My friend's summation struck me at first as the report of some other men's actions. I looked at my hands. They are quite presentable hands, but nothing out of the ordinary. I marveled at what Barnar and I had done thus far, even leaving aside that which the Privateer had made possible for us.

As for Wimfort's reaction to these words, it was like watching Barnar speaking sentences into a tunnel. After a long lag, answering lights of comprehension flickered from the darkness of the boy's eyes. His breathing grew stronger. More fear showed on his face, and he brought his hands up to touch it. Then, with a tremor, he thawed out. Tears bulged from the corners of his eyes – slow in emerging, then falling with that surprising quickness that tears have. Barnar patted his shoulder.

'We have a hard trek home, Wimfort,' he said, 'but we have an excellent chance of making it.'

The boy looked at him and me, beginning to breathe more slowly. He looked at Gildmirth, whose plum-red orbs were like two terrible sunsets in the grinning ruins of his face.

'Your freedom's real, son,' the Privateer said. 'To talk to you of odds, of numbers, would never make clear to you the magnitude of your good fortune. So many like yourself are here forever.'

'You two,' Wimfort said. It was a croak, a voice almost erased. He cleared his throat. 'You two. My father sent you?'

Seeing someone is half of meeting him, and hearing his voice the other half. I liked the voice – still a treble, with a gravelly shade of manhood to come. An un-self-conscious voice that said exactly what it thought. He probably had an ungentle tongue toward servants, but perhaps also a sense of humor, and imagination. He looked wonderingly about the sky and sea.

'How long have I been here?' he asked.

Barnar shrugged. 'We cannot say how long we've been atraveling. Perhaps you have been here two or three months.'

'Three months!' Wimfort said it hushedly. It was poignant, for we knew that he was reviewing what had filled those months for him. He shuddered, and then shuddered again more powerfully. He looked at us with what might have been panic drawing in his face.

'You two walked that long to reach me?'

'No,' I said. 'The trek was probably something more than a month, and you had been down here for a similar period before your father was able to ... obtain our services.'

'My father sent you ...' echoed the boy. I was getting alarmed – his stare was so wide. 'Three months here!' he groaned. 'Three months. And my father sent *you*. He waited two months, and then sent a pair of baboons on foot who took another two months to get here!' His voice was rising to a howl as uncontrolled as his arithmetic was getting. 'A good wizard could have had me out in a *day*. That dung-heap! That greedy, stingy dung-heap! THREE MONTHS!!'

XV

Wimfort recovered swiftly. My God, the resilience of the young! Within an hour to step back into your own mind and character after months of the Bonshad's intricate violation of your inmost thoughts. But that is the essence of youth – to believe soundly and fixedly in its own destruction. Soon we found, full-blown before us, the lad Charnall had described, with the same ambitions – intact, invigorated even by their grim miscarriage.

We cut the sack into a tunic for his temporary comfort. He dressed very surlily after I had told him he was a young idiot and that he was not to call us baboons. I tried not to be harsh about it, remembering he was convalescent. As he dressed, by way of setting things at ease, Gildmirth explained to him the erroneous tradition that made so many people summon Bonshads, and assured him that the Elixir of Sazmazm was nowhere near the sea, nor could any marine power hope to possess it, though such would treasure it as much as any primary demon would.

Wimfort had squatted on a rower's bench, with his back very straight and his face half-averted from us. When the Privateer finished the lad scowled and shook his head pityingly at the waters, then looked round to deliver this answer:

'I'm really an idiot, eh? As that one says? Do you think I'm so stupid I don't know the situation of the Elixir? Of course it isn't in the sea. It is obtained from somewhere outside it *by* the Bonshad, which as everyone knows lives *in* the sea.'

'You just know that better than most by now,' I put in, disgusted with the boy's impenetrability. He disdained to notice me and continued setting the Privateer straight:

'Just for your information, grandfather, I've read all that's known of the matter. The Elixir of Sazmazm is obtained in the prime subworld where the Giant Sazmazm, of the tertiary subworld, lies captive.' Wimfort had adopted that bored off-handedness with which smart students reel off authoritative texts which they have memorized entirely and – in their opinion – mastered completely. 'If you are curious as to the manner of the giant's captivity, it's relatively simple. Sazmazm sought ascension to the prime-subworld where he meant to enjoy empire, and unholy feasts upon the lesser demons. He bargained with the great warlock, Wanet-ka, the greatest in all the Red Millennium, and generally held unscrupulous enough to wreak any harm for the right price, even that of bringing a tertiary power within one level of the world of men. Wanet-ka accepted the giant's advance, a stupendous sum, and then swindled Sazmazm. Using a loophole in the re-assembly clause of his pact, he transported the demon two levels up, as agreed, but everted him in so doing, and reconstituted him with fantastic whimsy and disorder. Sazmazm endures, a vast, impotent disjointment, his lifeblood pulsing through him in veins nakedly accessible to those who would brave the giant's tertiary vassals, who attend him, and laboriously transport his essence back down to his native world, fraction by fraction – a millennial labor.'

Something tickled my memory. The boy's words evoked some image, too ephemeral for me to resolve, which spidered uneasily across my mind. The Privateer laughed. 'Excellent. Two-thirds Ha-dadd – almost word for word – and the other third a loose rephrasing of Spinny the Elder. Both standard sources even in my day. Moreover, everything you have recited is true.'

'For this feat – ' Wimfort spoke with the outraged

emphasis of a lecturer who has been crassly interrupted. '
– the Grey League granted Wanet-ka the honorary epithet
of "the Benevolent," and included his biography in their
Archive of Optimates.'

'Just for *your* information, grandchild, in the Benevolent
Wanet-ka, you have chosen from the past the worst possible
hero on whom to model your ambitions. A great man and
warlock he surely was. But such a one as only greybeards
like myself, who understand how to distinguish his tri-
umphs from his lunacies, can intelligently honor. Wanet-
ka! For the reasons you admire him, you might as well
choose some great demon chief from these deeps to
idolatrize.'

'I don't idolatrize,' the boy said hotly, 'and you can just
keep your jaw locked from now on.'

The Privateer's jaw did indeed tighten shut. He reached
forth his hand toward the boy. He was back in the stern,
and so the boy didn't move, thinking the gesture a senseless
one – until the Privateer's arm elongated impossibly, and a
huge webbed claw half-engulfed the lad's head. Wimfort's
horror was plain. Gildmirth said, 'Your father didn't send
me after you, boy. I live here, and may do so forever. For a
false copper I'd take you back down and hand you to
another Bonshad. Don't yank on my old grey beard, boy. I
hurt all over in ways you'll never learn enough to understand. I'm in a nasty mood, grandson, and you watch your
tongue most carefully with me, at all times.'

Gildmirth's pique was surely forgivable. To hear such a
squall as the boy had made raised over a three-month term
in hell, for one who has stoically borne a sentence of three
centuries, must be unimaginably irritating – especially
when the short-term wailer makes his complaint en route
to his freedom. Perhaps he regretted his anger, however,
for he brought his arm back to its proper form, and went
on in a gentler tone: 'You must grasp, my boy, that I'm
not disparaging your ambition. I admire your spirit. And

237

when I force unwelcome information on you, I'm just trying to amplify your understanding, give you vital data on whose basis you can proceed to fulfill your dreams of sorcerous power. Do you think that I or my friends here are jealous of the greatness you propose for yourself? Why should we care one way or the other? We have our own pressing concerns. Since I happen to know something of the matter – a circumstance I regard as purely an accident of time and experience, and of which I am no-wise vain – I'm simply telling you that no serious wizard, save for some hard to imagine and highly specific aim, would meddle with the Elixir of Sazmazm. It's power is far too unwieldy – too great for accurate mastery and utilization – while its immense attractiveness to all the demons of this world makes the mere transport of it highly dangerous, assuming that it could be wrested from Sazmazm's vassals in the first place. I am told that you bear a spell of incorporation for the Elixir. Can you believe that making your body a jar for this substance could be anything but the rankest suicide down here? The first demon that caught you would make a fire and render the Elixir from you as casually as if you were a chunk of whale fat.

'You must understand. This Elixir is a powerful drug to the denizens of this world. It enhances their sensual and cerebral universe to a pitch of paradisiacal ecstasy. From even the most vanishingly small potations of it, they taste an amplification of spirit to which the intoxications of human prey are but the feeblest premonition.

'But leave all this aside. Suppose you brought the Elixir safely back to the surface-world? Your plans for its use might be unexceptionable – temperate, benign, creative – still the smell of it would be on you, so to speak. Within the first day of your homecoming, all the most powerful wizards on earth would know you had it – know who you were, and how to find you. Consider that phrase, please: "all the most powerful wizards on earth." In my day, that was a crew that contained some great and remorseless predators. Whether or not many of those men still live – and many might – their like have surely been appearing throughout the intervening centuries. I'll say no more than to remind you of the chunk of whale fat.'

The boy said nothing, but clearly it was only the demonstration that his preceptor was no mean magus that stilled his tongue. He squirmed and twitched with unspoken rebuttal throughout the Privateer's remarks. Gildmirth sighed, and the three of us returned to our wine while the boat, under his covert direction, returned us to his manse.

I sat facing the sea through an archway in the colonnade where we sat. The Privateer, sitting behind me, touched the back of my head. A whiteness and nothingness occurred. Then again, there was the archway and the sea beyond it. I was faintly dizzy, but this passed almost at once. I looked around, and saw that a cloudiness was just clearing from Gildmirth's bloody orbs. When he spoke his jaw at first moved numbly.

'You've lived much, Nifft. You leave me quite a world to be explored once I'm alone again.'

His eyes mused a moment, and he chuckled and swore. I felt my past had been as air to his present imprisonment, and it made me glad. Barnar took his turn, and I saw that Gildmirth's touch lasted less than a minute. Again the Privateer rested, and marveled. When at last he looked at us, there was no self-consciousness in our looking-back. What would have been the point? Gildmirth smiled and said: 'How tired I am of what I know of this world, my friends. How I crave to return to the learning of that more evanescent and various lore, the lore of living men.'

'Listen,' Barnar said, 'Nifft and I have talked. We've agreed that if there's any way in which we could help you

239

win your freedom from this place, we will put off our return until this is accomplished.'

Gildmirth smiled again, and shook his head. A loud snort from Wimfort reminded us all of his presence. The Privateer had given the boy leather leggins and a byrnie of light mail from his own stores. The gear hung a bit roomily on his frame, which caused him an irritation that betrayed a habit of infallibly correct fitting-out – something the Rod-Master's pride of place would surely have seen to.

The snort was a prelude. The boy had been developing his strategy, and was now going to expostulate with us as though we were rational beings with at least as much say in the course of events as he had. He made a reasoning gesture with both arms, a very political bit of flourish which he almost had the hang of, and which a few more years of observing his father would make him perfect in. He addressed himself to the Privateer.

'I'm *convinced* that you aren't seeing the true advantages of an expedition for the Elixir. You've probably been down here a while. You seem to know your way around down here, you have some powers – guide us from here to scout inland for the Elixir! You have yourself, sir, given a hint of the immeasurable value it would have, even here among demon-kind. What could it not purchase? Impressive though your establishment here might be, surely you don't have absolutely everything you wish! Surely there is something you lack that you desire. Who has everything he wants?'

The Privateer had paled. Knots of murderous intention were forming at the corners of his jaw. Then, in his eyes, I could see the dull rage give way to more self-command – to a realization that the irony of the boy's words was accidental, and that Wimfort had no conception of our protector's situation – indeed, had surprisingly scant *attention* to spare for it, considering that Gildmirth manifestly commanded an outpost of influence in the sea itself. The Privateer expelled the last of his wrath in a deep sigh. Looking earnestly for a moment into the boy's eyes, he ended by laughing. 'Oh Junior Rod-Master, it is truly well for you that you have these men for your escorts. If anyone, on your route home, can protect you from the consequences of your fatal misapprehensions, they can. Pray for the wit to appreciate their services, and to aid them in every way you can. Gentlemen – ' Here he took our hands in turn. ' – I honor you for your worth, which just lately I have come to know in detail. I thank you for your generous offer to help me. May all luck go with you. I cannot hope – for your sakes – that I will see you again, though the affection I bear you makes me wish it. For the trifling service I have done you – ' (Here he glanced at Wimfort.) ' – I am amply repaid.'

Walking away from the Privateer was as hard as disarming would have been – piling my weapons on the ground and setting forth without them. When we had scaled the salt cliffs we raised our hands to him. He was far below, but I saw him nod very slightly as he stared back up at us. Then he turned and entered the manse – I think to spare himself the spectacle of our endlessly gradual disappearance as we dwindled from view along his clifftop skyline.

XVI

On first reaching the sea we had noted an offshore crag for a landmark, and thither we now doggedly bent our return course. We knew that by walking a diagonal path inland from the manse we could cut many weary leagues off our march, but the convenience of this was not worth the risk it entailed. The route we knew offered dangers we had proven to be survivable, and for all we knew it was, in this, unique.

Naturally, Wimfort began gaping at the baubles down on the beaches, and immediately started demanding we stop, and go down for this or that trinket. I say 'naturally' because I believe I understood him perfectly. He didn't really need to hear the answer we gave him: that such treasure-hunting would mean a dangerous re-entry of the sea's zone of influence, and that most of those riches were merely bait for man and demon alike. He didn't truly want those baubles; what he couldn't forbear to do was push at us. He was furious with us – not for anything we had done, but simply because we were the tardy, powerless drudges that we were. What he wanted was rescue by a wizard astride a golden griffon – an immediate plucking from the imprisoning waters (and *not* three months late, thank you) followed by a swift jaunt to pick up some of the Elixir of Sazmazm, and concluding with a prompt, painless return home, and the heating of Master Wimfort's bath.

And after all, how could the boy be otherwise? All he knew was to order us to do what he wanted. Reality, for him, did not run any other way than that. And here we were, telling him he was going to have to walk with us, through mire and peril, for more than a month, and that there was going to be no stop for some elixir en route. We offered mere escape – ignominious, arse-bare escape escorted by two scoundrels of unromantic appearance.

Rage and wounded pride look painful on a young face. Sixteen is a difficult age to get on with. There's much to like – the freshness, the force of conviction. But there is also a certain arrogance, an inevitable concomitant of development, perhaps, which one must always struggle to forgive. Wimfort had a great deal of freshness and enterprise, but he also required huge amounts of forgiving. He lashed us with pejorative epithets and sneers when we denied his will and bade him march on.

Verbal rebukes were powerless to curb his hectoring. At length Barnar and I conferred aside. We took some of the rope which Gildmirth had included in our provisions and rigged a humane though not extremely comfortable cradle. In this we trussed the boy. We hung him from one of our spears and carried him between us as hunters will a bush-pig they've bagged upcountry. An hour of this convinced him of our sincerity in telling him that henceforth he would cease to vilify us, or he would make the entire journey thus. Though successful in the short range, this ploy proved a mistake. When liberated the boy did, strictly speaking, stop vilifying us, but in insult's stead he muttered endlessly varied rehearsals of our punishment and death at the hands of his father, the august Kamin, Rod-Master of Kine Gather. Whenever this paled, the boy had only to scan the beach till he found some new thing there to demand and be denied. This accomplished, he was able to resume his vengeful soliloquy with fresh gusto.

Meanwhile his surroundings, the fabulous nature of his present position, were dawning on him. At times he fell silent, and caught his eyes marveling at the sea's horizon, exulting in its shore's tangled wonders. At these moments we glimpsed an impressive strength of will in the boy – an ambition sharp and forceful as a man's hatching within a heart and mind still childish in their scope and capacity. These glimpses did not increase our peace of mind.

When at last we approached our landmark, Wimfort, gathering that we were near our inland-turning, began to find the attractions of the beach ever more urgent. I could feel him winding himself tight for some absolutely peremptory requirement that could give occasion to an outright defiance of our will. Then he saw some amphorae of burnished copper.

We were above a particularly lush stretch of beach. The cliffs here were luminously white. On the shingle footing their waxen wall, on the wave-worn stones as black as boiling tar, a flock of thralls lay in the surf. Each of the flock was two – a man and a woman, fused at the waist into a limbless, two-headed sausage – and each of these, when the surf came in, bent up in a U of revulsion, hoisting its heads out of reach of the erratic, leap-frogging foam. On all sides of this flock tide pools dappled the rocks, and these were clogged with such lurid riches as would mock the greediest imagination with its littleness. The amphorae were strewn through several such pools, and some were battered and ruptured, like storm-wrack. The plug sealing each of them bore a deeply graven, S-shaped rune. Wimfort stood stock-still, then opened his mouth. Furious in advance, I forestalled him: 'Can you be such a fool, Wimfort?' I shouted. 'Would it be sealed in jars and stamped like a bottle in a perfumer's stall?'

'Yes!' he shrilled. 'If it were some demon's booty – some elixir *successfully stolen*, and jarred for storage in the demon's cellars!'

Barnar groaned. 'Wimfort! Did they all lie to us when they called you well-read? That could be a snake-rune! It could be the High-Archaic demi-sigil. I mean who even knows how "Sazmazm" is rendered in demon callig – '

'Look!' shrieked Wimfort in horror. I blush to report that Barnar and I, green as bumpkins at a fair, whirled round as one man, and the boy sprinted for the cliff.

The bluffs were mostly sheer, but above the amphorae a deep gully split the cliff. Wimfort jumped into it and rode down it on a little avalanche of loose salt. He was halfway down before I could uproot my feet. As I ran for the cliff I called back to Barnar: 'A line! And brace yourself, I want a good haul coming back!' I jumped into the gully and skied down as Wimfort had done.

The boy was nimble as a fox pup. He took some tumbles I vowed to myself had killed him, only to see him get his feet beneath him at the last instant. I couldn't match his speed, and saw the inevitability of the thing I least desired – a struggle with him on the shore, down in the reach of the surf, and whatever lived in it. He hit the cove and

pelted for the amphorae. I sprang off the bluff and took the
last fifteen feet by air. Wimfort was wrestling a jar from
one of the pools, and I saw how suddenly the surf came in,
like an extended paw, to swirl teasingly round his ankles.
He dragged the jar – half his own size – onto the shingle
and began frantically to pry at its stopper with a sharp
stone.

I was on him, seizing his shoulders. He hugged the jar
with both legs and arms. I was in urgent dread of the sea,
and so I gave up trying to pry him off the jar, and dragged
them both back toward the cliff. Meanwhile just offshore,
the water was beginning to fold and peak in a dozen places.
The peaks were sharp, and did not move with the rhythm
of water, but fitfully, like things scurrying around under a
sheet, all of them coming erratically but steadily nearer the
beach. I looked up at the clifftop. Barnar stood and
brandished a noose, beginning to move down the gully for
a nearer cast. I nodded and bent down to pry at Wimfort's
grip in earnest. I would have to stun his arm with a
blow to the shoulder. It was not going to be an entirely
disagreeable task. The boy sensed my preparatory movement and wrenched himself with unexpected violence to
one side, dragging the amphora down with him to the
shingle, and knocking the stopper out of it.

What poured out of it was a reeking black fluid – and far
more than that. For in the fumes that instantly tangled up
through the air, my mind and soul went twisting and
reeling into an utterly other being. The sky over me,
though it did not alter physically, became something different, became an agelessly familiar thing. The black and
white shingle was the only floor my feet had ever known,
except that I did not possess feet, but some giant raptor's
talons. And my tongue was charged with curses in a
language never heard in the world of the sun. I poured these
curses from my hooked beak upon my deadly adversary.

This enemy of mine was a crablike thing, half my size.

245

Fluid fire were his eye-knobs upon their ghastly stalks, and his pincers were likewise of flame. We joined battle, as we had done, world without end, whenever we had met in the long eons of our being. He clawed and tore at my chest and legs as I took his eye-stalks in my forepaws and lifted him, shaking him in the air.

When my mind goes back, now, to that battle, it is like stepping into a great shadowed corridor endless in either direction, a hall of memories and dark hates. For in those moments I possessed the entire past of that other being – its shape and senses, its deeds and lusts, all were mine, and I fought for them all. There was a touch, a pressure around my upper body, and then a tightening around my neck and under one of my forelegs. As this was happening, so was something else. The surf arched itself up off the stones, just like a carpet lifted by children who are playing beneath. Crouched forms with merry red sharp-cornered eyes rode mats of coiling slime out from under the shadow of the lifted water blanket. They winked at us. I knew them, and I knew what they wanted, but I was powerless to do anything other than fight my close-embraced enemy to the death.

And then something began to lift me. Haltingly, I rose up the cliff face, and my enemy, whom I could not loose, rose with me, clawing wildly at my body all the while. The sharp-eyed things swarmed onto the shingle. My heels rose just barely clear of their ropy palps, entreatingly upreached.

Somewhere in that jerky climb I began to shed somewhat the being which had engulfed my own, but the madness of battle remained upon both of us. When Barnar landed us on the clifftop he had to act fast to save Wimfort's life. The lad, who had the fight of a drenched cat, was obliviously kicking my shins and clawing my face as I, singlemindedly, throttled him, while trying to grab his hands and stifle their assault. His face swelled above my fist, purple as an eggplant, but he didn't seem to care about being strangled

– he wanted my life and nothing else. I began doing my lunatic all to fold him up small enough so I could pound him flat with a rock. My legs had more lumps on them than a mile of city street has cobbles, and the little beast had clawed my arms to such a tatters they looked like I'd been scrubbing them with rose-bushes. I'm not sure how my friend managed to pull us apart, but fortunately the fit waned almost immediately after we were separated.

The boy sat up groggily and set about, cautiously, trying to get some breath through his bruised windpipe. He sounded like a bellows with the nozzle rusted half-shut. I limped about until some of my blood had forsaken my many bruises and returned to my veins. I hobbled to and fro, marveling at the disastrous condition of my shins.

When Barnar saw we were at peace, he sat down to rest from his exertions. As he sat there, he started to laugh. Once he got started, he warmed right up to it. He set himself to laugh in a big, methodical way, sending a great, stately braying sound out across that festering sea. It took more and more of his strength, that laugh, and finally he had to lie on his back and give it his all. I didn't join him at first.

'Just look at you there,' I snapped, 'just haw-hawing away, snug as a hog in muck.'

Barnar fought to breathe, to speak: 'You should have . . .' (Some further struggle) '. . . You should have seen yourself!' (A gurgle, and some more braying.) 'You looked like two puppets . . . whose handler was having a seizure! . . . I almost . . . *dropped* you!'

This last amusing thought was too much for him, and he went off again. I began to join him, half just to irritate the boy, who was taking on a pout of bitterness and injury as he came back to himself. 'You rotten, swaggering bullies!' he shouted at us. It was meant as a preamble, but he stopped short, snagged on the fact that we had just pulled him out of a very deadly mistake. It didn't soften him toward us. As any spoiled child will do, he punished us for making him feel guilty by hating us more. The incident didn't really prove anything to him, since he had only half disbelieved our warnings against the amphorae in the first place. And it left intact the hateful fact of our control over him. After staring at us a moment, he said bitterly: 'You just *refuse* to see the importance of the Elixir! It's worth any risk. Don't you see that if we brought some back, you would be rich beyond your most insanely greedy dreams?'

Barnar and I traded a look, and then stared back at him. Our humor had left us. It was more than sad, the eternal unteachability of youth.

'Wimfort,' I said at last, 'I speak this with all gravity – without malice or ill will. But may all the nameless dwellers in the Black Crack itself prevent you from ever accomplishing your desire. I swear that we will always do our utmost to thwart your efforts in that direction. And now we must march. We crave the sun, Barnar and I, and the wind and the stars. Our souls are perishing to take up the thread of our proper lives. And so would yours be too, if you were not the young idiot you are.'

XVII

The essence of nightmare lies less in the simple experience of horrors than in the unpreventable fruition of horrors foreknown. And when we turned inland from the sea, we entered our ordeal's most nightmarish phase.

We knew, in large part, what awaited us, and consequently we advanced armed with strategies – bleak-hearted, but murderously determined to dispense more damage than we endured, and to endure far less than our coming hither had caused us. In such a spirit, I say, we advanced. We advanced to encounter a perfect series of disasters – to meet each of our wisely prepared-for enemies with collision force, and come off twice as scathed as our first encounters with them had left us. The reason? The reason, in a word, was Master Wimfort, Rod-Master-apparent of the city of Kine Gather.

To evoke that train of extravagant missteps in any detail is a task from which my hand rebels. Calamity struck us with such ruthless regularity that those hours of fevered scrambling achieved – for me – the quality of Damnation itself, of entrapment beneath the Wheel of Woe where it grinds out its eternal reiterations of misery and peril.

The boy lost no time hitting his stride. The salt dunes' only predators were big-jawed beings which laired like ant-lions in plainly visible funnels whose avoidance was easy. Then we hit the first rough spot, announced by greasy black smoke which overlay and stained the dunes for miles in advance of its actual frontier. And the roaring of it outreached its smoke, for it was a place of furious conflagration. Flesh was the universal material of that jumbled terrain, knit of welded bodies both human and demonic, and all that flesh was toweringly aflame. Crazed, veering winds raised the flame into peaks and harvested it, tearing it up by its sizzling roots of skin and blowing flesh and flame alike to rags and tatters that came driving at you like a blizzard. The living fuel sundered, body fragments wheeled before the gale till they were re-welded by impact against the first feature of that landscape that intercepted their flight, while roaring within the roaring of the fire were these victims' million voices, which rose in grieving unison, intact above their molten, broken bodies.

Our tactic here was to run shoulder to shoulder ahead of the boy, the two of us forming a kind of prow to cleave the wind, while the fire-clots splashed off our joined shields. Wimfort ran close behind in the lee we made him. The wind's shifting had us staggering and stumbling. We had to run as much as possible against the wind in order to

249

keep our shields between us and the burning flesh. This, when it struck us, clung to us – sometimes in the most literal way when hands, claws or entire limbs of it hit us and tried to wrestle the shields from our grips, and wherever that flesh touched ours, ours came away.

We were well across this zone, and were keeping the bulk of the fiery carnage off our charge, when a few bits of flame began to get round to him on a back-draft – negligible bits, no more than we were constantly being singed with all over our bodies, but they caused Wimfort such a lively sense of discomfort that he panicked, and bolted from our cover. He began a lateral drive which he almost immediately aborted at the onslaught of a big fragment – a whole blazing torso, in fact, which spun toward him, its arms spread to wrap him in a crackling hug. Barnar had turned and reached out his free arm to pull the boy back to cover, and when Wimfort ducked, the burning body sailed over him and smashed into my friend's embrace. The boy, mindful only of his own stinging flesh now that we no longer covered him, seized my shield and tried to wrestle it from me while I was helping Barnar peel the pyro-nomad from his chain mail, which was already cherry-red with the heat. Whole steaks of our skin came off in that grisly grappling, while the boy's wild assaults endlessly frustrated my efforts to use my sword as a prybar on Barnar's tormentor without killing my friend in the process. When pain and desperation grew too much, I knocked Wimfort senseless, and then I was able to help Barnar to a quick disentanglement. I tossed the boy across my shoulder and we fled.

The fields of fire gave place to orchard country – squat trees of leatherlike, veiny foliage studded with wrinkled blue fruit that gave off a delicious fragrance. We had no unguents, and our burns were an agony beneath our armor. With scant ceremony we told Wimfort that he was not to pluck or even touch this fruit – that we were going to make a brisk, direct march through this territory, that he was going to hold the position we assigned him throughout, and that there was no more to the affair than that.

Naturally, there proved to be a great deal more to it than that. We'd cut Wimfort a staff for the trek, and he expressed his resentment of things in general by prodding curiously with it at this fruit or that whenever our eyes were not on him. We learned he was doing this because, inevitably, one of his idle, resentful little pokes brought the fruit down. That which we had been too weary and curt to describe to him came to pass – with the first fruit, every other one on the tree dropped off. The leaves came with them, for these were the wings of those plump little monsters, all of whose bodies split open in fang-rimmed mouths as they converged in a ravenous swarm upon the three of us.

For this particular eventuality we had formulated a very clear strategy, and Barnar communicated this to Wimfort: 'Run for your life!' he bellowed, and he and I set the boy an example which, at that moment, we didn't really care whether he followed or not. But in fact, he outstripped us, and nearly knocked me off my feet in so doing.

By the Crack, how that lad could run! He was, in all seriousness, an unusually gifted runner – just how gifted we had yet, to our sorrow, to learn, though we were beginning to realize it. He was long-legged and, though not quite yet at his full frame-size, already deep-lunged. In him, we saw the image of our own plight ahead of us during that long sprint beneath those trees all fat and gravid with the clustered swarms of razor-fanged hungers. Given even the briefest contact, they clipped a bite of skin off you as big as an Astrygal twenty-gelding piece. They taxed us sorely, though we swatted them with our shields, which grew heavier with their fig-soft, impact-flattened bodies, and dragged at our flight. When near at hand, the loathsome things smelt putrescent, and as they swooped at us they hissed feverish little curses, and derogatory personal remarks. Even when we had thinned them out till they posed no further danger, it remained a pleasure – indeed, a vindictive obsession – to smash them, and when we were at last outside the frontier of the orchard-land, we shed our gear, arranged ourselves back to back, and proceeded, methodically, to hammer every last one of the stubborn little abominations flat. We stood thus – our arms, cheeks, shins all spotted with red bites, our eyes insanely bright – and feasted on their annihilation. Wimfort, finding himself similarly beset with hangers-on, ran back to us and howled at us to kill his too, and so enthralled were we by the task, that we actually did this for him.

After that we rested, hid, and lay still for a time. It was perhaps a day or two, for our wounds had begun to scab, and the sharpest edges of their pain had dulled when we again proceeded. Just before we set out, we had an earnest talk with Wimfort. We were in a gully in a low hillside, and I pointed out to the plain before us.

'Do you see, Wimfort, yonder there, where those flatlands get so much paler?'

'I suppose so.'

'Well, that's where we start running into the bog. It's a kind of swamp, teeming with men and women, you understand? With males and females. Tens of thousands of them, all of them . . . moving together.' I paused, feeling that this sounded lame. 'Listen Wimfort,' I said, 'don't be offended, but I must ask you. Do you know how babies are made?'

He gave me a look of enormous scorn. He looked up at the luminous murk that was our sky, as if to call witness to his trials at the hands of dolts. He disdained to answer.

I was relieved. He didn't know, then, or at least, knew only in a remote way. At his age the question is tricky, but I had read him as a prudish boy like many privately extravagant and ambitious types – no young tom-about-town he, fascinated by the flesh perhaps, but still feeling some compromise to his dignity in it. I handed him a cudgel I had whittled him from a thorn root.

'Well,' I said, 'that's what the men and women and girls and boys and other assorted creatures in the bog are all doing – that, and variations of it. The danger is not really great, if you just remember not to be attracted *into* their activities. Anyone who's really trying can make his way through them, though it takes some hard struggling in the thickest places. Just remember that the fun is all on the surface there – if you let yourself be pulled deeper into the matter, you'll find yourself being swiftly destroyed. As before, momentum is everything. Don't pause, just drive forward, whacking away like a thousand devils.'

It seems to me now that I hardly need to describe what ensued. When we reached it, we entered the swamp at a run, zigzagging among the mossy knolls and black, weed-slick pools where the small, outlying knots of nude humanity mingled with miscellaneous demonry in orgiastic combination.

And our momentum held even after the orgiasts grew in number, lay ever more profusely heaped till sweaty hills of them coalesced, and the muddy earth was blanketed by their lascivious coalition. A whinnying, jabbering clamor arose from that voluptuary fen, a vast, ragged oratorio of lust, with a muffled accompaniment of something else. We reached the thick of it, and it was time to clear ourselves a path with club-work.

Coming down, we'd lacked knouts and had used our spear-butts. On either trip our swords would have been the most efficient weapons, but it was humanly impossible to use them. It was horrible enough using the clubs, even on the men, and inexpressibly so on the women. To stir the arm for such an act – not once, but countless times – was dead contrary to what every fiber of my being wanted

– nay, *demanded*. In a certain way, that may have been the worst mauling I got on the entire journey – wading through the slippery shoals, hammering through the hot, coaxing embraces of urgent arms and pleading fingers. It was a violence to my soul. Each bruise I gave, my own nerves wore.

For the first long moments of this excruciating immersion, we kept a fair pace. Then the lad, who went between us, started lagging. He would fall behind me until Barnar would catch up to him and thrust him on. Ever more balkily he advanced. Then I looked back and saw his eyes, even as I watched them, grow rapt, his gaze become dangerously entangled in the carnal weave. Snap! He came to a full stop, dropped his club, and dove into the squirming heap.

The succeeding frenzy, just at its fullest pitch, caused me an eerily calm moment of remembrance. I had done fisherwork on the Ahnook trawlers when I was young, and there had been one late afternoon when we made a stupendous strike. Our greedy skipper plied the nets with epileptic ardor and buried our decks with a spill-over haul, in a mad race to ship every possible ounce before it grew dark. Half of us had to stand the decks with spars in our hands and club the fish like a devil with his arse afire. They were shadfinns, big as dogs with the fight of wild pigs. In the dimming light, on the heaving, slithering decks, walloping and dancing berserkly, I had for a short eternity fore-lived what I lived now.

The boy hadn't noticed anything below the upper layers, and kicked at us furiously as he wormed himself into the endless grapple. Instantly, he had a dozen allies aiding his immersion. I felt for a horrified time the certainty that we wouldn't get him out in time. For even in our distraction, we got many glimpses of the deeper action of the fiendish congress. Several layers down you saw a kissing mouth that suddenly grinned and sank its teeth in flesh. A hand with a thumb and four bleeding stumps was seen to pound helplessly against a massive thigh. A rib broke under a powerful knee. From down there you heard the smothered undercurrent of a different oratorio, one of horror covered by the chorus of lust.

Wimfort gave us great thumping kicks of painful authority. When we could spare a blow from the rest, we parried him and struck at his legs to stun them. He sank under the first layer of stroking hands and worshipful lips, and suddenly pain stamped his face, and he howled. He began to fight like mad to become free, but now his allies had become his captors.

In desperation I drew my sword. I lopped off a man's arm, another's foot. Mercifully, this sent a shock through the massed orgy – arms recoiled and torsos writhed away. This helped Barnar as much as it did Wimfort, for several thralls had gotten arm-locks on my friend's neck, and in the last instant before he was freed I saw his left ear bitten off flush with his head.

I must say that Wimfort, when he had his feet under him again and his club restored him, began to ply this weapon with a vigor that greatly sped our passage through and exit from that region. This performance had purchased him a measure of forgiveness from our hearts by the time we had sat down in a safe place to bind Barnar's wound.

But then Wimfort, that prodigal youth, managed to squander all he had purchased in a few brief words. He was looking at us absentmindedly when suddenly his eyes narrowed, and a look of pleased discovery dawned on his features. He laughed triumphantly, in innocent enjoyment of his enemies' defects – for I must mention that, some years prior to this time, I had had the misfortune to lose most of my own left ear.

'Your ears!' Wimfort cried, and laughed again. 'Now the two of you match!'

XVIII

We gave ourselves another, shorter period of rest, until Barnar's wound had scabbed cleanly and stopped throbbing, and then, once again, we marched. Endlessly.

Long and long we marched. Unendingly we marched. We marched, and Wimfort nagged us.

The boy was unquestionably a great natural talent, if not an outright genius, in the art of complaint – tirelessly inventive, and completely shameless in the matter of interpreting his dissatisfaction as someone else's – *anyone* else's – criminal failures to content him.

And so we marched, and Wimfort, marching too, also nagged us, and at length the sheer influx of his voice, relentless as the surf's assault on the rock, began to expunge my mind, scour away any thought of my own that tried to sprout from my fast-eroding brain.

'STOP!' I bellowed. 'Stop right here, sit down, shut up, and listen.'

Wimfort skidded down the slick, pink knoll I had just descended, and obeyed three of my commands. Given the loathsome wetness of this spongy terrain, I didn't insist on his sitting down. I said to him, 'Now. Your mouth will remain shut, and your ears open, until I'm finished. First: you are aware of the Life-Hooks in us which bind us to Charnall, who is in your father's power. Second: you were present – though you may not have been listening, since the discussion concerned persons other than yourself – when we asked Gildmirth to remove the Hooks for us. He told us that, as the Hook is a primitive, strongly talisman-linked spell, we stood a two-to-one chance of having our hearts ripped out if he removed the Hooks from us without

using the control-ring. Now here is the new bit of information I want you to have. A while ago Barnar and I had
a lengthy conversation out of your hearing in which we
pondered, *at length*, the relative merits of abandoning you,
returning to the Privateer and taking our chances on the
operation, so that we could win the freedom to escape this
place without the burden of yourself encumbering our
efforts. We weighed the merits of this course of action for a
long time, Wimfort. Do you understand my meaning? I am
in no manner joking.'

We marched on. I knew my speechmaking had bought
us only a morose and temporary silence from the boy. I
was undefinably uneasy, aware of a peculiarly sharpened
rancor toward the boy, and aware that my patience with
him was dangerously frayed, while at the same time I
acknowledged that, though intolerable, he had been no
worse than usual lately. Moreover, I deeply disliked this
zone we had recently entered, and yet so far it had been
remarkably free of dangers and difficulties alike.

I couldn't discover what it was about the place that had
my back up like this. It had quickly become clear that the
impossibility of precisely retracing the path of our descent
had resulted in the deeper penetration of an area which,
evidently, we had encountered only peripherally before.
And though this left the dangers of the leagues ahead an
unknown factor, at least the unfamiliar territories were
proving no more perilous than the remembered one had
been. Here, for instance, in these wet, pillowy fields of rosy
tissue, it was easy enough to fall, so ridged and seamed the
stuff was, so scalloped, wrinkled and whorled – but then it
was nearly impossible to suffer hurt from a fall on such
moist, blubberous ground. The prospect was wide and
unthreatening. Here and there from the twisted, velvety
billows rose huge buttes and mesas of the whitest, smooth-
est stone we had ever seen. Out toward the limit of our

vision the plains could be seen to grow smoother and paler, and to be thinly forested with some kind of growth.

We found that whiter zone to be sharply demarcated from the pink one. It was a wholly different material, tough and dry, and faintly resilient. And it was quite smooth, save for a system of shallow striations that printed on its surface vast, swirled patterns reminiscent of the wave lines the wind engraves on untrodden sands.

As for the treelike things that sprouted from it – quite sparsely at first – they were harmless things, but inexplicably repellent. Their substance – wet, purple twists of bundled fiber – resembled nothing so much as raw meat, thick strips of it all torqued and braided together in rubbery stalks and flaccid branchings. Pythons of translucent, silvery cord were complexly spliced throughout this treemeat, and their network corruscated faintly, with a rhythm roughly matching that of the trees' movement. For all these growths stirred vaguely in the windless air, and faint, intricate shudders of torsion incessantly agitated their limber frames.

The ground began to rise. The trees grew ever denser and ever bigger. As the sticky forest closed in above and around us, my oppression of spirit grew almost crushing.

'Listen,' Barnar said. 'Do you hear something?' I shook my head angrily, and didn't answer. I *had* been hearing something, a slow-cadenced booming – vast, but also soft, diffuse. The grade got steeper. We wound through the carnal jungle up toward what promised to be a major ridge-crest.

When we topped that crest, I saw everything in an instant – my own stupidity first and clearest of all. The land fell away before us in a broad, shallow valley more thickly forested than the ridge, and with a different growth – with black hair, jungle-high. Erupting from the valley's basin at its farther end was an immense mountain. Its crest was lost in the phosphorescent gloom of the sub-world's vaulted ceiling, but its smooth and tapered shape was immediately identifiable. One stark vein ran up across this mountain's face, and a swarm of aerial entities hovered near the vein at about its midway point.

It was the mountain we had been hearing, and whose thunder now rolled unhindered across the shaggy lowlands – a thrumming, buzzing knell: a sound as of a million bowstrings simultaneously loosed. Wonderingly, Barnar said: 'We've found – we are *in* – the Giant Sazmazm.' I nodded, still gazing. Then we jumped, our wits returning to us at the same moment. We whirled around. Wimfort was gone.

Though we failed to pick up his trail, there was at least no doubt about the direction the boy would be taking. He would be impossible to spot until he reached the clear ground at the mountain's foot, the very threshold of his lunatic desire. Seeking him en route in the giant's snarled pectoral pelt would be futility itself, giving the young idiot plenty of time to destroy himself – and thereby us – unhindered when he reached the perimeter protected by Sazmazm's tertiary slaves.

So down we went, and threw ourselves into the arduous, oily struggle, which was hard enough to let us hope that our greater strength would enable us to reach the mountain before the boy. Our bejungled approach denied us any chance to view the situation we were nearing. When at length we stepped onto clear ground again, we were in a scorched, war-torn zone, hideously heaped with the wreckage of war, and beyond these intervening dunes of dead, the visible part of the mountain bulked huge, fearsome in its nearness.

We stood numb awhile. Some high point had to be reached from which we could overlook this cyclopean disorder.

'The best thing seems to be to look at what we're dealing with,' Barnar said bleakly. 'And then try to anticipate where he'll choose to make his rush.'

I nodded, and another silence passed. I answered: 'If he has formed a plan at all, and doesn't just rush in on a blind faith in his luck.'

We sighed. All was speed now, but a melancholy languor was on us. Insistent despair, soliciting yet again our weary hearts, woke no more fight in us. We were almost emptied, and beginning at last to accept our destruction.

Glumly, with audible loathing, Barnar said, 'That seems to be our only adequate vantage.' He nodded toward the hirsute carcass of a gigantic slothlike beast that lay on a debris-hill of smaller corpses and their broken chariots of war. Somehow, we started walking toward it. 'Yes,' I said, we can climb up that spike it has strapped to its head.'

It appeared that the beast had died among – *upon* – its own cavalry. The eyeless, beetle-jawed apes whose multitudes underlay it had died in a wreckage of chariots whose prows projected great spikes identical in all but size to that the giant wore. These eyeless charioteers were small only beside their monstrous ally, for their vehicles were the size of galleons, and they, when standing, could have spread their nasty jaw-scythes and clipped the crow's nest off an Astrygal windjammer's mainmast.

The sloth's flesh, puddling in cheesy wrinkles around each huge shaft of its hair, stank. Dead fleas the size of yearling horn-bows lay half sunk in the charnal mire. We kept to the spine-ridge, which was a little balder of this stinking pelt. 'Corpse-fleas!' Barnar raged as we clambered past an ear, and stumbled onto the knoll-top of the cranium. 'That vile, willful little moron makes corpse-fleas of us!'

Death had frozen the giant's head at only a slight forward droop, and the steel spike strapped to his forehead jutted a hundred feet farther out at the half-vertical. We started shinning up the bright needle. Already we saw all we needed to, but we climbed mechanically, up and out, our eyes lost in what confronted us.

The dreadful grandeur of that monstrous, chambered muscle, shapely as a Shallows wine-jar, bottling the colossal vintage of the demon-giant's vitality, thundering endlessly with the stoppered power of these contents – it was more than a life of looking could truly take in. The great vein serpenting up its flank was itself a thing of awe. The pulse and volume of more than one mighty river charged through that gargantuan blue pipe.

And we now saw just how that vein was tapped, and saw more clearly too the genesis of those things which tapped it. A tough, glassy capsule both sheathed and vaguely displayed the fibers of the heart's underlying sinew. And all this inmost, toiling demon-meat was infested – riddled with encysted shapes, slimly tapered ellipsoids like sarcophagi of carven wood.

These could be seen at every stage of growth, in fluid-filled bubbles that slowly swelled with their growth, sundering the muscle of the giant's tortured, consenting heart. Ultimately the bubbles' swelling ruptured the heart-sheath. Everywhere across the living wall, stilt-legged, stingered monsters were to be seen wrenching their drenched and folded wings from broken natal husks. They hatched, they spread and dried their wings, they took flight, and moved toward the vein.

Around halfway up its length, at perhaps half a dozen different places, the vein had been clamped by vast brazen collars, each of which bristled with steel couplings. It was upon these couplings that the winged Regatherers converged. Each one in its turn sank its caudal barb into one of those sockets and waited as its hive-mates worked spigot-wheels, which diverted into its tail-bulb its alloted iota of the Master's blood. Not infrequently, the strength of the current they tapped mocked their precautions. Spigot-wheels would stick, and helplessly coupled individuals would claw the air with panicked legs, their bodies swiftly burgeoning, then exploding in a fine, red mist. Then every nearby worker flew crazily, lapping the bright spray from the air till others succeeded in reclosing the spigot, whereat – unfalteringly – another would take its turn at the coupling.

They had emerged only to drink in this manner, and, having drunk, each immediately set about the work of its return. Each engorged Regatherer began a steady, hovering descent toward the war-strewn flesh that floored this cosmos. Each settled on this floor in the zone closest to the heart and clearest of debris. Settling on this floor, each sank its jaws into its master's skin and chewed until its head was wholly buried. While its front end ate this anchorage, each monster's stern half compacted – its legs and wings folding up tight – and started a rhythmic convulsion. Swiftly, the folded body began to split. Now it was a husk. A great, shining maggot's body moulted from the husk and started worming its way underground after its sunken head. The obscene, ribbed barrel of its new body was little more than a cistern, a tiny-legged tank wherein to convey another jot of the tyrant back to his dominions. And though these grubs ate their way all the way under with truly sickening speed, their tapered body-casks did protrude defenseless for several minutes during the process of their descent. We came to this realization at about the same time.

'Hmph,' Barnar muttered. 'Notice the next-highest ones waiting their turn to settle down and moult – they hover on guard over their siblings while they wait for them to dig in.'

'Yes. Still, it has that first-glance look of feasibility. If the boy takes note of it, his eagerness will see it as a sure-fire tactic.'

Barnar nodded, somewhat disinterestedly. It was the spectacle as a whole that absorbed him. 'Such a labor,' he mused. 'Since the Red Millennium, did he say?'

'Yes.'

'Did they ever sing you that cradle song when you were small?' Amazingly, he began to sing me the song he meant. His frayed basso rendered the simple tune with surprising sweetness:

'. . . And that Neverquit bird, though small and weak,
Lights again and again on Neverend Strand.
And he packs into his narrow beak
One little bite of that infinite beach,
And recrosses the sea till he reaches that land –
That land of his own he is building to stand
In a sun-blessed place beyond harm's reach,
That land he is making with stolen sand
And a will that will not be denied what it seeks.'

It made me smile to hear those lines, which I knew, sung here by my friend as we hung there dreamingly, hugging the great sloth's spike-tip, looking rather like sloths ourselves, I suppose.

'And when they've regathered his essence,' I asked, 'when the Elixir's been brought below again? Though Sazmazm's spirit might live in the brew, what freedom will the titan have if he must lie in a vat, a bottled ocean of bodiless soul?'

'You know, I asked Gildmirth that question. He didn't have an answer. He'd heard a rumor that the giant's slave-hosts have long been at work building him a second body out of stone.'

I shuddered, trying to throw off the stupor that lay on me. 'Come on,' I said. 'We have to try. The effort is utterly pointless, but inaction seems an even greater agony.'

We shinned down the spike and repeated the verminous traversal of our dead host. We reached the major claw of its left hind paw and, with a leap, departed from its rankly meadowed slopes. We jogged toward the naked mountain, carrying our shields and spears at half-ready, watching for ambuscades – for we had noted that many of the giant dead surrounding us had been quarried for their meat. The carrion-appetites that haunt all battlefields most surely haunted this one. Mechanically we jogged toward the moulting grounds, near the heart of the thunder that filled this morgue-ish world.

And we had almost reached it when we came across a corpse worth pausing over. It was one of the stingered, stilt-legged giants, a dead Regatherer. A toppled siege-tower had, in falling, sunk a spur of its broken beamwork through the middle segment of the creature, which was the segment its legs and wings were jointed to. The spur had pierced it laterally so that the corpse lay on its side. It was huge partly in its great lengths of leg and wing, for its slim-built, tri-part body had perhaps somewhat less overall bulk to it than the hull of a mid-sized merchantman.

We took our lances to it, climbing to prod its body for vulnerable features. It was everywhere as supple as leather and as unpierceable as steel. Finally we stood near its head, looking up bitterly at its face. I saw in the black moons of its eye-bulbs, in the cruel barbs and shears of its mouth-tool, a pitiless amusement with our littleness, our urgent, dwarfish ambition to do its demon hugeness harm. In my gloom and mortification I contrived, unthinkingly, an excuse to hurl my hate against the thing.

'You see between its eyes and jaws that "X" of muscles, or nerves, or whatever they are? X marks the spot.'

I got a lot of run behind my throw, and heaved the stick up toward the alien planets of its extinguished eyes.

Instant death missed Barnar by somewhat less than a handsbreadth, for that was how far he chanced to be standing beyond the arc of the stinger's thrust. Whip-quick, the great, pinned corpse folded in half on the iron axis of its impalement. Its caudal barb stabbed forward with a force that imbedded it deep in the chestplates its legs were jointed to. I saw, above the spasmic working of its mouth-tool, the butt of my spear protruding from the softness it had found to enscabbard more than two-thirds of its length.

We did not risk the convulsions that might attend retrieving my spear, and found me another among the weapons so profusely littering that waste of carcasses and martial engines.

A short time later we were edging out to the limits of our cover amid the battle-debris, and viewing the more barren moulting-ground's vast perimeter. Looking out over the impossibly broad frontier we planned to prevent the nimble, determined Wimfort from crossing, Barnar burst out with a short, disgusted laugh. 'Let him be damned,' he said. 'He'll break cover where we can see him in time to catch him, or he won't. I'm going to sit here awhile, and sooner or later we'll find out which of these it is to be. To hell with everything else. I'm going to enjoy the simple pleasure of sitting still for as long as the opportunity lasts.'

I thwacked his shoulder consolingly, but couldn't come up with any comforting reply. I wandered around a bit, looking listlessly along the frontier. And, a quarter-mile or so down that border, across a little clearing that separated two large heaps of wreckage, a small shape moved. The movement was abrupt and dodgy, like that of a lizard sprinting from covert to covert. I was already running, half-crouched, weaving toward the place, keeping all the cover I could manage between me and it.

So fast I went, more flying than afoot! On what strength, drawn from where, I'll never know. I'd more than half reached him when I saw my quarry again – back of a last trash heap bordering the open grounds. There Master Wimfort crouched, and gathered himself for the spring. Just then he put me in mind of a young lion on a first kill.

There was that clownish lack of finesse alloyed with mortal seriousness in precisely equal measure. The boy was no longer, in strict truth, a boy. He was abundantly ridiculous, and he was also truly kill-ready. He had been at work on a weapon of scavenged parts. He'd gotten a seven-foot fragment of heavy spear-haft. He'd lashed a battle-ax by the handle to one end of this, and had spiked and lashed to the other the broken blade of a splendid sword – like a falchion, broad and razor-edged at the point. Around his haft's balance point he'd wrapped himself two hand-grips of leather cording. His strategy was plain from his weapon's design. This was no casting-spear – it was to be used like a jousting-lance, the ax at the other end providing an option of chopping blows as well.

Even as I studied him I neared him at a mute-foot sprint, praying for the few seconds' luck that would suffice to get me within range to outrun him before he could bolt far enough onto the moulting-ground to bring the titan slaves down on us. Four seconds would have done it, and of course, I didn't get them. He saw me, and without the shadow of a hesitation, leapt out on the wounded, wormy plain below the mountain. We pounded across that meaty resilience, our desperate drives converging toward one of the tertiary monsters lying in full moult a scant three-hundred strides ahead of me.

Alas! A scant two hundred and fifty strides ahead of Wimfort. But our ruin was already accomplished – I saw it then, though I couldn't curb the insane persistence of my legs' pursuit. The boy was oblivious. Still running at full tilt, he raised and couched his lance. Beyond and above him, a stingered giant hanging five hundred feet off the plain swung around to us the remorseless black globes of its eyes, and sank gigantically toward us.

The great abdominal cask that was Wimfort's target had thrashed itself clear of its parent-husk and gotten about half-submerged. Up-ended, it towered ponderously, rocking with its gluttonous labor. The boy, uttering a shout of rapture, drove his point full against it.

Obliquely, I noted his weapon's fragmentation, his collision with the grub, his stunned fall – foreseeable details. Primarily, I watched the Regatherer's dive toward the boy as I ran to intercept it. It loomed down, its spike drawn up and under, strike-ready. I vaulted up with the cast, flung myself into free-fall after it to put some heft behind the stick's flight. My eyes popped with the snap I put into the toss. My fall back to the ground seemed almost leisurely as I watched my spear take root, watched the giant's dive become a death plunge as it folded convulsively in the air and sank its stinger hilt-deep in its own swollen underbelly. I tucked my head, hit the ground, rolled to my feet. The Regatherer's cargo spilled in black cascades behind it as it tumbled toward its ruin. I ran toward the boy, stumbling once at the shock of the giant's fall.

The Regatherer's torrential wound had drenched him, yet he was almost dry by the time I got to him. Not from that black brew's running off him, but from its soaking into him. It drained into his skin as quick as water melts into dry sand. But his hair was still half soaked, and in picking him up, I slipped my left hand under the back of his head to support it, and the demon blood sizzled on my palm.

I had to put him down again – he was coming around in any case – and dance around trying to shake the pain off my hand. The stuff couldn't be rubbed off; it burnt me for a bit, and then it became a painless black dust which I blew on, and was cleansed of. Yet I must testify to an unnatural thing the Elixir bred in the part of me it touched – for since that occasion I have been what I never was before – perfectly ambidexterous, and have long behaved right-handedly from habit only.

Seeing the boy gain his feet, I seized his arm and hauled him back toward the cover of the battle-zone's mortuary maze. He promptly had his legs well under him and was running with a will. Having what he sought, and craving to get it safely home, the boy now became scrupulously cooperative. At least two Regatherers were moving toward their fallen sibling already, and scanning around for an enemy. I told Wimfort where to dive and he did it instantly and flawlessly – under a toppled chariot. I flung myself supine on a heap of relatively anthropoid dead, and ceased to move.

We were not discerned – the stingered giants were soon patroling the area in force, but not knowing what they sought, they seemingly spared scant lookout for things of our order of magnitude. How many whales ever die of fleas? And once a second squad of Regatherers had completed our victim's obsequies – completed that is, the lapping-up of all that its broken belly had spilled – these patrollers retired, and returned to their hovering-places above the moulting-grounds.

Just as we were setting out to find Barnar, he came stealing into the clearing. Together we guided our now obedient charge to a clearing farther back from the unspeakable mountain. Barnar had seen what had happened, and we found nothing to say to each other. We sat ourselves down, not knowing what else to do. Listlessly, I began a minor repair of my boot-binding. My friend sprawled back against a broken battering-ram. He balanced his ax on the toe of its handle on his finger's ends. He would hold it upright awhile, shifting his hand to keep the balance, and then he would let it fall forward through one full turn and bite into the cheesy white world-floor – into Sazmazm's vastly mislaid skin. Then he would pry it free, and repeat the process.

For a while, Wimfort poked around cheerfully in the debris, savoring his deed, his successful rite of passage into the pantheon of heroes. He sang, he whistled, he whispered to himself, like a carefree child gathering shells in a beach.

But soon his exaltation began to fill him, swelled in him unendurably. Big with the sense of being already in possession of everything the Elixir could obtain for him, continued calm became a visible agony for Wimfort. He'd been poking with a mace he'd found among a heap of armor, and muttering ever more feverishly. I saw him pry out of the heap a particularly fine piece of work – a brazen shield, graven with a stylized earth-wheel surrounded by astronomical symbols. I thought he was going to try its weight. Instead, he began to hit it with the mace. Each blow released an even greater shout of triumph from him. He danced like a demon, whooping and smiting the shield till it rang like a gong, marring the artful metalwork. By the time Barnar had wrenched the mace from his hands, he was entirely transported. He grinned unseeingly at us, who were at that moment in his eyes but two more of the legion of scoffing oafs who had long mocked and thwarted his ambitions, and who were now, with the rest, about to witness his vindication.

'*Ha*!' he shouted. '*Ha*! *Now* who's going to be laughing, and who's going to be gnashing his teeth, eh? How's it going to be *now*? What about the jabóbos, hey my friends? Do those slimy Priors *argue* and *debate* with us about our ancestors' sacred herds? Do they presume to *tell* us who our herds belong to? Will they still presume, now that there's no tract of earth I can't encompass with the mere spreading out of my ten fingers here? Oh, mark me now, my friends: Let my return be on First Market Day; and if that's the day I get back home, then on Second Market Day, let them step outdoors and look about their country-side, and see if they can find anywhere in all Prior Kairnlaw one jabóbo, one blade of grass, or even one muddy stream-let in all their parched dominions. They won't find any of those things – but then, they won't even get outside their doors to look for them either. Because before first light on that same morning, their own swords will jump from the

269

scabbards on their wall-pegs, and hew them all to pieces in their beds, and spare not a babe or a greybeard among them!'

There was more, much more. When his histrionics ceased to be dangerously loud, they abated nothing in intensity, and we sat down again, unspeakably melancholy, and let them roll through our ears. There was a lot about Kine Gather's great future as its nation's capital of rivers, prime pasture-land, and jabóbo herds. There was a good deal about which of Kine Gather's sister cities would share but subordinately in her fortune, and expiate their various crimes against her with shovel-work in her offal-yards. Following this, there was abundant information about every folk or city the wide world over which had ever had dealings with Latter Kairnlaw, and about how their fates were to accord with their treatment of his beloved fatherland.

We sat morosely as this wealth of data was lavished on us. With our eyes we questioned one another, and saw no answers.

XIX

Freedom! That belabored word! It is a big, empty word, and yet, when some experience reminds us what freedom is, how clear and particular its meaning becomes, how unspeakably sweet, and full! I once had the experience of walking up to that word, and gazing into its measureless amplitude, upon all that it contains. I could see the word as I approached it – it looked like a small, raggedly square patch of blue. I walked through a stony, steel-paved dimness. My mind was mostly numb, with little more than one idea in it, which I muttered to myself for my own instruction: 'That is freedom.'

I kept walking, and as I got closer to the word it began to fill out. A minute blackness swam into the blue patch. Its shape told me it was a hawk, and its size – in telling me its distance – reminded me of the depth of that blueness. With a pang, I remembered that depth.

'That is the sky,' I pointed out to myself. I began to walk faster. Beyond the hawk – far beyond – was one small, gauzy scarf of cloud. Steadily I approached. Distant mountains sprouted from the bottom of the sky's frame, then the intervening plains unrolled toward me from their feet.

And then I stood on freedom's very doorstep, and looked directly into it. It was made of stone and sand and tough, green scrub, and was studded with blunt, grey mountains on whose crests unmelting snows lay, sugar-white. And over these lay a blueness so deep and rich you felt it like a chill down to your bones. Across all of this the winds moved at liberty, and these winds were inhabited by japes and corbies and hawks and crooked-winged finches.

'The thief! The lanky one! He's back!'

The garrison, all rousing at once to the soldier's cry, swarmed to assemble. I nodded to myself. The thief, the gaunt one, *was* back, and the thick one too. I believe I beamed down at them one brief, idiotic smile before I went back to beholding freedom. I viewed the inching movement of a herd of horn-bow being driven across a stream out on the plain. I noted the low, tender hum the wind made crossing a patch of dry spar-grass just down the slope from Darkvent. And, observing that the sun was westering toward a fragile net of cloud-wisps on the horizon, I foresaw the red-and-gold fire-trellis that would frame its setting in half an hour or so. After these few brief discernments, it startled me to find that the garrison was all mounted and drawn up a few yards below the shaft-mouth, with Charnall and Kamin mounted at their head, and Kamin looking as if he'd been waiting awhile for my attention. The necessity of focusing my attention on the Rod-Master caused me to heave a deep sigh. I did it unthinkingly, and the moment after, realized its agonizing ambiguity to a father all coiled up to seize on my first expressions for the report of his son's fate. I almost smiled.

'We've got your boy back for you, Rod-Master.'

Perhaps some private resolution had frozen his jaw till I should speak the first word, for it thawed now and his lips parted. Still, nothing came out of them.

'Hello, Charnall,' I smiled. 'How does it go with you, my friend?'

He looked absently into my eyes, rubbing his baldness gently with his left hand, as if to force into his brain the reality of my return.

'We knew you were near,' he said slowly. 'I knew it through the Life-Hooks.' Suddenly, he smiled back at me. 'Didn't I foretell it? Didn't I have a feeling about it? You *found* the Privateer of Sordon Head?'

'We did indeed. He is a rare man, Charnall. A great man.'

'Yes. So I thought he must have been – must *be*.'

'Show me my son!' It was a choking roar. We looked at Kamin. His beefish face was congested with rage. He thought we were playing with him – that there was nothing else in the wide world but his particular concern to occupy anyone's mind. So like his son he was! But his concern, at least, was for someone other than himself.

'I'll show you your son,' I told him quietly. 'And only that – show him to you. When our Life-Hooks are removed, your men withdrawn and our payment arranged before us, when these things are done, we will release him to you.' I turned, and called back down the shaft: 'Barnar! Bring him out to the light!' I turned to Kamin. 'Come in, you and Charnall. You can bring two guards for your person if you distrust us, but no more.'

I almost laughed at the needlessness of the last admonition. Kamin had to use his most compelling scowl to get even his captain and one other man to attend him. I led them in, and felt them grow tense behind me when they heard a rumble welling out toward us. I led them a few strides within and bade them halt. We watched a murky bubble of torchlight rise at us from Darkvent's gullet. In the bubble was Barnar, the torch in one hand, and his other hand on a rope across his shoulder. Beyond him you could just make out the ore-cart he was hauling up the gentle grade.

He stopped a short distance from us, lashed the rope to a beam, and waved cheerily to Charnall. To Kamin he said: 'Here's your boy, Rod-Master.' Holding his torch above it, he reached one arm into the cart and sat the neatly trussed boy upright on the shredded cable we'd packed him in, so Kamin could see him plainly.

'Father,' the boy said.

Barnar drew his sword. 'And here is our safeguard against any treachery you might intend. Note the tautness of this rope.' He laid the sword's edge upon it. 'The slope here is gentle, but constant. In a few seconds he would be rolling right along. Farther down, the pitch grows exceedingly steep.'

'Before anything else,' I said to Kamin, 'the Life-Hooks. Here and now.' The Rod-Master nodded to Charnall. The mage plucked from his tunic a bit of parchment which his lips voicelessly rehearsed before he set his hand to my chest and spoke the spell. I did not despise this in him. On the contrary, in matters of sorcery give me every time the careful plodder over the slap-dash man. I felt a terrible pain which at first made me think I had been betrayed. It was the Hook coming loose from my heart like a rusted-fast spike from dried wood, and I recognized what had seemed agony to be an intense pang of relief. When

Charnall had done the same service for Barnar, my friend took the control-ring from him and pocketed it.

From the mouth of the shaft, I showed Kamin where we wanted beasts with our gold and weapons drawn up, and how far off his men must be deployed, before we'd let him lead his boy out of the shaft. The Rod-Master didn't move at first. He looked at me with hate and scorn. 'How cooly you carrion-birds barter with the life of a defenseless boy.'

I was paralyzed with rage myself a moment. All that I might say to him surged into my throat, and died away there, since I knew its futility. At last I said: 'I tell you this, Oh Rod-Master, and no more than this. In paying what you do, you underpay us shamelessly. I do not cavil – we asked as much as we could carry and still outrun you if you proved treacherous. I don't expect to convince you, but I simply tell you, for the record, we shall always consider you and your people to be greatly in our debt. And now, let us have done with one another, for in all truth, I loathe the very sight of you.'

Stolidly, Kamin turned, then checked himself and, as if in afterthought, disdainfully waved to Charnall his dismissal. The mage jumped up, clicked his heels in the air, and then solemnly bowed to his former captor. Kamin strode out into the waning light – all red and gold on the hillside – and the three of us, as from another world, watched his arms waving and his soldiers dispersing to his will.

Then Charnall looked at us. 'I do not believe you have done this,' he said. 'And I never really believed you could do it, save in brief flashes of irrational excitement.'

'We've just had a great deal of irrational excitement,' Barnar nodded. 'We'll tell you about it on the way to Shormuth Gate.'

Charnall nodded, smiling. 'Shormuth Gate sounds just fine.' He turned to notice the boy then, and made a half-step to approach him. I stayed him gently.

'Best not, my friend. He is in a serious kind of shock – as you might imagine.'

The mage's face darkened. He nodded gravely. 'It was something I thought of when I went so far as to imagine you might find him. How ... *much* of him, psychically speaking, you would be able to bring back after he had suffered such a captivity.' The three of us regarded the boy, who sat in the cart and stared back at us, his eyes dark and frightened.

'We've brought you back as much as you see,' Barnar said solemnly. The answer grieved the mage. It startled me – though I had never doubted the man's bigness of heart – to see his eyes fill with tears just short of spilling over. He brought himself a little straighter and cleared his throat, sighed and wiped his eyes briskly on his sleeve. 'I remember,' he said, 'once having a particularly clear thought about the boy. He was, at the time, unwillingly practicing his High Archaic hand by copying over one of the spells I had just procured him. If he had a copy of the spell and knew how to read it aloud, he had all he needed, he would tell me. He saw no point in learning how to form the letters on the page.

'So I was watching him there. He sat hunched over, scowling closely at his hand as it performed the detested calligraphy, and the thought came to me: He carries selfish ambition almost to the point of selflessness. And now, poor boy, he is selfless indeed.'

I squeezed Charnall's shoulder. 'Don't feel so badly. The boy's full self persists, undestroyed, although the rigor of his experiences may have rendered it remote from us at present.'

The sun had set. The movements of men and beasts, framed for us in Darkvent's mouth, seemed – in the gold-shot cerulean light – a kind of swimming, as if the frame held a window into an immense tank of oceanic light. Their liquid jostling began to show pattern – the mounted

275

forms retired, and a rank of riderless beasts remained, hobbled together near the shaftmouth. Three of them were saddled and had packets of arms lashed to their pommels, and the rest were saddle-bagged, and tight-legged with the strain of heavy loads.

I nodded to Barnar. He lifted the boy from the cart, cut his bonds, and brought him to stand between us on Darkvent's threshold. Kamin was already climbing toward us. We stood aside from the boy and urged him forward.

He stepped out uncertainly, seeming to cringe from the open air, as if it was thronged with harmful presences. 'Father,' he said to the man who sped to embrace him; his voice was small, its tone wavering eerily. 'I was with the Bonshad, Father. I was his. I breathed the water, and all the black smoke that was in it.'

Kamin reached him, grasped his shoulders. Strangely, the boy was not looking at him now, but at the full moon which had just risen from the ridgeline directly opposite the still blood-smeared zone of the sun's vanishing. His father, frightened by the oddness of his look, embraced him.

It was an embrace from which the Rod-Master quickly recoiled. The boy's limbs never stirred, but his whole frame made a terrible, fierce movement, a growth. His body swelled to almost twice its mass, and lost an inch of its height. His eyes grew bigger, his mouth sank within a pale, brambly beard that sprouted twisting from his jaw.

Kamin took a slow, staggering backwards step; his soldiers, across the dale, reached uncertainly for their swords, all of them watching Gildmirth as he drew a dagger hanging from what had been Wimfort's middle, and slashed the front of the boy's doublet to give himself breathing-room. Then, reaching behind him, he made two vertical slashes in the fabric covering his shoulders. The Privateer, turning his plum-red eyes to Kamin, then smiled courteously, and said: 'Be at ease. I'll do none of you any harm.'

Kamin lunged, and his soldiers started forward. Gildmirth raised his left hand, and all of them froze – the very beasts they bestrode became as stone. Kamin's sword, which his arm had been in the act of swinging forward, spilled from his petrified fingers. Barnar and I signed Charnall to follow us. We went down to our pack-train, got him mounted, and mounted ourselves.

Gildmirth stepped close to Kamin, whose eyes alone could move. Those eyes blazed – they all but *clawed* – at the hideous face that had usurped the face of the boy.

'I am heartily sorry for you, Rod-Master.' The bloody pools of his sad eyes looked more than deep enough to contain the Kamin's outrage. 'Your son was rescued in good faith, and brought halfway back to you. And then an accident endowed him with a large quantity of what he had been seeking all along – the Elixir of Sazmazm. Rise if you can for an instant above the terrible pain I know you feel. Fight for the detachment to ask yourself: would you bring the Great Plague to the cities of your fellow men? Would you be the man to do this, even supposing that this deed purchased the freedom of someone dear to you – of a son? Would you make such a fool's bargain, and buy his release into a world universally blighted by your act? Liberate him into a raging inferno of catastrophe that has been enkindled solely by your loving emancipation of him?'

The father's eyes wavered, seeming dazed by these words. They sharpened again. They explored the face of the Privateer, wonder and loathing shining from them. They said, as plain as words: 'You are not my son. You stole his chance of escape from him. You are here in his stead.' Gildmirth sighed, and patted his shoulder. He turned away and, his eyes rediscovering the moon, forgot Kamin – instantly and completely.

I roused my mount, and came around where Kamin and

I might look eye to eye. I said, 'I'm sorry, Rod-Master. Truly I am. We got him out for you – and we only did it through the Privateer's help, which he gave us gratis – we got him out, and all but got him back to you. And then, in an evil moment, your son became something which – listen. If Wimfort had simply *resided* in your city, undertaking none of the cataclysmic things he planned – if he had simply *stayed* here for the space of a day, possessing what he possessed, then your precious Kine Gather, by the second day of his residence, would have been nothing but a smoking blister, a black death-scab on the face of a total desert. Such are the powers of those whom your son's booty must inevitably have brought down upon himself and all near him.'

I faltered, searching the magnate's eyes for some way to break through his hate to his dispassion. Barnar geed his mount up the slope, and into Darkvent. Kamin's eyes followed him, and so I watched with him, as all the rest of us save Gildmirth were doing – fettered and free – and so fixedly there was nothing to choose between the two groups.

A grinding noise began to swell from the shaft. Barnar emerged, a line stretched taut behind him, his mount's legs etched with effort. He spurred the beast down the slope. Just as the cart he was towing came plunging from the shaft, he cleared his pommel of the line, tossed it free and wheeled leftward from its line of fall. The big steel box turned turtle as it dove. It crashed just above us and settled crazily on the glittering heap of its vomited cargo: a hillock of barbarous splendors – subworld artifacts of wrought gold and everbright, weapons scabbed with jeweled onlays, gear and gauds of rarest demon-work.

I sighed, mortified by the inadequacy of the gesture. Unwillingly, I met Kamin's eyes again: 'It's yours. Twenty times the worth of what we take from you on these beasts. Your bullion is enough for us, and its portability is a convenience, for which we thank you. This doesn't buy

278

your son back, I know. Take heart at least in the fact that, though he is a thrall, he suffers no torment. He lies like a . . . wine bottle in the cellar of a minor demon, a reclusive weft. This keeper of his hides and secures the boy with fanatical care, you may be sure. Wimfort suffers at worst an endless ennui, as a jar for his master's most treasured potation. Meanwhile the boy, who couldn't safely be returned to the sunlight, has at least restored to it a man of great and deserving spirit. He's one whose liberation will surely bring men more good than harm.'

'Some day,' the Privateer said. 'I'll bring him back for you, Rod-Master. But when – forgive me – I cannot say.'

In facing round to say this, Gildmirth turned his eyes from the moon for the first time since it captured them. His cheeks were wet. The red of his eyes had a terrible, vivid purity I had not seen before, and, in some subtle way, his body was quieter. 'Master Charnall,' he said with a slight bow, 'I have spoken with your friends of you. There is a certain post which, before very long, I will be seeking a man to fill – that of scribe-apprentice. It requires a mastery of High and Paleo-Archaic, as well as the five primary branches of Runic scripture. Would you perhaps be a man of latent ambition? The post involves a great deal of work, but is handsomely paid both in gold and in advanced instruction in major thaumaturgies. Do you have some spit left, honest Charnall, for grueling and chancy work if it offers you the power to walk the sky and the ocean's floor as easily as you could these hills we stand in?'

'Yes, Privateer. And again, yes.'

'Then, after a time, I'll come seeking you in Shormuth Gate. This gold will maintain you opulently until I come. In the interval, you can do no better than to read – anything and everything, though always bearing in mind that neither Ninefingers nor the immortal Pandector ever fails to repay a thoroughgoing review.'

The Privateer turned now to Barnar and me. 'So now

it's time to part ways,' he said. As he smiled into our eyes he raised his right hand as for oath-taking. 'Let it be witnessed, by all the powers that bind men to their vows, that I salute as my saviour this Nifft, called "the Lean" (and justly so as anyone will swear who's seen what a weasely, gaunt oddity he is); and that I likewise most feelingly salute this Chilite hulk, Barnar his name, whose measure of ungreedy goodwill is more than great – who is a cask, a very *vat* of that . . . elixir. And also let my promise to them be witnessed, that my life will never be worth more to me than their salvation, whatsoever danger I might chance to find them in.'

As he turned away he paused by Kamin, but whatever he meant to say could be seen to die on his tongue, and he murmured only: 'Be of good heart. You'll find yourselves free to move at sunrise.'

The Privateer walked away from us now, out onto the open slope. As he walked, his back swelled, and his legs wasted and shriveled under him. But instead of falling, he thrust from the slits he had made in his doublet two broad, tar-black wings. The wings bowed, then pressed down powerfully on the night air. His legs – talons now – tucked themselves up under his chest. He half-turned his griffon's head and sent back to us a brazen hiss of farewell. And then the Privateer rose up against the moon, and sped from our sight in its direction, as if its silver hugeness were the home he had for so long been denied.

Part 4

Shag Margold's *Preface to* *The Goddess in Glass*

Perhaps the only pertinent information I can offer about the source of this document is that I am not its author – for some of my acquaintance have charged this, on the grounds, I suppose, of my own brief appearance in it. Who its author was, or even when and how it came among my papers, I do not know. Nifft himself could have secreted it in my (securely locked) files, but so could a number of our mutual friends. Certainly none of them lacked the particular skills requisite for such chicanery, and neither the manuscript's style, nor its hand – some scribe's of indeterminate nationality – offers any clues to its authorship.

As to what it reports, there must by now be few who have not caught wind of Anvil Pastures' misfortunes, and many will doubtless find here much to render comprehensible what must have seemed an utterly fantastic and unaccountable rumor. Perhaps it will seem callous in me to say that I do not grieve for that city. My feelings about merchants of war are made plain enough. I think, by my prefatory remarks to *The Pearls of the Vampire Queen*. Even granting this prejudice in me, I doubt any informed person would deny that, among purveyors of arms, Anvil Pastures' commercial history has been the most shameful of the century. So decayed are the morals governing the professional activities of merchants of arms, that the mere simultaneous sale of arms to both belligerents in an ongoing war is such a matter as only the ignorant or naive would take the trouble to deplore in print. Witness the offhandedness with which Anvil Pastures served Hallam and Baskin-Sharpz. But the records of Anvil's activities afford more than one instance of what even the most cynical cosmopolite would blush to countenance. I will presume only so far as to remind the reader of the most publicized of these travesties to occur in recent decades. The occasion I refer to was Pythna's 'crusade' against the city of Taarg.

Pythna's posture in the conflict was undeniably laughable. She *is* an Astrygal, but one of the chain's cluster of small islands that is often called the Seven Little Sisters. The wizardry that prevails on Pythna – as on any of the Little Sisters – is by no means comparable to that of Strega, Shamna or Hagia, for it is the thaumaturgy of the three mountainous Big Sisters that gives the Astrygals their deserved name as the world's great nursery of the lore of Power. Indeed, little Pythna is quite aptly described by Deenwary the Traveler in his otherwise sensationalized and distorted (though, admittedly, highly diverting) account of his experiences in the seas off southern Kolodria. 'The inhabitants of Pythna,' he says, 'are a motley, half-wise, half-crackpot lot.'

Pythna's much-trumpeted *causus belli* was also laughable. An edition of an obscure Pythnan philosopher's summa (all four volumes of which I have read, and which piracy of any kind could only flatter) was pirated by an equally obscure publisher in Taarg, to what end I have not been able to discover. And perhaps most laughable of all was the ambition which Pythna's seizure upon this pretext was meant to mask: to snatch some thaumaturgic renown and status by crushing a power so wormholed and rotten with invasive demon influences as Taarg. Pythnans, every half-wise crackpot of them, were tired of being little sister to Strega, Shamna, and Hagia.

One might smile, but perhaps only moderately, and then, reflect. Taarg, so near the Vortex that bears its name (see *The Fishing of the Demon Sea*) *is*, in the estimation of all informed commentators on the subject, and all those who have been there (and I am one of the latter, howbeit some might contest my being one of the former) – is, I say, eaten all but hollow by the demon influence that flows out with the rotten exhalations of the Vortex's ragged, spuming mouth. If crusades are to be mounted, whatever fools may mount them, let their blades be drawn against such a city Taarg was then, and to some extent continues to be. So I feel, at least, though the reader must, of course, side as he chooses.

Anvil Pastures entertained the embassies of both parties, exercising her traditional discretion, which spared either party the painful knowledge of its rival's entertainment. The Pythnans purchased from the Aristarchs a formidable weapon: a flock of spring-steel harpies, clockwork airborne carnivores guided by such basic spells as their field marshals could command, and able to scour the largest ramparts bare of defenders in mere moments. The Taarg embassy, with its demon-augmented coffers – and all the world knew the subworld source of those coffers' contents – purchased from Anvil Pastures a perfect defense against *any* aerial assault, for thus much had they divined of their enemy's tactical plans: a marvelously light, strong system of steel netting, erectable on a vast framework by spring-powered spreaders that could operate in mere seconds.

Taarg's fleet lay prepared for a counterassault, which it launched the moment the Pythnan assault had been crushed. The Pythnans reeled home with an armada quite large enough for a full-scale invasion scant miles astern. And indeed, the failure of its crusade against Taarg threatened to be followed directly by its homeland's invasion and conquest. Taarg's pursuing flotilla must, in truth, have offered a spectacle of grim majesty, for Dami-ergs commanded the flagships, and a century of their Galgath Assaulters stood in every prow. Before this many-hulled marine juggernaut Pythna's broken navy fled, lacking even enough lead once they reached home to blockade their harbor before the Taargian fleet broke through. And, as is widely known, Pythna was not then saved by any powers of her own, but by powers that came down from Strega. These latter, incensed that demon-kind should presume to touch their keels to any shore in the Astrygals, bent upon those invaders such attentions as shortly sent them wheeling and bleeding straight back to the Vortex, and back down its clamorous throat.

But whatever one's views on these matters, and on the proper apportionment of blame between those who resolve to make war and those who, by supplying the needs of the former, effectuate their sanguinary ambitions, I hope there are few who would dissent from calling one historical consequence of Anvil Pastures' fate a good one. Shortly after Anvil's catastrophe, the trade war between Hallam and Baskin-Sharpz ceased, and the belligerents achieved a composition of their differences that has endured until the day of this writing, and produced a number of cooperative ventures that promise to usher in a new era of collaboration between the two cities' economic spheres.

If it is anything, the story of Anvil's disaster is a poignant illustration of the tragic insularity of consciousness that mankind is so much a prey to. The extant information about Anvil Pastures' remote past, while not abundant, is such that any man who spent a few weeks researching the matter in the proper places would be sufficiently informed that he would have found many of Dame Lybis's oracular directives to her townsfellows most alarming, and would have deemed their *fulfillment* of those directives to be downright astonishing. Moreover, my own compilation of these data, of which Nifft carried an abstract on his errand for me, was and is not the only such scholarly treatment of the matter available in the world, if one but seeks diligently for other scholiasts' productions.

The geography of Lúlumë's Southern Spur, where Anvil Pastures is located, is worthy of notice. The highly metal-rich composition of that great massif has been noted by many writers. The troubled waters of the Sea of Agon, for all the ceaseless power of their erosive assaults, manage only to emphasize the obdurate imperviousness to weathering of the Spur's majestic cliffs. These, as our nameless author tells us, are very little worn, for all the millennia of their endurance, and oppose an almost flawlessly vertical wall of more than five hundred miles' breadth to the ocean's futile siege. Several authors, the Learned Quall most reliable among them, report an ancient tradition that the Spur is not of earthly substance; that it is the remnant of a fireball which, in some immemorial era, fell from the stars upon Lúlumë's southern rim. There is at least a poetic felicity in this conception, for when, later, on Anvil's site that legendary foundry of star-vessels was built, it was said that the starry visitants seeking the services of the forge rained down upon the place in meteoric showers, lighting the night-buried ocean bright as day for hundreds of leagues in every direction. Fitting, that those cosmic mariners should have been refurbishing their craft with materials native to those trans-stellar gulfs it was their task – and triumph – to navigate.

Shag Margold

The Goddess in Glass

I

When the thief Nifft, of Karkmahn-Ra was near thirty (which side of it is not known), he had achieved the first plateau of mastery in his art. That is, his style had been defined but he still lacked certainty about the proper canvases for his efforts. He knocked around more than he worked.

And one summer when he was hunting hill-pig with Barnar Ox-back in the highlands of Chilia, a letter reached him from his friend Shag Margold, the Karkmahnite cartographer and historian. Margold, knowing that Nifft meant to strike out westward across the Sea of Agon when he left Chilia, entreated his friend to stop in Anvil Pastures on the Southern Spur of Lúlumë on his way out. Margold had an important treatise in hand, to which information on that city's primary religious cult would be highly pertinent, and he had enclosed a packet in inquiries he wished Nifft to give the oracle of the Flockwarden's shrine.

The most current news in the scholar's quarter of the world was that the city had for more than a year been enjoying a period of astonishing prosperity, resulting from a revelation made to the citizens by the goddess through her oracle. The city was supposed to have benefited throughout its history from similar benevolent theophanies on the part of the Flockwarden, and the present boom period in Anvil Pastures seemed an excellent time to make some respectful investigations of this matter.

So from Chilia Nifft took ship, some two weeks later, for

Anvil Pastures. He had already been aware of its prosperity. Anvil's weaponry had dominated the Great Shallows markets for decades, and quite strikingly so during the last nine months. Blades, body-armor, arbalests, seige-machinery – everything from byrnies to scabbard-chapes, and all of a superlative quality of steel both impossibly flexible and all but unbreakable, had been pouring from its foundries and forges at such modest prices that all competition on both sides of the Sea of Agon was overwhelmed. Nifft expected no trouble finding ships bound for that port.

But it did surprise him that the most convenient option that he found was a big Gelidorian troop-shuttle bound for the city with no less than seven hundred mercenaries requisitioned by the Aristarchs of Anvil Pastures. These troops included a large contingent of pioneers and field-engineers. None of these troops knew the city's object in retaining them, but they had other news for him. Anvil Pastures' luck had just recently taken a very nasty turn. One of the huge, contorted mountains flanking the city had suffered an uncanny form of collapse. Its peak had been fractured and the entire mass of it had for some weeks lain poised on the brink of a collapse that must utterly obliterate the city beneath it. The Aristarchs – the body of commercial oligarchs which governed the city – had beseeched the Oracle of the Flockwarden for some remedy to the civic anguish. The Goddess-in-Glass – for this she was called as often as Flockwarden by the mercenaries – had, through the oracle, declared that her aid in this crisis could be procured, but first the Aristarchs must, in pledge of earnest allegiance on their part, procure for the Goddess this sizable expeditionary force of first-quality professionals.

At the evening mess Nifft sought a seat by the First Captain of Pioneers, a man named Kandros, whom he had found the most concise and enlightening of his informants about Anvil Pastures' dilemma. By the time the grog ration went round the two men had exchanged a variety of anecdotes and philosophical perspectives, and had found that they rather liked each other. Kandros was a slight, leathery man, not quite forty, but with the eye-wrinkles of a desert tortoise, the wrinkles of eyes that had studied two eventful decades' worth of encampments, fortifications, seigeworks and battles. The hands that hung from his wiry arms were great knobbed and tendoned pincers. These big, hammer-knuckled paws which he seemed to move so seldom were uncommonly direct and neat in the movements they did make. Nifft sipped his aqua vitae and said:

'Kandros. Am I right in feeling that this company of yours presents an unusually strong component of engineers and sappers and the like, given the number of combat forces?'

'Quite right. We've conjected no end what place we might be hired to besiege, but we are too few to attack any city of real consequence. Besides this, it's hard to see what help for Anvil Pastures there'd be in the capture of some fortress or town.'

'Though the Aristarkion has engaged you, I gather that august body is as much in the dark about your precise commission as you are.'

'So I conceive it. The Aristarkion is not always piously prompt to fulfill a directive of the Flockwarden. For instance, more than a year ago, the Goddess announced through her oracle that her flock had returned to the world of the sun, and that – I quote exactly now – she must have them by her, every one, for it's long and long that they have been gone. The oracle asked, in the Goddess' behalf, for an expedition to bring her flock back to her from somewhere on the southeast coast of Kairnheim, where apparently they had re-emerged from some long burial under the earth. And the Aristarchs, after mature consideration, declined to undertake so great an expense for so vague a behest.'

'It would seem that the Goddess is forgiving. It must have been shortly after that refusal that she pointed the city the way to its recent bonanza.'

A certain watchfulness had entered Nifft's manner, as if Kandros' last remarks had a connotative undertone that he was not quite catching. The captain's reply was in a meditative voice.

'In religious matters, my understanding is that the city-fathers are somewhat inconsistent. When the Goddess gives them oracles that hint of profit, they are piously convinced of the deity's potency. There resides in her corpse a strange attunement to the earth, its deep and secret structures, and the oracles have preserved the secret of interpreting the Flockwarden's revelations, though their mysteries remain inviolate. You're right about the Goddess' generosity. Her revelation to the Aristarkion followed its rejection of her demand by little more than a week.'

Nifft was smiling absently at his cup. 'I get the feeling,' he said, 'that there is a certain irony in the city's state of affairs which you have yet to reveal to me.'

Kandros nodded, conceding. 'To someone not intimately affected by the situation it might be amusing that it was the Aristarkion's intemperate haste to capitalize on the bonanza the Goddess revealed to them which, through an unforseeable fluke, created the deadly flaw in the structure of the mountain which now threatens the city.'

Nifft and Kandros stood by the rail amidships. 'You know,' Nifft said, 'no matter how I tried to imagine it, it all sounded preposterous.' Gazing at the mountains surrounding the bay into which they sailed, and smiling, Nifft shook his head. Kandros nodded.

'Descriptions never convey it.'

'What is that jetty made of?'

'Steel, or something like it. It's called Pastures' Staff. It is a relic of the age of the Flockwarden.'

'Pastures' Staff . . . And how remote was that age?'

Kandros shrugged. 'It was when this bay was formed, and these mountains gnawed from the coastal massif. It was when these mountains were almost twice as high as you see them now, and far more terrible in their form.'

The Staff, jutting a quarter mile into the bay, was the spine of the harbor's system of docks. The gentle slope of the bayfloor submerged its seaward end, so that its full length was not determinable. Though entirely caged within the skeleton of masonry and timber that crowned and branched from it, the cyclopean axis immediately engrossed the eye, as though all that encumbered it – not quite as real as its immemorial metal – lacked the necessary solidity to obscure it. It drew the viewer's gaze shoreward, to its inland end, which the city's architects had incorporated in the foundation of one of the towers of the imposing city-wall. But once there, the eye again neglected the nobly-proportioned masonry of Anvil Pastures, and was drawn upward to the mountains that embowered the city.

Kandros was not given to fanciful turns of speech, and he had called the mountains no more than what they were – terrible in form. The Southern Spur as a whole was essentially one vast block of extremely metal-rich stone two hundred leagues in length, opposing huge, blunt cliffs to the Sea of Agon's troublous waters. Erosion had flawed and featured those cliffs, but nowhere really breached the general smoothness of their mighty wall. But at the site of Anvil Pastures something more powerful than the wind and the tides had torn into it – had gouged the deep embayment that was the harbor, hewn the rocky niche that was the city's seat, and chewed the continental buttress into mountains stark as a rack of bones, and stretching sixty miles inland in all directions. They reared up two miles and more with fearful steepness from the sea's threshold. They were gaunt, disjointed peaks. Something in their contorted multitude suggested pain and calamity.

Nifft said, 'I remember a certain battlefield I saw some years ago. The war had moved on from it two weeks before, and many cavalry had died in that engagement. It was a fiercely hot mid-summer. I remember those acres of sun-hardened, leathery carcasses, their crooked legs sticking up from the earth at every angle.'

Kandros made a mouth of wry assent, and nodded at the peaks. 'Imagine them twice this stature, their carving not yet softened by eons of rain and wind.'

The two men lounged on the rail absently watching the harbor as they approached their berth in it. They passed a pair of warships which, while ignoring in-bound craft, appeared to be stopping and boarding every outbound vessel, once it had cast off and pulled into the bay.

'Hallamese,' Kandros said in answer to Nifft's look of inquiry. 'Rather an amusing matter. Hallam is at war with Baskin-Sharpz, near the equator upcoast here on Lúlumë. I suppose you've heard of the conflict?'

'Yes. Hallam's on Moira, the next isle east of Chilia. A trade war, no?'

'Correct. You'd think the Sea of Agon big enough to share between them. Anyway, it turns out they only *went* to war because both had discreetly sent diplomats to Anvil Pastures and both sets of diplomats negotiated what they thought were exclusively advantageous arms contracts with the Aristarkion. So they find themselves at each others' throats, and each finds the other twice as well-armed as he had been gambling on. If their war wasn't going so hot and heavy the discovery would've made a truce between them and they'd have joined forces to enslave Anvil here, despite her mighty walls. Even as it is, this harbor is now a zone of truce for both belligerents. In a few days two Baskinon warships will probably arrive here to relieve these Hallamese vessels. There are to be no emigrants from Anvil, you see. They intend that the inhabitants of the Pastures will stay here to fulfill those arms contracts they so doubly sold. Naturally both belligerents have staffs of diplomats obligatorily hosted by the Aristarchs in the comfort of their own homes, and these diplomats keep a daily roll-count of all the city's rich and powerful men and of their liquid assets, to ensure that both remain at home. It's the only reason that splendid metropolis there isn't a ghost town.'

They regarded the ramparts under which they were now docking. Wealth and power radiantly incarnate – such were the hugeness and the resplendent masonry of the walls, as well as of the great buildings which, farther upslope within the city, overtopped them. Nifft, musingly, said, 'Pastures' Staff. Is that the name of that thing in the water, precisely? I mean, I have the impression I've heard it referred to, but pronounced differently.'

'No, Pastures' Staff is what I've always heard it called.'

'Well. Shall we share a maxim of wine while we're waiting to go to the temple?'

'I'll take you to the Hammerside Inn, but I insist on the privilege of buying the maxim.'

'That is kindly spoken, and gladly accepted.'

II

The wiry Captain was to join the rest of the mercenary commanders when they reported to the oracle of the Flockwarden to learn their commission. Kandros was of the opinion that Nifft's interview with the oracle stood a better chance of success if she first met him in company with the military gentlemen whose services her Goddess had enjoined her to procure, and Nifft thought this very likely.

'We probably have time for another of these before we

must leave,' Kandros said, hefting the empty maxim. He signaled the ostler of the Hammerside.

'Only if it comes from my purse this time,' Nifft said.

'Absolutely not. If you are obsessed with repaying me, you can do so on some other occasion.'

Nifft smiled thoughtfully. 'Very well. On some other occasion.'

'Your eye dwells on the fireplace,' Kandros said a bit after the fresh wine had been brought.

'It's odd to see one whose inner wall is of iron rather than brick.' Indeed, the wall glowed with the heat of the blaze. Kandros nodded with the satisfied smile of one who has achieved a calculated effect. 'It is in fact a far larger piece of iron than the little fragment of it visible there. That whole wall of the inn is built against it.'

'The Hammerside Inn . . .'

'I will show you when we go out.'

'So be it, oh thou military man of mystery.'

A large, sleek man in a fur-hemmed robe came into the common-room, his manner one of dignity in haste. He stood in the entryway, simultaneously clapping to summon the ostler, and scanning the room for him. The ostler was not overly quick to terminate his conversation with some patrons at a corner table, and when he came, exhibited only a perfunctory deference. Kandros nudged his friend and said, 'I think this fellow is from the temple.' Indeed, the ostler directed the stranger's eyes to their table. The smooth-faced could be seen to consider summoning them to him from their table, but something in their aspect decided the stranger to approach their table.

'Good afternoon, gentlemen. Which of you is Captain Kandros?'

'That's me. And you are Sexton Minor, are you not?'

The man nodded, looking both pleased and vaguely miffed, as if announcing his identity were one of his habitual pleasures. 'The shrine-mistress would have her interview with you a trifle earlier than she indicated. I told your fellow officers of this, and they asked me to bring you to the shrine. My conveyance waits outside.'

'Will you have a glass with us?' Nifft asked. 'It seems shameful to waste so much good wine.'

The Sexton's oily black eyes, resting on the maxim, plainly agreed. 'Dame Lybis bade me hurry . . .' He hesitated. His own words decided him. 'Bah! I'm her Sexton, not her lackey. Thank you, gentlemen.' He took a chair and signaled the ostler for a cup. With evident relish he decanted and sampled the wine. Kandros said, 'I heard from one of the other captains, friend Minor, that your shrine-mistress is an irascible sort. I hope she doesn't make the honor of your office a burdensome one.'

This sally visibly warmed the Sexton. He grimaced confidingly and leaned nearer his hosts, regaling them more liberally with the scent of his pomade.

'The honor, as you so graciously term it, is positively *onerous*. I thank the stars that I'm a near connection of Aristarch Hamp – through whom I have the sextonship – and that I can make some modest claim to civic position and consequence without it. My first cousin, in point of fact – '

'Indeed I have heard a great deal about you, Master Minor, and I'm pleased I have a chance to benefit from your knowledge of the situation here. I've passed through your city several times, but have to confess I have no deep understanding of Anvil's affairs.'

The Sexton nodded sympathetically, a great depth of understanding shining in his large, black eyes. Nifft refilled all three cups.

'One puzzlement of mine has never been resolved,' Kandros went on. 'Dame Lybis, for all her eccentricity, must be a priestess of genuine power, for is not the Goddess she serves, and speaks for, dead?'

'How could the Flockwarden not be dead?' asked Minor. 'Have you seen her?'

Kandros nodded. 'Precisely. And how then does Dame Lybis obtain her insights from the divine corpse? How do the dead, though they be gods, communicate anything at all?'

Minor smiled indulgently at his glass, and drained it with gusto. 'You must forgive my amusement, Captain, but your talk of divinity – though we call the Flockwarden a goddess – strikes me as naive. What is a god or goddess? The notion is so vague! Surely you are aware that the consensus of enlightened opinion holds these beings popularly called gods to be visitors to our world from the stars? Their alien attributes, their powers so incommensurate with our own, are the source of the mysteriousness which the cults make so much of. The Flockwarden while she lived was not unique, but one of many others of her breed. Her body has by chance survived the holocaust that killed the rest of her fellow-colonists on our world. Whatever faculties her kind possessed for reading deep into the structures of stone and earth are preserved in her body, and through some means the shrine-mistresses over the generations have kept secret, the dead alien's eyes – so to speak – can still be looked through, and some of her powers of geologic insight can, erratically, be tapped. You noticed that the Goddess' antennae extend forward, and their tips reach to a point quite near the surface of the glass block?'

'Indeed, it was as you say.'

'Well, the oracle's mode of communion with the Goddess is not known, since the operation is veiled, but it is generally believed that it involves placing her hands against the glass at just the aforementioned place. This action, by the way, is called the Solicitation of the Goddess. What passes between Dame Lybis and the Flockwarden is not known outside the guild of the shrine-keepers. You may be sure that many an Anvilian entrepreneur has put his hands

297

to the glass in the small hours of the morning, when the temple is empty, and strained to feel some million-lictor clue of the Goddess' posthumous knowledge – ' Here the Sexton raised his eyebrows in an expression of ironic self-communion. ' – but to no avail. But is this *divinity* we are dealing with here? Surely it is technique, historical knowledge – mysterious to most of us, surely, but mere technique, in essence, nonetheless.'

Nifft had refilled their glasses, and Minor paused to empty his at a breath, before concluding: 'Well, my friends, shall we go? Dame Lybis will be quite harsh if we are *too* late . . .'

As they left the inn, Kandros raised a hand to detain the Sexton, who was opening the door of their landau. 'A moment more, if you please,' he said. 'I want Nifft to see the Hammer.'

The pair had approached the inn from the direction opposite that in which Kandros now led Nifft. They rounded the corner of the tall, old building and Nifft saw that it adjoined a major gate in the city-wall. The wall was ninety feet high, and the gateposts more than forty feet higher still, supporting battlemented towers designed for the gate's defense against siege. But, while the left post's entire bulk was of massive stonework, the right post as well as much of the tower that topped it, was of a single piece, an immense block of iron, roughly rectangular in profile, which stood on one of its narrow ends. It was starkly distinct from the stonework that embraced it, and made the inn that abutted it – grand and venerable though that structure was, seem an inconsequential thing, hastily made, and destined to be dust when that immense ferrolith still stood unaltered by millennia of storm and sun.

And a hammer it plainly was, for from a point somewhat less than halfway up its height there sprouted a horizontal bar of iron which ran for more than half the distance to the wall's sea-ward turning – incorporated in the wall, yet seeming rather to pierce and destroy it than to contribute to its substance.

'And that,' said Nifft after he had gazed a moment, 'is Pastures' Hammer?'

'It is indeed,' Kandros replied, his own eyes dwelling on it with fresh awe and appreciation that contradicted his cicerone's role in this revelation. Nifft nodded, and looked to Sexton Minor, who had followed them round the corner, and who was not so nervous at this delay as he was gratified by Nifft's query: 'Forgive my troubling you with what must be a boring question, good Sexton, but I am not a well-schooled man, though your city fascinates me. This is called Pastures' Hammer, as who should say, the hammer of the Pastures?'

'That is perfectly correct, my friend, in every detail.' The Sexton smiled at the wit of his reply, and blandly awaited further droll questions. But the one which Nifft murmured a moment later, gazing at the mountains, appeared at first to baffle, and then to irritate him: 'It is hard to imagine terrain that looks less like pastureland than this, don't you think?'

Minor shrugged, frowned. 'No doubt, in the usual sense. Naturally, the city's name refers to the historical facts. The Flockwardens' herds were lithivores. Their grazings carved the bay and made these mountains where before there were only great cliffs of metaliferous stone. The flocks' excreta provided purified metal for the Flockwardens' industry, as well as a kind of coal to fuel their forges. These *are* pastures, though not such as horn-bow or jabóbos graze on. Please, gentlemen – we really should be on our way.'

III

Near its inland border, the city rose toward a central
eminence, a great table-topped monolith crowned with its
most august edifices. These surrounded a vast, colonnade-
bordered plaza, in which Minor's landau discharged its
three passengers. Minor turned to guide the other two
toward a huge, blunt-terraced building, the acropolis'
second-largest structure. Nifft, however, set out rather
dreamily in the opposite direction, walking a ways out
toward the center of the square, and stopping at the tip of
a jagged blade of shadow that lay upon the flagstones.
This was the greatest salience of a vast wedge of shadow
which the noonday sun printed upon the plaza, darkening
more than half of its upland side. Minor lifted his arm and
began to call some remonstration, when he and Kandros
saw the gaunt Karkmahnite lift his gaze from the shadow's
tip toward the megalith that cast it. The Sexton's arm fell,
and for a moment the three stood looking silently up at the
hammer of ill fate that overhung the prosperous city.

The half-destroyed – and potentially all-destroying –
mountain was so like its grotesque fellows that its condition
endowed them all with added menace. They would not
have lacked this quality in any case. The noon sunlight
blazoned forth the dynamic of their making, showing well
over half their material to be disparate metallic veins,
wildly torqued and twisted together, as if the varied metals
had once been molten in one cauldron together, and stirred
there by some cosmic ladle. This structure was the source
of the mountains' tormented and skeletal shapes, for it had
been gnawed into prominence by millennia of 'peeling' –
spiral quarrying of various individual veins, as well as of
the rock between the veins. This latter material was not so

variegated as the metals which it interleaved. Most of it was a dense, fine-textured stone of brownish black – the fecal coal, in fact, which Minor had mentioned. This had been as heavily quarried as any of the metals were.

The damaged peak resembled many others in having been so deeply scored that the intact veins supporting the mass of its higher parts were clearly discernible. At a place perhaps four-fifths up the mountain, just about where its 'neck' might be said to be, a large landslide had exposed the scrawny spinal veins holding up the massive, gnarled summit. The three twisted shafts of metal ore that did this looked surprisingly slight for the task, and indeed, had buckled under it – had bent to an angle halfway between the vertical and the horizontal, bowing titanically in the city's direction. Raggedly surrounding the point of breakage, a system of wood-and-steel buttresses had been built – colossal enough on the human scale, but pathetically inadequate to sustain the mass they encircled.

Nifft turned and rejoined his companions. As Minor led them toward the temple, Nifft murmured: 'Those supports. They must have been undertaken more as a psychological palliative than a seriously-believed-in preventive measure?'

Minor nodded sourly. Nifft went on: 'How big is it, in terms of the city? I mean, if it hit the city – or say, if it were just *set down* on the city – would it cover it?'

Minor gave Nifft a look of wide-eyed irony. 'Heavens no! It's been carefully computed, you understand. Look out there, down near the harbor. Do you see that little bit of shanty-town by that farthest corner of the wall?'

'That little brownish-grey patch, like huts of weathered wood?'

'Precisely! Well, if that – ' (he pointed at the peak without needing to look toward it) 'were set down here – ' (he spread his arms to indicate the city around them) 'then that – ' (he again indicated the little harborside zone) 'would be entirely uncovered. As for the rest . . .' Minor shrugged, as who should say that one couldn't have everything.

The pair waited by the temple's entry while the Sexton stepped within and conferred with one of the shrine's attendants. He came back out to report.

'The other officers are already within. Shrine-mistress Lybis is just now conferring with the Aristarchs. If you'll join the party inside she will be with you quite soon.'

Kandros nodded, but Nifft laid a hand on his arm and said, 'I wonder if Kandros here might be prevailed upon to indulge a bumpkin's curiosity and give me a brief tour of this magnificent acropolis of yours while we're waiting for the oracle's arrival.'

'Very well. Please be conscious of the time. The attendant just within will direct you to the Warden-shrine when you get back.'

When Minor had gone inside Nifft said, 'Is not the Aristarkion one of these buildings?'

'It's that one yonder.'

'Most impressive! Could you show me the interior of it? We might even be so lucky as to hear some of the priestess' remarks to the Aristarchs.'

Smiling slightly, Kandros answered: 'That would probably not be difficult. Though theirs is not strictly a public meeting, there are many galleries that should allow a discreet vantage on the proceedings.'

The Aristarkion was the only building on the acropolis larger than the Flockwarden's temple. For a seat of governmental deliberations, it was rather an open structure – an extensive, roofed system of porticoes and pillared promenades with a single great chamber, the Aristarkion proper, at its center. There was a broad and doorless portal in each of the chamber's walls, and thus from almost anywhere in the galleried periphery a view of its interior could be had, as well as a clear hearing of what was said under its echoing vault. Nifft remarked on this before they had fairly

302

mounted the steps up from the plaza, and Kandros smiled faintly.

'The design,' he said, 'expresses the oligarchy's upright-ness. The Aristarchs, you see, since they never allow considerations of personal gain to bias their legislative policies, have never had anything to fear from public audience of their proceedings. Besides, it's long been their custom to do the real work of governing at informal convocations in the privacy of their homes, and when they gather here it's usually to solemnize enactments whose awkward elements they have weighed beforehand, and worded in the seemliest, least troublesome terms possible.'

They found the corridors and forested columns surround-ing the assembly chamber were populous. Talk was sub-dued among all these strollers and loiterers. Most seemed to be listening to a woman's voice that came spilling out of the Aristarkion – strident, though not yet distinct to the pair.

'Nevertheless,' Kandros concluded, 'certain persons, under certain conditions, can oblige the Aristarchs to assemble here even when their sense of delicacy might prompt them to prefer a more discreet kind of conference. The forgemen's Guildmaster, for instance, can demand one session yearly to debate forge conditions. And the Goddess' oracle can convoke them whenever an important communi-cation from the Flockwarden seems to her to require it.'

They were making for the nearest of the assembly room's portals, and the voice of the woman within now grew distinct amid the reverberations it spawned among the marble shafts and pavements without.

'. . . because once again it's *money* I'm talking to you about, gentlemen. And you needn't fidget and squirm, because we've talked about money before – we talked about it a little over a year ago, for instance, do you recall the occasion? Anvil, Staff, and Hammer! What possessed you then, gentlemen? Our heaven-born Flockwarden, whom you all revere, whom you have thanked for a score of benefits within my term of service alone! – our Goddess asked something of us, and that led – did it not? – to this previous occasion I refer to when we also talked about *money*, just as we're doing now – you *do* recall the occasion, gentlemen? What's that you say, Director Pozzle? Forgive me but I didn't catch your remark – will you repeat that a bit louder, please?'

If any voice other than the woman's had sounded within the chamber, no peep of it had reached Nifft and Kandros. They turned into a promenade that approached the chamber's portal straight-on, and saw the speaker for the first time. She stood on a high rostrum, half-ringed by marble tiers where the Aristarchs sat. She was wild-haired, short. She had her fists thrust into the pouch of an apron, below which hung her shabby tunic, its skirts crookedly caught up with pins to mid-shin, perhaps to free the movement of her restless, sandaled feet. She leaned forward, her posture elaborately solicitous to hear Pozzle's alleged remark repeated, and even in this attitude, she paced, her impatient feet shifting her leftward, rightward, leftward. A florid man in the center of the highest tier shook his head gloomily. In a voice resigned to harassment he said, 'you're mistaken, Dame Lybis – I said nothing.'

'You said nothing? Oh, you mean just *now* you said nothing! I see! Because in last year's discussion about money you said a great deal – perhaps that's why I mistook you, for I thought you might be going to quote to us now the very elegantly worded remarks with which you *closed* last year's discussion. And dear me, but that *was* an effective little speech you made, Pozzle; one point in it I particularly remember. You were helping us to appreciate just how great the *cost* of bringing the Goddess' flock to her would be. You'd computed that, if the beasts of her flock were as big as she had indicated, then it would cost more to retrieve just one of them from southern Kairnheim than it would to construct three large public buildings. Very cogent, that was, a very telling way of putting it, especially since you gentlemen at that time were so eager to subsidize the building of a new guildhall for the forgemen – and heaven knows you had good reason for wanting to appease them, considering the remarkably creative ways you'd been putting their portion of the municipal revenues to work for yourselves! Ah me! How perspectives change! Each one of the Flockwarden's beasts would cost three buildings to bring home to her. And how many buildings will it cost us if, a second time, we do nothing? How many buildings are there in Anvil Pastures?'

She had, in asking this, turned aside from her audience, but now she whirled, fiercely re-confronting them. 'Note well!' she almost bellowed. 'Mark me, and mark what I do *not* say to you!' She grinned at them a moment, savoring the opacity of this admonition. Her hair was the color of dirty honey. She wore a kind of skull-net of wire. Long past containing her pelt, it was deeply sunk in it, and her hair thrust from its gridwork in soft spikes reminiscent of the half-erected feathers of an angry hawk. Her nose was, like most of her person, small, but strongly aquiline, and due to the neighborhood of her eyes – large, black, bright and restless – had the look of being a keen nose for trouble. Her compact mouth was delicately ripe of lip, and would have been sensual in repose, but it was always either tight with purpose or ironically awry. Both Nifft and Kandros, leaning against opposite sides of the portal, could be seen idly discovering within her tunic the womanly emphasis of her pelvic curves and the plump buoyancy of her little breasts.

'What I do *not* say,' she all but crowed, 'is that the Goddess intends to send us after her flock as the means to our city's salvation. I am the Flockwarden's humble servant – I do not presume to foretell her will. *But what seems more likely,* eh? And if she does send us to Kairnheim, what more

305

perfect reparation than that for your criminal stinginess a year ago, eh?

'Enough, then. I have but one thing of importance to tell you. You've commissioned the mercenaries, as she demanded. Thus much, at least, you've paid up, and without inordinate whining, I must confess. Therefore, beware lest you falter now. Whatever use she should direct you to make of them, see you do it and damn the cost. I'm going now to talk with their commanders. I don't plan to do any dickering or mealy-mouthing about costs. They are crack professionals from Gelidor Ingens. When they learn their task, they'll bid the highest figure that a reasonable and well-informed customer could be expected to pay for the work in question. And it will be your business, gentlemen, to accept their bid, and muster the funds for them with all dispatch. Since there's nothing more that lies in your power to do for your own salvation, then you must do nothing less.

'I will make the Solicitation in one hour. Please be prompt.'

IV

As the pair re-crossed the plaza toward the temple, they saw the oracle's litter already some ways ahead of them, and they quickened their pace. Nifft, watching the palanquin, smiled, saying, 'I like her manners.'

'Yes. They were perfectly suited to her audience.'

They walked. Nifft's eyes grew abstracted. 'Tell me what you know of the historical circumstances, Kandros. How was it that the flock came to be lost in the first place, and that it still survives?'

'They were lost in the same assault that exterminated the Flockwarden and all her race.'

'Competitive visitants from . . . abroad?' He waved sky-ward. Kandros shook his head.

'Men. Seemingly, this was one of our race's epochs of greatness. I've even heard that in those days men tolerated such visitants as the Flockwardens the more equably because they themselves had crossed to and colonized worlds not their own.'

'Hmm. But toward the Flockwardens, toleration ran out?'

'Apparently, greed supplanted it. It is said the colony here prospered mightily. One tradition has it that this was a kind of smithy servicing the great steel vessels that conveyed men and gods alike from world to world among the stars. At any rate the men of some neighboring city – then great, since vanished without a trace – attacked the Pastures. Such was their onslaught that the Flockwardens were obliterated. In fact, the Goddess in the temple yonder, having died in one piece, was unique. Hence her preservation – a kind of monumental trophy, I suppose. Anyway, the battle caused a tremendous landslide above the slopes where the flock were grazing. The beasts were buried en masse, and in consequence, the conquerors took command of a ghost-smithy starved of metal and fuel alike. But as for the flock itself, these lithivores needed no air, it seems, and burial was not death to them.'

'And so they fled underground? And since then have dwelt subterraneously, until their recent emergence?'

'Apparently.'

'And there was none with them to . . . shepherd them?'

Kandros raised his brows at the question, and Nifft laughed by way of retracting it. 'If you mean to suggest,' said Kandros, 'that a Flockwarden might have escaped destruction by burrowing down with her flock, you will have only to behold the Goddess within to know that hers was not a digging breed.'

At the entry they were met and ushered within by an

acolyte, an exceedingly elderly man who muttered and groaned faintly as he moved. As Nifft stepped into the Wardenshrine – an immense, softly lit room at the temple's heart – he faltered just perceptibly. Both the Goddess' form and her posture had the effect of making her hugeness seem to leap toward the beholder.

She resembled a titanic dragonfly. Her long, slender stern segment curved up and forward above the four angular archways created by her eight impossibly delicate-seeming, jointed legs. She filled the block of glass containing her, and this was at least six stories high. She had two pairs of antennae. Two were short and fanlike, intricate trellises that antlered her spheroid head just back of her faceted, pyramidal eyes. The other two were slender, plumate, and tremendously elongated. These bowed forward and down, their tips plunging to within inches of the glass surface at a point close enough to the floor to lie within the enclosure of a small cubicle of drapery. The drapes were at present drawn back.

From a postern near one corner of the glass monolith Dame Lybis marched, her hands still completing behind her head the knot of an embroidered fillet with which she had bound her brow. Coming to stand directly before the first row of pews, and plunging her hands into her apron pouch, she bowed gravely, meeting every man's eyes.

'Gentlemen, you are most welcome here, and that is putting it mildly. Please forgive a haste that might resemble discourtesy, but this isn't the time for a genuine conference. It's a chance for me to give you the outlines of our situation, and answer the most general kind of question, no more.

'So first: When I've made the Solicitation and you've learned the task for which we'll want to engage you, then set yourselves the most generous wage that fairness allows you. The Aristarchs will only remain cooperative if they are dealt with firmly and unequivocally from the start.

'Second: Though we don't strictly *know* the Flockwarden's will until I *have* made the Solicitation, I can't pretend to have the least doubt of what it is, and so I can acquaint you with the parameters of the task. For surely, the Goddess' flock is what she herself has wanted since the day their re-emergence became known to her more than a year ago, while they are also the only credible antidote to what ails our city.' Lybis gestured ceilingward without withdrawing her eyes from those of the mercenary commanders.

'So what is the flock? Its numbers aren't clearly known – hundreds, but nowhere near a thousand. They are giant lithivores. I gather they stand about knee-high to the Goddess.' (Eyes rose gaugingly. Each of the Flockwarden's legs had three major joints. The lowest was fifteen feet from the floor.) 'Their bulk is that of a good-sized whale. They are highly tractable. They've surfaced in the hills of Kairnheim's southern promontory – a region both so mountainous and so jungled that the Prior-Kairns have never troubled to annex it. This season it's a ten-day crossing over the Sea of Catástor. And before you start computing the number of crossings needed, know that the beasts are phenomenally tough-bodied, all but undamageable, and that they can live entirely without air. They can, in fact, be lashed together in groups of four or five, buoyed, and towed behind a transport of moderate size, which the while can be carrying one or two more of the beasts packed in its hold.'

She paused and raised her brows to invite remark. One of the infantry commanders, Menodon, murmured: 'Twenty ships could carry a hundred and forty a trip. Will we have twenty ships?'

'We'll have thirty-five. The Aristarchs can levy twenty from our own merchant fleets alone, and they'll willingly underwrite the procural of fifteen more from the Shallows or the Aristoz Islands.'

'Mmm. Forgive me, Dame Lybis, but you must let me rephrase some of your remarks in what I can't help feeling is a more accurate manner. Ages past, the remote *ancestors* of this flock *were* highly tractable to the commands of their *Flockwardens*' – he nodded significantly at the frozen colossus – 'but what we must deal with will be beasts which have never known either a Warden or her rule. In this rather different light, let me repeat a question you have already answered by implication. Will the collection and transport of these huge things involve any dangerous difficulty? Please be frank. We don't shrink from danger or hardship, we merely seek to assess it properly and price it fairly. Surely these nomadic, long-ungoverned behemoths will not be tamely tethered, marched into the sea, bound and dragged across it, without offering some opposition. With no offense intended, how can you plausibly promise such a thing?'

Lybis stood smiling serenely, hands restfully pocketed in her pouch, head slowly shaking a benign negative. 'You don't grasp the entire picture, my friend. Toil and difficulty there'll certainly be in crossing the terrain in question. Other claimants to the herd might also be met, and need fighting. These things excrete in purified form whatever metal they ingest, along with very high-quality furnace fuel, man, and if they're noticed they won't go unclaimed! But as for resistance to our will from the flock itself, we shall encounter none at all. For a Flockwarden *will* be commanding their obedience. What you might think of as the Goddess' voice will prompt their compliance through-out the expedition. For does she not speak from my mouth, and declare her will through my presence, and shall I not be with you? Though speech, in this case, will not be the medium, nevertheless her commands will be channeled through myself and the flock will feel them. And the latter's ilk, however long at large, are so made that they can never be impervious to a Flockwarden's behests.'

There was a fractional silence, in which all eyes posed a question which Lybis, by her smiling silence, benevolently challenged them to articulate, and then Nifft asked: 'With apologies, Dame Lybis, do the dead, then, not only reveal hidden treasures, and discover the remote emergences of long-lost beings, but govern expeditions as well, with hourly attention and providence?'

The Aristarchs had begun to file into the shrine, a subdued group. The priestess did not turn her eyes from Nifft's, which she studied for a moment with an air of speculation. Then she said: 'You know that the Goddess does the first two, sir. Whether or not you believe she can do the third is for yourself, and the rest of you gentlemen, to decide, before you accept this commission.'

V

The assembly was silent. Aristarchs and mercenary commanders alike studied the slack folds of the drawn Veil of Solicitation, which Sexton Minor had closed behind Lybis when she had stepped within it, and before which he now stood, awaiting the priestess' word that the Solicitation had been completed, whereat it was his office to unveil her again.

Though identical in their silent concentration upon those pleated drapes, the Aristarchs watched them with a queasy premonition of painfully large capital disbursements, while the soldiers' faces betrayed a covert complacency as they kept the same vigil. But given this difference of attitude, it could still be said that for both groups, the slightest stirring of the ceremonial curtain emitted the same ghostly sound – the subliminal music of five-lictor gold pieces hefted by the palmful, a melody melancholy to half its auditors, and dulcet to the other half. Meanwhile the eyes of the men in either group showed an identical tendency – whenever they forsook that pregnant drapery – to flicker upward at the coffined giant. Her great antennal bows, plunging to receive her dwarfish petitioner's query, were given looks of uneasy calculation. Seemingly, the Goddess' active sentience was being given some thought by the congregation. A caw of triumph rose from within the Veil:

'Ha! I knew it! And you shall have it, Mistress, on my very life I swear it! Ha!'

The Sexton's feet shifted; embarrassment marred the decorous blank of his expression. Near silence followed in which a very faint noise, a soft, erratic pattering and squeaking, was audible from within the Veil. Then Lybis cried: 'Her will is known! Her will be done!'

The Sexton, as his post seemed to require of him at the pronouncement of this formula, turned suavely to withdraw the Veil for the oracle's emergence, but he had no more than turned when the drapes flew apart – one of them rudely enveloping his head and shoulders – and Lybis strode out, holding a wax tablet and a stylus. The stylus she pointed vindictively at herself, while she hammered the tablet against the air at the assembly.

'Didn't I foretell you this, gentlemen? Eh? Didn't I now?' She stabbed the stylus into her hair, where it vanished. Then she patted the tablet against her free palm with a menacing smile. 'Harken,' she said. She read from the tablet, her voice dramatic, and clarion-clear:

> From ancient murder buried deep, like seed,
> A harvest has arisen in the sun –
> So men may reap what once they did lay down
> When they entombed the thing that sparked the greed
> Their murderous action had been meant to feed.
> In south-most Kairnheim murder is undone;
> If you do but restore to Anviltown
> Her lately un-killed issue, thus you'll speed
> The lifting of that doom that weights you down.

'Well, gentlemen?' Lybis burst out, as if astonished that they all sat silent after hearing this exhaustively foretold revelation. 'Can you really be so chill-blooded? So unmoved by heroic sentiments and cosmic phenomena? Come, you're all playing stoic, as men so love to do. One of you, at least, must show that he has heard me, in token for the rest of you, or else I'll think you're all deaf, or dumb, or both. Mint-Master Hamp! You sir! Let it be you, of estimable, agile-witted Aristarch! Come, Lord Hamp. What did you discover from the Goddess' utterance?'

The man in question, by allowing only a grey stubble to occupy the pate of his otherwise severely shaven head and face, had made the more manifest an unusual squareness of visage. Hamp regarded Lybis morosely, the glumness of his mouth complaining in advance that his answer was going to be mistreated.

'I entreat you, Lord Hamp,' the oracle urged, 'can't we dispose of the obvious with more dispatch? What did the oracle tell you?'

With the prompting of many supportive gazes, Pozzle's among them, Hamp cleared his throat, and availed himself of his jaw's massive hinge. 'Well, what she *means* essentially, as you predicted she was going to in the Aristarkion, is the interpretation that the way to solve the problem is to go and bring her flock back, which again as you were saying was exactly the same situation of a year ago.'

Hamp cleared his throat again, with a faint note of optimism engendered by Lybis' silent, thoughtful gaze. She shook her head slowly, still looking at him. She grinned. Her head tilted back and she emitted a big, braying laugh. At length she brought herself more or less under control.

'Oh, my dear Lord Hamp,' she said. 'Anvil, Staff, and Hammer bless us all! Mind that I don't say this disparagingly, for knowing you and hearing your views has always given me the liveliest kind of pleasure, but that's precisely the kind of cretinous irrelevance I've come to count on from you over the years. *Obviously* she wants the flock brought back home! What could be plainer? But does no one see what the *significance* of this will be, once it is accomplished? Why has her thought and will endured throughout the countless centuries of her death? Why has she always helped us? In short, why has she held this posthumous sentinel's post *all along*, if not precisely for this moment? The return of her flock to its home, the restoration of her world as it was when, anciently, men destroyed it? And whose luck is this? Who *inherits* those long-lost mountain-makers and mountain-destroyers and mountain-*miners* now? To think that we had to be *forced* to accept this staggering enrichment! So greedy you all are in the short term, so lazy and unimaginative!'

'Yes, *forced*!' erupted Director Pozzle. 'That's exactly what I'm talking about!'

'Eh? Have you been whispering to yourself, Director Pozzle?'

Pozzle had surged to his feet with an accusing finger thrust up toward the Goddess, but in the same instant that he struck this posture the huge countenance of the accused caused his legs to wobble slightly, and the voice to leak out of his throat momentarily, as if the Flockwarden's mute giantism confuted anything he could say.

'*Extortion*,' he managed at last. It came out muted, like a comic attempt at confidentially addressing the whole chamber without the giant's hearing. 'It's blackmail. We talked in the Aristarkion.' His challenging look elicited some uncomfortable nods and murmurs of support from his fellow Aristarchs. 'The Goddess *knew* about the deceptive support-vein – that it wasn't nearly as thick as it looked from outside. The lode she revealed to us lay *deeper*, and if she knew about *that*, she must have known about the support-vein we were counting on to – '

Lybis had held up her hand, and was nodding calmly. 'Lord Pozzle. The Goddess doesn't condescend to discuss her divine motivations with her humble servitor, but do you think I'm a fool? Isn't it more or less staring us in the face? And I will say to you what I told myself when I had the same realization: *So what?* Will *you* gentlemen undertake to punish her? And if she has seen how to make a mountain bow down above our city, surely she's the only one who can help us *decapitate* a mountain. Who else will you go to for help? But of course, the city's purse is yours to command. I will leave you to reach whatever agreement you see fit with our military friends here. Do let me know what you decide. I'll be in the atrium.'

Nifft followed the shrine-mistress from the chamber. 'Dame Lybis, could I speak with you?' He held out to her a string-tied packet of vellum. 'A very dear friend of mine in Karkmahn-Ra, a scholar of the highest reputation, sends you this. Perhaps you have heard of Shag Margold?'

Her brows rose and she took the packet. 'Margold? His *History of the Kolodrian Migrations* stands on the shelf of my most prized books. Why has he written me?'

'He's at work on a history of the world's most prominent religious cults. He's always followed yours with interest, and has gathered a fair amount of information on it.' Nifft paused, dropped his eyes, and cleared his throat. 'He's asked you a number of questions which he hopes you'll be so good as to answer for him, to fill out his account of Pa – of Anvil Pastures. Forgive my impertinence, but that's a charming ring you have on. Is that an anvil?'

'Yes.'

'It's a beautiful piece of silverwork – by the same artisan as made your staff and hammer?'

Lybis, whose eyes had grown rather remote, absently touched the latter two miniatures, which hung from a chain around her neck. 'I presume so. They are temple heirlooms, made long before my time.'

'Well. I'll be in the city for some time – frankly, I'm looking for a bit of employment – and perhaps you'll find it

315

convenient to answer Shag's letter in time for me to take your reply back with me.' Lybis nodded, not speaking. 'So! Thank you again. I think I'll go stroll around a bit and take the view from this marvelous plaza outside. Good-bye for now.'

Nifft had loitered outside the temple for perhaps ten minutes when the Aristarchs came out, and after them, the commanders – the former grave, the latter rather buoyant, in a decorous way. Nifft told Kandros to go on without him, and that he would meet him back at the quarters where the mercenaries had been housed. When he had been alone again for perhaps another ten minutes, Dame Lybis came hurrying from the temple, spied him, and made straight for him, wearing a rather strained smile.

'Still here, then? You know, I'm curious – have you read your friend's letter?'

Nifft straightened indignantly. 'Why – well, certainly not!' His awkward expression did nothing to repair the lack of conviction in his tone.

'Naturally not,' Lybis said. 'Forgive me for asking. You know, I'd like to express my admiration for Margold in some more substantial way than merely answering this. You mentioned you were looking for employment? You seem to be a handy and active sort of man – it would be my pleasure to secure you a commission on our expeditionary force, at an officer's pay, if that would suit you.'

'You are extremely kind! I would undertake it most gratefully and faithfully!'

VI

The expedition, being lucky in the winds, had crossed the
Sea of Catástor and found the nearest suitable anchorage
to their goal by the afternoon of their ninth day out of
Anvil Pastures, with seven hundred leagues of their journey
accomplished. To cross the remaining fifty miles, and then
re-cross it with the Goddess' flock in tow, took three weeks.

This sloth was, in part, due to the mountainous jungle
they had to penetrate with every step of their inland
journey. Partly, too, it was their mode of pathfinding. On
the open sea, the directive emanations of the Goddess –
her extended filament of sentience – though attenuated by
distance, reached unobstructed over the level seas. But
crossing the fern-choked gorges and vine-webbed groves –
following the narrow water-courses slick with mist, mud,
and moss that were often their sole means of traversing the
ridges that opposed them – here, Lybis was often forced to
diverge from this psychic connective to the point of so
diminishing her sense of it that she must find high ground
whence she could relocate its course, and correct their
tedious path accordingly.

And a third circumstance retarded them – the fact that
when they reached the flock, they found an army in
possession of it, and a second army besieging the first.

The first army was in possession of the lucrative monsters
in a technical sense only. The beasts were in a kind of
fortress of their own making – they had eaten a broad, flat-
bottomed gulf out of the flanks of two adjoining hills.
Raggedly vertical walls some ninety feet high encompassed
them, easily enough descended from the hills with ropes,
but impossible as an escape route. Consequently the
besiegers bent their main effort against the impressive

317

wood-and-stone wall the defenders had strung across the pit's one open side: the narrow valley-floor whence the herd had approached the hills they found so appetizing. And the defenders possessed the giants only in the sense that those behemoths were gnawing too leisurely at the hills' flanks to be very far away by the time the battle was likely to be decided, and were too torpidly indifferent – if not, indeed, blind – to events of so small a scale as human warfare to contest the claims of the army that had strung the wall behind them.

They had tough, laquered-looking bodies, plated so that they appeared staved or planked, and they were shaped like the overturned hulls of ships. They hauled themselves along on clusters of crooked, relatively dwarfish legs, and swinishly pushed their black, four-lobed mouthparts – when closed together, they resembled tulips – against the nourishing bones of the earth.

Both armies were Prior-Kairns, natives of the continent's lush, cattle rich southern half, competing for the enrichment of two rival provinces. This was learned from the survivors of the besieging army who, while the mercenaries encamped to debate their approach to the siege, attacked them. They had been alert for the arrival of a relief force expected by their enemies, and in the dense jungle had not recognized that they were engaging – not the small contingent their spies had described – but a force larger as well as more seasoned than their own.

The mercenaries now found their tactical problems simplified. The next morning they advanced to the rampart. There they compelled the surrender of the skeleton force the besiegers had left to mask their withdrawal from the defenders, and prevent a sortie and assault on their rear. Menodon then called on the defenders to make a peaceful withdrawal, as his force represented the claims of the flock's lawful owner. This suggestion was rudely declined by the army upon the ramparts.

318

With this eventuality in view, Kandros had already commenced the construction of a single, slender siege-tower. This was brought within some hundred yards of the wall, and Lybis mounted it, Menodon and Nifft accompanying her and covering her with their shields. She identified herself as the viceroy of the flock's rightful owner, and repeated the request for her property's surrender. Being scornfully invited to come get them, she replied with a smile that this would not be necessary. She stretched her hands, palms out, toward the herd.

The beasts showed a swift unanimity frightening in things so huge and slothful. They turned their backs upon their meal and proceeded thunderously in Lybis' direction. The considerable number of soldiers who were too stunned to abandon the rampart in time were crushed along with it.

Though the expedition did not have to grope for its route back to the coast, the bulk of the five hundred colossi they now had in train compelled them to weave one that was often extravagantly serpentine. Detours were maddening, but failing to find them was worse. Many steeply pitched and densely overgrown ridges were so lubricated by topsoil and wet foliage that even the fearsome, rock-splitting traction the beasts' queer little louse's legs could exert was powerless against the instantaneous obedience of their huge, mud-buttered masses to gravity's imperatives. And all too often a squad of lead-beasts had to set to gnawing through muck into base-rock, and eating a slow-rising trench of rough stone up to the crest, along which the rest of the flock could be channeled.

They returned, at least, to find that the detachment of pioneers Kandros had left with the ships had completed the structures necessary to overcome the difficulties of the flock's embarkation. The greatest of these was getting at least one of the beasts into each hold, as the urgency of hastening their delivery compelled the expedition to make it in only two crossings. For this, a huge, arched ramp stretched from the beach, out along a line of offshore rocks, to deep water a hundred yards offshore – a half-bridge, from whose bowed terminus a giant crane thrust out over the water.

For the binding of the herd into flotillas of a half-dozen that could be towed astern, thirty-five corrals of six-whale capacity (the overall bulk of the beasts had been accurately expressed in terms of whales) had been built on the intertidal sands. Made of thirty-foot posts, their seaward walls were hinged to swing out, gate-wise. When each corral's huddle of tenants had been lashed together and hung with floats by teams working at low tide, high tide would be awaited by the fleet – their holds all loaded previously – at which time they could tow out their stern-cargo simultaneously, and make full sail to convey to Anvil Pastures her deliverance.

The flock marched with clockwork obedience through every phase of the loading operation, and their perfect inertia once in the holds or tied astern gave everyone involved a sense of vast power in total, uncanny vassalage to a governing will that was, after all, thousands of miles distant. Indeed, the Goddess now enjoyed, with only the open ocean separating them, unobstructed governance of the flock's will, and could, Lybis said, perceive the beasts' environment unambiguously, and dictate to them the behavior necessary for their defense against whatever beset them from the inlands. So the half of the flock that could not be taken with the first convoy were left to wait, with a substantial garrison, the fleet's return, and Lybis went back to Anvil Pastures with the first half.

En route, about two days out of Anvil Pastures, the convoy encountered a fleet of Baskinon men-of-war. Their pilot-vessel hailed Lybis' flagship, and a boarding was requested politely enough, given the belligerents' customary brusqueness with the citizens of their shared arsenal. Lybis' strident cordiality scarcely required the hailing-trumpet she used to invite them aboard. The visiting admiral, sufficiently nonplussed by what he saw astern of the Anvilian craft, was even more disconcerted by the inspection of the hold to which his blithely garrulous hostess exhorted him. Afterward she invited him to a glass of spirits in her cabin. By this time the man – a stolid, scar-faced great-uncle, doubtless a merchant in peacetime, according to the pattern in Baskin-Sharpz – had caught the idiom of her insolence and begun to warm toward her. Draining his second glass, and rising to go, he reached forward without the slightest hint of awkwardness, and patted her arm.

'You've got seven devils-full of nerve in you, Priestess, and you're so small! I hope you come out of what you're doing all right. You know, I half believe that if your city is destroyed, we could end up at armistice with Hallam. And I must tell you, my dear, that there's many a place in this world where your city-saving efforts are talked of, and not cheered on. I'm sorry, but that's the truth.'

Lybis smiled at him with a strange glee: 'But my *city* cheers me on, Admiral.'

Back in the city, Lybis left Kandros with instructions to build a system of ramps encircling the peak just below its breakage, and to incorporate the existing shoring in its foundation – a function for which the latter was adequate, laughably insufficient though it was for its original purpose. Both going and returning, Lybis kept Nifft on her ship, and occasionally would drink with him in her cabin. At such times she would question him about his life, and she found much to laugh at in his answers.

VII

The morning after the expedition's return to Anvil Pastures, Nifft, Kandros, and Minor strolled across the plaza of the acropolis toward its major salience, whence they would have an excellent view of the flock, assembled on the little plain outside the city's main gate. Meanwhile they did not lack for spectacle, for up on the mountain, on the rampway collaring its broken neck, a swarm of tiny figures sent down to them a minuscule, belated noise of construction.

'They'll be off it by noon,' said Minor, squinting impassively up against the sky's brightness, 'and we'll see if it'll hold the brutes.'

'If the brutes will be on it by then,' Nifft said. His friends looked at him, and he smiled. 'I have a feeling there's to be another Solicitation.' He nodded toward the temple, across the square behind him. A procession of coaches was pulling up in front of it, and already several of the Aristarchs were stepping down.

'Damn the woman!' the Sexton cried. 'I'm the first functionary on her staff! She told me nothing! She insists on baiting me and slighting me.'

Nifft clapped him on the shoulder. 'I hope it doesn't make it worse that Kandros and I were told to expect it. The priestess has a feeling, you see, that the Goddess is going to want something that will require my friend's engineering skills again. Come on – let's go on and take our view. We've got almost half an hour.'

As they proceeded, Minor continued to grumble, until Kandros burst out: 'Can her hostility surprise you, Sexton Minor? Does she love the Aristarchs? Your connection with them, your debt to their influence for your very position, is a major point of pride with you. You're frankly skeptical of the Flockwarden's divinity; indeed, that's putting it mildly. Meanwhile, the Dame herself is nothing but devout toward – '

'Ah-*ha*! You see *there* you're misled!' It was a point on which the Sexton seemed prepared, fervently ready, with an answer. They had reached the balustrade facing the north-most tip of the plaza at the terminus of its slender projection in that direction, and he gave it a slap for emphasis. 'View it objectively. There is an object, the corpse of the so-called Goddess, which emanates undeniable power. Like a heated poker, its power beams forth from it, shines out in rays, long after the death of the fire that endowed it with this radiant power. Heat we all know how to use. But suppose it's a *power* that there's a *trick* to using, to tapping? You are in a hereditary guild that bequeaths you this trick, in exchange for lip-service to some divine cant that legitimizes your exclusive possession of that vital trick. What would *you* profess then? Yet it remains raw, residual power in an accidentally preserved alien body, and no more than that. Would a *goddess*, who could beam her will across the ocean, be unable to send it curving through a bit of rough terrain to reach her servants' minds? Is such laughable limitation a divine potency? Ha! But a simple beam of power, like a poker's heat and glow, *that* might well need reflecting, focusing, as a mirror might reflect and aim the poker's glow around a corner.'

'But there's a *sentience* in this reflected power,' Nifft said. The amusement in his eyes was lazy, remote, perhaps, from the precise question at issue. 'There's directive consciousness in it.'

'But who knows what energies these beings from the stars glowed with?' cried the Sexton. 'It's still a brute, mechanical thing, and Dame Lybis is as callous and realistic in her manipulation of it as the most cynical unbeliever.'

'Well well,' sighed Nifft. 'Who's to say your description, in its main outlines, is wrong?'

All three fell to gazing where their eyes had dwelt for some time – upon the Flockwarden's cattle. Seen from this vantage, the flock might have been a little town built just outside the city wall – a bizarre settlement of loaf-shaped buildings, perhaps just such an alien-looking town as might be found on other worlds. Its background of tortured, carcass-gaunt peaks, wherein strands of a half-dozen bright metallic colors – silver, copper, bronze, brass – were twisted inextricably with black ribbons of the flock's age-old fecal coal, did nothing to dispel the illusion. Indeed, it was the mighty, walled city of pale stone, Anvil Pastures itself, which struck all three witnesses as the least 'real,' most ephemeral fraction of that panorama.

'"By Anvil, Staff and Hammer,"' murmured Nifft. 'Where's the Anvil, Minor?'

'Eh? What do you mean? What Anvil?'

'The Anvil that goes with the Staff in yon bay, and the Hammer in yon wall. "Anvil, Staff and Hammer." Your mistress is always saying it.'

'Oh!' The Sexton chuckled. 'There isn't any. There in the harbor is Anvil's Staff. There, in the wall, is Anvil's Hammer. There before you, you have Anvil's Staff and Hammer.' He seemed quite pleased with the neatness of this, and Nifft laughed in his turn, catching a look from Kandros.

'I see. Silly of me. You know, huge though the Goddess is, one wonders how she, or even all her race together, wielded such tools.'

Minor snorted, but his answer was not as immediate as before. Finally with a shrug he said, 'A curious thought. I suppose they were a kind of statuary, memorial landmarks – perhaps together they formed a sort of signboard identifying the town to its airborne customers as they flew near!'

The Sexton was pleased anew by this explanation. Nifft nodded. 'Now that's ingenious,' he muttered, smiling still.

They returned to the temple. As they mounted the steps to its entry, it was the elderly acolyte already encountered by Nifft who ushered them through the door, and on seeing him, the Sexton flew into a rage.

'Krekkit! You senile weasel – I suspended you for two weeks!'

'Rig a noose and suspend yourself from a rafter beam,' the old man answered, still leading them onward. Minor seized his shoulder, detaining him in the sanctum's doorway where, in the same instant, Dame Lybis appeared.

'Unhand my acolyte!' she blazed.

Minor obeyed before he protested: 'I disciplined him! I caught him peeking through the Veil at the Goddess' . . .'

'At the *Goddess*' what?'

'Her private zone, her *veiled* part which only yourself . . . I mean, does it not clearly say in the protocol that – '

'Be still! Is there one shrine-servant out of the whole two score of you who *hasn't* peeked there? Including yourself? *And* put their hands, experimentally, to her . . . *private parts*?' Lybis grinned wickedly. 'I tell you, oh Sexton Minor, acolyte Krekkit came here after working forty years in the forges, and volunteered his services out of piety, and has served here since then for twelve of the fourteen years I've served. You understand? It was out of respect for *her* power – ' (the priestess pointed toward the sanctum) 'and not the Aristarchs'. And if anyone is going to be peeking at the Flockwarden's privates, I'd rather it were Krekkit than you, given the nasty, acquisitive frame of mind I'm sure you *do* it in. Now you're to attend to the Solicitation and stop making trouble. I have a feeling that today's oracle is going to leave us all with much new business.'

In singing tones, the shrine-mistress – raising from time to time enraptured eyes from her tablet – read out the oracle:

Oh, bear the brood-nurse to her hatchlings' side!
Though she within her ancient death be pent,
Deliver her – herself, her hearse – beside
Those on whom her former life was spent.
To the nursery of those tender innocents
Bear her so that they, of Knowing void
May with fruit of her Great Knowing be supplied,
And fully may conceive of her intent.
What though in death her frame stand vitrified?
You know her Knowing part doth yet abide –
More nearly let it work their government!

With unwonted tenderness the Priestess tucked the tablet
into her apron pouch. Her stylus she did not put away, but
turned slowly in her fingers as she gazed at it, and began
to speak. Her voice was a supple, compelling current of
calm ardor:

'Ye gods, gentlemen! If our interest didn't lie in fulfilling
her desire, how could our hearts resist doing so? I've often
been moved by the Goddess, in touching the living flow of
her emotion, her immemorially ancient knowledge and
desire. But this time . . .' Now her eyes flashed upon the
mute congregation. 'I tell you, it's almost as if she were
alive! The soulful urgency of her will to be near her children,
as she seems to call them – yes! She seems almost to feel
toward them as a mother to her children. So deep must her
caretaker's bond have been with the flock! I promise you
that I haven't managed to translate even a tithe of the
emotional resonance, the motherly passion there was in
her wordless behest!

'And I can understand this, gentlemen, though there be
no blood kinship between her and those beasts! Have I not
known the service of an alien being, known a devotion to
the excellence and beauty of an entity foreign to my kind,
and known this devotion to achieve a degree of joy and
proud commitment that's like love itself? I make bold to
detain you with these personal sentiments, but I tell you I
rejoice that the Goddess will at last enjoy in death that

nearness to her beloved charges which was once so central to her life.

'For she must have what she wants, of course. It's a tricky bit of surgery she's going to be doing with those brainless giants of hers and her hand must be set as firmly upon the scalpel as possible, that's mere common sense . . . It's obvious her glass-muffled emanations will benefit from all the amplification they can get. The sweet maternal propinquity she craves, honest Aristarchs, is also our greatest security. It's also obvious she will not command them to our salvation until she has the conditions she specifies, and so it is scarcely a matter of choice. What remains to be done is clear . . .'

VIII

The Goddess' multitudinously attended procession out of the city was a stately one. It took four days and, despite the most cunning devisement of its route, necessitated the partial or complete dismantling of nine sizable buildings to make passage for the cyclopean corpse. Before this laborious pilgrimage could even be undertaken, the Goddess' equally arduous descent from the acropolis had to be accomplished. The vitreous megalith was lowered with an immense block-and-tackle from a boom of unheard-of proportions, whose skeleton the city's forges had finished and assembled in less than forty-eight hours of cacophonous, febrile toil. It was just before dawn when her hugeness inched down from the blocky plateau's beak-like promontory. The catwalks built up against the plateau's sheer wall swarmed with torches of workmen attending her descent, and the plaza was also teeming with lights, so that a shower of sparks seemed to be spilling down from the great mesa as the Goddess deserted it for the first time in recorded history.

At length the great crystalline block had ground its way – rollered on the countless trees which its vast bulk devoured by the hundreds in its progress – out through the main gate. That giant portal admitted its exit by scant inches only. The sun had been down for an hour by the time it had been positioned in the field where the flock was gathered, and cordoned round with a screen of temple tapestries draped from pole-strung cables to designate the periphery of sacerdotal privilege, into which lay-folk must not penetrate. Dame Lybis, already half-veiled by the deepening shadows, entered this screen under the silent gaze of the townsfolk, whose torches washed the field with unsteady orange light, and made the immobile herd seem to stir and shift restlessly. And indeed, before ever she reappeared from her sequestration with the Flockwarden, a shock went through the crowd as those nearest the beasts leapt and cried out in startlement. The flock had begun a shambling progress toward the mountains.

Darkness masked their ascent of the slopes and occupation of Kandros' monumental feeding ramp, but both proceeded in flawless order, as the contingent of mercenaries sent up to observe the beasts reported during the first lightless hours of their watch. Sunrise revealed them to the city already well at work.

For the next ten days, the spectacle was tirelessly observed by Anvil's citizens. The beasts' huge forms were plainly visible even at that remove; less so was the small army of men endlessly clearing the rampway of the giants' waste products and – since these consisted of pure metals and tons of furnace-nourishing fecal coal – conveying them down the slopes to the city. In this period the mass of the great natural hammer that threatened the city was substantially reduced – by as much as a fifth to a quarter, according to the best estimates of Kandros and his staff.

The lofty rampway became the focus of many a festive gathering of friends. Anvilians began to make a pastime of congregating on the acropolis or out on the field before the north wall to eat, drink, disport themselves with music and dancing – all the while rejoicing in that magical, miniaturized activity upon the peak which was so steadily and painlessly reducing the lethal menace that had for so many weeks overhung their rooftops.

Therefore when, on the morning of the eleventh day, things went awry, it was before the complacent gaze of thousands of such happy spectators. The first panicked contingents of workmen reached the city with the news half an hour after the catastrophe had begun to develop, and even by this time the city at large had not yet grown alarmed. At the most, a certain hyperactivity on the part of the scarcely perceptible swarms of workmen had been here and there observed, and some people had thought they noted a faintly erratic quality enter the movements of the flock. By the time the disaster had been reported throughout the city, its effects were just becoming visible. The rampway was beginning to sag and buckle, and little avalanches of loose earth had begun to stream down the neck of the mountain. An ever-growing efflux of panicked citizens began to swell the near-hysterical multitude thronging the meadow round the Flockwarden.

The flock had run amok. They had not only abandoned their orderly feeding pattern round the outermost edges of the peak, but they had begun a restless, almost rhythmic milling about on the ramp which had already caused a vibrational break-up of its pilings. Worst of all, several dozen of the beasts had turned their ruinous appetites upon the naked metal of the already bent mountain spine itself. This last news almost caused the assembled Anvilians themselves to run amok.

Dame Lybis had stepped within the hieratic screen to

perform an emergency Solicitation of aid and enlightenment, and she had not yet emerged when the entire rampway was seen to collapse, and the monstrous peak itself bow down a farther heart-freezing three yards. The mutinous giants were already tumbling down the slopes when the roar of this ruin fell upon the ears of the multitude. Eternal moments unfolded during which the peak – universally, breathlessly regarded – settled no farther. Meanwhile, the indestructible behemoths, having ceased their uncontrolled plunge down the slope, began to extricate themselves from the jumbled jack-straws of the fallen timbers and sluggishly – unwillingly, one might have said – to assemble and descend the rest of the way to the city. It was then Dame Lybis emerged from her colloquy with the Flockwarden and proclaimed what she had learned. The Goddess, who for some days had exerted her control of the flock with ever-growing difficulty, had at last become exhausted with the effort, and the mammoth brutes had slipped her control. It was only through the most titanic efforts that she was now reasserting her government sufficiently to bring them back down to the plain.

IX

Sexton Minor, on every feature of whose face was stamped distaste for his mission, walked into the forge room of one of Anvil's larger foundries, which stood not far from the main gate in the north wall. He threaded his way through it, vainly shouting requests for attention from various of the thousand sweating devils producing the fire and brain-numbing clangor that made his efforts so futile. Each man moved like a single, task-concentrated muscle in the toiling body politic of the desperate city. The feeding-ramp had to be rebuilt around the peak, presuming the priestess' current efforts to secure some kind of aid from the Flockwarden produced a remedy for the flock's sudden recalcitrance. To ponder in the interval whether she *would* provide a remedy – indeed, to ponder whether the enfeebled arm of the mountain-hammer would hold long enough to *permit* remedy – was far more agonizing than even the most infernal labors, and every smith and furnaceman was demon-eyed with his absorption in his work upon the braces, bolts, collars, groinings and crossbeams the new ramp was going to require. Sexton Minor wove his way, glaring resentfully at every hiss of steel in tempering tub, every gasp of a down-draft forge – as at some intentional impertinence.

In one corner he found a smith snatching a nap atop his anvil while his forge was a-heating. The man was curled peacefully on his side, his ankles neatly crossed upon the anvil's horn, his head on his palms. Minor could see that a forge-hammer leaned against the wall just beyond the man. He shook the smith awake. The man, balding and tuft-jowled, gaped glassily as Minor bellowed in his ear: 'There has been a new oracle. Dame Lybis sends me here to get a forge-hammer. Give me *your* hammer!'

Having shouted this, Minor stood tight-lipped in the inscrutable majesty of his office, trusting that the man's sleep-drugged amazement would procure him the hammer without the pain of further howling. The man rolled off the anvil and fetched him the hammer. Minor, mistaking the weight of the tool which the knotted arm tendered him by the handle-tip as one might a spoon, gave his arm a painful wrench in taking it.

His eyes only lost the look of pain this put in them when he raised them, upon exiting the main gate, and viewed the Flockwarden's grotesque, jerry-built encasement. Scaffolding now enveloped the glass block. Lybis, still robed for the Solicitation, stood about two-thirds of the way up the vertical maze. She was attended not only by the detested acolyte Krekkit but by Aristarchs Pozzle, Hamp, and Smalling. The entire population spread upon the plain, though its flock-ward border stayed well withdrawn from those unpredictable beasts. The Sexton appeared to derive little pleasurable sense of consequence from this fact. Nifft received the hammer from him and passed it up to workers higher on the scaffold. He grasped Minor's shoulder encouragingly.

'Be comforted, honest Minor. Can't you see, from the way she treats the Aristarchs, that there's no way to win if you argue with her eccentric demands: Confront it, friend – she enjoys rubbing your set's faces in your covert cynicism toward the Goddess all these years. I mean, it's an unlovely, vengeful act, but surely understandable in someone who's been dedicated to a covertly ridiculed mystery for years?'

'There was simply no need to insist on a used forge-hammer, especially if one light blow *is* sufficient for the job,' the Sexton sulked. But the Priestess now had the hammer, and despite his professed scorn, Minor seemed to catch some of that breath of apprehension which swept faintly through the entire multitude at that moment.

In the manner – oddly, under the circumstances – of one who gives comfort, Nifft said: 'Oh, I'm sure it will do the job, Minor. If she can trace the deepest mountain-bones from where she lies, she can surely find one faint seam of critical weakness in her own coffin? Come, come. The Goddess is about to be, in her own term, "divested." Ye gods, Minor, wasn't that a rousing set of lines – I mean for their expressiveness, apart from its import to all of us.'

Nifft cocked his head back appreciatively, like one about to recite some admired verses. It was unlikely that the Sexton was going to hear him, for at this moment he watched fascinated as Lybis, with an address surprising in one of her diminutive stature, was hoisting the hammer above her shoulder, hefting for the swing. Nifft, instead of reciting, pointed to one of the copies of the latest oracle, which had already been posted throughout the city, scant hours after its delivery. He read aloud from it:

> Can shackled Mistress bind and rule her slave?
> Unsheathe my limbs, so long the air denied –

(Lybis now carefully took a wide-legged stance, and calculatingly applied the hammer nose to the ribbon-circled spot of any impact's maximum disruptive effect upon the glass.)

> – Divest me, that my power, which never died
> Might flow undammed, as when, before the grave
> Did cover me, I governed in my pride!

The priestess slowly drew back the hammer for a second time above her head, and swung the steel slug lustily to the marked spot. A dull, disappointingly flat *whack* echoed over the heads of the crowd. The people roared softly. The entire crystalline vitrolith had grown milky, utterly opaque. And then it collapsed – smoothly as dry, heaped sand, it rivered off the giant, alien frame.

The scaffolding had been built rigid and close to the block, in order that it might catch and at least partially sustain the Flockwarden's pithless remains once their support should have fallen away. The precaution was needless. The Flockwarden did not fall. She stood springily upon her jointed legs, and her iridescent wings delicately essayed the air.

The noise this raised from the crowd was such that it brought Nifft's head around in sudden, surprised appraisal. For the outcry was a curiously relief-tinged groan, as might greet a thing that has been all but foreknown. The Flockwarden's wind-spawning wings sped up. They were now scarcely visible, yet for all their power of vibration they did not even graze the narrowness of her enclosure.

Smoothly vertical she rose, and cleared the box of scaffolding. Smoothly across the plain she moved, bearing the message of her mastery directly to her refractory herd.

And as her assault commenced, her mastery proved never for a moment to be contested by the swinish giants. It seemed a strangely ritualistic scourging she gave them, too – not to all of them, but to perhaps a hundred individuals, one after the other. Over each of these she hovered, and bowed downward – dead contrary to her tapered abdomen's normal bent – her caudal prong. This she thrust into the beast beneath her, and thus linked, she did no more than hang in the air a moment, her body shuddering rhythmically. Then she unanchored herself and flew to another, seemingly randomly chosen member of her flock.

When at length she returned from the scourging, the Goddess seemed dreadfully enfeebled. She wobbled in her flight, and in settling on the grass not far from her shattered coffin, her legs buckled under her on her left side, and her head drooped.

It was soon learned from Lybis that the city's benefactress lay in grave weakness, and her life – that long-kept secret – was waning within mere hours after its last, long-prepared for vital service. It was not known how long she might survive, and the only assurance she could give the city was that the flock was, at least for now, subdued, and would return to work when the ramp was ready. Her beasts would in any case be showing a marked slowing down, as they were nearing their natural calving-season, but while they approached that period, they should at least obediently – if not energetically – pursue their task.

At least, they should do so while the Flockwarden lived. Their possible behavior if she should die became a matter of terrified conjecture. A great pavilion was erected over the Goddess. Her moribund vastness was constantly visited by the piously solicitous townsfolk, and an outdoors shrine blazed with votive candles as the indoor one had never done. A further oracle was besought, and given.

In her pronouncements, there were some dim fore-shadowings of what aid the city might seek in the melancholy event of the Goddess' demise. These could be read on any street in town, as the posting of the oracles had become at this point an invariable procedure:

> My life doth gutter, darken toward its close.
> If death my governance of the flock o'erthrows,
> One there is, not far from here, whose name
> His ancient nearness to our city shows –
> Pastur. His tomb I'll teach you, should the flame
> Of my remaining life grow yet more dim.
> Before that time I nothing will disclose
> Lest some too greedy man uncover him
> And use the butied giant for selfish aim –
> Vain consequence and power – for among those
> I shared my world with, Pastur could dispose
> Their giant bulks to suit his lightest whim;
> He drove them as he listed, unopposed
> By me or mine, who cowered when he came.

X

The herd resumed its lofty pasturage, but in a manner that nourished among Anvilians gloomy speculations on the Goddess' diminishing strength. The flock's obedience was sluggish, balky, and its appetite was dull. Apart from the approach of its breeding season, some of this torpor seemed a plain token of its warden's wavering life-flame. No one could bring himself to seek the abatement of the beasts' remedial labors, nor could they allow themselves to contemplate the result of a second anarchic frenzy, should such again possess them. So throughout a two-week agony of ambivalence, the citizens stared themselves dizzy at the thronging rampway, and in that time saw the lapsed peak's bulk dwindle by inches to a mass that was still more than two-thirds what it had originally had – and this supported by a spine rather less than the same fraction of *its* original thickness.

And then the flock abandoned its work en masse. The city woke one morning to find the peak deserted, and the plain outside the north wall again encamped with the motionless colossi.

The populace had soon thronged the walls and the ground outside them to view the prodigious biological event that was occurring out on the plain. It had soon become evident that far more than half the flock were females. Perhaps four hundred of the mammoth livestock on the sward were seen, by noon, to be engaged in the generative process.

The promised breeding was unquestionably in progress. Each female, after establishing a caudal link with the soil for at least an hour, inched her tail-tip up from the earth, hoisting its rubbery apical mouth from around what she had so laboriously, and with so many a shudder, been implanting: a shining, white, ribbed ellipsoid with a barbed peak – and, presumably, barbed tail, the which was snugly planted in the earth, and must have been what permitted the wobbling anchorage that each newly deposited egg exhibited as it rolled lazily with the assaults of the onshore winds that arose at dusk. Each of the giant cows produced a minimum of a dozen eggs, and several huge old cows produced more than fifty apiece.

The egg-laying marked the beginning of an alarming decline in the Flockwarden's already diminished vitality. She had been lying with her legs half folded under her, her abdomen more tightly curved above her than it had been during her endless immurement in the glass. Her antennae were almost her only active part. They could be seen to move in feeble conference with the veiled priestess during the several non-oracular communions Lybis held with her, during which she acquainted the priestess with the state of her diminishing vigor. Now, however, the Flockwarden's great head hung forward, and her major antennae trailed almost touching the ground. They could be seen to stir now and again. The priestess, prevented by the Goddess' posture from a full and formal Solicitation, could do no more to ease the tormented hearts of her townsfellows than assure them that the Flockwarden, should death truly come for her, would rouse herself a last time on behalf of her human flock (as, said Lybis, the Goddess had come to regard the Anvilians) and speak again, imparting to them the cue to their salvation – the means of raising the giant from the past to work their deliverance.

During this suspension of the herd's activity – for though they milled restively from time to time, they were generally almost comatose, each cow standing stupidly, flanking her egg-cluster – the city agonized ceaselessly over the oracular implication that the beasts were indeed capable of a second anarchic outburst if the Goddess should die. An assault upon the city itself was not thought impossible. Within four days of the egg-laying the Aristarchs had dwelt so vociferously upon this topic that a plan was developed, in concert with Kandros and his staff, for the city's defense in the event this hair-raising possibility should eventuate.

As the powerlessness of stone to oppose the advance of the flock was the original cause of worry, ramparts or other vertical barriers were discounted at the outset – they would go down too quickly, by mere pressure alone, unless the town should be given an unlikely amount of time for construction on a major scale. A great, straight-walled trench was deemed the best thing to slow them, and the digging was commenced by truly massive gangs of conscripted citizens, working side by side with the mercenaries and swelling their numbers to an extent that made it possible to finish the trench in less than a week. It ran almost a mile and a half, dividing the north wall from the little plain. It was more than a hundred feet broad, and as many deep, and from its inner, wallward lip a thick palisade of spike-tipped timbers projected at an angle above the pit, wherefrom the defenders could harrass the ascent of the besiegers. A short time after this impressive feat of engineering was accomplished, while gangs of grimed Anvilians still lolled in the parks and squares of the city, numbly awaiting the next dreadful exigency that should come to rouse them to maniacal efforts, the priestess sent out a city-wide summons to a Solicitation – for the Flockwarden had lifted her antennae, and feebly besought the oracle's attendance. It appeared this might be the Goddess' last revelation for her human flock. There was the more reason for hasty attendance, the message added, in that the eggs of the flock were beginning to hatch, and the congregated giants showed signs of waking from their torpor – indeed, showed signs of advancing upon Anvil itself.

When Lybis emerged from the Veil, her pallor, and the cold, impassioned determination on her face were such as to distract the populace for some moments from the dreadful organic unfoldings out on the plain, a short quarter mile beyond the just-completed trench.

'The Goddess, the Flockwarden, is dead. Long live the Goddess! Long live the Flockwarden!'

With a vast, low grumble, the multitude repeated her words – a hopeless outcry of shocked piety, for all now saw what, in their absorption flockward, they had missed: the Flockwarden's slack neck, her antennae like dead pythons on the grass.

'We have done well to defend ourselves,' Lybis said, gesturing toward the spike-rimmed ditch. 'They will advance – they begin already, do you see? Those which are hatching now – soon they too will advance. Watch them. Give me your ears only while you watch them. View what

338

threatens us – behold in all its meaning the calamity that descends on us, while I speak its remedy in your ears. And then upon your own heads let it be if, after hearing, you do not spur hell-bent directly and speedily to accomplish the great labor which must purchase that remedy.'

And so she brought her tablet from her pouch, and read the Goddess' last oracle to the city. As she read, they watched the plain, whereupon there was much to be seen. For though all the flock's eggs were identical – each the size of a four-passenger coach, tapered top and bottom, identically ribbed and colored – two radically different kinds of creature were erupting from their rupturing husks.

The most numerous of these were clearly infants of the flock. Though their leg-clusters were rudimentary, scarcely more than blackish nubs, their overall conformation was that of their parents, in bud.

But there were some egg-clutches, perhaps a hundred of them, whence very different hatchlings dragged themselves out amidst these bona fide calves. These had spiny black barrels for bodies, leg-clusters that were much more developed and elaborately jointed and barbed, and jaws of an equally elaborate structure, entirely distinct from the rock-guzzling snoutlets of the more numerous calves.

Both breeds of hatchling began to feed instantaneously once their heads were free, even though the rest of their bodies had still to be dragged free of the shell. The calves fed upon the first bare rock they found beneath them. The black hatchlings began with equal speed to feed upon the calves.

It was a stunning, gaudy carnage, for the babes in question were on the general scale of a large battle-chariot with its team. The calves seemed to lack all awareness of, or powers of resistance to, the assaults of their carnivorous nestmates. They squirmed ineffectually, some even continued to devour the stone as they were flensed to blubbery fragments by their scissors-jawed siblings, and guzzled down. Meanwhile the parent beasts displayed no more reaction than did their victim offspring, but continued an inchoate, milling advance in the general direction of the watching city. Long after Lybis had finished reading the oracle, the multitude watched, and saw the pattern emerging in the flock's movement. The hatchling carnivores remained more or less stationary, usually surrounded by a blood-spattered mess of half-a-dozen calf carcasses, where they continued feeding methodically on their swiftly captured feasts. At the same time, the calves that had escaped their predation – never ceasing to graze – gradually completed their eclosions, and began following the movement of the adult beasts. These latter now made steadily, in an ominous unison of apparent intent, toward the recently completed trench.

Strangely, few of the townsfolk afterward found that they needed to read the posted copies of the Flockwarden's last oracle. Sunk in astonishment as they had been while gazing on that vast unearthly and disaster-pregnant spectacle, Lybis' voice seemed to have imprinted itself upon their minds, and most recalled both the burden, and the sweet, ambiguous music, of her message:

> In Ossuaridon, where priest and seer
> Seek insight, and in visionary gloom
> Within the giant's bones themselves inhume,
> And dwell in dark that they might see more clear,
> There seek great Pastur's catastrophic bier.
> Exhume him and return his remnants here.
> For his bones – if from their accidental tomb
> You take, and with them work his frame's repair –
> Have might to master those that threaten doom,
> Seek the magic of my murdered more-than-peer!
> Haste to find him and convey him where
> Great Anvil-town doth offer greatest room –
> Oh, haste! Lest that should fall which now but looms!
> And the flock my death leaves lawless, do not fear.
> All things their hungry jaws have power to tear,

Save gold alone – this can they not consume.
Weigh then your wealth, and judge if it's more dear
To you than life. If not, your course is clear.

XI

Dame Lybis, in the company of Kandros and Nifft (generally recognized now as being her chosen strategic counsellors for the many emergency labors her position was imposing on her), went on the expedition sent to retrieve Pastur's bones. She stayed there long enough to see the work commenced, and then sped back to the city to oversee the last phases of its wall's 'thickening.'

If she had made a special effort to rouse an energetic responsiveness in her fellow citizens, her success was striking. A sort of de facto communalism had developed. The city's material stores were disbursed city-wide on a strict basis of need according with amount and importance of work done, and people of every class joined in a whole-hearted furtherance of whichever aspect of the city's need they were assigned to assist. At work on the wall, or on the arduous convoy of hugely laden wagons bearing back Pastur's bones from Ossuaridon, or on the work-gangs frenziedly constructing the wagon train's roadway (and working a scant league ahead of the vanguard's rumbling advance) the townsfolk struggled shoulder-to-shoulder with the mercenary squads, distinguishable from them only by a peculiar, taut-faced singlemindedness, a rapt concentration that was almost glassy-eyed, like the look of a desperately driven slave.

By far the most herculean labor fell to those sent to exhume the bones. Ossuaridon – until now no more than the name of an obscure hamlet of religious fanatics to most Anvilians – was a mere five days' journey inland through the mountains fencing Anvil Pastures against the sea. But this was the time that a mobile expedition of foot with lightly laden wagons took to traverse that distance. Their return necessitated the highway already referred to, and even this it took the burdened wains more than eight days to traverse. The hamlet, built against the flank of a sheer, glacially carved escarpment, was founded upon the giant's bones themselves, in both an architectural and cultural sense. Its inhabitants all had in common, despite the diversity of their origins, a shamanistic turn of mind. The age of ice which had seemingly intervened between the era of Pastur's death, and the historical past, had sheared away most of the rock that encased his bones. These had been even more fully exposed by subsequent erosion, and many of them thrust gigantically from the escarpment. In particular the skull had been frontally exposed to an extent that made it possible for the mystic devotees to enter either of the orbits of the eyes and, within these bony caves, enjoy the dream-producing vigils which had for centuries drawn others like themselves to the place and, effectually, created Ossuaridon. And yet, though all the meagre structures of this religious outpost clung variously for support to the ribs and femurs of the broken titan, their inhabitants never offered the slightest opposition to what amounted to the complete (and swift) dismantling of their habitations, nor to the extraction and removal of the object of their cult.

Once the mining-out of the skeleton was well begun, and the first of the great wains were laden and on their way back to the city on the still embryonic highway, Lybis led Nifft and Kandros, along with a small group of mercenary officers, back toward Anvil on horseback. Just as she was setting out she abruptly turned her mount aside, and rode to the shamans' encampment. They had quietly removed their belongings out on the plain to some tents provided them at the oracle's orders. A man was standing in front of the nearest of these, and she reined up on reaching him.

His eyes, which were flat and flinty black, were old, though he did not seem particularly aged in the rest of his lean, raggedly garbed person.

Lybis leaned forward in the saddle. 'You are content that this – ' she swept her arm toward the sprawling, scaffold-decorated exhumation – 'should be?'

'I am content, Mistress.'

'May I ask you why?'

The man's mouth smiled, an operation that did not involve the rest of his sun-blackened face (Ossuaridonites' days-long vigils were not restricted to the cult-object's skull). 'Are you not restoring him? Would this, in us, be thanks for his infinite, history-spanning insights, to obstruct his resurrection?' Lybis smiled, and nodded as if to herself. Then, delicately, she cleared her throat, and said, 'I am glad and grateful. I am especially glad you do not mingle with our workmen, trouble their labors . . .'

'Nor speak to them either, about anything at all, Mistress,' the man nodded calmly, not even his mouth smiling now. 'And that is as we shall keep matters. We do not wish to obstruct your labors in any way.'

'Bless you, shaman.'

'Equally to you, oracle.'

When she had rejoined her companions, and they had been some moments on their road, Nifft murmured wonderingly: 'Marvellous, those caves⁻ of his eyes. Did you go inside, Kandros?'

'No. Somehow I didn't get the chance.'

Nifft glanced a smile at his friend, then resumed his musing. 'So warm it was in there! And once they'd broken out some of the overhanging rock that shadowed the interiors, you know what we saw? The back of the left socket is cracked – there's a hole in its rear wall – and you could see just a bit of a huge metal sphere, imbedded in the bone where the brain would be. I'll tell you, my friend, that's going to be the heaviest piece of all.'

Back in the city they found the civil defense project well in progress. It had not been initiated without the most anguished and repetitive deliberations up in the Aristarkion. The agonized Aristarchs, from whose pockets must come the bulk of the protective gold, pointed out that it was a futile defense, as the flocks, however effectively a layer of gold might repel their destructive appetites from the wall itself, could always simply tunnel *under* any gilded bulwark that opposed them, and bring it down by collapse, as sappers do.

As the days of debate lengthened, the flock advanced. They and their greedy, ever-growing calves, appearing to dread a precipitous fall into the trench (though many of the adults had survived a far more dizzy plunge when the ramp had collapsed under them) had eaten their way down into it at an oblique angle. And then, once down in it, they had begun to eat their way out again, creating a second oblique rampway, and proving impervious to all the missiles hurled down on them by the troops on the log palisade. As this rampart began caving in and had to be abandoned, and as the time before the beasts should regain ground-level outside the wall shortened, the urgency of the citizenry for concerted action grew so ardent and demonstrative that the dilatory Aristarchs yielded. Huge bellows-powered pumps were constructed. These fed off of melting-vats into which, with pathetically evident reluctance, the Aristarchs fed their hoarded bullion, along with all the specie they had cached in the several banks of the city. When Lybis returned, the first quarter of the wall had already been gilded with the finest lamination of gold the Aristarchs had been able to procure from their closely overseen staff of engineers. Lybis quickly put the rest of the task in the hands of Kandros and his staff, with Nifft assisting their efforts. It was a labor to which the workers engaged in it welcomed any additional support, as the flock had already eaten more than half their way up from the pit, and those constrained to work the bellows and the melting-vats did so in the most urgent anxiety. Nifft and Kandros ordained some alterations in procedure, and the gilding of the walls moved ahead apace. Pastur's bones began to reach the city.

The relative lightness of these bones was the one fortunate circumstance the gangs of laborers on the caravan had encountered. Those citizens at all conversant with such matters vowed that the cyclopean remains had to be less than a third the weight which normal animal bones of similar size would have possessed. The acropolis was still crowned with the derricks that had facilitated the Flockwarden's abandonment of it, and as that great square was the only place in the city that appeared adequate to accommodate a skeleton of the size they were dealing with, these machines were once more enlisted in the city's salvation, hoisting up Pastur's fossil as fast as its pieces could make their progress through the city from its eastern gate. Further demolitions, which largely or completely destroyed some thirty-seven buildings, were required to create the necessary passageway for the broken skeleton's approach to the base of the great eminence, and before the work of reassembly up in the plaza had progressed very far, it was evident that supplementary support must be created for the huge *memento mori*. A gigantic platform was extended from the broad end of the elevation. When, about two weeks after Lybis' return, the skull arrived, it was, with vast effort and exquisite care, laid upon that north-projecting horn of the acropolis from which Nifft and his friends had formerly viewed the flock out on the plain. With the spine largely completed, and the legs and feet assembled on the platform at the eminence's opposite end, it became evident that Pastur, when he lived, had stood about eighty stories high.

At this point the Aristarchs brought in to Dame Lybis a very shrilly voiced complaint against her generalship of the city's defenses, most particularly as regarded the wall-gilding project. Their mathematicians had scrupulously worked out a volumetric equivalence of unit gold per area of wall coverage, based on the desired thickness of application per square foot, and the wall, now all but covered, had consumed more than one and a half times the gold computed as adequate for its surfacing: Nifft's and Kandros' crews pursued their labors even as their rectitude was being subjected to these lofty (and heated) examinations up in the Aristarkion. It was well this was so, for long before the Aristarchs, under the moderation of Dame Lybis, had brought their deliberations to any conclusion, the wall had been completely gilded and, in the same hour, the ravening columns of the besiegers had swarmed out of the trench and attacked it. The citizens fled within the gates, and crowded anxiously atop the walls, manning the defenses there and breathlessly watching for the first decisive contact of the flock with their now priceless defenses. The giants crowded to the wall like pigs to a trough, applied to it their all-destroying snouts, and recoiled.

Their will to assault the citadel never flagged in the tense days that followed this first rebuff. The flock, recoiling sullenly and undamaged from the projectiles and boiling oil the defenders poured down upon them, tirelessly returned to their attack, but this never involved the use of their dreaded jaws, which indeed the gold appeared to inhibit their use of. Instead, they reared as high as their short legs permitted, and butted thunderously against the barrier. This was far from a futile ploy. As the days passed, there were several points in the wall where cracks began to develop, and even inward bucklings of an ominous appearance. The herd could fairly be numbered at around two thousand now – the calves had speedily swelled in size, and at present had half their parents' bulk and most of their adult bodily features. An army of these proportions, which never ceased its ramming, was bound, eventually, to

346

break down an even more considerable bulwark than that of Anvil Pastures. The citizens toiled unremittingly, manning the battlements or shoring the wall from within wherever it showed signs of weakening.

Two small mercies were discerned in the situation by some of the more optimistic Anvilians. First, the herd never seemed moved to resort to the under-tunneling tactic which the Aristarchs had dreaded, and which would surely have brought the walls down in swift and utter ruin in half the time that had thus far elapsed since the flock's onset. And second, the menacingly carnivorous co-hatchlings of the calves had, far from showing any disposition to join in the siege, shown a reassuringly passive temperament. All of them, shortly before the battle was joined round the wall, had burrowed themselves halfway into the ground and lain perfectly dormant. In the course of the first few days following this occurrence, observers from the wall noted that the beasts' exposed upper bodies had developed an opaque ensheathment of tough, dark material. A kind of second eggshell, it seemed, was enveloping them. Now, after more than ten days had passed, they showed no sign of further life, and their new encapsulations had grown quite rigid-looking.

Meanwhile, the bones of the city's savior-to-be passed one by one through its eastern gate and, amid the shouts of men, the grunts of dray-beasts, and the rattle and groan of massive tackle, inched their way up the vertiginous side of the acropolis to join the steadily growing framework of the recumbent titan that crowned it. The work never faltered, even at night, when the great plateau was draped with torch-swarms, and seemed, once again, to shed cascades of sparks.

XII

Late in the afternoon, Aristarchs Pozzle, Hamp and Smalling stood outside the temple, talking gravely with Sexton Minor. To stand where they did, or indeed, anywhere on the acropolis, was to stand under a monstrous, stark forest of megalithic shafts and arches, one where swarms of men on ramps and crane arms were – not timbering – but supplementing, multiplying its growth. If this overlooming industry caused the Aristarchs to cringe somewhat, to crouch resentfully, it seemed to add something to Minor's stature. Perhaps this was due to a certain unconscious pride he was beginning to take in this stupendous productiveness of his hitherto disregarded temple. Power, in his understanding, was clearly taking on a broader definition than he had formerly accorded the term. His posture lacked the deferential tilt it normally exhibited when he was in the company of the power-elite, and he looked particularly fresh and spruce. This trio of the elite, on the other hand, looked gravely worn, almost shabby, as though mired by the exhausting defrayal of endless costs.

'I am very sorry, gentlemen,' Minor was saying smoothly. 'Dame Lybis is at this very moment searching the repository of sacred texts for some clue. We can do no more than wait. Believe me, I regret the anguish this subjects you to. But try to be comforted. Hasn't the temple proved to be the source of an astonishing variety of powers and insights, just in these past few months alone? I must confess to you, gentlemen, that I feel an irrepressible optimism myself, however grim things are in a general way. After all, every danger the Goddess and her cult have gotten us into, they've gotten us out of again – try to be encouraged by that.'

348

Pozzle regarded the Sexton with a just-barely repressed bale. Members of the power-elite tend to keep a close accounting of all the little taxes of deference and flattery they levy from their subordinates, and the Aristarch looked particularly incensed at being short-changed in this regard by the Sexton – and short-changed with an impunity bestowed by the very cult which had so deeply involved his finances in the general ruin. In a thick voice, but managing an even tone, he said: 'To have done so much, Sexton Minor – ' he gestured overhead ' – and then to find the skeleton imperfect in so relatively small a way, and its power entirely unavailable as a result, and when it's so incomprehensible in the *first* place how simply reassembling a skeleton is going to help us in any way against those monsters outside – it is all exasperating in the highest degree. It is *infuriating* in fact – '

Aristarch Smalling, a slight, dapper man, laid a soothing – and preventive – hand upon Pozzle's arm. 'It is not difficult to observe, Sexton,' he said, smoothly in his turn, 'from the north promontory – ' he pointed toward the giant's skull, its orbits aimed skyward ' – that the wall under attack is now deeply buckled in several places, and that even the most extreme counter-bracing measures will not hold some of those ruptures for more than a few days longer. Is it certain the hand does not lie somewhere in the same stone as contained the rest of the remains? If need be, we'll tear the entire escarpment to rubble to find the thing, and damn the expense.'

Pozzle emitted a low moan of impotent anger here, and the square-faced Hamp looked distinctly greenish at the corners. Minor shook his head, his brows rising in a regretful shrug. 'That's the heart of the trouble, gentlemen, but, like so much else in this affair, it's also going to be our salvation. You see, Dame Lybis was assured of the hand's separation from the rest of the giant's body when she remembered a part of her instruction as a tyro that mentioned Pastur's loss of it – indeed, it was so obscurely referred to that it took our failure to find the hand to recall it to her at all. But do you not see? Once she has found the textual foundation of that tradition in the archives, she will also find therewith, in all likelihood, a description of the place where the hand may be found.'

'If it has survived to *be* found at all.' Pozzle murmured this almost to himself, looking a trifle feverishly up at the great work above him.

And, toward the end of that day, as the sun neared its setting, that work was essentially one of final adjustments. By that time, all of Pastur's bones thus far exhumed had been put in place – and this comprised the entire skeleton except for the right hand. Throughout the day Aristarchs in various combinations had come, stood outside the temple, stepped into it and out of it again, and departed. Now, as the skeleton's shadow reached its maximum elongation across the rooftops of the eastern half of town, and lay upon them like a cage of vast and alien design, a large number of these dignitaries had collected before those – hopefully – pregnant doors.

The doors burst open. Out of them, and halfway down the steps, the shrine-mistress stormed, brandishing a scrap of parchment. Her tiny figure too cast a long shadow, and the swarm of notables condensed close to her. Her voice, a small but strident sound audible from afar though indistinct, wandered through the forested acres of stone, weaving itself into the cathedralled ossuary. The rapt flock of other miniatures stood paralyzed, and close to her. Then her voice changed key, her arms moved expressively and, shortly, the swarm of Aristarchs dispersed, as if exploded by some verbal bomb. Nifft turned to Kandros, with whom he shared a seat upon a length of scaffold draped across the crest of the giant's high-arching ribs. Nifft's eyes, which had lazily abandoned the scene directly below them, had risen toward the wall on the northern side of the city. 'Do you notice, Kandros, beyond the parts of the wall not directly assaulted by the flock, there still seems to be a kind of assault-like activity, but one carried on by small, shadowy forms?' He handed to the captain the wineflask they were sharing. Kandros applied himself comfortably to this before he answered:

'Yes. Men, I make them out to be. One wonders what they're after. Perhaps some of that gold smeared all over the wall. They're certainly drawing a lot of fire from the archers.'

Nifft nodded with the solemn, enlightened expression of one who hears a very ingenious theorem propounded. 'Thieves. Of course. They've probably been swarming here from every city on the coast since the word went out about the gilding.' He was returned the flask, and paused to utilize it. 'You know, Kandros, in the spirit of the great friendship I bear you, I must declare something to you. I am myself not unacquainted with the workings of thieves.'

Kandros nodded in his turn, receiving the flask. 'No man who is acquainted with the world at large, is unacquainted with the workings of thieves,' he said. He utilized the flask.

By the time full dark was settling on the city, a large party of belanterned wagons was speeding from the base of the acropolis, down to the harbor. There, with that day's end, was the beginning of new labor.

By dawn, a big raft was launched from the dockside. It supported a massive crane, whose boom overreached its side. Heavy pontoons of welded metal casks gave it counter-support for its work. This work, which began with the first rays of the sun, was the retrieval, assisted by divers, of a series of large, weed-bearded, shell-crusted blocks, the longest of them some eighteen feet in length. A considerable heap of them soon accumulated on the dock. All were found in one narrow zone quite near the Staff, about midway out along it. Indeed, half of these objects were winched out from under the Staff, whose underlying sand and muck had to be laboriously sucked away with bellows-driven pumps supported by several auxiliary rafts, and serviced by dozens of additional divers and mechanics. Once deposited on the dock each piece was scraped by crews of men with saws and scaling-axes used by fishermen on the larger marine reptiles. The cleansed products that ended up loaded on wagons to make their way through the harbor gate were rather remarkably identifiable as bones; so undamaged were they, beneath the ocean's encrustation, that once cleansed, they were to be seen even by a man innocent of anatomy as the building blocks of a gigantic hand.

As night drew on again, most of the city was massed on the walls, expectantly attending the results of the completion of Pastur's skeleton, for this would be accomplished, all were informed, within the hour. Pozzle and Smalling stood in the privileged spot near the pylons of the north gate, an area reserved for the Aristarchs as one of the best posts for observation, and one of the rampart's strongest parts.

'Where *is* the little weasel?' Pozzle rasped, squinting toward the fossil-encumbered plateau. Smalling, who did likewise, answered: 'I believe that temple landau just coming down from the acropolis bears toward us the unctuous little eel. Seems to be making remarkably fast time too. I wonder what it was he was so mysterious about "investigating."'

A murmur of concern swept along the wall. Someone down the line reported seeing one of the hummocks containing the dormant carnivorous hatchlings stir, and tremble where it lay. For an indeterminate, unbreathing time, everyone watched the plain. The hillocks marking the self-inhumed monsters seemed universally unmoving. The thunderous impacts of the flock against the wall, never having ceased, returned to the general awareness. Missiles and hot oil resumed their rain – all but ineffectual except in a temporary way – upon the assailants. Pozzle and Smalling returned their gaze to the route the landau must be following to reach them, and when it came into view they found it to be remarkably far advanced toward them.

'Why such haste?' muttered Pozzle. 'Some *new* catastrophe?'

'Here he is.'

Breathless, Sexton Minor pitched from the landau and floundered up the causeway to the gate-side battlements. His manner, once he appeared, was of extravagantly elaborate discretion, and this drew all eyes upon him as he ushered the waiting pair over to a corner.

'A dreadful catastrophe has befallen us,' he moaned. 'Dame Lybis, in her excitement, didn't find the *whole* passage. I had a feeling about it. I went into the Archives . . . and I found the rest of it, right near where she had stopped looking when she discovered the first page. Look. Read.'

Smalling seized the document. He held it so that he and Pozzle could read it together. When they had done so, both went to the posted copy of what Lybis had discovered in the archives the night before. They reread this, and then reread what Minor had just handed them. Taken from the beginning, the entire passage ran:

> By foes disarmed, in death unhanded,
> Though all disjoint, still Pastur clutches
> The staff that he, in life, commanded,
> And still with moveless fingers touches
> That which shall make all harm be ended.

(Here the published fragment ended, and the Sexton's supplement began.)

> For once each bone to each attaches
> Thereby is his death rescinded –

Thus both his mind and might are mended,
And 'ware ye then, lest down he reaches –
What he pursues, great Pastur catches.

When they had finished their perusal, the two Aristarchs
looked dazedly at Minor. The crowd of their fellows was
now curiously following their actions.

'Where's Lybis?' Pozzle asked in a small and distant
voice, his shock as yet embryonic, not fully born in his
mind. 'She must be shown – '

'Listen!' Smalling said. So closely did the pair have their
fellows attending to them that his command was obeyed
by the entire company of Aristarchs. Their heads rose, ears
tilting inquisitively. From all along the wall a blurred roar
of consternation welled. And nothing crosscut the sound.
It was distinct from the most distant points of the wall –
because the flock's crashing assault had ceased utterly.
The Aristarchs surged to the battlements, whence the rest
of the city already gaped upon the universally quiescent
behemoths below. Even the dogged parties of thieves
engaged in stripping the gold from the wall paused, astonished, in their shelters where they melted down their
peelings. Somewhere a cry arose, and here and there it was
taken up in accents of hoarse terror:

'Out on the field! Look out on the field!'

The hillocks holding the self-encoffined carnivores were
trembling and heaving. Loose soil drizzled from shining
sarcophagi of black plates which were beginning to split
open even as they wrenched themselves from their shallow
socketings in the earth. The one most advanced in its
struggles lay also among the nearest to the trench. The sun
was just down – there were no more shadows on the earth,
and the light was red-gold. Clearly the populace saw the
encasement split lengthwise, and clearly too saw what
dragged itself forth and gigantically unfolded itself, beginning to winnow dry its wide, membranous wings as it

stood fully revealed before them. It was a Flockwarden, and relatively small though the secondary egg had been, it stood a third as large as the Goddess herself, whose pavillioned corpse, lying not far off, had carried for so long the undying seed from which it had sprung.

XIII

By the time the light had faded, a legion of her kind had risen from the plain – and by that time, they had stood long enough, and their restive wings had so gained in dry resilience and eye-eluding speed of oscillation, that nothing appeared to hinder them from taking flight. But grounded they stood, vibrating with readiness, while their flock, separated from them by the chewn-down trench, shared their paralysis.

Once it was grasped that a heaven-sent hiatus (some obscure feature of these breeds' biological cycles, no doubt) was to be granted the beleaguered city, the multitude turned and bent its gaze on the acropolis, where the repair of Pastur's ancient amputation was being prosecuted energetically.

It was a dramatic vision that greeted the throng, and wrung a hopeful cry from it, a shout of excited discussion – for the crane erected for the hand's assembly, working from a platform built on the edge of the giant's pelvic bone, was at that moment but one step from finishing its task – raising what appeared to be the last joint of the last finger, and dangling it some few yards from its point of juncture with the condyle of the next-to-last phalanx. Though the light was fast dimming, the sketch of lanterns and torches in which the scaffolding ensheathed the skeleton starkly displayed its form. It was more anthropoid than not, but with certain striking exaggerations or diminutions of the human scale in some of its features.

Its arms and hands were almost simianly massive and elongate, but withal the fingers were extremely prehensile-looking, the fingers being four-knuckled, and the thumb connected by an exceptionally mobile-seeming joint to the metacarpal. The rib cage bespoke a stupendous chest of topheavy outline, with most of its mass displaced in an upward bulge. This was an arrangement that doubtless gave the arms a basis for the exertion of truly enormous leverage. Waistwards, the giant slimmed and his legs, though strong and shapely, were comparatively small. As to the skull, while in sum it was more bulky than human make, it had its excess of bulk exclusively in the cranial bulge, whose ampleness seemed divisible into four distinct lobes of bone. Toward the tiny, delicate jaw the lower skull shrank radically. The giant's face must have been eerily, gnomishly small under the swelling of its brainpan. As for the delicate tapering design that marked every aspect of Pastur's hugeness, it was evidenced even in this final phalanx now being lowered to its assembly-crowning lodgment. For the bone was scarce four feet long, spare and graceful, completing a digit identical to its fellows in its limber strength of design.

But just then, perversely, the movement of the crane suffered a hitch, then paused abruptly. The bone, light though it was, had been faultily wrapped with the cable, and its sudden slippage in its noose brought the crane up short. The phalanx was swung back again to the platform and lowered to be reslung. On the wall the people groaned, and shuffled like a herd growing nervous to the verge of stampede.

Alone among the crowd a group of three men standing near the gate showed a doubtful, retrogade cant of body in their gazing up at the skeleton. The million leaned toward it, as if from a distance to impart their own strength to the

356

effort of the crane-crew upon that culminatory bone. But Smalling, Pozzle, and Minor, through each moment that they regarded it, cringed anew from what they saw, or from something they were thinking of as they watched.

The crane rose again, and swung the now perfectly balanced fraction of the giant across the cerulean, torch-lit sky. The crowd yearned, in a movement as multiple and unanimous as phototropism in a variegated garden, toward that elevated spectacle. The phalanx drifted across and down. Two workmen were poised on catwalks to either side of the near-finished finger. They received it in the air and guided it downward, applying its condyle with delicacy – almost tenderness – in its proper orientation to that of the penultimate bone. The piece rocked into place, making a gentle, solid crack of impact, belatedly but crisply audible across the deserted city. A much vaster noise succeeded this one.

First there was visible a slight, sharp tugging-together of the skeleton, a magnetically simultaneous tightening that rippled through the whole immense fossil. This was followed, an instant later, by the noise: like that made by a vast, well-drilled army performing a turning movement, it resembled the oiled rattle of a hundred thousand shields, spears, and swordbelts. This washed down to the stunned multitude. And then the orbits of the recumbent skull filled with saffron pools of light, and sent two towering, powerful beams of illumination into the sky. The right hand gently closed upon the workmen perched on it.

A new cry was arising, overtopping even the uproar this had kindled. For the legion of new Flockwardens was taking wing. In the next instant the herd had renewed its assault on the walls, and the staggering force of their impacts was such as made their prior efforts seem a curiously restrained performance. In the anarchy of mind that engulfed everyone for the next few moments, the approach to the north gate by a large aerial form went unnoticed. And then this apparition swept down and hovered just above the Aristarchs, to add to their already multifaceted astonishment. Astride the back of the creature – it was a new-hatched Flockwarden – sat Dame Lybis and, behind her, Nifft the Karkmahnite. The shrine-mistress cried out: 'Aristarchs! Townsfellows! Hark you, all my venal devotees, my greedy congregation – harken all ye dear, doubting, ducat-minded delvers into Pastur's rightful wealth and realm! I bring you the last sacral Pronouncement of my priesthood, indeed, of my cult itself. First, behold, if you will, Great Pastur!'

The injunction was ironic. All saw the giant sit up, saw it, with a curiously delicate gesture both deft and dismissive, reach down from the plateau to liberate the workmen he had captured amid the empty buildings below. They saw him, with quick, finicking movements of his fingers, brush from himself like cobwebs the scaffolding encumbering him. The weighty shards rang as they rained on the rooftops of the buildings below the acropolis, and the queer, delayed musicality of this was, in the crowd's stupor, as enrapturing as any of the more prodigious things they witnessed. For then, the giant stepped down from the plateau, spread his hands upon the plaza where he had just lain, and leaned there, his eye beams playing, as if musingly, upon his recent bed.

'And then, if you will – ' Lybis let her voice echo and create a listening silence, then repeated herself, voice resonant: 'And then, if you will, behold Pastur's *Anvil*, whereon he will work again as he once worked, and this time he will fashion, not the star-vessels of others, but his own, for he has wearied of our world, my erstwhile parishioners! Exceedingly and abundantly is he weary of it. The Wardens will now marshall his flock, to whom gold is no real obstacle, to the swift and – if you choose it – peaceable dismantling of the city's walls. A squad of the goddesses now guards the harbor, and others patrol the other walls. You will work for Pastur, and you will work surpassing hard, and long though your toil will be, you'll suffer no harm from him if you obey him, and serve his forges. And now I bid you a farewell that is not untinctured by a sour satisfaction with your fate. Since I was sixteen, I have served an unthanked shrine where you regularly came scavenging whenever the Goddess chose to throw you the lucrative offal you craved. I have known the proverbial aloneness of the dedicated artist. I will grant that my solitary tenure was not unleavened by laughter, and I have had the further incomparable compensation that the flock, and the Goddess' unfettered will, were resurgent during my humble term of service. Of these circumstances I have taken unflinching advantage, and am grateful that the honor of doing so has fallen to me, out of so many thousands who have served here. And now, Sexton Minor, you are to accompany me. Step forth!'

The Aristarchs recoiled from the Warden's smooth approach, which accompanied these words. Minor began to retire in equal confusion.

'What?' boomed the priestess. 'Do you think you would survive residence in this vast slave camp, now that your complicity with me is thus widely published? Climb aboard or die here, it's as simple as that. Pastur has greater work in hand than the guarding of one miserable life.'

The Sexton's passionate denials died in his throat. Gaping, he climbed up via one of the Warden's spiny legs. The Goddess bore them upward, and Lybis shouted: 'Now, farewell. Your new master will be setting to work now, and he will need his tools. You near the gate would do well to clear the wall when he comes for his hammer!'

Pastur swept his hands across his anviltop. This one brief gesture cleared it of all that crowned it. The Aristarkion mingled with the temple in the general wreckage he sent cascading down. Then, setting his feet with titanic delicacy upon the broadest open places amid the buildings, very few of which he crushed in his progress, he walked down to the harbor. He reached over the sea for his staff. His hand slipped into the same waters from which it had so recently been raised, and with a great tearing and sucking noise the rod came uprooted from the harbor-floor and towered in the starlight, shedding in fragments the dockworks that encrusted it. Its upper end, immemorially masked by the waters, was arched like a shepherd's crosier. A dozen of the Flockwardens swarmed upward and perched atop the crook of the staff. The giant turned the beacons of his eyes upon the north wall of the city, and gestured toward it. The Wardens sped thither, and commenced clearing it of the astonished Anvilians, while Pastur advanced to take up his hammer, so long laid down.

'And so none of them had ever read that ancient variant of their city's name? Nor of Pastur himself? How very curious.'

'Hm! I'll tell you, Shag, it's always been an exceedingly curious thing to me, just how incurious most people are about all save their own little island of time and place in the world.'

'Yes. If the cult was guilty of systematically obscuring its own origins and traditions, it was at least not hiding anything that anyone was inquiring into very energetically. Indeed, the scholarly community at large has been none too vigorous in recording that temple's history . . . Well! You've come well out of it at least. You understand of course that there's absolutely no question of my accepting a gift of that size.' The scholar sternly indicated a little stack of gold bullion on the floor in one corner of the study. 'The way you spend money, you're going to need that yourself before long.'

'Well, if you're going to be stonefaced about it, you're just going to have to get rid of it yourself. Those bricks are *heavy*. I recommend that you only carry them out of here one at a time, and at long intervals. And anyway, what about this new treatise – has the Academy gotten richer, or aren't you going to have to help subsidize the printing of this excellent work, wherein my own humble name appears repeatedly, in ample footnotes?'

Margold glowered mulishly at his square, rather battered-looking hands. After a while, glancing up at Nifft's eyes and finding them both sarcastic and resolute, the historian sighed.

'And so. Where is Dame Lybis now?'

'Somewhere in the Aristoz Chain.'

The scholar nodded, impressed. 'I see. She sounds like one who will go far with that caliber of thaumaturgic training.'

Nifft's assent to this was accompanied by marked restiveness. He got up and went to the window as he answered. 'Absolutely my own opinion. It's caused me some worries, too, I'll confess to you. I love Dame Lybis dearly – I have the highest admiration for her person, her pluck and her artistry. But then too, she doesn't lack cynicism. Power she'll surely gain. She has the love of achievement, and the will to drive herself. If she will remain benign as she grows in power, that's the question I can't confidently answer.'

Margold guffawed. His thick grey hair was wispy in a flame-like way, and for a moment his sea-weathered face seemed to corruscate with his enjoyment of Nifft's remark. '*Remain* benign, you say? By the Crack and all that crawls out of it – by Anvil Staff and Hammer! I like that! I truly do. Remain benign. When I tell that to my colleagues, I'll have to get it just right, the earnest way you said that!' The cartographer sat chuckling. Nifft arched a brow at his nails. Presently he chuckled a bit himself.

'I don't deny it was a grim game. Though they didn't suffer the death they marketed abroad so blithely, some of them at least might have learned what it was like to wish they would.' The pair enjoyed this sally equally, and at some length.

'You know,' Margold said at last, 'your description of the giant, his bones' lightness . . . it is an odd thought, but perhaps those bones of his never did have flesh on them. Perhaps he was *himself* . . . the product of a forge, some distant foundry far vaster even than his own?'

'You mean, that he was some kind of vast . . . automaton?'

The historian nodded. 'Remember, if we may trust the tradition, how he was destroyed. It is said that the landslide created by his ambushers did not . . . kill him – that he'd worked both hand and staff clear of the rubble, and would have used that formidable weapon to free himself in a short time more, had not their amputation of his hand broken his bodily integrity, and therewith his life. Care was taken to remove the hand far from the body, and cast it in the sea. A man who loses a hand does not necessarily die of it. But a clock with even one spring removed ceases to work, and will start up again should the spring be restored to the rest of the mechanism.'

Nifft looked dreamily from the window. 'So that all his work was for yet greater masters on a greater world? Why not? A slave himself? But a terrible and beautiful creation all the same, Shag. I recall the last look I had of him – like some of those engravings you showed me of scenes from Parple's *Pan-Demonion* – whose were they again?'

'You mean Rotto Starv's woodcuts.'

'Starv's. The same. Anyway, a day before we set sail, Kandros and I took Minor and Krekkit up on a Flock-warden just after sunset, to take a sort of good-bye look at the city, I suppose – as much for ourselves as for the old man and Minor, both of whom we'd come to like. At any rate, we flew up over the peaks to the south of town, and hung there looking at it as the light faded. It was something to fill you with awe, Shag, the armies of them, their desperate unison.

'The townspeople, I mean. They thronged the streets,

and moved in that steady, always-changing-yet-the-same way a stream has. They served the same forges and foundries the town has always served – but they *all* served them. The flocks were off working a distant mountain, quite near Ossuaridon, in fact. Half the Flockwardens were with the flock, and the other half were patrolling the streets and the perimeter where the rubble of the walls was heaped. They were scarcely needed. Pastur's sole presence commanded every man and woman of them. He was resting from his labors. His anvil still hummed with the recent blows of his hammer, and glowing crumbs of metal were strewn atop it. He sat back on the hillside, his huge arms draped over his knees, the hammer held casually in his right hand. He was watching the city as a sightseer might watch a view. The chimneys smoked and the firestacks flamed as I, nor anyone else, had never seen them do before. His eyebeams played across the rooftops and the crowded streets, and from time to time, he raised them toward the stars.'

After a silence, Margold murmured: 'He had the flock working where he was buried with their ancestors? Perhaps even then he was beginning his preparations to return home.'

'Yes. One wonders what he will find there, after so long an absence. He seemed to be wondering too.'

The world's greatest science fiction authors now available in Panther Books

Philip José Farmer
The Riverworld Saga

To Your Scattered Bodies Go	£1.95	☐
The Fabulous Riverboat	£1.95	☐
The Dark Design	£1.95	☐
The Magic Labyrinth	£1.95	☐
Gods of Riverworld	£1.95	☐

Other Titles

Dark is the Sun	£1.95	☐
Jesus on Mars	£1.50	☐
Riverworld and other stories	£1.50	☐
The Stone God Awakens	£1.50	☐
Time's Last Gift	£1.50	☐
Traitor to the Living	85p	☐
Strange Relations	£1.95	☐
The Unreasoning Mask	£1.95	☐
The Book of Philip José Farmer	£1.95	☐

To order direct from the publisher just tick the titles you want and fill in the order form.

SF281

The world's greatest science fiction authors now available in Panther Books

Ursula K LeGuin

The Dispossessed	£1.95	☐
The Lathe of Heaven	£1.95	☐
City of Illusions	£1.25	☐
Malafrena	£1.95	☐
Threshold	£1.25	☐

Short Stories

Orsinian Tales	£1.50	☐
The Wind's Twelve Quarters (Volume 1)	£1.25	☐
The Wind's Twelve Quarters (Volume 2)	£1.25	☐

Ursula K LeGuin and Others

The Eye of the Heron	£1.95	☐

A E van Vogt

The Undercover Aliens	£1.50	☐
Rogue Ship	£1.50	☐
The Mind Cage	75p	☐
The Voyage of the Space Beagle	£1.50	☐
The Book of Ptath	£1.95	☐
The War Against the Rull	£1.50	☐
Away and Beyond	£1.50	☐
Destination Universe!	£1.50	☐
Planets for Sale	85p	☐

To order direct from the publisher just tick the titles you want and fill in the order form.   **SF481**